Book Three of the Jack

RIDING WITH THE

KING

DAVID G. KIRBY

Riding with the King

Trilogy Christian Publishers A Wholly Owned Subsidiary of Trinity Broadcasting Network

2442 Michelle Drive Tustin, CA 92780

Cover design by: Cameron Olson

For information about special discounts for bulk purchases, please contact Trilogy Christian Publishing.

Manufactured in the United States of America

10 9 8 7 6 5 4 3 2 1

Library of Congress Cataloging-in-Publication Data is available.
ISBN: 979-8-88738-359-0
E-ISBN: 979-8-88738-360-6

TABLE OF CONTENTS

To

Dawson David, Judah Otto, Lila Reign, Emrie Joy, baby Kirby on the way, and all who will enter this world through physical birth in the years ahead. I am so thankful for you!

You are not accidents. You bear the image of the sovereign God within you: glorious treasure in jars of clay. Unlike Him, you have been made. Like Him, you are eternal beings.

My prayer for you is that you will always remind yourselves of this truth from God's Word:

> *For you formed my inward parts; you knitted me together in my mother's womb. I praise you, for I am fearfully and wonderfully made. Wonderful are your works; my soul knows it very well. My frame was not hidden from you, when I was being made in secret, intricately woven in the depths of the earth. Your eyes saw my unformed substance; in your book were written, every one of them, the days that were formed for me, when as yet there was none of them.*
>
> *~ Psalm 139:13–16*

Know, then, that He designed you and brought you into this world. Do not look around you or inside of you to know who you are. Found in the Creator alone is your life, your purpose, your identity.

But also know that even though your body is alive, your heart is dead and needs to be resurrected. Jesus, who loves you with His life, came for you so that He might give you a second birth—a spiritual one.

> *But God, being rich in mercy, because of the great love with which He loved us, even when we were dead in our trespasses, made us alive together with Christ—by grace you have been saved—and raised us up with Him and seated us with Him in the heavenly places in Christ Jesus.*
>
> *~ Ephesians 2:5–6a*

So, remember that you are designed. Rehearse the truth that you are loved. Memorize the fact that you are here on purpose for a purpose. Why be so intentional? Because heaven's truth will be opposed in this dark world. By now, you see this.

Lastly, my sons and daughters, know that one day you will Ride with the King on vast and verdant plains, breathing the air of heaven.

I'll be waiting for you.

"To be born again is, as it were, to enter upon a new existence, to have a new mind, a new heart, new views, new principles, new tastes, new affections, new likings, new dislikings, new fears, new joys, new sorrows, new love to things once hated, new hatred to things once loved, new thoughts of God, and ourselves, and the world, and the life to come, and salvation."

~ J. C. Ryle

"There are two kinds of beauty; there is a beauty which God gives at birth, and which withers as a flower. And there is a beauty which God grants when by His grace men are born again. That kind of beauty never vanishes but blooms eternally."

~ Abraham Kuyper

"If then you have been raised with Christ, seek the things that are above, where Christ is, seated at the right hand of God. Set your minds on things that are above, not on things that are on earth. For you have died, and your life is hidden with Christ in God. When Christ who is your life appears, then you also will appear with him in glory."

~ Colossians 3:1–4

"Then I saw heaven opened, and behold, a white horse! The One sitting on it is called Faithful and True, and in righteousness He judges and makes war. His eyes are like a flame of fire, and on His head are many diadems, and He has a name written that no one knows but Himself. He is clothed in a robe dipped in blood, and the name by which He is called is The Word of God. And the armies of heaven, arrayed in fine linen, white and pure, were following Him on white horses... On his robe and on his thigh he has a name written, King of kings and Lord of lords."

~ Revelation 19:11–14, 16

RIDING WITH THE KING

CHAPTER 1

THE RETURN TO TELEIOS ACADEMY

The old greenhouse that was converted into a library on the fourth floor of the Edifice is awakening from its six-week hibernation. Today it is flooded with sunlight that pours through its many windows and filled with the sounds of life. Winter break is in the rearview mirror, and both students and professors have returned to the small campus.

The Screaming Eagles, reunited once again, are gathered in a corner of the musty library, sharing stories about their unique adventures while they were away. Some of the events that transpired over the break have already been communicated via texts and social media while they were unfolding, but now the graduate students are sharing face-to-face and filling in the details.

Aly folds her petite hands on the old table in front of her and speaks at length about her unexpected trip to Jerusalem with Moussa that is forever branded on her memory. With tears in her eyes, she recounts the tragic death of Daniel and his fellow soldiers but also tells about the gospel being shared with hundreds of men and women, many of them from the Muslim faith. She mentions the amazing coming to Christ of Abdullah Khan, the imam from Saudi Arabia. As she talks, she makes more than passing references to Moshe Abramovich, Kameel Majdali, and, of course, David.

When she speaks of the colonel's son, Aly's five peers sitting around the table easily detect by the excitement in her voice and the gleam in her eyes that she has developed an affinity for the young Israeli Mossad agent.

Aly concludes her account by informing the other members of the micro-cohort that her brother, Mahmoud, who is now Moussa, has decided to remain at the school near Atlanta for the spring semester. Professor Madjali has personally taken the new Christ-follower under his wing and is committed to his spiritual growth.

When it is Rachel's turn, she explains recent updates about her discipling of Drew, something that Jack especially is excited about. She informs her fellow students that she had the opportunity to meet the university student four times during the break, including one trip to his parents' house in Lake Luzerne, New York. Several astute members of the micro-cohort detect in Rachel's eyes the same twinkle they saw in Aly's eyes when she spoke about David Abramovich but quickly dismiss the notion. Rachel's excitement is certainly attributable to the growth of Drew's young faith.

Stewart offers a summary of his time in Two Harbors, Minnesota. He makes no mention of Michael, limiting his comments to the sojourn in the remote cabin, including his encounter with the record-setting blizzard. When he is done, he mentions that he has something else he wants to share later before they leave the greenhouse library. As Stewart shares, everyone around the table thinks the same thing: he's different; he seems notably less wooden than in the past.

Jack and Armando have shared multiple group texts and emails with their fellow classmates concerning their amazing encounter with Sniper but have not posted anything on social media sites out of concern for Miguel's safety. They reason that even gang bangers might access social media.

Jack mentions that before they left the new believer in his backyard several weeks ago now, they reassured Miguel that they would be praying for his future now that he had surrendered his life to Jesus. They also spent over an hour discussing some difficult issues with him: Should he immediately share his faith with his fellow gang members? Should he leave the gang for his own safety? Should he remain with his homies and pray for them to come to faith as they witnessed his life change during the weeks and months ahead?

Jack and Armando reveal to their fellow Screaming Eagles that they learned just that morning that Sniper-become-Miguel has decided to remain with his gang for the immediate future as he grows in faith and seeks wise counsel from his new mentor. Yes, Miguel has connected with Juan Ortega, the man who led Syko Loco to Christ and then helped Armando grow as a new believer. Carmelita and Angela Rosa are also meeting with Sniper regularly to assist him in his journey of faith in Jesus.

Jack mentions that he and Armando have talked frequently about Jim Elliot before and after their experience in the jungles of the barrio. In fact, they have recently read some of what he wrote before his death. Jack's favorite quote from him is, "Lord, make my way prosperous, not that I achieve high station, but that my life may be an exhibit to the value of knowing God."

Armando confesses that he went from initial dislike for Jim Elliot to deep respect. The man's exemplary courage is partly what inspired him and Jack to go into gangland in the first place. The words of the martyred missionary that Armando has embraced as a life challenge are, "Live to the hilt every situation you believe to be the will of God."

Armando concludes that he witnessed a great miracle in Sniper's back yard because he and Jack were obedient to God's will.

"So never turn away from God's calling," the young man says, "even if the path appears dangerous. Didn't God Himself say in Joshua 1 that 'This Book of the Law shall not depart from your mouth, but you shall meditate on it day and night, so that you may be careful to do according to all that is written in it. For then you will make your way prosperous, and then you will have good success. Have I not commanded you? Be strong and courageous. Do not be frightened, and do not be dismayed, for the LORD your God is with you wherever you go.'"

Emily is last to share. Her comments are brief, vague, and leave everyone hungry for more. She discloses nothing about her assault on the beach.

Jack experiences her summary as similar to eating a small appetizer before a meal and then being denied both the entrée and the dessert. She is clearly withholding something. Her face and voice have a defiant edge. No one pushes against her defensive posture. Her "no trespassing" sign is the size of a highway billboard.

After three hours of talking, the students are done catching up. The greenhouse is now overrun with shadows as the February sun sinks lower in the sky. Jack suggests that they conclude their time together with prayer, giving thanks to God for the marvelous things He has done, especially in the lives of Drew, Abdullah, and Miguel.

The six students spend the next forty-five minutes approaching God with gratitude on behalf of His three new children. Then they go on to pray for Drew's parents and Pete's grieving parents, for their own parents and siblings, for Moussa (who is no longer Mahmoud), for David, Moshe Abramovich, and even Miguel's fellow gang members back in Valinda. Aly prays for Mahmoud Dajani, the friend of the colonel in the Old City of Jerusalem, and for the family of Daniel.

Lastly, they pray for each other.

Jack ends the time of prayer by reading from Psalm 145:4–7: "One generation shall commend your works to another, and shall declare your mighty acts. On the glorious splendor of your majesty, and on your wondrous works, I will meditate. They shall speak of the might of your awesome deeds, and I will declare your greatness. They shall pour forth the fame of your abundant goodness and shall sing aloud of your righteousness."

When Jack is finished reading, the Screaming Eagles chat and laugh and reminisce some more.

"Jack," a voice says on the periphery of his consciousness.

It takes a few seconds for the voice to register in his awareness, but eventually, Jack turns to the person who has spoken his name. He finds himself looking into the face of Stewart. He stares at the Intellect for a while before the man's raised eyebrows jog his memory.

"I'm sorry, Stew," he says, "I forgot. You said you wanted to share something with us."

Jack gets the attention of everyone around the table and announces, "Stewart has something to say."

When all eyes are on their classmate, the young man intones, "There's a new development relative to the journal. I discovered another entry penned by JLS after we thought we had read his final word." Stewart pauses to open a folder sitting on his lap. He pulls out sheets of paper and distributes them to the other students gathered around the table.

"You have in your hands a copy of this new entry," Stewart says. "As you can see, it is dated 16 April 1899, two days after what we assumed was Jacob's final journal entry detailing his account of the murder of his wife and children. As you can also see, the content of this entry is a cipher. Its message has been encrypted, encoded in numbers and letters, some of them capitalized. I'm not certain why Jacob felt the need to embed his message in the form of a cipher, but he must have had his reasons. I haven't been able to decipher it yet. Of course, I've only been able to dedicate several hours to it so far."

Rachel, who has always had a soft heart for her relationally challenged classmate, leans toward him and smiles. "Where in the world did you find it, Stewart?" she asks excitedly.

"I was examining the journal on my return flight from the Twin Cities just yesterday," he replies, "when I noticed a slit in the back inside cover. When I explored the opening, I found a folded piece of paper that contained the entry."

"Wow, Stew, well done!" Rachel exclaims. "I wonder if we'll ever be able to decode it."

"If it's mathematically based," Aly interjects, "Stewart will be the one to solve it."

"Is it anything like a Caesar cipher?" Jack inquires.

"Actually, Jack, it is similar, just more complex," Stewart responds, adjusting his glasses. His face and voice are emotionless, but his eyes betray excitement. "A code would have been easier to decipher except that their representational nature would preclude the use of mathematical analysis. But it appears that your great, great grandfather had a mind for mathematics. So, he availed himself of a cipher.

"The good news is that in the twenty-first century, I have the advantage of using a computer to facilitate the development of encryption schemes. My cryptoanalysis of Jacob's entry is also assisted by logical reasoning based on algorithms. I'm confident I'll solve it soon."

Armando clears his throat and speaks words that do not come out of his mouth easily, "I agree with Aly—if anyone can solve it, it will be you. Stewart."

Everyone stares at the young man from LA, but no one says anything. Armando's positive words stand in sharp contrast to the customary irritation and even unapologetic anger he has directed toward his intellectual classmate in the past. On his part, Stewart stares at Armando from behind the familiar mask that seems to have been permanently pulled over his face.

Jack breaks the silence. "It's amazing to see all of you again," he announces as he glances at Emily. "Who could've imagined that a few weeks apart would bring so many unforgettable adventures?"

"God knew," Aly interjects with her usual unapologetic confidence. "He knew the plans He had for all of us, not to harm us, but to give us a future and a hope so that we might live for the praise of his glory."

"Well said, Aly," Rachel replies.

Armando, whose brain is connected more closely to his stomach than the average person, says, "Hey, dudes and dudesses, it's time for supper. Let's get down to Agatha and grab some *comida*!"

Jack nods his head in agreement and says, "When Stewart cracks this cipher, let's get together again and figure out the next step in this journal journey. Who knows? This latest message from Jacob might bring more clarity to our next step. Maybe we'll decide it's time to dig up that grave."

Jack begins to rise but then sits back down again. "One last thing," he says, looking into the faces of his peers with his clear blue eyes. "As you already know via my texts, I ran into the Cemetery Man just before break—not by choice, of course. He was very insistent about getting his hands on the journal. So, watch your back. He's dangerous and seems willing to do anything to get the journal—even bodily harm to anyone who stands in his way."

Jack pauses and then adds, "He claimed he was a relative of Jacob's. I think he said he was Zeke Sutherington."

Armando breaks into loud laughter. "Seriously?" he asks. "He said his name was Zeke?"

"Sounds a bit 'dodgy' to me," Aly adds. "At least that's the word my friend in Australia would use."

"Around here, we say 'sketchy,'" Rachel comments with a smile.

"Yeah, it sounded very sketchy to me, too," Jack admits. "He just wanted the journal, and he was willing to tell me anything to get it."

"We just need to figure out what he wants with it," Emily interjects. "I doubt that he's looking to acquire it as a family heirloom or bequeath it to the local historical society."

"Maybe he knows about the coins," Stewart suggests.

"He must know that the journal holds clues to something valuable," Jack agrees. "But how would he know about the coins?"

Rachel's face brightens, and she says, "I'll bet he's not a Sutherington but a DeFoe. He's a relative of Philip and knows that Jacob took his great-great-grandfather's coins."

"That's an idea, Rach, but does anybody know that Jacob was responsible for Madeline's death and the disappearance of the Lady Liberty coins besides Philip?" Jack asks.

"Of course, that's something we can't know," Armando says with a smile, "since it happened in the nineteenth century. But what we do know is that whoever this Cemetery Man is, he knows about the journal. How he knows it exists is a total mystery."

Jack looks at the Intellect and says, "Until we know more, you'd better put that journal under lock and key, Stewart. Don't take it anywhere out in public. Don't let anybody see you with it."

Stewart nods his head and says, "Understood."

"Especially if you see a gray pickup truck following you or someone who looks like the Cemetery Man," Armando adds.

"Can you remind us what 'Zeke' looks like?" Emily asks.

Jack shakes his head and laughs without mirth. "How can I forget that dude? First, I encounter him in a nightmare, then I hear about him in Violet's dream, and finally, I meet him face to face at the university. He's big, maybe six feet four inches", broad across the shoulders and chest. The front of his head is totally bald, while the sides and back have long hair. I only got one good look at his face that night in the moonlight. He has a scraggly beard, bad teeth, and a crooked nose. He didn't strike me as exceptionally intelligent."

"He's probably the guy who followed us when we went to the university," Armando offers.

"That's what I'm thinking," Jack agrees. "Anyway, if you see him, get away from him as fast as you can and move to a safe place. Run if you have to."

"Shouldn't we call the police?" Emily asks, irritation in her voice. The assault she experienced on the beach—an event she has chosen not to share with the cohort—is still vivid in her mind.

"I'm more and more inclined to do so," Jack replies as he glances at the girl with emerald-green eyes.

"But didn't Mr. Fagani say that a relative of Philip DaFoe is the police commissioner?" Aly inquires, ever the not-so-subtle nay-sayer.

Jack nods his head. "Yeah, that's what he said. We just need to decide at what point we can't handle this issue on our own. The whole police department can't be corrupt, right? Maybe there's just a few rotten apples in the barrel. And that's assuming the police commissioner is crooked. Maybe he's actually a good apple."

"I've got an idea," Rachel volunteers. "Dr. Greenlay told us he has a brother-in-law who works for the highway patrol. Maybe we could call him and ask his advice."

"Not a bad idea," Armando interjects as he turns to look at his roommate. "If this whole thing blows up, we need to have someone in our corner."

Jack nods his head and says, "I feel like I'm always asking you to do the legwork for us, Rach. But do you think you could talk to Dr. Greenlay about his brother-in-law?"

"Not a problem, Jack," the woman with the rich auburn hair replies with a smile. "I'm here to serve."

"To 'protect and to serve,'" Armando quips, "like the motto of the police academy in LA?"

Everyone laughs as they get up from the table.

"Oh, one more thing," Jack says. "Manny—sorry, I'm calling you by the name Carmelita used—do you remember what we talked about earlier? You were going to show them something."

The olive-skinned young man with close-cropped black hair and brown eyes stares at Jack for a moment before he smiles and says, "Ah, yes, I remember, mi amigo."

The man who formerly was known as Syko Loco pushes his left sleeve up to his shoulder, revealing a tattoo of a male face twisted into a snarl. His exposed teeth are sharp like those of a wolf, and his eyebrows are twisted in rage. Everyone in the room knows immediately that they are beholding a representation of Sniper, the cold-blooded killer of Armando's half-brother.

Beneath the man's unpleasant face, a cross has been tattooed over the older letters, "CFY—Coming For You."

Above Sniper's face is a new inscription. It reads, "Miguel, brother in Christ."

CHAPTER 2

THE INTELLECT STRIKES AGAIN

Silently, the dark creature makes its way upward, rung by rung. It moves quickly, like a cat. It reaches the top rung and slowly pushes up against the door. When the trap door hits the bottom of the bunk bed, the creature becomes enraged and beats the door with its head, screeching, "Jack! Jack!"

Jack sits bolt upright in bed. His heart is racing. He is preparing to peek under his bed when his foggy brain registers that someone is knocking on his door and calling his name. He is instantly relieved when he realizes that the noise and the voice are not from his nightmare.

He glances at his phone: 4:20 a.m. *Why in the world is Stewart pounding on my door in the middle of the night?* As the fog lifts from his mind, he has a hunch why his friend is there.

Jack slides out of the lower bunk and glances up at the sleeping form of his roommate. Jack shakes his head and mumbles, "That guy gives a whole new meaning to 'sleeping like a rock.'" Then he stumbles over to the door and opens it.

In the dim light of the hallway, Jack is greeted by the Intellect, who is dressed in the same clothes he was wearing the previous evening in the greenhouse. It appears that he has not slept at all. His face is drawn, but his eyes are amazingly alert.

"I have good news, and I have bad news," Stewart announces as he glances down at a notebook in his hand. "The good news is that the cipher is decoded. It turned out to be more difficult to solve than I first thought since it involved less than one hundred characters, and there were no spaces between words. Also, your great-great-grandfather created a polyalphabetic substitution cipher which, as you probably know intuitively, is more difficult to decrypt than a monosyllabic substitution cipher. But it is now intelligible."

"What's the bad news?" Jack inquires as he groans and rubs his eyes.

"The message is a riddle," Stewart announces gravely, as if informing Jack that his mother had just died.

"A riddle," Jack repeats impassively as he stares at his nocturnal interruption.

Stewart nods his head. "It is a riddle, wrapped in a mystery, inside an enigma, but perhaps there is a key,'" the Intellect replies.

"What?" Jack says, frowning.

"It's a Winston Churchill quote," Stewart says.

"Oh," Jack says, sighing loudly. "So, what's the riddle?" he asks, stepping out into the hallway and closing the door behind him.

Stewart opens his notebook and thumbs through pages of scribbling and letters and numbers. When he finds the right page, he glances up and down the deserted hallway as if someone might be watching them. Jack does not criticize his friend's hypervigilance in the least. After being attacked by the Cemetery Man on the university campus six weeks ago, he is totally sympathetic with a high level of caution.

Stewart glances at Jack and then reads, "*He who is wise will consider habitation by the water to be more pleasant than by the forest. But do not habitate alone. Heaven brings light and glory, while hell brings darkness and death. Listen to your soule and grow up with the country. Seventh heaven in hell will bring you to what you seek when you remember the number of Abraham's address. Peer behind the confluence of heaven and the place of the dead."*

"What?" Jack asks for a second time as he rubs the back of his neck. "What's all that supposed to mean?"

Stewart peers at his friend from behind the thick lenses of his black-framed glasses. "It's a riddle, Jack. We need to solve it just like I solved the cipher."

"I know it's a riddle, Stew," Jack replies with more impatience. "I'm just thinking out loud. One more hurdle," he adds, shaking his head.

"What should we do, Jack?"

Jack runs his hands through his flaxen hair and then rubs his eyes again. He is silent for a long time. Finally, he looks over at his friend and says, "We have to get the Screaming Eagles together again in the fireside room just like we did after Violet's funeral. Figuring out this riddle will take a group effort. We have a good track record for solving mysteries together."

Stewart nods his head, and his eyes light up. "I concur with that idea. When should we meet?"

"Why not tonight?" Jack says. "I'll send out a group text to everyone and see who can make it. If we aim for 11:00 a.m., I think just about everyone should make it."

Stewart nods his head conspiratorially. "I'll be there," he states. "Back at the fireside room?"

"Sounds like the place to be," Jack replies. "I'll see you there tonight, Stew."

The human cipher solver nods at Jack then turns and walks away. Jack's eyes follow him as he retreats down the deserted hallway.

Standing alone in the hallway, Jack ponders the fact that his intellectual friend lives alone in his dorm room. He wonders if the isolated arrangement was by Stewart's request or if the professors decided that being alone would be conducive to his growth. Jack watches Stewart walk to the far end of the hall next to the umbilical cord and disappear into his room.

As he turns to reenter his "blind" room, a deep sadness sweeps over Jack for his friend from Minnesota. He cannot begin to imagine what it must be like to be so alone in the world. In that instant, he decides that one of his objectives for the semester ahead will be to draw Stewart out of his solitary world.

All six members of the micro-cohort, only days removed from their winter adventures around the country as well as the world, gather in the fireside room that is familiar to them for several reasons. First, it is where they gathered after Violet Windsor's funeral to discuss the Sutherington family gravesite and to read the journal of Jacob Lane Sutherington. More importantly, it is the classroom where they met with Dr. Hawkstern three times a week during fall semester to endure his atheistic teaching and intimidating presence.

In just a few days, they will trudge back into this academic arena once again to begin a spring course with the giant professor entitled, *Why the Science of Evolution Eclipses the Irrationalism of the Supernatural.* Jack is anticipating the new course with enthusiasm because he has already decided that a second objective for the new semester—inspired by Emily—will be to befriend the unapproachable professor and love him toward the kingdom of God.

When Jack and Armando saunter into the room rendered royal by the deep red carpeting, a waning fire flickers in the mammoth fireplace. As they walk toward the lounge area on the far side of the room, Armando salutes the large painting of Moses, who is standing, arms raised, at the edge of the Red Sea. As he gestures toward the patriarch, he remarks, "When I meet you in heaven, Mo, I'm going to ask you what it was like to stand on that rock, lift your staff, and then watch the Red Sea part before your eyes. I can't begin to imagine how awesome that must have been!"

Rachel, Emily, Aly, and Stewart are already sitting on the couch and overstuffed chairs, waiting for their two counterparts to arrive. The six students greet one other with hugs and handshakes—the latter are for Stewart—and then settle into their seats. Jack ends up in the same spot on the couch where he sat the night they began to unravel the mystery around his great, great-grandfather, Jacob, and the cemetery.

"Thanks for coming on short notice," Jack begins as he scans the faces he has grown to love over the last six months. "As you already know from my text, we're here to solve the riddle that Jacob hid in the back cover of his journal." Jack pauses and looks at Stewart. "But before we dig into this thing, I want to thank our friend and resident decoder for solving the cipher that got us to the riddle in the first place."

Everyone in the intimate gathering claps for Stewart. Jack notices that Armando claps the loudest and the longest. He alone knows why.

The Intellect simply nods his head once and presses his lips together. No one can know the elation that stirs in the young man's chest since he learned a long time ago that he is to be seen but not known.

Stewart hands out copies of the riddle to everyone and announces, "Here it is—the riddle of Jacob Lane Sutherington, Jack's ancestor."

Jack glances at his printed copy of the riddle and then looks up and says, "Emily, could you please read this to get us started?"

The green eyes flash at him as if she is not pleased with his request. Nonetheless, the young woman with the wide white headband that obscures half of her golden hair looks down at her copy and begins to read the one-hundred-twenty-year-old riddle:

"He who is wise will consider habitation by the water to be more pleasant than in the forest. But do not habitate alone.

Heaven brings light and glory, while hell brings darkness and death. Listen to your soule and grow up with the country.

Seventh heaven in hell will guide you to what you seek when you remember the sacred number of Abraham's civil address.

Peer behind the confluence of heaven and the place of the dead."

"Thanks, Emily," Jack says as he smiles at the woman who represents the most difficult riddle he has ever encountered. Then he announces, "Well, this is it, gang—the riddle that must be unriddled. This is our mission tonight if we decide to accept it."

"No sleep for the present company until we solve it," Armando says with his familiar buoyancy. "No rest until we resolve it. No fun until we figure it out. Don't you guys love my alliteration?"

Aly shakes her head at Armando and grimaces. Then she says, "I have no idea where to begin. The words don't seem too difficult to understand, even for me, but what it means is totally hidden from me."

"That's why they call it a riddle, Aly," Armando quips.

"Ha-ha," Aly replies with a weak smile.

"We need to start by putting ourselves in Jacob's shoes," Rachel offers.

"He probably wrote this in the Citadel catacombs, right? What would he be seeing and thinking in his mind's eye at that location?"

"And at that time in history," Stewart adds, "in the late 1800s."

"He refers to water," Emily says, unusually engaged in light of her recent detachment at the Academy.

Jack has noticed that the young woman from Florida does love solving mysteries, possibly explaining her investment in the moment.

"Could he be writing about Silver Bay Lake?" the woman thinks aloud. "It's the only body of water around here."

"I think that's a great place to start," Jack replies. "Let's plug it into the riddle. What do you think he means when he writes *habitation by the lake and not alone?*"

The six Academy students sit in various states of concentration. Rachel is humming aloud as she rests her chin on her hands. Stewart is staring across the room toward the Old Testament paintings. Emily's eyes are closed, and her forehead is furrowed in concentration. Armando is sitting with his fingertips pressed together, chewing on his lower lip.

Aly's face reflects deep passion as she prays, "Jesus, give us wisdom as we seek to understand this riddle. We know we're all at the Academy for a reason and that solving the mystery around the journal of Jacob Sutherington is part of that reason. Holy Spirit, please open our eyes to the mind of the Father as we pursue serving you instead of the powers of darkness. In everything, may you be glorified."

A few "Amens" are uttered after Aly's prayer. Then there is silence in the fireside room for a long time. A few random pops and crackles from the Hawkstern-sized fireplace punctuate the quiet, but nobody hears them. The intense, bearded face of Moses the Patriarch stares down at them from the far side of the room.

"When was the Silver Bay Lodge built?" Emily asks, finally breaking the silence. "What are you thinking, Emily?" Jack asks.

"I'm wondering if your great-great-grandfather could be referring to the lodge when his riddle says to *not habitate alone*," Emily replies. "After all, the lodge is a place where people come together, sort of, maybe."

Rachel's face brightens suddenly. "Yes, that must be it! His riddle is pointing us toward the lodge! Stewart, when was that place built?"

Stewart's nose is already in his phone. He raises a finger at Rachel while the index finger of his other hand slides across the screen. Soon, his eyes are scanning data in front of him.

"The original lodge was built in 1867," he replies, looking up from his phone. His glasses have slid down his Roman nose, and he looks like an absent-minded professor.

"Okay, then," Jack says, "the lodge was in existence in 1899 when Jacob wrote his riddle."

"Your great-great-grandfather could be referring to the Citadel, but the word habitate sounds like it might apply more to the lodge where people would eat and sleep," Aly comments.

"Sounds reasonable to me," Rachel says. "Let's run with that. Let's fix our sights on the lodge and see where the riddle takes us next."

"*Heaven brings light and glory while hell brings darkness and death*," Armando mumbles aloud. "*Listen to your soule and grow up with the country. Seventh heaven in hell will bring you to what you seek ...*"

"Well, that's a bit obscure," Rachel remarks. "It sounds like we should avoid hell and go to heaven, but then he says that 'seventh heaven in hell' is what we need to seek."

Emily leans forward in her chair and glances around at her classmates, who are tightly gathered around the table in the middle of the lounge area. "If we've narrowed the location to the lodge, then what comes next is either looking outside the lodge on the grounds or inside the lodge somewhere," she reasons. "If we go with Jacob's earlier modus operandi, he seems to prefer hiding things inside structures, especially in the basement."

"Or outside in cemeteries," Armando adds with a chuckle.

"I vote for inside the lodge," Jack says. "If he hid whatever we're supposed to find outside the lodge, good luck finding anything there, especially after they dug up half the lawn when installing the sprinkler system."

"If we decide to look inside the lodge," Aly interjects, "won't we hit a dead-end there, too, because of the fire Steve Slotter told us about? When did that happen anyway, in the late 1990s?"

"1998," Stewart remarks. "But the good news is that the fire was limited to smoke damage only. If Jacob did hide anything inside the lodge, odds are that it survived the fire."

"Okay, so we're looking inside the lodge," Armando says. "Now we need to figure out what he means by heaven and hell. Is he referring to physical location, as in up or down—to one of the floors above ground or to the basement?"

"Again, if we go by Jacob's habits, he likes to bury things," Emily observes, "whether inside or outside. I say we look in the basement."

"Ay caramba," Armando remarks with feigned disgust. "The answer to every mystery around here is found in a tunnel or a cave or a catacomb or a grave. Why is the light always found in the middle of the darkness?"

Everyone laughs. No one offers a dissenting opinion.

Jack begins writing something down in a notebook he extracted from his backpack. As he writes, he says aloud, "At the lodge, by the lake, in the basement, then *listen to your soule and grow up with the country*. What in the world does that mean?"

"Let's see," Rachel says as she looks at her phone. "'Soule' with that unusual spelling could refer to a lawyer with an office downtown, or a province in France, or a restaurant in Chicago, or an obsolete spelling of 'soul.' Or it could be a singer, or—the list goes on. We certainly can rule out the names of people alive today whom Jacob would've never met."

"*Grow up with the country*," Stewart mumbles aloud as he stares at the ceiling. "*Grow up with the country*," he repeats. "I know I've heard that somewhere before. In high school, I think."

Jack smiles at the Intellect and then winks at Emily.

"I've got it!" Aly remarks excitedly as she holds out her phone toward the other members of the micro-cohort. "The words are from a man named John Babsone Lane Soule. It says here that he is responsible for the quote, 'Go west, young man, and grow up with the country.'" The young woman from Thailand pauses, tilts her head, and adds, "Whatever that means. It must be something only understood in the context of American history."

"That's correct, Aly," Steward remarks. "It referred to the recommendation by many people living back in mid-nineteenth century America to settle in the uncivilized western region of the country."

"What does the quote mean for us?" Emily inquires as she adjusts her gigantic headband that obscures her golden mane. "Is Jacob saying we should go to the west side of the basement?"

Armando looks at Jack and says, "The most westward part of the basement is the storage room, where all the broken and forgotten things are deposited. You know, the old wheelbarrows, extra irrigation hoses, unused light fixtures, some old furniture, and even a few ancient pinball machines.

It's like a junkyard down there."

"So, what we're looking for might be in that storage room?" Rachel asks. "Like, buried in the floor?"

"Hopefully not under the floor," Jack comments. "It's solid concrete."

"Let's not forget the number of Abraham's civil address," Stewart reads aloud.

"Are we talking about Abraham from the Bible?" Aly inquires.

"Good question," Jack replies. "Jacob didn't seem particularly drawn to the Bible, though. He was running from divine accountability and what he perceived were God's stifling commandments. So, I don't think Jacob was referring to the patriarch in the Old Testament."

"Who, then?" Armando says. "And what does he mean by a 'civil' address? Is he talking about the address to a house or a business as opposed to a military location?"

The six members of the Screaming Eagles fall silent. Aly looks totally defeated by this portion of the riddle. Stewart scratches his head and then mumbles, "When in doubt ..."

He picks up his phone and inquires of the wise sage who lives inside the device, "Who was an important Abraham in the nineteenth century?"

There is no response for several seconds until the female voice in his phone responds, "Abraham Lincoln was a pivotal character in the shaping of America in the nineteenth century. He—"

"Of course!" Emily exclaims. "Abraham Lincoln! He was president during the Civil War. Jacob must be referring to one of Lincoln's public addresses he gave during the conflict between the north and the south!"

Jack sits forward on the couch and says, "What would we do without the information highway and Emily?" he says with a smile. "I'll bet my great-great grandfather never thought someone would solve his riddle so quickly. But now we have the world's information in the palm of our hands."

Rachel stands up and walks over to the small ice chest she brought with her and extracts a cold coffee. As she tears off the plastic from around the cap of the bottle, she says, "One of Lincoln's most famous public speeches is the Gettysburg Address."

Unscrewing the lid, she takes a swallow of the mocha coffee and then lifts a finger into the air. "Do you guys remember how that address begins?"

"Of course," Stewart replies. "Four scores and seven."

"Eighty-seven," Armando says, translating the words into a more familiar mathematical sum. "That's our number—the sacred one Jacob's riddle is referring to!"

"Eighty-seven," Aly repeats aloud. "What does eighty-seven mean? And how do we know we have the right address or the correct number? Maybe he mentions another number in his Gettleburg address."

"*Gettysburg*," Stewart says, correcting the young woman who spent most of her life in Saudi Arabia and southeast Asia.

Jack gets up from the couch and begins pacing slowly around the lounge area. He muses out loud, "Okay, at this point, we believe that the riddle is directing us to the Silver Bay Lodge, into the basement, and then toward the west end of the storage room. Next, we're supposed to find or go to seventh heaven and remember the number eighty-seven. Is he referring to degrees of latitude or longitude or maybe even a compass reading? I don't think those numbers work for any of those things."

"The riddle says we're supposed to *peer behind* something," Stewart reminds Jack, "*behind the confluence of heaven and the place of the dead*, which seems like a reference back to the eighty-seven years."

"*Correcto* and *verdad*!" Armando says with enthusiasm as he continues to exhibit an unprecedented positive regard for the Intellect. "The only thing to peer behind in that room is all that junk or—" the young pauses and massages the tear drop below his eye.

"What is it?" Jack asks as he stops pacing. The room grows very quiet, and everyone leans in toward Armando.

"Or the stone wall," the young man says slowly. "That storage room is huge—the size of a small soccer field. The walls are constructed of blocks that are larger than bricks but smaller than the stones in this Citadel. They must run, maybe, twenty courses high and over a hundred bricks long. The riddle might be suggesting that we locate the seventh row of stones up from the floor and then find the eighty-seventh one across."

Jack nods his head, and his eyes narrow with conviction. "I think you're on to something, Manny!" Jack says. "You have just identified where we need to look for whatever Jacob wants us to find: behind the basement wall."

"But how do we do that?" Emily asks, speaking the words everyone is thinking. "How do we dig behind a stone wall?"

"I imagine the basement stones are held together by mortar," Stewart remarks. "We just need to find the correct stone, chisel out the mortar that's holding it in place, and then remove it. I assume Jacob selected a stone that was easy to extract from the wall."

"Will Steve Slotter give us permission to do that?" Aly asks, always the rule follower.

"Why does he have to know?" Armando says, fixing his clear brown eyes on Aly. "It's not like we're stealing anything or otherwise sinning against him, right?"

"I suppose not," Aly responds with some hesitation. Everyone in the micro-cohort knows that the young woman is a stickler for following the rules.

"And we'll put everything back just how we found it," Armando adds, nodding his head vigorously and looking around at his fellow students.

Jack walks back to the couch and sits down. "Once again, you've demonstrated that Sherlock Holmes has nothing on you sleuths," he says with a laugh. "You all played a huge part in solving Jacob's riddle!"

"And thanks again to Stewart," Armando says as he nods his head toward the Intellect, "for decrypting the cipher in the first place."

Everyone around the coffee table tilts his or her head at some angle to express their ongoing surprise at the transformation of their classmate from LA. Then they offer their own words of affirmation to Stewart.

The bespectacled young man looks around at his peers with his usual impenetrable countenance. He remains a closed book, a locked safe. Except for his eyes. They are more transparent than ever before and betray something between happiness and elation.

"The next step in this riddle wrapped in a mystery inside an enigma," Jack comments, glancing at Stewart with a knowing smile, "is for Manny and I to scout out that storage room. Since we have a shift at the lodge tomorrow night, we'll check to see if the seven rows and eighty-seventh block idea is a winner. Then we'll proceed accordingly. Does that sound good to the rest of you?"

There are no dissenters in the fireside room.

"Okay then, let's bring this riddle-resolving-session to a close with prayer. Jack bows his head and says, "Thanks, Jesus, that you call us to great adventure in this world beyond what eyes can see. Help us to hear your voice, know your will, and then obey you. Obeying you will bring us the greatest joy possible not only in this world but also in the next because you always know what's best for us. Holy Spirit, fill us with your power so that we might trust and obey. Amen."

———

The next evening, after their shift at the Silver Bay Lodge hotel has ended, Jack and Armando run down the three flights of ancient pine-wood stairs to the basement. The massive subterranean space is deserted and silent except for occasional creaking and groaning noises coming from the ceiling.

Fortunately for them, the director of maintenance, Zeke Caldwell, went home hours ago. He was the only person Jack worried about bumping into since Zeke is as attentive to the lodge as a smitten man is attentive to his girlfriend. In fact, the lodge has been his paramour for forty-two years.

In the second year of their marriage, Zeke and his wife, Marilyn, began to grow apart, and the distancing continued unabated over the next four decades. Marilyn married Zeke because he was nice, but then later experienced the niceness as passivity, which she found emasculate. Zeke initially enjoyed Marilyn's assertiveness but later found her to be excessively nagging—like his critical mother. So, sadly, Zeke chose to do what too many husbands do: he stayed in the marriage, yes, but he built an emotional wall around himself to keep his wife out and instead pursued an affair to spice up his indentured existence, namely, his work at the lodge.

The two roommates from across the lake navigate the massive, labyrinthine basement and eventually arrive at the pitch-black storage room. Jack flips on the wall switch, and dozens of fluorescent lights flicker momentarily before they explode and flood the massive room with light. The glaring illumination exposes a tired and worn army of miscellaneous items, including bird houses, hoses, plumbing pipes, old six-panel doors, mill-work, rolls of carpeting, dozens of ancient headboards, a few toilets, and even a huge clawfoot bathtub. Some of the items are organized on shelves resting against the walls, while others are lying on the floor in a state of organization that only Zeke would understand.

Jack leads the way across the cement floor to the other side of the room, a hundred feet away, where the gray *western wall* rises toward the ceiling. This part of the basement is especially musty and dank. Fortunately, the familiar weight that often descends on Jack when spiritual darkness is close at hand does not present itself. Nonetheless, there is something about the room that feels surreal—a strange mix of creepiness and expectancy. It feels like a living thing, waiting for something or someone to penetrate its deep aloneness.

When they arrive at the wall that is the epicenter of their mission, they are relieved to see that there are no shelves on this side of the room. A field of exposed stone blocks stares back at them like a giant face of oversized tesserae, silent and brooding. The blocks are fixed in place with pale-white mortar dulled with age and dust. The two men count the courses of stones that rise from the floor to the ceiling—twelve. Finding the "seventh heaven"—the seventh row—will not be a problem. They set their attention to the more challenging task of identifying Abraham Lincoln's eighty-seventh block.

As they examine the wall beneath the bright fluorescent lights, Jack muses aloud, "I wonder if Jacob was counting from left to right or right to left."

Armando rubs his goatee thoughtfully and says, "I'd say he was counting from left to right. Isn't that kind of a universal thing?"

"Not necessarily," Jack remarks. "The Hebrew language, for example, is read from right to left. But let's go with left to right since that likely was most familiar to Jacob," Jack remarks with a chuckle.

"Unless he was a Hebrew language scholar," Armando says, his brown eyes twinkling.

Jack shakes his head as the two men wend their way around the items scattered over the floor until they reach the south end of the storage room. They easily locate the seventh course up from the floor and then begin counting the gray blocks as they move back toward their right. After only a dozen blocks, however, Jack stops suddenly. He turns to Armando and says, "We may have a problem."

"What's that, Juan?"

"It just struck me that this south wall of the storage room is not the actual end of the basement. It's a wall built of studs and wooden paneling, not the stonewall that marks the end of the basement. So, the question is—"

Armando finishes Jack's sentence. "Was Jacob counting the eighty-seven blocks from the partition wall or from the stone basement wall?"

"Exactly," Jack says as he runs his fingers through his hair, sighing.

"I've gotta believe that this partition wall wasn't here a hundred years ago," Armando offers. "It certainly doesn't look like it's weight-bearing."

"I have to agree with you," Jack replies, eyeing the partition. "That means we have to get behind this wood paneling and start counting from the stone wall."

A few minutes later, both men are standing in a much smaller room set aside for small tool and equipment storage. This room is gloomy, even depressing, lit only by two bare bulbs attached to cords dangling from the ceiling. The walls are much less accessible than in the larger room, covered almost entirely by cabinets, shelves, and peg board.

"Ugh," Jack says, biting his lip. "This isn't going to be easy."

The two roommates spend better than half an hour removing the various obstructions that obstruct their view of the wall. Then they begin counting the rough-cut stone blocks of the seventh row that vary in size from 1' to 2' square. They count ten blocks along the seventh course up to the paneled partition. Here, the tenth block disappears behind the wooden wall. Jack and Armando return the shelving and cabinets to their previous positions and then make their way back to the larger storage room.

When they arrive at the other side of the partition wall, Armando rolls his eyes to the ceiling and asks, "How many blocks did we count on the other side, Juan? Nine? Eleven? Fourteen?"

Jack laughs and punches his friend in the arm. He says, "*Silencio*, Syko Loco! It's ten, and you know it. I wrote the number on the back of my hand just so I wouldn't forget."

"You're a wise man, Juan," Armando says with a wry smile.

Still laughing, Jack counts seven rows up from the floor and then begins counting the first whole horizontal block beyond the wooden partition wall: "Eleven, twelve, thirteen ..."

It does not take long for the two men to arrive at block number eighty-seven.

It is the second to the last one in the wall and sits at a height of over nine feet above the floor. The two young men eye the object of their search with silent reverence. The gray block is surrounded by a frame of pale mortar.

"We're going to need a ladder," Armando announces.

"I'll grab one from the shop room," Jack volunteers. "In fact, I'll grab two. Why don't you see if you can track down a couple hammers and chisels? We might as well see if we can finish this mission tonight instead of returning a second time."

Five minutes later, the two young men are back with two of everything—step ladders, small sledgehammers, and chisels. They both open a ladder and position it in front of the wall. Then they climb up several rungs until their faces are level with the eighty-seventh block.

"Are we crazy or what?" Armando comments as he looks at Jack. "What if the riddle is referring to the granary over on the other side of the lake? What if we're supposed to be up on the second floor in room two hundred eighty-seven? What if we've solved the riddle correctly but that when Jacob was down here, there was only a dirt floor, and since then, cement has been poured that covered up the first two courses? What are the odds of us finding anything at all behind this wall?"

As he examines the block and rubs his finger over the rough mortar, Jack replies, "Under normal conditions, I'd agree with you, Manny. But there's good news here. The mortar around this block is slightly different in color than what's around the other ones. See?" he says, pointing first to the mortar frame around block eighty-seven and then to the block next to it. "The mortar is a hair lighter."

Armando looks back and forth at the two shadings of mortar, and his eyes widen. "Sure enough, vato. You're right. The mortar around block eighty-seven is different!"

"The other piece of good news is that all the stone blocks in the wall are offset, so it's not like all the blocks above this one rest on it alone," Jack observes. "Theoretically, it shouldn't be that hard to extract."

"Especially if it has been removed once before," Armando adds, "and if Jacob didn't add the nineteenth-century equivalent of super glue into his mortar."

Jack places his chisel against the line of mortar on the left side of the block and prepares to strike it with his hammer. "Bless our efforts, Lord," he says. Then he strikes the chisel hard. A small piece of mortar chips away.

Jack squints at the line of mortar and remarks, "That broke off way too easily."

Excited by Jack's success, Armando draws back his hammer and strikes his chisel even harder. His blow does not chip off any mortar; rather, it drives the chisel through the mortar and into the cleft between blocks eighty-seven and eighty-eight. Elated, Armando announces to Jack, "Who thought I was such a strong dude! My father was wrong after all!"

Jack smiles at his friend and says, "Either you're a mutant, or this mortar runs only several inches deep. It's more of a façade than functional."

Jack turns back to the wall and strikes the mortar again and again. Soon, his chisel drives into the space between blocks eighty-six and eighty-seven.

Within minutes, the two men punch through the mortar around the top and bottom of the block as well. As they drop their hammers to the floor, Jack looks at Armando and observes, "That was way too easy."

"So, what do we do now?" Armando asks after unsuccessfully attempting to move the stone block with his fingers.

"I think if we insert our chisels on both sides of eighty-seven and use them as claws to pull the block toward us, we can dislodge it," Jack recommends.

It proves to be difficult, but with much pulling and leveraging and grunting and groaning, the two men slide the stone block out far enough from the wall to get a good grip on it. At that point, they each grab one side of the block and slide it all the way out of the wall. Then they carefully descend their respective ladders, each with two hands under block eighty-seven. When they reach the concrete floor—only two rungs down—they set the block next to the wall.

Jack wipes perspiration from his forehead and says, "How in the world did Jacob remove this block by himself?"

"He must have been a world-class weightlifter," Armando replies. "He could probably lift a small pony above his head."

"He must've been," Jack agrees, shaking his head at his roommate's relentless humor, "or he had help."

There is a brief silence before Jack inquires, "Well, are you ready?"

Armando's face lights up, and he places his foot on the first rung of his ladder. But then he stops and says, "Your great-great-grandfather is the one who brought us down here, so I believe the honor is all yours, Juan. Climb on up there and find out what's so important to hide down in this dungeon."

"Have it your way," Jack says with a shrug and a smile. He climbs two rungs up the ladder and peers into the space where the stone block had sat untouched for one-hundred and twenty years. When he sees nothing, he pulls out his phone, turns on the flashlight, and examines the vacated cavity.

Almost immediately, he cries out, "Jackpot!" A moment later, he adds over his shoulder, "Forgive the pun."

He reaches into the space behind the extracted block and pulls out a slender wand about a foot long. It is made of a darker wood that appears to be walnut. "I don't know what it is," Jack comments as he descends the ladder to the floor, but there's little doubt this is the object Jacob's riddle was speaking of."

Both men eye the dark wand with wide eyes as Jack rolls the object around in his hands.

"It looks like it has a cap on that end," Armando says, pointing.

"Sure enough," Jack says, examining the dark wand more closely. "It's some kind of container, like the one people store maps in after they roll them up—except a lot smaller."

"What are you waiting for, Juan?" Armando cries. "Let's open her up!"

Jack's fingers begin to explore the cylinder, but then he hesitates. "I've got a better idea," he says, glancing over at his friend. "Let's get the block back into place before Zeke shows up and makes us work overtime all semester for destroying his home away from home. Then we can take our find back to the fireside room and check it out with the other Eagles. I think it's only appropriate to open this baby up together since it took all of us to solve the riddle. I think Stewart, especially, would love to be there for that moment."

"You're going to make me wait, Juan?" Armando says with a frown. "Okay, okay, you win," he says with a frustrated sigh. "You know how I struggle with delay of gratification. But it's the right choice. Harder can often mean better."

After Jack locates some white silicone caulk that he dispenses liberally in the bottom of the open cavity, the two men pick up the heavy stone block and slide it back into the wall. Then, once the eighty-seventh stone is back in its place, Jack squeezes more silicone into the spaces on either side of the block as well as into the space above it. He uses his chisel to push the silicone farther back into the crevices and then smooths the surface with his finger.

"Not bad, Juan," Armando says, examining his friend's work. "It looks lighter than the other mortar but shouldn't be noticed by anyone unless they get up real close like we did."

As Armando steps down to the floor and folds up his ladder, he says,

"This whole thing went too smoothly to be accomplished merely by human effort, Juan. The sovereign God was clearly behind it. We indeed serve a mighty God."

Jack nods his head in agreement. "I think it is more than coincidence that I read Psalm 32:8 this morning. It says there that "I will instruct you and teach you in the way you should go; I will counsel you with my eye upon you."

"Amen, Juan, amen," Armando replies. "The Holy Spirit is in the middle of this just as He was with us when we went into the barrio. Wherever we go, His presence goes with us."

The two men put the ladders, hammers, and chisels away where they had found them—Zeke will know something is amiss if his equipment is not in its correct place—and scan the basement to ensure they have not left any evidence of their presence. Then they turn off the glaring fluorescent lights and run up the stairs and out into the night. They have left nothing to suggest that anyone had been in the basement except possibly the new caulk. But who will ever give a bother to the old stone wall?

The only thing the two cautious men overlook is the single video camera hidden in the shadows of the northeast corner of the large storage room.

CHAPTER 3

DUEL TO THE DEATH

It is an unusually cold evening in April of 1899. The advance of spring has run up against a formidable foe that opposes it for mastery.

Jacob Sutherington emerges from the basement of the mammoth church and trudges toward the stone quarry only a hundred yards away. He, too, is about to face a formidable foe.

But he is not afraid—at least not at this moment. His heart is a repository for sorrow and an incubator for revenge.

When the grieving and raging man arrives at the birthplace of quarried stone, he pauses and examines the scattered blocks waiting to be transported to their assigned building sites. He stares at the deep channels cut in the quarry floor while he absently grinds the souls of his shoes into the carpeting of limestone flakes beneath his feet. The sun is setting behind the hill in front of him that forms the back wall of the quarry. The light of the dying day paints his face golden one last time.

Soon, darkness will swallow him forever.

Jacob glances down at the map in his hand, crumpled earlier by anger, then shoves it recklessly into the vest pocket of his jacket. He moves forward again, picking his way through the labyrinthine jumble of blocks, some redeemable, some destined to be discarded—like his life.

He is ready to die. Life promises him nothing that inspires him to keep living.

When he approaches the southwest corner of the quarry that is engulfed by shadows, he scans the area until his eyes settle on the object of his search—a 3'x 3' slab lying flush with the stone floor. He plods over to it and bends down slowly, as if he might break if he moves too quickly.

After searching its edges for a grip, he falls to his knees in the stone dust and attempts to lift the heavy rock. Eventually, it yields before his hands, and he leans it up against the back wall of the quarry.

He turns his attention back to where the slab had rested moments earlier and finds himself gazing down into a black hole. Immediately, thoughts of his visit to the accursed Devil's Lodge several months earlier rush into his mind, kick down the door to his storehouse of memories and resurrect a ragged recollection. It was the night of his first encounter with Philip DaFoe, offspring of darkness. It was the accursed night he opened Pandora's box of evil. His grief and rage are momentarily overshadowed by an inconsolable remorse.

Jacob takes a deep breath and rips his eyes away from the dark hole that is summoning him to hell itself. He studies his surroundings: the peaceful quarry, the majestic castle-church he has known since his youth, the glistening lake, the spring sky melancholy with the coming night. He is memorizing everything because he knows this is his final moment in the world above the ground. He is going to his death, to his tomb. The time has come for him to join his wife, his children—even Madeline—beneath the earth.

It is his penance.

He feels around in his jacket pockets—ever so carefully—until his groping fingers locate the two objects that will deliver him from his agony and serve as the executor of his burning wrath against Satan's seed. Then he swings his foot into the dark orifice and locates the first rung of the underground ladder. After yet another sigh, he begins his descent.

Sadness stirs in his chest and constricts his throat as he goes deeper into the shaft. He finds himself weeping. Why, he does not entirely know. He has no fear of death now that his loved ones are gone. Philip DaFoe is the only one he fears, as one might fear the devil incarnate.

But fear can be eclipsed by other emotions.

Jacob reaches the bottom of the ladder and steps down onto the floor of the tunnel. He imagines that he is in hell. He pauses and listens carefully for some sound, any sound, but hears nothing. Eventually, he kneels on the damp floor and feels around for the carbide mining lamp that the devilish Philip had promised would be waiting for him. His searching fingers soon locate the torch and the wooden matchbox lying beside it.

He fumbles in the darkness with the two-chambered device until his fingers find the knob that releases a slow drip of water into the lower chamber housing the calcium carbide. He turns the knob and waits for the acetylene gas to form. Then he strikes a match and lights the hand lamp. Grudgingly, the flame comes to life, and the new-born light reflects off the reflector and flows out into the tunnel.

Here, then, is the bright torch that will lead him to the dark man, Philip, and—if all unfolds according to Jacob's morbid plan—the final resting place for both murderers. One of the murderers is a cold-blooded premeditated assassin, and the other...an adulterous man who regrets everything he has done since he walked away from God.

Jacob pulls the map out of his pocket one more time and holds it before the light. He counts the cross tunnels on the paper one by one—eight total. After the sixth intersection, he will look for the next passage that branches off to the right. At that point, he will be near his destination, close to his final encounter with Satan's man—if the murderer's map is accurate. He trusts nothing about DaFoe, so he will not be surprised if the seventh passage is booby-trapped or contains a dozen venomous adders.

He begins walking forward through the tunnel with heavy steps, recalling the events of the previous three months. So excited at the onset of his journey to be untethered from law and authority, he now has profound, irreversible regrets. In fact, he rues the day when he decided to live out his libertine manifesto.

In retrospect, he admits that the word "experiment" was simply his euphemism for hedonism. He wanted what he wanted with no restraining deterrent. He was dead-set on defying morality and abandoning himself to reckless pleasure—a river without banks. Now he is about to drown in that river, the river of sin.

So much for the experiment that promised freedom and pleasure.

Jacob navigates the tunnel for a long time as it descends deeper into the belly of the earth. The walls are damp beneath a ceiling that rises from six to ten feet in height. The passage of time is difficult to assess in the subterranean night, but he estimates that at least an hour has passed since he left the world of light.

A while later, he passes the sixth intersecting tunnel. Then, shortly after that, he arrives at his destination.

He extracts his map one last time and studies it in the light of his lantern. After he has determined that he is in the correct location, he does something he has not done in years: he talks to God. His plea is simple. "Jesus, I don't know if you actually exist or if you are but a figment of desperate men, but if I ever needed your existence to be true, this is the day."

As he turns into the smaller tunnel on his right and begins walking through the cramped passage, he recites the 23rd Psalm, or at least as much of it as he remembers from Sunday school.

"The Lord is my shepherd," he recites from his memory of the King James Bible. "I shall not want. He maketh me to lie down in green pastures, he leadeth me beside still waters; he restoreth my soul... Even though I walk through the valley of the shadow of death, thou art with me."

A few minutes later, the walls and ceiling of the passage fall away, and Jacob finds himself in a huge cavern that could house a small village. The broad swath of light from his lantern reveals dozens of stone teeth hanging from the ceiling. For a fleeting moment, Jacob imagines that the sinister stalactites are the incisors of a prehistoric creature ready to rip him asunder.

As he looks around the large room, the unmistakable sound of gently flowing water greets his ears. He decides that it is generating too much volume to simply be a trickling spring.

Navigating his way among the rocks on the floor of the cavern (and between the dangling teeth), he eventually espies the source of the sound—an underground river!

Approaching it, he lifts his lantern above his head and sees a dark sheet twenty feet wide flowing over the floor. Its surface is so smooth that it appears he can walk across it to the other side. He follows the path of the river with his eyes until it disappears around a bend in the gloomy cavern.

"Utterly amazing!" he whispers to himself in the underground cathedral. "In all my years, I never possessed a notion that a river was flowing beneath my feet." He shakes his head and repeats, "Amazing!"

He stares at the river for a long time, moving his lantern up and down its visible length. For a fleeting moment, he wishes he was not going to die. But he has no choice; he must embrace his fate and rendezvous with Philip DaFoe. The man will never leave him alone until the matter between them is settled. Jacob believes that even if he were to move far away, the Satan man would follow him to Timbuktu to transact his evil business. No, it must end—in this place, on this night.

Jacob comes to his senses and remembers that danger is near. Immediately, he becomes vigilant to his environment. His nemesis cannot be far away—possibly even hiding behind one of the boulders on the floor of the cavern.

He knows where he must go. He follows the river for a hundred yards as it bends toward the right until he comes to a large rock painted with a small white cross—an inverted cross, of course. Here Jacob stops and lifts his lantern as high as possible. Sure enough, on the other side of the river, he sees a small portal in the wall of the cavern—his final destination. He shivers as he envisions the end of his life.

Jacob examines the water that hurries forward with only a whisper, then wades into the river. The water is cold and flowing more rapidly than he had anticipated. He moves forward slowly, steadying himself as the water rises above his knees.

When he is halfway across the subterranean river, he remembers the objects in his jacket, and he is filled with terror. He glances down and is immensely relieved when he observes that the water has not reached them.

He slides his right hand into both pockets, one after the other, and extracts the heavy objects that were custom-made by an acquaintance he met at the Watering Trough Cantina—two sticks of dynamite twelve feet long and three feet in diameter. He lifts them high above his head next to the lantern he grips in his left hand. The small box of matches supplied by Philip to light the lantern remains dry in the vest pocket of his jacket.

At one point during his crossing, he panics when a depression in the riverbed throws him off balance. He lunges forward, attempting to right himself. Initially, he is horrified that the dynamite and lantern will plunge into the river; however, he is fortunate to regain his footing, and the potential disaster is averted.

After he has righted himself, Jacob looks up and notices that the explosive sticks are touching the side of the carbide lamp, only inches from the lantern flame. He cries out in fear.

Once again, however, disaster is averted as he jerks the dynamite away.

Moving forward more carefully than before, he reaches the other side of the river and stands cold and wet before the portal that is no larger than the lid of a coffin. It is the doorway to the tomb of Philip DaFoe. It is also the doorway to his own tomb. He will enter but never leave.

How ironic that Madeleine and his mother inhabit the same tomb, and now he and Madeleine's husband will do the same.

Jacob replaces the two sticks of dynamite into his jacket—the water rose no higher than mid-way up his thigh, so his pockets are dry. He sighs deeply and whispers from a throat choked by emotion, "This is for you, Martha. This is for you, Ezra and James, and Delilah. Witness my faithfulness to you all." Then, with adrenaline crashing through his body, he walks through the coffin door.

The passage to the adjoining room is short. After only a few steps, he enters a chamber dimly lit by several torches jammed into crevices in the walls. For a fleeting moment, he is back in the altar room with the hooded members of the Devil's Lodge, and he feels a wave of nausea rise into his throat. His heart begins to race, and everything in him wants to flee back to the surface where there is light and fresh air instead of dark shadows and the smell of wet rock and—death.

He does not run. He remains. He is dedicated to his mission of revenge on behalf of Martha and his three children.

A voice booms in the cave, and Jacob jumps so violently that he almost drops the lantern.

"Well, well, well," the disembodied voice of Philip DaFoe utters. "You decided to come after all. I feared you had deferred to your weaker nature, my dear Jacob. From the first time I met you, I smelled your fear. I discerned in my soul that you were a yellow-bellied coward."

Jacob lifts his lantern high and scans the room. He does not see his adversary but suspects that he is hidden around the corner of what appears to be an L-shaped chamber. He begins to walk toward the sound of the voice. His legs are shaking.

When he reaches the turn in the dogleg, he slowly swings the lantern to his right and peers into the darkness. As the light floods the room, he sees a small mountain of objects at the end of the room, maybe thirty feet away. In the middle of the pile is a chest four-feet high. On top of the chest is his worst nightmare, sitting calmly and staring at him. A thin smile plays on the macabre face.

In the light cast by the carbide lantern, Jacob recognizes the spear-shaped beard, nose, and eyebrows. Yes, it is the 'sharp' man. Everything about him is cutting, threatening, murderous. His eyes stare at Jacob, sinister in their sockets.

Before Jacob can spit out a venomous accusation, Philip states offhandedly, "Behold the man who mercifully escorted your dear wife and sweet children to the afterlife."

"There was nothing merciful in those dastardly actions!" Jacob shouts as his hands form fists of rage. "You cruelly robbed me of my wife and children!"

"Tsk, tsk," the man says, shaking his dreadful head.

Jacob wants to crush it with the rock that is lying on the floor at his feet.

"What I meant was that the execution of my executions was not painful to your dear ones," he says with a cold laugh. "I rendered them all unconscious with one skull-fracturing blow before I surgically cut their throats from ear to ear. I began with Martha and then moved from room to room to complete my errand in the name of justice—an eye for an eye and all that rubbish.

"Rest assured, Jacob, I was as silent as a snake. None of them knew what was coming to them. One minute they were dreaming of social gatherings, and spring flowers, and puppy dogs—then their lives were severed like clusters of grapes from the vine."

The devil man pauses and then adds thoughtfully, almost pleasantly, "Oh yes, your littlest one—what was her name, Delilah—as I raised my ball-peen hammer to bludgeon her, she mumbled something in her sweet sleep. I believe she said, 'Daddy, Daddy.' Then I tucked her into bed forever."

A surge of rage explodes in Jacob's brain. A curtain the color of blood descends over his eyes, and he takes a long stride toward the sitting man. "You're the wickedest man I've ever known, DaFoe!" he snarls. "You're a beast dressed in human clothing. You're the devil himself!"

"Don't judge me, O murderer of my wife!" the sharp man screams loudly, his face contorted with an emotion that makes Jacob's passion pale in comparison. "You killed first. You stole the love of my life from me!"

"Love of your life!" Jacob dismisses with a sneer. "You only wanted her like a raccoon wants an egg in the chicken coop! You didn't love her, and neither did she love you. She knew you were plotting to kill her. Did you know that? She was planning to flee from you the first chance she had."

Philip extracts a pocket watch from his trousers and glances at it calmly, his rage gone as fast as it had come. He comments matter-of-factly, "Madeline was unfaithful to me. Repeatedly. Nothing came to her that she didn't deserve. You simply struck before I was able to follow through with my plan."

"I didn't kill your wife!" Jacob counters. "She fell and hit her head on the hearth. It was an accident."

"I believe you, my friend," the spear man comments blithely as he returns his watch to his pocket and looks up at Jacob. "I know you didn't take her life by intention. You're not capable of homicide. Truth be told, as I said before, you're a weak man, Jacob."

The murderer smooths out a wrinkle in his pants with his fingers and then says, "Besides...I know she loved you, and you loved her—if what you two had could be called love. She confessed that to me one night as she was beating my chest with her fists—that she loved you, not me. She was simply too afraid to leave me. She knew I was capable of loving her to death."

"So why in tarnation did you murder my family if you knew I didn't kill your wife by intention?" Jacob cries out. His fingers, that tremble as much as his voice, reach into his pockets and touch the two hidden objects. He feels a small level of comfort.

"The Devil told me to do it," Philip replies with a smile.

"You told me you don't believe in the Devil," Jacob retorts.

Philip pauses, and his eyes narrow. "I *am* the Devil," he says.

Jacob feels a shiver run through his body, but it is not enough to deter him from asking again, "Why did you have to kill them? They didn't deserve to die."

"The truth is that I simply felt like depriving you of them, so I did."

Jacob stares at the man in disbelief. "You murdered my family because you felt like it," he repeats dumbly.

"That is what I said," Philip replies impatiently, clearly weary of the topic.

"How can you kill a woman and three innocent children simply because you feel like it?" Jacob asks, breathless with rage. "You're unhinged!"

Philip raises his eyebrows and rests two fingers on his right temple. "I am not unhinged in the least," he says evenly. "When God is dismissed as myth, humans exist not by divine design but by evolutionary accident. There is no compass, no morality. Better yet, there are no fences or walls to limit our choices. We are free to do what we wish. Subjective experience is our god and what we desire is our morality."

Jacob punches the air in front of him and screams, "What you did to my wife and children was evil! Some things in this world are inherently wrong!"

The devil man considers Jacob for a while before he smiles knowingly and replies, "Who says?"

Jacob begins to speak but abruptly stops.

"Who says?" Philip repeats with his maddening smile. "The Bible? There is no God, so there is no Word of God that holds us accountable. The government? Where do they acquire their authority? Is it not their own minds, their own opinions, that are the source of truth? So why would I listen to them? Are not my opinions as valid as theirs? Who rightly holds any authority over me?

"Have you not heard, Jacob, that our morality now is the survival of the fittest? To survive, I must put myself first. I will run roughshod over anyone who gets in my way—man, woman, or child. My survival is primary."

There is a short silence before Philip continues, "Even the madman, Nietzsche, saw the awful consequence of killing off God. He prophesied that the result would be war and death, and chaos. He discerned that when there is no revelation to direct us, we will throw off moral constraints, whatever be their source, and do what's right in our own eyes. Killing your wife and children was right in my own eyes. So, there you have it—I felt like it was the right thing to do for me, so I did it."

Intellectual dissonance warring in his brain and emotional chaos crashing in his heart threaten to undo Jacob.

"Common sense tells us some things are wrong!" he protests half-heartedly, his argument compromised by the hypocrisy of his own actions with the devil man's wife. "Yes, it's that fundamental. It comes down to common sense!"

Philip laughs sardonically and arches his eyebrows. "Whose common sense? Yours? Mine? If God is dead and there is no truth, then there is no morality or common sense. Don't you see the logical end of it all? There is no yardstick to measure anything by; no plumb to determine what is straight. We are animals living for what we feel and want. And animal life is cheap, my friend. If something exists by accident, what value can it have? I kill a deer to feed my stomach, and I kill a human to feed the primitive impulse of my heart. Both are satisfying to me."

"You're a poltroon and a madman, is what you are!" Jacob exclaims as he points a shaking finger at the man. "A filthy murderer of innocent women and children!"

"No one is innocent," Philip remarks gravely. "Not even you," he adds as he sits up straight on the wooden chest. "In fact, my friend, you have just insulted my honor, referring to me as a poltroon. You have committed slander. No one calls me an ignoble coward without consequence."

Jacob's heart is pounding like an iron hammer on a rail. He snaps, "I'm more committed to calling you a madman. 'Poltroon' is simply an afterthought."

Philip snorts and dismisses the comment with a wave of his hand. "You are now boring me. Enough of this nonsense."

He pauses and then announces, "It will come as no surprise to you, my good man, that I have summoned you here for a reckoning of sorts. Your slanderous pronouncement against my honor as a gentleman only further demands a reckoning."

"You called me here to this dungeon of hell to murder me like you murdered my family," Jacob counters in a voice breathy with fear and rage.

The spearman lifts his chin with its sharp beard and looks down his long nose at Jacob. "You're only partially correct," he replies thoughtfully. "I have no intent to murder you, but I do have every intent to kill you."

"What do you mean by that nonsense?" Jacob asks sharply as he rubs his fingers over the dynamite in his pocket. "Speak clearly, not in inane riddles."

Philip rises to his feet and smooths out the legs of his trousers with precision. "This cave is not a dungeon of hell but a field of honor," he explains as he looks at Jacob. "As an honorable gentleman, I'm challenging you to a duel. Neither of us has a 'second' here to ensure the properness of this location or the equity of our weapons, but I believe we can resolve such matters on our own."

"A duel?" Jacob asks incredulously.

"But of course," Philip says. "After all, you're the fornicator who coveted my wife and stole her affections from me. You have despoiled my honor, and so I am challenging you to a gentleman's duel to gain a just resolution of said offense. The matter will then be satisfied in my eyes."

Jacob swallows hard and stares at the man standing twenty feet away from him. Then he clears his constricted throat and announces, "I refuse to engage in a duel on the grounds that you are not a true gentleman."

Philip cocks his head and stares at his adversary. Then he bursts out laughing. He closes his eyes when he laughs, granting Jacob a brief respite from looking into the twin depths of evil.

"Unless you truly are imbecilic," the sharp man says, "you must know that accusing me of not being a gentleman is a high insult against my character. Now I have absolutely no other recourse but to challenge you to a duel, you fool. If you refuse, I'll simply kill you outright."

Privately, Jacob is aware that there will be no avoiding the challenge. He knew the minute he received the invitation from the devil man that Philip's intent was to kill him one way or another. He just never imagined that it would come in the form of a duel. A glimmer of hope flickers in his heart because he has been familiar with guns since he was a boy. Long guns are his favorite. He is not as practiced with pistols, but neither is he a stranger to them. But maybe the weapons for the duel are not even guns at all.

He remembers the objects in his pockets, and he feels a strange comfort. *How far my life has sunk to be comforted by the prospect of my own death.*

"I am a man of honor," Jacob's mouth speaks even while his mind is elsewhere. "To refuse your challenge would be a loss of face for me. Consider your challenge received and accepted."

"Very good," Philip says as a smile parts his beard and mustache. "I anticipated your acceptance. Now you have an opportunity to attain revenge against the madman who executed your family."

"As you know, the rules of dueling dictate that I choose the weapons," Jacob informs his adversary. "What are my choices down here in this hole?"

Philip smiles his wicked grin and says, "I happen to have two weapons for you to choose from: dueling swords or pistols. Come here and see," he says, gesturing toward the pile of boxes behind him.

Jacob hesitates and licks his lips with a tongue that has suddenly gone dry. He wills his legs to move and, several moments later, they finally obey. He wobbles as confidently as he can toward the spear man.

As he draws close, he forces his attention away from Philip. For the first time, he examines the pile at the end of the gloomy chamber. His widening eyes travel over sealed boxes and open boxes. The open wooden containers overflow with gold coins and jewels. Piled up haphazardly among the boxes are bars of silver and gold. There are dozens of them, some more than two feet in length. Jacob knows that by themselves, the coins and bars he is beholding are worth millions of dollars.

"What is this?" he inquires without taking his eyes off the treasure trove. "Where did you acquire it, DaFoe, from some shipwrecked pirate vessel?"

Philip laughs and replies, "Not far from the truth, my friend. Some of what you see is recovered treasure. Some has been collected over the last century from around the world by my father and grandfather. And some is from the Great Western Pacific Railroad. The sealed boxes are full of stock certificates I've obtained, legally and illegally. I'm not above 'acquiring' items that are not well-monitored, shall I say. As one of the vice presidents of the railroad, I have access to many valuables—even a few gold spikes!"

"Wherever did you lay your pilfering hands on the bars of silver and gold?" Jacob inquires, momentarily forgetting his imminent mission.

"Aah, now that's a secret I could not share with you unless I was going to kill you after I told you. But since killing you is my exact intent, I can tell you. It has to do with Robert Louis Stevenson and an island you have probably never heard of."

"I'm familiar with Stevenson's book, *Treasure Island,*" Jacob replies as he looks sidelong at the bearded man.

"Well, then, you will most certainly understand what I am talking about when I tell you that fifteen years ago, my father, Balak, was reading *Treasure Island*. The book inspired him to go on a quest to find his own treasure." Philip speaks animatedly, as if Jacob is the only person he has ever confided in about the trove.

"My father contacted a friend who had sailed the world and was privy to many tales of pirates and hidden treasures and sunken ships. They scoured libraries from London to Lima and studied countless documents and maritime accounts. They also spoke at length with many old sailors. Eventually, after five years of painstaking research, they decided to concentrate their efforts on the lost treasure of Captain William Kidd. All their research and anecdotal information pointed to Oak Island off the coast of Nova Scotia."

"Up Canada way," Jacob says.

"Exactly," Philip confirms with a nod as his tented eyebrows rise upward, "a small island no larger than 140 acres. My father, along with his business partner and a shipload of men, sailed to Oak Island and searched carefully for the treasure. They possessed special knowledge about the site gleaned from a descendent of one of Kidd's deckhands. There was no map, of course, only a landmark that had to be located.

"Whereas previous treasure hunters focused their digging at a site that long had been suspected of concealing Kidd's pirate hoard, my father knew that the site was located further to the west. One night, under the cover of darkness, my father and his crew located the landmark that had been disclosed to them by the pirate's descendent. Digging like the devil was their taskmaster; they uncovered the treasure in only four nights. What you see in front of you is the whole of that treasure after the deck hands were paid."

"The whole?" Jacob inquires, raising an eyebrow. "Shouldn't this be but half? Didn't your father's partner receive the other half?"

"One would assume that," Philip replies, his eyes narrowing and his tongue flicking over his lips. "The story goes that my father's partner fell overboard on the return trip from Oak Island. Such a dreadful accident," he says, shaking his head.

"A dreadful accident, I'm sure," Jacob says, pronouncing the third word with disgust. "As much of an accident as my death will be in this cave."

"You are a man of rare perspicacity," Philip replies.

"What will you do with it all?" Jacob asks as he nods at the small mountain of treasure. "Share it with the members of the Devil's Lodge so you can finance your unholy crusade?"

The man repeats his obnoxious habit of staring blankly at Jacob for a moment and then bursting into laughter. "You're such a child, my good man," he chides, "such an innocent child. No, I will not share these riches with anyone," he insists in a voice hard with resolve. "A few people know this fortune exists, but only my father and I know that it waits here, in this cave. Those who transported it down to this vault all met untimely deaths. Their bodies are somewhere at the bottom of the river you crossed, weighed down with rocks."

When Jacob opens his mouth and begins to make a retort, Philip speaks over him. "However, you are correct that I will use this wealth to advance my unholy crusade, as you call it. Already, my father has influenced a political election of high importance with money from this cache. I will go further than that. I will use this fortune to influence the whole country. I will build an organization that will advance secularism and deliver America person by person from the clutches of religion, morality, and rigid authoritarianism."

The men stare at each other for a long time in the uneven light shed by

Jacob's lantern and the torches.

Then, abruptly, Philip waves his hand dismissively and says, "Enough prattling. What weapon do you choose to deliver you from this world, swords or pistols? We do not have available to us, of course, what some duelers have chosen in the past—billiard balls or hot air balloons."

Jacob has already decided. "I wish to see the pistols," he announces.

"An excellent choice," the man says as he displays his perfectly straight, white teeth. "They're directly behind me."

Philip turns and opens a rectangular mahogany box, then steps aside just far enough away that Jacob cannot grab one of the guns and strike his adversary on the head with a death blow.

Jacob steps forward in the gloomy cave and takes one of the pistols in his hand. The walnut half-stock looks like the crook of a cane that has been half-sawed off. It has an octagonal barrel that is very attractive to the eye. The whole gun is around fifteen feet long.

"What you have in your hands is a barrel-scratched rifled forty-bore percussion dueling pistol fashioned by the famous gunmaker John Manton of England in 1822," Philip announces proudly. "It fires more faithfully and true than any flintlock pistol ever wielded. My father purchased this pair of handguns during his travels in Europe. If you know anything about fire-arms, you know that the rifled barrel on these pistols leads to greater accuracy than a smooth-barreled pistol. The quality of higher accuracy coupled with the larger size of bullet ensures devastating bodily damage, especially at a shooting distance of only thirty-five feet."

The devil man strokes his sharp beard and says, "In this cave, our field of honor will be limited to thirty feet. Due to the shorter distance, I estimate there is a hundred-percent chance that at least one of us will be wounded." The man pauses and then adds ominously, "And to be wounded here in the womb of the earth far removed from medical assistance is most assuredly a death sentence."

Philip reaches over and picks up the other pistol. He holds it up above eye level and slowly turns it back and forth in the air, admiring it.

"Both guns have been loaded with powder and ball," he announces. "All that remains is to position the percussion cap, pull back the hammer, point the gun—not aim—and then pull the trigger. Please, do note that these guns are equipped with hair triggers. If you accidentally fire it, your single shot is spent. I am then at liberty to shoot you at my leisure."

Philip smiles pleasantly at Jacob and announces, "As in the Bible, today, on this field of honor, it is David against Goliath. You are David, of course, and I am Goliath. But unlike the biblical account, there will be a different ending in this cave. Today, Goliath will triumph over David and sever his head from his body."

The man who is Goliath pauses and sneers at David. He divulges, "I did a little research and discovered that you rarely fire a pistol, my dear Jacob. Long guns—yes, you are familiar with those—but not so much the pistol. I, on the other hand, am an expert marksman with a pistol who has vanquished my foe in four previous duels. So, without doubt, Goliath will emerge victorious on this day. Your blood will spill on the rock floor of this cave, my friend."

Jacob examines his pistol and then glances at the one in the hand of his foe.

"Do you suspect I am a cheater, Mr. Sutherington?" the man asks, lifting his chin. "In your darkest imaginations, do you believe I've deceived you by gaining some sort of advantage with my gun, or maybe that I carelessly forgot to place a bullet in yours?"

Philip DaFoe pauses and then holds out his pistol to Jacob, "Take my weapon as a sign of good faith and put yourself at ease. Take it, I insist."

The two men exchange pistols and then eye one other. Jacob is imagining Philip's shot penetrating his forehead. Philip is imagining the exact same outcome.

"I still believe your choice of a duel is bad form," Jacob says. "Ever since the atrocious carnage of the war between the North and the South, the duel as a way to resolve a matter between two men has largely fallen into disrepute. Often, in this more civilized age, it is even met with strong opposition. Too many young men have senselessly died. We are now living in a modern age where offenses are settled in a court of law instead of on 'the field of honor.'"

"Simply because a slice of America's citizenry has altered its sentiment relative to the honorable practice of the duel does not necessarily condemn it as an inferior or primitive practice," Philip counters. "The majority is not always correct, my friend. Allow me to read to you from *The Art of Duelling Manual.*"

The son of Balak turns and retrieves a black book sitting on top of one of the wooden boxes behind him. He turns back toward Jacob and rifles through a few pages of the small book. Then he reads, "'The man who falls in a duel, and the individual who is killed by the overturn of a stagecoach, are both unfortunate victims to a practice from which we derive great advantage. It would be absurd to prohibit stage-traveling because, occasionally, a few lives are lost by an overturn.'"

"I do not understand this parallel between stage-coaching and dueling. What is this 'great advantage' of dueling that is mentioned?" Jacob inquires with distaste.

"Why, for no other reason than to remove lowlifes and miscreants from the face of the earth," Philip says without blinking an eye. "Above all, to bring justice into this world," he says as he returns *The Art of Duelling Manual* to its place on top of the wooden box.

"How can you believe in justice if you don't even believe in God?" Jacob retorts.

"One does not need to call on the name of a deity in order to believe in justice," the devil man parries as he lifts the spear on his chin and points it toward Jacob. "We can practice evolved ethics that are commonsensical to the human race."

Goliath waits for a response from his opponent. When none is forthcoming, he exclaims, "But on to more pressing matters! I do not wish to address human morality or the survival of the fittest today with our words. Instead, we will soon enact and validate Darwin's science by our actions."

Philip clears his throat and says, "Since we have no 'seconds' to direct us, it is up to you and I to implement the Royal Code of Honor for this duel in a calm and dignified—"

"One last thing before we duel," Jacob interrupts as he feels emotion rise in his throat. "I need to know if you are speaking truth when you claim that my little Delilah spoke my name in her sleep before you...slaughtered her. Or are you simply manipulating my emotions with your demented mind? Tell me."

The leader of the Devil's Lodge considers the man before him for a long time with eyes that would be equally at home on the face of a rabid wolf. Finally, he shakes his head, and the spear slides back and forth in the air. "No, she did not," he replies. "I misspoke about that. However—" Philip stops himself and falls silent.

"What?" Jacob insists. "What were you going to say?"

"I should not be so honest as to tell you this," Philip utters with a thin smile playing on his lips.

Jacob is not so certain he wants to know what the wicked man is withholding from him. But in the end, he inquires against his better judgment. "Tell me if it has to do with my family."

"If you insist, my good man," Philip says. He pauses and then reveals, "I did awaken your wife before I brought the hammer down on her skull."

"What!?" Jacob exclaims. "Why in blazes would you administer such torture?"

Philip runs the fingers of his left hand over the barrel of his pistol in a distracted fashion as he replies in a sing-song voice, "I awoke your dear Agatha to inform her that you had been secretly in love with my wife for months. I also told her that you were planning to abandon your marriage and your children and move to St. Louis with Madeline in two months' time. Of course, that was before you ravished her, strangled her, and burned her body in the woods."

Jacob clenches his jaw and shakes his head. "You didn't tell her that! You're lying again, you crooked snake."

Philip shakes his head slowly as he continues to rub his gun thoughtfully. "Sadly, this time, I'm telling you the truth, the whole truth, and nothing but the truth."

Shock is replaced by rage, and a growl escapes Jacob's throat.

"Don't you wish to hear what your dear Martha said to me?" Philip asks as he looks up from the gun and turns gleaming, insane eyes on Jacob.

When Jacob does not reply but prepares to strike out at his torturer with his pistol, Philip chuckles softly and says, "Sweet Martha said her life was worth nothing now, and that therefore I should strike away, swing my hammer of justice. Her last words to me were, 'Deliver me from my unbearable suffering.'"

If Jacob had not known that the devil man was lying yet again, he would have attacked him in that moment, most likely to his own quick demise. But he knows his wife too well. He is certain that Martha would have fought the devil to the death to protect her children.

With great effort, Jacob quiets the fury beating against the wall of his chest by meditating on the courage and integrity of his wife. A sob awakens somewhere deep in his heart, and he cannot hold it back. He despises the fact that his dark adversary is witnessing his pain and, no doubt, reveling in it, but he can no more prevent it from escaping his throat than he can stop himself from breathing.

He rues the day he ever set foot in the cantina where he met Philip DaFoe. What deadly offspring can one seemingly innocent decision birth in a man's life?

Jacob holds the side of the pistol against his forehead as if the touch of the cool barrel will soothe his sorrow. He thinks of his wife—now dead only four days—a few moments longer. Then his mind trains his full attention on the man standing only a few feet away from him.

If Jacob had not known it before, he now knows for a fact that everything about his opponent is a lie. Every time the man opens his mouth, he lies. There is not a drop of truth in his words or in his heart. Jacob's mind races to find a way out of his certain fate that will soon erase his family's name from the face of the earth. He settles on one thought.

"Do you need more time to grieve your poor Martha, who now sleeps with the worms?" the executioner asks with feigned sorrow in his voice and a mask of compassion on his face.

Jacob wipes away the tears that had misted his eyes and shakes his head. "No, I need no more time. I wish to get on with this dark undertaking.

But without the presence of seconds, I insist on one thing—that you read the Royal Code before we engage. I wish to be apprised of any and every advantage available to me."

Philip sighs and narrows his eyes in disgust. "Seriously," he states as the right side of his mustache quivers. "I must read you the rules like you are some imbecilic school lad?" He stares at Jacob with his tented eyebrows that make him appear even more dastardly than he already is.

When Jacob lifts his chin and stares resolutely at his Goliath, the executioner abruptly slams his pistol down on the gun box and turns to reach for the manual. When he wheels back to face Jacob, he begins rifling through the pages of the small black book.

"I see no need to review the specifications of the weapon or the section on how to charge the pistol," he snaps in a voice an octave higher than earlier. "I've already attended to these details. And the section on the position of firing is common sense—don't expose more of your body than necessary."

Philip pages quickly through the manual and comments so rapidly that Jacob struggles to comprehend his words. "The section on practicing for the duel is completely irrelevant to our situation, and the chapter on 'chances' simply tells us that death commonly occurs only once every fourteen duels and injuries one in six. Of course, the possibility of death or injury in the confines of this cave is much higher due to the smaller distance between us and the advanced accuracy of our weapons. I have already told you that," he remarks with irritation.

Goliath bites his lower lip as he continues to scan the contents of the small manual.

"We have no seconds, so that section is irrelevant," he announces in a voice that is growing in volume. "We have not arranged for a medical assistant because this duel is to the death...You and I have not imbibed too much alcohol, I am certain, and have instead consumed coffee and a biscuit this morning...The paces of the two participants are to be three feet in length. On this small field of honor, we will both take five paces before we turn."

"I believe there is only one last thing to read to you," Philip shouts as he glances up at Jacob, his eyes now fiery. "Listen closely, for this will apply to you."

He turns his attention back to the manual and reads, still shouting, "'I cannot impress on the individual too strongly, the propriety of remaining perfectly calm and collected when hit: he must not allow himself to be alarmed or confused, but summoning up all his resolution, treat the matter coolly, and if he dies, go off with as good a grace as possible.'"

Having completed the review of the manual, Philip tosses it on the floor where it lands open, looking very much like a shot gunned duck with wings spread in death. Then he picks up his pistol and reaches into his trouser pocket, and extracts two caps. He throws one to Jacob and holds the other one in his hand.

"The moment of judgment is upon us, my friend," he announces gravely. "Let us position ourselves in the center of the room."

The two men stare each other down as they walk to the spot Philip had marked earlier on the cavern floor. Soon they are standing back to back.

The devil man speaks toward the pile of treasure that lies in front of him, "Cock your trigger and place your cap on the nipple at this time. Then hold your pistol toward the floor and take five paces on my command. Once you turn, raise your weapon and fire at will when ready. I will be aiming at the second button of your shirt that lies over your heart."

Even though Jacob's hands are trembling, he somehow manages to position the cap in its proper place. His mouth is dry, and his stomach is churning. The moment seems surreal. He squeezes his eyes shut and thinks of Madeline and Ezra and James and Delilah. He calms a bit. He opens his eyes and examines the floor of the cave in front of him, searching for the preordained object he will need to defeat his self-designated executioner.

"Ready—on my count," Philip announces, still speaking in the loud, higher-pitched voice that sounds deranged to Jacob. "One. Two. Three..."

Jacob strides forward through the gloom of the chamber, his chest heaving as he gasps for air. He cannot erase the image from his mind of Philip's bullet striking one of the sticks of dynamite and blowing him to pieces. He attempts to steady his shaking arm.

In that moment, an unrehearsed, calming vow forces its way into his conscious mind against stiff opposition: "God, if you deliver me from this devil, you have my oath that I will serve you the rest of my days."

"Four. Five."

Jacob blows the air out of his lungs through his nose. He turns and raises the pistol out before him at arm's length, being careful not to expose too much of his body to Philip's shot. His chest on fire with a chaotic blend of undefined emotions, his eyes focus like field binoculars on his opponent. Thirty feet has never felt so close in all his life.

Everything that ensues occurs in less than two seconds.

Jacob depresses the trigger, and his gun discharges. Smoke bursts out of the end of the pistol, and the lead ball is sent hurtling toward the Satan man. The cave of shadows explodes with the report of his weapon. A cannon fired in the parlor of a house would not have been any louder.

Almost simultaneously, he sees flame erupt from Philip's gun, and another artillery shot rings out in the gloomy chamber—the most unlikely field of honor in the history of dueling. Jacob remains on his feet long enough to observe his adversary's shoulder jerk backward and the pistol fly from his hand. Then he crumples to the hard, damp floor on his right side. His own pistol falls to the floor of the cave and cartwheels away.

"By George, you actually grazed me, you lucky devil," Philip laughs as he probes his shoulder with his left hand. "But I can see that I have mortally wounded you. Do not fear too much, my friend; the bullet is large enough that your blood will spill quickly. You might be dead even as I speak."

Jacob hears the shoes of hell's wraith scraping across the stone floor, and he knows his foe is walking toward him.

"You were so naïve to trust me, Jacob Sutherington," the devil man says, sneering. "I gave you the pistol that fires left and high, you buffoon. I reserved for myself the pistol that fires straight and true. You should never have agreed to exchange weapons with me. How predictable you are. You're nothing but a fool."

Jacob watches through narrowed eyes as his adversary retrieves his pistol from the floor using his left hand and shoves it into his waistband. Then the man comes closer and stands over his supposed victim. Jacob lets out a low groan for good measure.

As Philip reaches out to roll his fallen opponent over and examine the damage his pistol has inflicted, he says, "Haven't you yet discerned that I play by no rules but my own?"

Jacob's right hand—the one hidden beneath his body—closes around the rock he had seen on the floor before he had turned and fired on Philip. It is the same one he had discovered earlier with his roving eyes. He clutches it tightly. He will have only one chance. A thought flits across his consciousness—*As David killed Goliath with one stone, so must I do the same with the devil's giant!*

As Goliath rolls him over, Jacob swings his right hand with its jagged weapon toward the side of Philip's face. He does not hold back. Empowered by the adrenaline that is screaming in his body, his blow is fierce. The rock strikes his adversary on his left temple, and he collapses as if he had been struck by a bullet. The sharp man's body falls across Jacob's legs.

Jacob lets out a ragged sigh of relief, and a feeling of euphoria rushes into his heart. He lies there in the damp cave panting like a wild animal, until he hears the devil man mumble, "I will now kill you, my friend."

The wicked demon from Hades is not dead!

Spurred to action by dread, Jacob shoves the motionless body off his legs and scrambles to his feet. He is able to move quickly because he is uninjured. Philip's bullet fired from the untrue pistol had not found its target.

Even as Jacob reaches into the pocket of his jacket to retrieve his secret agent of death, the devil man somehow manages to push himself up onto his hands and knees. A red river rushes down Philip's face and over his spear beard. The tip of it is crimson and already dripping blood, adding to the pool flowing from his shoulder. Staring down at the growing red puddle, the man mutters, "Tarnation! How—"

"Two can play your game of deception, Mr. DaFoe. When you turned to retrieve the dueling manual, I switched pistols," Jacob explains breathlessly as his fingers fumble to execute the coup de grace.

The victor of the duel pauses to wipe perspiration from his forehead, then says, "You give me far too little credit, Philip. Even a slow learner like me finally discerned that everything you do is a treacherous stratagem, so, naturally, I assumed you had altered one of the pistols to your advantage. When you were so quick to exchange weapons with me, I was certain you wanted the pistol I had in my hands because it was the true one."

Philip pushes himself up on his knees and shakes his head groggily. He touches his left temple gingerly and then stares at his bloody fingers. "By

George, you struck me well," he mutters. "But unfortunately for you, the blow was not fatal. You have simply awakened the raging beast within me."

The seemingly invincible man reaches a hand inside his jacket. It moves smoothly, like a serpent on a rock. A moment later, the 'snake-hand' slithers out with a large knife in its grip. A smile that reminds Jacob of the devil himself contorts the man's bloody face, and he opens his mouth to speak.

However, when he looks up, and his eyes fall on the object in Jacob's hand, his countenance alters dramatically.

"What—"

Jacob strikes the match, and it blazes to life in the gloomy chamber that is thick with smoke and the smell of sulfur. "'My friend,'" he announces with sarcasm, "your destiny awaits you. This morning, I was fully resigned to my fate—that I would die with you in this dungeon from hell—but now it appears I may yet live to see the light of heaven."

Jacob smiles grimly and adds, "You were correct in your assessment— it's not in me to kill a man with my bare hands, even if he is the monstrous executioner of my wife and children. Instead of directly being the agent of your demise, I will entomb you here with the treasure trove you are so enamored of."

Jacob pauses briefly, then pronounces the final, unholy benediction: "Farewell, Mr. Philip DaFoe. May your spirit find its rest—in hell."

There is no hint of pleasure in Jacob's voice, only the certitude of a judge announcing the just sentence to the offender.

Jacob holds the match up to the fuse and lights it.

"No!" Philip screams as he attempts to get to his feet. Amazingly, he succeeds and staggers forward. But his foot slips in the puddle of his own blood that is spreading over the floor of the cave, and he falls hard on his right shoulder.

"I cannot die!" the devil man shrieks, lunging up and swinging his weapon at his dueling partner with shocking agility. The large knife grazes Jacob's jacket. "I am Philip DaFoe the Great!"

Jacob backpedals quickly and stares at the man sprawled out grotesquely on the floor before him. Most of the spear man's body is now covered with blood. His teeth and the whites of his eyes are the exception—they stand in sharp contrast to his crimson-stained face and clothing. Jacob cannot decide if he should be terrified by the murderer's appearance or feel deep pity for him.

He momentarily forgets the burning fuse.

Then he looks into the devil man's terrible eyes and witnesses the hatred that must have smoldered in them the night he bludgeoned his wife and children and cut their throats. All pity abruptly vanishes from Jacob's heart. This wicked man must face his judgment day to pay for all the evil he has perpetrated and to prevent him from committing additional hellish deeds. Some men are incorrigible in their evil bent. Philip is one of them.

Jacob remembers the weapon in his hand. He looks down at the flame that is rapidly devouring the fuse toward a doomsday that Jacob will no longer share with Philip. He panics when he realizes that he only has seconds left before the weapon delivers its irreversible justice. He grabs the lantern that had been set aside during the duel and runs to the entrance of the room. He hurries through the short passage and sets the heavy stick of dynamite on the floor of the portal. Then he runs to the bank of the underground river.

He crashes through the cold waters like a rabid beast, clawing with his hands and churning forward with his legs. When he reaches the other side, panting, he wheels around and rivets his eyes on the entrance to the room.

For the briefest of moments, panic surges in his chest when he hears Philip's voice coming from the treasure room. "I will come for you, Jacob!" he screams dementedly. "I will—"

A bright light engulfs the portal followed an instant later by a deafening percussion that roars a hundred times louder than the earlier pistol reports. Flying rock fragments strike Jacob, and he throws himself to the damp floor, clutching the lantern to his chest. He lies there for a long time as the blast echo reverberates down the length of the cavern like a fierce growl in a mammoth dragon's throat.

When the cave is silent, he gets back on his feet and holds up the lantern with its weakening light. Peering through the dust and gloom, he makes out the dim outline of a pile of rubble covering the entrance to the "field of honor" room. The portal is sealed as if with a giant stone plug.

For the first time since the night of Madeline's death, Jacob breathes a sigh of relief. The chains of the hundred-pound millstone that had been pulled tightly around his body for weeks finally break. The giant boulder rolls off his back, and he takes a deep breath. Unbidden by his conscious mind, he raises his eyes to the dark vault above him and unleashes a primal scream that is part victory cry, part anguish for his dead family, and part rage for the devil man.

Jacob does not linger. He navigates the floor of the cavern with its shadowy stalactites and scattered boulders as quickly as his shaking legs and the dimming light of the lantern permit.

When he reaches the far side of the massive room, he hurries through the passage to the main tunnel. Here, he removes the other stick of dynamite from his jacket pocket and lights it with the matches Philip had provided for the lantern. Setting it on the floor of the long tunnel, he turns and travels up the dark passage. This time, he runs as fast as he can.

When he has covered only thirty feet, the flame in his lantern wanes rapidly and then extinguishes altogether. Jacob throws the lantern aside and slows his pace to a walk. He stretches his arms out on either side of him so his hands can feel the walls of the tunnel.

Not long after the lantern goes out, the flash from the second stick of dynamite illuminates the tunnel. Aided by the brief burst of light rushing toward him from behind, Jacob breaks into a run. An instant later, the roar of the second blast reaches him, and the ground shakes beneath his feet. His ears have a moment to register the sound of falling rocks behind him before the shock wave smashes into his back, and he is thrust forward into darkness.

Then there is nothing at all.

CHAPTER 4

STEWART SHEDS ANOTHER LAYER

Stewart sits in the old leather chair in Dr. McNeely's office. His posture is rigid, his hands are on his knees, and his eyes stare unblinkingly at his listener. He has spent the last hour speaking to his mentor about what Miriam had told him in her prophecy last semester, as well as about his experience in the Cave of Dread. This time, he even reveals his encounter with Michael in the cabin in the northern Minnesota wilderness. His level of vulnerability is unprecedented. Milner McNeely is listening carefully, well aware of the rarity of his student's transparency.

The president of the Teleios Academy leans toward Stewart, and his desk chair shrieks out in resistance. "Sorry," the man says with a smile. "This is one squeaky chair that doesn't get the oil."

When the young man with the large black glasses displays no reaction to the facetious remark—not even a twinkle in his eye or an upward twitch of his lips—the professor clears his throat and says, "Well, then, it does appear that God is repeating the same message to you, namely, to come out of your internal fortress. In that hiding place, you can neither receive love nor give love. You're simply a machine."

The professor folds his hands under his chin and announces, "Always remember, Stewart, that evil is anything that interferes with you being and becoming who God made you to be for His family. The enemy has separated you from the community like a cowhand culls a steer from the herd. He

STEWART SHEDS ANOTHER LAYER

has driven you into the wilderness, where he has lied to you and convinced you to exile yourself from all others. You've been alone for a long time. But now the time has come for you to escape the trap of the devil and become the true self that God created you to be."

Stewart continues to gaze at his mentor as he replies, "Yes, I've heard the message loud and clear that I need to return from exile. It's just that...I don't know how to come back. Also, I keep asking myself if I honestly *want* to come back."

The professor's eyes burn intensely from inside their dark caves. "If God calls you out of your captivity, He'll provide the way and the means for you to escape. Remember, He's the God of the Exodus, the great I Am."

Stewart licks his lips and adjusts his glasses. "My belief is that God is already delivering me from the dungeon of my own heart," the young man admits dispassionately. "In recent months, I've felt things I've never felt before. I just don't like how strong they feel—whatever they are. When Michael left me, my stomach ached, and my eyes were wet. When I saw Armando yesterday, I wanted to punch him in the throat. When the members of my micro-cohort clapped for me the other night, I wanted to hug them all—except Armando, who I still wanted to punch. These responses are all highly atypical for me. They feel embarrassing to me and out of control. I hate feeling out of control. I fear that I will destroy others."

Dr. McNeely reaches over to his desk with its towers of tomes and retrieves his mug of tea. He takes a sip and then says in his uniquely deep voice, "As best as I can tell, Stewart, you've already been born again spiritually. Now God is calling you to another rebirth, so to speak. This next one is emotional and psychological in nature. After all, the enemy has kept you imprisoned on every level, not just spiritual. One way to visualize this second rebirth is to imagine that your true self has been held in captivity for decades, and now God is calling your emotionally dead self out from the dungeon just as He called the physically dead Lazarus out from his tomb."

The professor pauses to finish his tea with one big gulp, then says, "The rebirth of self is not a smooth journey, Stewart. It's messy and unpredictable. Along the way, you'll feel emotions so strongly you won't be able to contain them. That's what happens when you've suppressed those parts of your heart for twenty years, young man. Sometimes they'll emerge in quiet tears, sometimes in volcanic eruptions of boiling lava. Believe it or not, that's normal. That's how it works.

"The anger usually shows up first announcing the return from exile."

Dr. McNeely sets his mug on the one available spot on the cluttered desk. "It's not just emotions that will rise up from the dark recesses and crevices of your true self," he says. "They're just a part of the rebirth. The awakening will include memories, thoughts, and aspects of your personality that have been held captive in the dark place for decades. Remember, Jesus came to set the captives free on every level: spiritually, relationally, emotionally, physically—you name it."

Stewart nods his head slowly. Then he looks up to the ceiling and closes his eyes. "I don't comprehend everything you're saying," he admits, "but it makes more sense than it did in the past. I understand it in my head."

"Accurately spoken," his mentor replies. "Your head is your strength, Stewart. Do you know why that is?"

The young man hesitates and then answers, his eyes still closed, "I believe so, yes. I've hidden my heart, so now all that's left to interact with the outside world is my brain. I'm all gray matter and no colors."

Stewart pauses for a long time and then adds, "I initially hid my heart to protect it. Now I hide it because it's full of dragons."

The professor eyes the young man carefully. Then he rubs his bearded chin and nods his head slowly. "When early childhood relationships are too unpredictable, terrifying, and rejecting, a child copes by finding a way to protect his heart because the pain is too much to feel alone. Your early pain, whatever caused it, was so great that you walled your heart off and stopped feeling anything. Instead, you learned to relate to the world, yourself, and even God through your brain.

"A psychologist would call that coping skill *intellectualization*. You defend against relational hurt and even self-awareness by reducing everything to a problem to be solved with your intellect. You think about everything instead of feeling anything. You depersonalize things."

"Then I'm experienced by those around me as the Tin Man or the wooden Pinocchio," Stewart remarks as he opens his eyes and looks down from the ceiling.

Dr. McNeely nods his head and says, "Yes, you're reduced to a body and a brain. The very parts of you that were created by God to love—your soul, spirit, and heart—are cut off and unavailable even to you. You know things and talk about facts and ideologies, but you won't—can't—connect with people at the heart level. So, you're very alone in the world even when surrounded by others."

Stewart stares at his listener with eyes that are as expressive as brown marbles and replies, "I've never heard me described in such a...'succinct' manner. You've just summarized my whole personhood. I sound...pathetic."

"No, Stewart, not pathetic. Protected. Highly protected. Sadly protected."

The professor pauses and leans toward the young man, who still sits with his hands on his knees as if he is posing for a nineteenth-century photograph. Then the mentor announces slowly, "If the level of your protection mirrors the level of your pain, you undoubtedly suffered significant pain as a child."

Stewart's passionless eyes continue to hold the professor's burning eyes. He is quiet for a long time. Eventually, he acts out of character and allows a sigh to escape. "When I remember the past," he confides quietly, "it hurts too much to make it my reality. I must distract myself and push it out of my mind. Besides, I don't want to feel sorry for myself. That version of Stewart is weak and, like I said earlier, pathetic."

The older man nods his head and says, "You're describing the Great Divorce, Stewart. Our hurt, shame, fear, anger, and even our sadness feel so painful and overwhelming that we're compelled to make it all go away. But when we send those things away, we send ourselves away; we send our hearts away. In effect, we divorce ourselves. Whenever divorce appears on the human landscape, we know that Satan is winning the battle for our hearts. He loves divorce. He's the architect of divorce."

The professor rubs his nose with the back of his hand and says, "Divorce goes against everything God desires, but it rules the universe in this present age. Fortunately, God has another plan for the world of men and women. He desires reconciliation, intimacy, presence, and love. These are the holy nemeses of divorce and separation and isolation."

"So, I need to reconnect with myself," Stewart observes from his brain.

"That's one way to say it," Dr. McNeely says as he repositions himself to the loud protests of his chair. "You can't love God, others, and even yourself until you raise your heart from the deep, dark trenches of the divorced place. Of course, if you died today, you would go to heaven since you've called on Jesus to save you. However, if you don't recover your heart, you'll go through your whole life in this world being saved but never really learning how to love. You'll never be close to anyone. You'll miss the most beautiful point of existence."

The president of the Academy pauses and adds, "Of course, once you surrender to Jesus, as you did in college, it's only a matter of time until He summons your heart from its hiding place, from its dungeon. He'll never leave His child in the divorced place for long. But as I said earlier, undoing the divorce will be a messy affair. Buried selves don't rise from the dead neatly. So, buckle up and be ready for a rough ride. Necrotic things take time to be fully restored."

Turning to one of his familiar comforts, Stewart fingers the pens that are neatly nestled in the green plastic shirt protector. He opens his mouth to speak but hesitates. He tries again, and a single syllable makes its way out of his mouth. His lips part a third time, but the Intellect shakes his head and looks away.

"What do you want me to hear?" the spelunking guide inquires as his eyes narrow with concern.

The professor waits a long time, but the student eventually turns back and looks at him. "I want to ask you a question," he states.

Dr. McNeely opens the palms of his hands invitingly and says, "Okay, shoot."

"It's not...that easy," Stewart states quietly.

"What do you mean?"

"I—I never ask questions," the student admits.

The president of the Academy tilts his head to one side and studies his mentee. He is attempting to hear what the young man is saying between the lines.

"I hate to ask a 'why' question," the professor eventually says, "but I'm going to do it anyway. Why don't you ask questions? Is it a pride thing—you know, you never want anyone to think you don't know the answer?"

Stewart considers the question for a while and then replies, "Sometimes, maybe, but that's not the primary reason." He hesitates and then adds, "I learned a long time ago that I wasn't supposed to ask questions."

"You weren't supposed to ask questions," the mentor repeats.

"Never. My parents made it clear to me early in life that I wasn't supposed to bother them," the Intellect informs his listener. "I couldn't show emotions, I couldn't have needs, I couldn't disagree with them, and I certainly wasn't supposed to ask questions. If I bothered them, they would get...quite angry with me."

"You were supposed to be seen and not heard," Dr. McNeely states.

Stewart nods his head. "They were inconvenienced by my mere presence, so I learned to go away. If I didn't show emotions around them or have needs or disagree or ask questions, everything was fine. Of course, I also had to have perfect grades and never break anything around the house—including the truck."

The professor lets out a low whistle and shakes his head. "Wow, I'm very sad to hear that, Stewart. You're basically saying that you couldn't exist in your own house. You had to become the person they could tolerate, which sounds like a non-person who would never cause a ripple in their fragile pond."

The Intellect stares at his mentor with his owl eyes and nods his head.

The president stares back at his student and clamps his jaws together tightly. He feels deep anger toward the parents who killed their son's spirit. He briefly thinks about a book he read recently called *The People of the Lie* and imagines that Stewart's parents are all over its pages. Their picture might even be on the front cover.

"Well, then," he eventually states in his deepest voice, "let it be known from this moment forward that you can ask any question you want in this room. And—I will not be angry with you. Never. I guarantee that. So, ask away."

"Okay," Stewart says, elongating the word to express his doubt. He pauses for a long time and examines his mentor's eyes as if to determine if it is safe to speak. "My question was about the divorce," he finally says. "I was going to ask you if I really want to undo it."

"Probably not," the professor admits. "At least not at first. But later, as you begin to emerge from the divorced place where your heart has been exiled, you'll never want to go back. The good news, even during the difficult beginning, is that overcoming the divorce is an act of obedience. It's a godly thing to do. It's what God is calling you to do."

"Well, then," Stewart says and then stops. There is a brief silence. The young man takes a deep breath and slowly relaxes his frozen posture. He leans back in the leather chair, a degree removed from his false self, the wooden Pinocchio.

The Intellect adjusts his glasses and looks down at his hands. "Ever since the cabin and Michael, I've been having dreams," he volunteers.

Dr. McNeely discerns that the young man is venturing into unprecedented territory, so he says nothing and continues to look steadily at him.

"You said that as I come out of Lazarus' tomb, metaphorically speaking, I'll feel more emotions—especially anger. In my dreams," Stewart admits after a short pause, "I'm often angry. Abnormally angry. Angry in a way I've never experienced before in my life. I break things and...hurt people. Like I said earlier, there are dragons in my heart, and they're not people-friendly."

The professor nods his head and says, "Yes, you've undoubtedly begun the journey toward the second resurrection."

"But I don't like being that angry," Stewart insists as he adjusts his glasses for the eighth time in the last two minutes. "I don't want to live on the edge of losing control."

"No, I would imagine not," the mentor replies. "That would be well outside your comfort zone."

"Yes," Stewart admits, "that's true. It's all very uncomfortable. But I really need you to hear that the anger is unusually strong."

"Okay," Dr. McNeely says. "How strong are we talking?"

"I know martial arts," the young man admits as if confessing a mortal sin to a priest. "I decided to learn self-defense when I was in high school back in Minnesota. I religiously attended a dojo in Duluth. During my training, I don't remember ever showing anger on the outside, but I often felt something violent inside of me when sparring, like an earthquake rumbling beneath the ground."

Stewart pauses and then looks down at the floor. "It sounds weird and maybe even psychotic, but sometimes I actually saw different faces on my opponents. What I mean is that I superimposed the faces of certain people onto my sparring partners. Not on purpose. It just happened."

"Certain people?"

Stewart nods his head. "The faces usually belonged to my father or to a bully at my school named Billy Reisch."

The professor clears his throat and observes, "That violent rumbling inside of you sounds like rage. You don't go around superimposing faces on others unless fierce emotion is being aroused."

Stewart nods and replies, "In the dreams, I'm not able to control my emotions. My fear is that this subconscious anger will one day explode into my outside reality. The dragons inside will escape into the world. I can't allow that to happen. They might harm or...even kill someone."

Dr. McNeely nods his head and massages his forehead with his finger-tips. "I can't say I blame you," he commiserates in his deep bass voice. "That divorced part of you is most likely quite primitive. But—" he pauses and then adds, "but there are no shortcuts on this journey, Stewart. There's no bridge over troubled waters. You can't get on a plane and fly over the swamp-lands with their quicksand and boiling geysers. You must go through it.

"The good news is that this initial awakening of your heart won't last forever," the professor says reassuringly. "Maybe only several months. And later, after you've opened the door for the 'messy' parts of you to rise to the surface where the Holy Spirit can work in you, then other, more desirable parts of your heart will eventually be liberated to rise to the surface as well; much more attractive ones like joy and excitement and creativity and a deep, growing ability to be loved as well as to love. That's when you'll begin to see the character of Jesus forming within you."

"There are no shortcuts," Stewart says, repeating Dr. McNeely's words.

The mentor shakes his head.

"I have to go *through* the troubled waters."

The professor nods his head.

As Stewart stares at his listener with his Pinocchio eyes, the Academy president finally says, "There's a word for this whole journey."

When the young man does not reply, Dr. McNeely says, "It's called growth. God doesn't save you and then take you directly to heaven, Stew-art. No, he saves you and then calls you to a life-long journey of change, transformation, and even metamorphosis. It's all about becoming more holy and godly. You were made in his image after all—in the beginning, before the Fall of mankind—and now he's intent on growing you back into that glorious image. He wants you to become the person He made you to be before your life was interrupted by sin and evil."

"You're talking about the concept of sanctification in Christian theology," Stewart volunteers from his intellect.

The president ignores the young man and says, "Growing to be more like Jesus means that you'll learn how to love better, manage your anger well, develop strong self-control, become more joyful, be increasingly patient, serve others as you count their needs as even more important than your own, think about God more often, experience more gratitude, have less anxiety and more peace, and even become more aware of your sinfulness. God wants you to be the best friend you can be, the best husband, the best father, the best lover of humankind even toward those who may hate you, the best citizen. He wants to grow you into the best version of Stewart possible, namely, the one He created you to be from the beginning."

"He's not going to let me stay in my hiding place," the young man reflects aloud.

"Never," Dr. Milner's deep voice replies. "You're the Titanic, buried under millions of tons of saltwater on the bottom of the Atlantic, and Jesus is the divine salvager of sunken ships. He's going to raise you to the surface, Stewart. He loves you too much to leave any part of you unrecovered."

The Titanic-Intellect sits up in the king-sized leather chair and dares to ask a question. "So, what do I do next?" he wonders aloud. "What's my role in the salvage process—if I decide to surrender to it?"

"Your part, Stewart, is simply to move toward God and others," the professor replies. "No more withdrawing. No more avoiding. You need to talk to God every waking moment and stop hiding from other people. Let them see you and know you—even the primitive parts. Shun the Great Divorce and let yourself be loved by God and other people. Then you'll witness the power of the Holy Spirit draw you into deep relationships, one degree of glory at a time."

Dr. McNeely pauses and leans forward on his protesting perch. "Never forget, Stewart," he insists slowly, his eyes burning like bonfires beneath his overhanging forehead. They fix on the young man as if he is the only object in the entire universe. "Never forget that it's better to be known and *at risk* than to be alone and *safe*. To be alone and safe is to be under the curse of the Great Divorce. It means settling for mere academic knowledge instead of heart knowledge, for sex instead of love, for embracing a spirit of unbelief, pride, and defiance instead of inviting the Lover of the universe to be your best friend."

The professor's eyes narrow as he announces, "Jesus came to rescue you from a terrifying eternal separation that masquerades as a place of safety. Behind it lurks separation from God, others, and even your own self. The enemy convinces you that your protection is a beautiful palace when, in truth, it is a penitentiary."

Stewart gazes at his mentor and nods his head. He says nothing, but his wooden face has been infused with some color. It appears softer, more alive.

A few minutes later, the spelunking journey into Stewart's heart concludes for the night. As he gets up to leave the sanctuary of books, maps, artifacts, and towers of papers, he turns to his mentor and says, "My heart is the Titanic. It's ready to be raised from the murky depths."

"Excellent!" the professor replies. "The best is yet to come for you, Stewart. Just wait and see. The best is yet to come. Never forget what God's Word says in Job 12:22: 'He uncovers the deeps out of darkness and brings deep darkness to light.'"

After the Intellect has left, Dr. McNeely falls to his knees in front of the chair that Stewart just vacated.

"Jesus, be with this young man," he prays earnestly. "You know what lies ahead for him. It will be the most difficult journey he's ever faced. Guard him from the lies of the enemy who will tenaciously attempt to convince him that hiding is always better than intimacy and self-protection better than surrender to your love. Yes, Lord, may he know your loving protection so he can stop protecting himself to a fault.

"Possibly even to death."

CHAPTER 5

———

LIGHT SHED ON THE DARK PAST

The Screaming Eagles do not assemble to open Jacob's mysterious wooden cylinder until several days after its discovery. Rachel is beside herself with curiosity. When they finally do get together, they meet later in the afternoon due to Emily's work schedule at the lodge. Since the weather is exceptionally mild, they decide to rendezvous at the small amphitheater on top of the quarry hill that they have recently dubbed the *Areopagus* after Paul's adventures in Athens.

The six friends arrive at the wooded venue and huddle closely together on the first tier of the amphitheater. After Armando gives an account of the adventure into the lodge basement, Jack extracts the tube—the subject of Jacob's riddle—from his backpack and holds it up for everyone to see. Barren branches that soon will birth buds stretch over their heads as if attempting to view the contents of the small cylinder.

"All the fuss is about that?" Rachel exclaims as she looks at the foot-long wooden cylinder that in diameter is about the size of a large test tube. She crinkles her nose and says, "I don't know what I was expecting, but certainly something more interesting than that thing."

"Tsk, tsk," Armando replies as he waggles his finger at Rachel. "One must remember that big things come in small packages."

"Not that small," Rachel says with a laugh. "But I will try to suspend judgment until we see what's in it."

"Well," Aly says with a shrug of her shoulders, "let's open it. It does appear to have a cap on that one end."

"Yup," Jack replies, "it does. And yes, let's open it right after this prayer." He holds the cylinder in front of the small gathering and says, "Lord, guide our steps even as we open this answer to Jacob's riddle. You are the God of truth, so may we discover truth today in the contents of this giant mezuzah. Be glorified in our time together, Jesus. Amen."

"Giant mezuzah?" Armando says as he opens his eyes.

Jack smiles wryly and remarks, "Sorry. I got carried away. Hebrew class. Dr. Silverstein. Blame it on him."

Jack looks around at his friends and says, "Okay, here goes nothing." He grips the top of the cylinder and attempts to pull it off. When it resists his efforts, he attempts to twist it off instead. This decision proves to be the correct one. On his first attempt, the head of the tube budges a quarter of a turn. In a matter of seconds, Jack unscrews it all the way. When he removes the cap from the mouth of the cylinder, he half expects nineteenth-century air to flow out like visible smoke.

"What's in there, Jack?" the brunette with the starry constellation on her face inquires.

Jack glances over at his classmate and says, "Really, Rach? Give me a second, at least."

"Sorry," the young woman replies sheepishly as she holds up her hands. "It's just that this thing has been waiting one-hundred-twenty years to be opened. We don't want to waste another second," she says with a smile that brightens her face.

Jack tips the cylinder upside down—nothing falls out. He shakes it gently—there is no sound. Finally, he inserts his finger into the narrow tube and runs his finger carefully around its interior. Then he begins to extract something that resembles a scroll.

"Careful, Jack," Stewart warns. "The paper may be vulnerable to disintegration."

Jack coaxes the scroll out of the cylinder until it is fully removed. He sets the wooden container on the amphitheater pavement and examines the object in his hand.

"Another journal entry?" Emily inquires.

"Could be," Jack replies. He unrolls the scroll as Stewart again cautions him.

When it is fully opened, the students find themselves looking at several pages of 6" x 10" paper yellowed with age. Some of the edges are cracking. Here and there, small pieces of paper break away from the pages even as Jack holds them in his hands. They drift to the stone pavement like tawny snowflakes. The first page of the scroll has a watermark imprinted in the top left corner and is covered with familiar cursive.

"It's Jacob's handwriting," Aly observes, glancing up at Jack. Jack nods his head and says, "No doubt about it."

"What does it—" Rachel begins to ask, then stops herself. "Sorry," she says with an embarrassed laugh. "My lips are now sealed," she insists, making a zipping motion across her mouth with her fingers.

"It appears to be written in blue ink this time instead of the usual black," Jack observes. "I suppose that detail is irrelevant. The entry is dated April 17th, 1899."

He looks up and scans the faces of the other Screaming Eagles, who are now leaning in close. "I'll go ahead and read it since we're all anxious to see what Jacob has to say."

"This could be huge, Juan," Armando comments, nodding his head. "This entry could tie up a lot of loose ends."

Jack pauses and then hands the scroll to the person sitting next to him. "I think you should read it, Stewart," he says. "After all, you are the official journal reader for the Screaming Eagles."

The Intellect's face reveals nothing, but his large eyes smile at his friend. He receives Jacob's journal entry with careful hands and soon begins to read.

I am not even certain why I am compelled to record this event. It only damns me further to confess that I am responsible for the death of yet another person. But my conscience demands a cleansing, and so I write.

The sinister Philip DaFoe with the Dr. Jekyll and Mr. Hyde personality is dead—or soon will be—unless delivered by some witchery inspired by the Devil himself! The wicked man is buried forever in the cave he lured me to with the intent of ending my life. He was sealed in his tomb only three hours ago.

The devil man summoned me to a cave system beneath the quarry by means of a second accursed letter that arrived at my home—my domicile that is now so terribly silent.

Deathly quiet. He invited me to the underground cavern to murder me. Accompanying his missive was a map that brought me into the cave through a different portal—not the Devil's Lodge entrance but one that gave me purchase through the quarry floor. An hour of caving brought me to the fateful spot where I eventually buried him after he challenged me to a duel, of all insane things!

To ensure that the devil would not rise from his grave, I sealed his tomb twice with powerful sticks of dynamite, first inside the "river room" and then a second time in the passage that opens into the main tunnel. I am all but certain that the world will hear no more of Mr. Philip DaFoe, ringleader of the Devil's Lodge.

I was rendered unconscious by the second blast. When I woke, I found myself in utter darkness and retching horribly. Momentarily, I was disoriented to both place and time. I had to strain even to remember my name. I am ashamed to admit that I panicked. In the end, I called on God for the third time that day. Thrice! Imagine that. The hedonistic pagan who had so recently embraced atheism is moving back toward theism!

After my entreaty to the divine—God does seem to answer prayers, at least on this day—I remembered that I was in the tunnel beneath the quarry. I got to my feet and followed the tunnel as it slowly ascended, knowing that the passage should take me back to the surface of the earth. My grave fear was that I might veer off into one of the passages that branch off from the main tunnel and fall into some bottomless pit.

I had gone no more than thirty paces when more of my memory returned, and I recalled that I still had the box of matches in the pocket of my jacket. I retrieved them and used them conservatively as I labored forward. I would light a match, then walk forward as fast as possible without extinguishing it, all the while memorizing the tunnel ahead so I could walk a fair distance even after the match went out. I had two matches left when I reached the ladder that delivered me from what I had been convinced would be my tomb.

"Juan," Armando interjects, "could Jacob be referring to the tunnel beneath our blind room? Could he be talking about the same ladder we've taken down into the cave?"

Jack looks up from the pages in Stewart's hands and nods his head slowly. "You could be right, Manny. Unless there's more than one shaft that leads down into the tunnel."

Stewart clears his throat and adds, "Do you remember when we were in the tunnel the first time—with Jonathan? He led us to a spot where the main passage ended abruptly due to a cave-in. Could that be where Jacob deposited his second stick of dynamite?"

Jack closes his eyes and considers the Intellect's question. "Wow," he says a moment later, "that makes a lot of sense. Let's keep reading because this final journal entry does seem to be explaining a few things."

Stewart's eyes travel back down to the scroll, and he continues to read:

Yes, the nightmare known as Philip DaFoe has finally ended. But as one ends, another continues. I know I have not yet grieved for my wife and children as I must. My rage and desire for vengeance have consumed me. Now that they have been satisfied, sadness and loss are beginning to arise within me—as well as guilt.

I precipitated the death of my entire family in the pursuit of my selfish desires...

How foolish could I have been? I curse the day I met Philip DaFoe at that hellish cantina! Little did I know that my encounter with that devil would spawn a nightmarish series of events beginning with the night I met his wife! Five deaths. No, six deaths now, counting Philip.

My grief is unspeakable. How does a man live with these memories?

I have contemplated day and night taking my own life since the murder of Martha and the children.

One last thing. No, make that two. In the cave where Philip is entombed, there is a fortune. How much, I do not know. I did not have opportunity to fully assay its value. It appeared sizeable. Massive. Do I regret not absconding with his treasure? Yes and no. The greedy man in me wishes I had carried out at least one gold bar. The wise man in me—if such a one exists—is thankful that I escaped with my life. Yes, I am most fortunate to still be casting a shadow on this earth.

Why would I desire anything that Philip DaFoe touched with his filthy fingers?

The second thing is that I will be relocating to a new city where I will start my life over. I can no longer sleep in the house where my children used to play and laugh and run to greet me when I entered the door. Oh, my dear little ones!

I plan to invite my father to join me.

There is one final thing I must mention: I will be surrendering my life to God when I lay down my pen tonight. Through the tragic events of the previous weeks, I have learned a lesson I will never forget on this side of the grave. Life is not about pursuing fleeting pleasures but about loving others. Pleasure pursued by itself is a sweet honey in the mouth that, once consumed, becomes a poison in the stomach.

I will fulfill my part of a vow I made in the cave. God did his part. Now I must do mine. I promise to spend the rest of my earthly journey seeking Him and learning to love others. I owe that to my Martha.

How terrible that she is not here for me to love as I should have from the beginning.

I did not appreciate what I had until it was gone. Until it was too late.

I plan to take special measures to hide this final journal entry. Quite possibly, I will protect its whereabouts with a cipher. Hopefully, it will not be discovered until long after I am dead. My part in Philip's demise is not something I regret. He is the type of demented man who would never have stopped attempting to kill me until he had completed the task. I honestly believe I am innocent of his death. I do regret what occurred with Madeline. Arguably, I do deserve punishment for her untimely demise.

Maybe no one will ever discover my journal. Quite possibly, it will be reduced to dust before anyone finds it. But if someone does discover it as well as the contents of this cylinder and is reading it at this very moment, I will speak from my grave and impart some final words of wisdom: Never conduct an experiment with your unrestrained desires. It will only lead to darkness and death. And never trust any descendent of Philip DaFoe. Both are conceived in darkness and will only lead you to the gates of hell.

Godspeed, my reader. I hope to see you in heaven on the last day— if God forgives me.

Sincerely yours in inconsolable grief,

~ Jacob Lane Sutherington.

"What a sad story," Aly comments when Stewart looks up from the scroll.

"I feel terrible for his children," says Rachel, "and his poor wife. They were all innocent victims in this whole evil affair."

Jack is looking at Emily when she glances up at him. Her eyes hold his briefly, then seek out the floor of the amphitheater.

"You do know what this means, Juan," Armando says with a smile. "Now we have two jobs to do: dig up a grave and excavate a tunnel. Ay, caramba, we're going to be busy."

Jack laughs and replies, "Yes, as my grandfather used to say, we need to 'put on our thinking caps' and figure out what we're going to do next."

Stewart clears his throat and says, "There are several other sheets of paper here beneath Jacob's journal entry."

Jack looks down at the two other pieces of curling, yellowing paper and says, "Thanks for reminding me, Stew. What do you have there?"

The Intellect carefully lays aside the journal entry and says, "The first paper here must be Philip's letter to Jacob, while the other one," he says as he slides aside the DaFoe letter, "must be the map that Philip sent to Jacob. There's something drawn on both the front and back."

Stewart holds the paper within inches of his fake lenses—at least, that is what Jack has concluded they are—a layer of glass to protect himself from the world. "This front side has a drawing of the lake and the quarry and the cemetery and the church building," the Intellect observes aloud. Several seconds go by before he looks up at Jack and says, "And sure enough, the entrance to the tunnel is located in the northeast corner of the quarry. You know what that means."

"That means," Armando interjects, "that he went down into the cave system through the shaft beneath our blind room!"

"We unknowingly followed in Jacob's footsteps when we went down into the tunnel," Emily says, suddenly engaged again, "one-hundred-twenty-years later."

"And I wouldn't be surprised if it was Philip DaFoe who placed that slab over the mouth of the hidden passage that Emily and Stewart found," Rachel suggests. "He wanted to make sure that people from the church who were snooping around in the tunnel wouldn't stumble across his hideout with its treasure."

"He probably also drew those occult symbols on the walls of the tunnel to discourage people from finding the 'river room' Jacob mentioned," Aly says.

"What's on the back of that paper?" Jack asks the Intellect.

Stewart turns the map over and scrutinizes the other side. "It looks like it could be the map of the tunnel," he comments slowly, "but the ink has faded badly. All I can make out is what looks like the main passage and then an X up here at the top. It must be where Jacob met Philip for the duel."

"So, we need to go back down the shaft beneath your dorm room," Emily says to Jack and Armando, "and follow the passage until we find the entrance to the large cavern."

"Exactamente," the young man from La Puente says. "We need to follow it to the passage that was closed off over one hundred years ago by Jacob's dynamite. Clearly, it wasn't a natural cave-in after all."

"I guess we'll have to listen to what Jonathan suggested and do some of that extra credit work," Jack says with a chuckle.

"What extra credit work?" Emily inquires.

"Jonathan jokingly told us that Dr. Greenlay might give us extra credit if we open up the blocked tunnel," Jack replies.

"Is there a valid reason to dig out the tunnel?" Aly asks as she gently pushes aside a black ringlet of hair that has fallen over her left eye. "Why do we need to locate Philip's body?"

"We have to recover that treasure," Armando replies as if it is a foregone conclusion obvious to everyone. "We can't let a good trove go to waste," he adds with a smile.

"So now there might be two treasures," Emily says as she adjusts her head band. "The Lady Libertys and Captain Kidd's treasure."

"And two bodies," Rachel interjects. "Madeline's and Philip's. Three if we count Jacob's mother's body."

"Okay, let's summarize what we know after reading Jacob's latest and, supposedly last, journal entry," Jack says as he sits up straight and gazes out into the woods.

Thinking aloud, he says, "First, we now know what happened to Philip DaFoe—he's buried somewhere beneath our feet. Secondly, we can assume that Jacob moved out of this area to start his life over. Thirdly, we have reason to believe that there is some type of treasure in the cave system that branches out beneath the Citadel and the quarry. We can assume that all these things are true if we trust the words purportedly penned by my great-great-grandfather."

"The previous entries in the journal were corroborated by contemporary newspaper articles," Stewart points out. "I see no reason not to believe this final entry."

"But we still don't know for sure where Madeline's body is," Emily comments.

Rachel says, "That's true. Nowhere in the journal does Jacob tell us what he did with the body of Philip's wife."

"But in that earlier entry we read, he talked about 'two for one,'" Aly says. "It sure seemed evident to us that he buried Madeline in a grave with another body."

"And his mother's grave seems like the best option since she was buried the same day Madeline went missing," Armando interjects.

Jack looks around at his five friends and says, "For the sake of argument, what if I recommend that we just walk away from the journal and this entire unholy saga and instead focus on school and our journey to become uncommon believers in Jesus? After all, we've got Drew to think of, and Miguel, and probably even Moussa," he says, glancing at Aly.

"What about the man who attacked you at the university?" Armando asks. "Do you think you can walk away from that and believe he'll leave you alone? I don't think so. He'll be coming after you or maybe even one of us in the future. We can't just sit around and wait for another attack."

Jack looks around at Emily, Rachel, Aly, and Stewart. "Do you guys feel the same way?"

When the four other members of the Screaming Eagles echo Armando's conviction, Jack says, "I was hoping you'd all say that; I didn't want to drag you into something dangerous without your full buy-in."

"Jack," Rachel says, "if you haven't already noticed, we're already in the middle of this thing with you. Front and center. There's no turning back now. Besides, I don't think we would've stumbled into this whole adventure if God didn't want us to pursue it. Jesus is all about bringing light into darkness. That's exactly what we're doing here."

Jack nods his head and replies, "Well said, Rach."

"So, when do we dig up the cadavers?" Armando says, rubbing his hands together.

"That's a good question, Manny," Jack says. "Now that we have this new information from Jacob, we need to figure out our next step."

"I think we need to start with first things first," Stewart says as he adjusts his glasses. "I recommend we consult with Dr. Windsor and Louis Fagani about digging up the grave of Jacob's mother.

"Immediately."

CHAPTER 6

MISS MARPLE AND THE FINGERPRINTS

Rachel glances at her phone yet again, trying to decide if she should leave or stay. She has been sitting at a table in a local fast-food restaurant two miles from the Academy for over an hour. Since she was working at the Silver Bay Lodge and missed yesterday's Tip of the Spear outreach, she felt compelled to go out and do her own personal evangelism today.

She is frustrated with herself because she simply cannot generate the courage to approach a stranger and begin sharing her faith in Jesus. Her lack of boldness explains why she is sitting at the table waiting for someone to come to her. She finds her timidity not only disappointing but also confusing since she can be so brave in other areas of her life.

Her prayer as she left the dormitory earlier was simple and direct: "Jesus, I believe you want my availability even more than you want my abilities, as Embee has told me. Therefore, today I'm going out into the world, making myself available to you. If you want me to share the reason for the hope that is in me, please bring someone across my path who needs to hear the good news. I'm ready and waiting. And I'm sorry I'm such a coward."

Rachel glances at her phone one more time and then scans the room. It is almost noon, and the restaurant that specializes in everything chicken is busy—so busy that all the tables are now occupied. Rachel sighs and decides to leave so that someone can have her table since she is doing nothing with it. As she zips up her backpack and prepares to stand up, a female voice says, "You have an open spot at your table that you're obviously not using. Is there any reason why I can't sit here?"

Rachel looks up and stammers, "Yeah, sure—I mean, no, I'm the only one sitting here."

The woman who promptly sits down across from her is thin and looks to be around thirty years old, although she also looks like she could be fifty. Her long, thin face is not smiling. It is severe, hard. She is wearing gray dress slacks and a plain white blouse from which sharp elbows protrude. Her brown hair is trimmed short around her gaunt face in a style that only accentuates the overall severity of her body. Rachel thinks the woman looks like "death warmed over," as her grandmother used to say.

The new arrival at the table busies herself with opening her container of special sauce and then methodically arranging her grilled chicken sandwich and fries on her tray. Her movements are precise and machine-like. Rachel decides that they are too rigid and controlled. It must be from the Holy Spirit that she hears in her head, "This woman is full of pain. She must control everything on the outside because everything on the inside is chaos. Love her."

Rachel swallows hard and says a one-sentence prayer. Then, after a long hesitation, she dives into the deep end of the pool. *After all, this woman did not sit down at the table by accident, right?*

"Life can be so harsh, can't it?" Rachel comments somewhat randomly but with genuine compassion that flows from her own past and present pain.

The woman across from her glances up but does not look into Rachel's eyes. Instead, she looks at her forehead briefly, then quickly looks back down at her food. She does not say a word, but she does jerk her head slightly downward in apparent nonverbal assent as she removes the grilled chicken filet from the bun and sets the bread aside.

Rachel recognizes an anorexic when she sees one. After all, she herself struggled with the disorder for several years before switching to bulimia. Besides, just minutes ago, she was reading several articles on her phone about the proliferation of ana/mia websites and the thinspiration movement. So, the whole topic of anorexia is fresh in her mind.

"By the way, my name is Rachel," she says with a smile as she extends her hand to the woman who is toying with her French fries but eating none of them. The woman does not shake Rachel's hand. "If you must know, my name is Julianna," she reports. Her voice is cold and discourages approach of any kind.

Rachel takes a deep breath and continues her uncomfortable advance into what feels like enemy territory. "You must be here to grab a quick lunch before heading back to work," she ventures haltingly, kicking herself mentally for her lame observation.

The woman glances up at Rachel's forehead again. Her eyes are stones. "You have the gift of observation," she remarks so flatly that Rachel is uncertain of the woman's intent. Her tone betrays no sarcasm, but her words drip with it.

Thanks, Lord, Rachel says in her mind. *I pray for a woman to share my faith with, and you send me a porcupine.*

Only briefly deterred, Rachel plows forward like an Antarctic ice-breaking vessel. "Where do you work?" she inquires.

Without looking up, the thin woman remarks, "The university."

Rachel watches as her table companion surgically opens a salt packet and distributes its contents into an organized field next to her fries. She has yet to take a bite of her food. Her movements are still rigid. She does not lift her gaze from her tray.

"Just so you know," Rachel says in a voice that is unusually subdued for her louder personality, "I don't judge you for a second, Julianna. I've struggled with my eating for years. And I'm not just talking about disordered eating. I've met the diagnostic criteria for ED since I was thirteen. My family placed such a huge importance on appearances that I turned to anorexia to control my weight. No surprise there. I—"

Rachel stops herself and then says, "Sorry. Too much information and maybe premature. I assumed, maybe too quickly, that food is—"

The young woman looks at Rachel's forehead and comments coolly, "You're not wrong. ED is my closest acquaintance. I've been obsessing about food every day and every hour for over a decade."

"Do you mind me asking why you're here at a fast-food restaurant?" Rachel asks.

"You're wondering how I dare show up in public when I'm so uncomfortable being observed while I eat?" the woman asks. "You should know why," she adds, her voice as sharp as a chef knife.

"You're right—guilty as charged," Rachel admits. "I was just wondering if you're working an ED program, and one of your assignments is to push yourself out of your comfort zone and eat in a public place."

"You're intelligent after all," Julianna replies, still looking down at her tray. After a short pause, she adds, "I've been fighting this disease for years, and I'm not going to let it defeat me. I really don't want to die and leave my two kids without a mother. Did you know that anorexia has the highest death rate of any mental illness?"

Rachel shakes her head slowly from side to side. Then she says, "I just met you, Julianna, and I certainly haven't earned the right to say anything to you, but I'm going to tell you anyway: I'm so proud of you for what you're doing—even today, in this restaurant. I know it's such an intimidating battle. I think you're amazingly brave!"

The woman across from her in the noisy restaurant looks up. This time she looks into Rachel's eyes instead of at her forehead. As Rachel gazes back at her, she sees a beautiful face that has been wrecked not only by her disease but also by entrenched shame and its ever-present partner—defensiveness.

In her android voice, Julianna replies dispassionately, "I suppose you expect me to thank you for your compliment. Okay, thank you. Now I owe you nothing."

The two women sit together in silence. Rachel debates her next move as she silently prays to Jesus for more wisdom. She eyes the prickly woman across from her and watches as she continues to arrange her food. She still has not eaten any of it.

"Maybe today isn't about eating food as much as it's about walking in the door, ordering a meal, and sitting down with someone," Rachel finally offers.

Julianna glances up at her and smiles without warmth. "You're taking care of me, Rachel—a classic ED behavior." She speaks Rachel's name derisively, as if speaking to a lesser person. "And while your observation about why I'm here today is correct, I resent the fact that you, a woman who has personally dealt with eating disorders and so is aware of the social anxiety triggered by being observed, continue to comment about my eating."

Before Rachel can respond, the woman rises abruptly from the table and adds, "I've accomplished what I needed to here. It was good to meet you, Rachel—I think. I don't want to prevent you from getting back to your job, if you work, that is. Maybe you sit here in this restaurant all day long waiting for people with anorexia to come in so you can observe them like a gorilla in a cage."

"Oh, I don't have to work at the hotel today," Rachel says, feeling both irritated and discouraged that her encounter with the woman that God brought to her is ending in such an unfulfilling way.

The woman turns to leave, tray in hand, but for some reason looks back at Rachel and comments, "You work at a hotel."

"Yes, I'm over at the Silver Bay Lodge," Rachel answers. "I'm working there while I attend the Teleios Academy."

Julianna begins to say something but stops. The woman, who Rachel can now see is not only very thin but also very tall, glares down at her and repeats, "The Teleios Academy."

"Yes, I'm in my first year there," Rachel says, forcing a smile.

Julianna stares at Rachel and says nothing. Then she sets her tray back on the table and slowly sits down. Her hollow cheeks are pale, and her eyes are lifeless.

"Do you have any classes with...do you know a professor by the name of

... Harley Hawkstern?" She utters the name in similar fashion to how she spoke Rachel's name earlier, only with more vitriol.

"Why, yes, I do," Rachel replies, surprised. "I honestly don't think I've ever heard his first name before, but I'm certainly familiar with the last name. How do you know Dr. Hawkstern?"

Julianna's granite eyes fix on Rachel's, and she comments distastefully, "Unfortunately, the man happens to be...my father. Or, more accurately said, he was my father at one time."

Rachel is speechless. Her first reaction is to scan the woman's face to see if she can detect any resemblance to the giant professor. When her efforts yield nothing, she thinks to herself, *It must be her height. She gets that from her father. And the way she looked at my forehead at first—that reminds me of Dr. Hawkstern.*

To Julianna, she says, "I don't know what to say except...except that I don't think it would be easy being his daughter."

The tall woman's severe countenance melts before Rachel's observing eyes. Her precise movements and robotic gaze give way to slumped shoulders, and her eyes soften with tearless emotion.

"I wouldn't wish him on my worst enemy," the woman says. "He's a nasty brute who cares only for himself. He drove my mother into depression and alienated me before I was even a teenager. It was all about him and what he wanted; and what Harley wanted, Harley got. Even if it meant sleeping with a student twenty years younger than him. He could not empathize with another person if he were given lessons. Vodka and pot and cigars and sundry other sensual pleasures were more important to him than his own daughter."

Julianna pauses and then adds through clenched teeth, "The worst of it all is that I'm upset right now that I'm even upset. I don't want to feel anything for the man. I don't want him to mean enough to me to arouse even an ounce of emotion. He doesn't deserve even a drop of my energy."

Rachel's eyes grow large, and she exhales loudly. "I'm sorry, Julianna," is all she can think to say.

The gaunt woman grits her teeth and growls what must be a familiar mantra, "I will not feel anything for the man. I will not feel anything for the man." Then she looks over at Rachel and, in the same breath, asks, "How can you even be in the same room with him?"

"I really don't have a choice," Rachel replies with a shrug. "He is my professor, after all. All of us students just try to fly under the radar as much as possible when we're in his class. Until he gets us going, that is."

"Ah, yes," Julianna retorts resentfully as her eyes transform into burning embers. "Until he gets you going, exactly! He's a master manipulator. He says the most outlandish things to draw you out and elicit a reaction. Then he mows you down like a sharpened scythe swinging recklessly in a wheat field. He used to do that to me all the time when I was a teenager. He'd suck me in with a remark he knew would irritate me enough to debate with him, then he'd tear me to shreds with his superior intellect. At least he thought his intellect was superior. I found it condescending and boorish."

Julianna pauses to take a breath and stares down at her hands. Then she says, "After growing up with a father like Harley Hawkstern, I'm surprised I ever married a man. When I was a teenager, I vowed I would be a lesbian when I grew up."

"I can't imagine what it was like for you," Rachel comments. "I mean, I can imagine what it was like for you from what I experience in the class-room, but I have no idea what it would be like living in the same house with him."

Julianna does not seem to have registered Rachel's comments. She pauses from her diatribe to take a breath, then starts up again. "In a weak moment, my mother confessed to me that Harley demanded that she abort me," the woman says with a bitterness in her voice that could corrode metal. "He didn't want me, his own flesh and blood! He wanted to get rid of me so nothing would disturb his precious life. He didn't even want my mother to inconvenience him. He demanded an open relationship in their marriage so he could be free to pursue any woman his eyes lusted after. He despised rules and commitment. He wanted to do whatever he wanted to do without any restrictions or consequences. In his eyes, he was god."

The volume of the woman's voice rises as she speaks venomously about her "ex-father" for the next twenty minutes. As she pours out her scathing tirade, her body movements become increasingly fluid, and her face transforms from stone to flesh. Color enters her cheeks, and she appears alive instead of cadaverous.

It is not difficult for Rachel to give this woman her full empathic attention because she can relate, at least to a small degree, to the feeling of being rejected by a father.

Eventually, the woman sitting across from her is spent. She falls silent.

Rachel is also spent from being the receptacle for Julianna's extensive exhumation of twenty years of deposited rage and bitterness. The academy student sighs quietly after absorbing all the vitriol intended for Harley Hawkstern and wonders, in comparison, how she could have been so upset with her adoptive parents.

"Your father is a hurting man," Rachel offers after a brief interlude of silence. "You know the old adage, 'Hurt people hurt people.'"

"Are you making excuses for him?" Julianna snaps abruptly. "Are you making the victimizer the victim?"

Rachel shakes her auburn head and replies, "No, Julianna, not at all. I'm just saying that some of us students have decided that Dr. Hawkstern's intimidation is a way to protect himself. At his core, he's a scared boy."

"Are you saying that—"

Rachel interrupts the woman with the flashing eyes and the snarling countenance and clarifies, "He might be a scared boy, but oftentimes emotionally, young people do incredible damage to those around them because they're only thinking about themselves. They have no idea how to love another person. They're angry, hyper-sensitive to their environment, and they live to feel good even if it's at great cost to everyone around them."

Rachel's words seem to mollify Julianna. She leans back and stares down at her tray with its neatly arranged food.

"Is it any surprise that I had to find a way to control something in my life?" she asks resignedly. "ED is a family systems issue, right? And my family is spelled d-y-s-f-u-n-c-t-i-o-n-a-l. In some ways, I don't want to blame Harley because then I give him power over me. At the same time, I do want to blame him for screwing up my whole family. He's made me so angry for so long. I hate that poor excuse of a man!"

There is silence at the table again. The restaurant is now almost empty. Only a handful of people still linger over their food.

Julianna has momentarily shed her sarcastic, condescending attitude that ironically reminds Rachel so much of professor Hawkstern. At her best, she still is not a warm person.

Looking at her listener, the daughter of Dr. Hawkstern surprisingly thinks of someone other than herself. "So, what's your story?" she inquires. "Why did you control food? Ah yes, you said you come from the classic family system where appearance is worshipped, and perfectionism is demanded."

"That's spot on," Rachel says. "In my family, I never felt loved for being me—only for my performance and my achievements."

"So, how did you beat anorexia?" Julianna inquires. "I don't know if you've mastered bulimia yet or not, but it sounds like you're on an upward trajectory."

Rachel clears her throat as her heart begins to beat faster. "Do you want the truest answer or an answer that's true?" she inquires with hesitation.

"Not sure I'm following you," the woman says, "but I think I'll go with what's behind door number one."

Rachel nods her head and says, "Okay, you want the truest answer." She looks down and examines the food on Julianna's tray without really seeing it. "I did several ED programs," she answers haltingly, "and I found them helpful. But what led to the most radical change in my life was...a new relationship."

"A new boyfriend?" the woman asks. "Or a girlfriend?"

Rachel shakes her head and pushes aside the embarrassment that rises so easily into her cheeks when she talks to others about her best friend. "No—it was...Jesus."

The woman with the severe face stares at the young woman across from her for a long time and says nothing. Her eyes are no longer hard stones or angry embers. Now they are inquisitive pools—large and reflective. It looks to Rachel like the woman is trying to register something she did not expect to hear.

"Oh," she finally comments as if awakening from a daydream. "Well, I guess that's better than being an atheist." The woman pauses and drums her fingers on the tabletop. "As you know very well by now," she says with clipped words, "my ex-father is one of those. My definition for an atheist—especially for Harley—is a person who doesn't want to submit to anybody else's rules. Abort your child, dismiss your spouse, kill God, make morality relative, and you're good to go. Nothing gets in the way. You're free to do whatever you want with no authority of any kind limiting your choices."

"Wow, that's an interesting perspective," Rachel comments, genuinely intrigued.

Julianna picks up a French fry and inserts it into her mouth. Rachel pretends she doesn't notice.

"So, isn't Jesus just another controlling man in your life?" the gaunt woman asks, still an edge in her voice. "Isn't he a domineering sovereign who demands perfectionism and gives you yet another reason to be enslaved to an ED?"

Rachel shakes her head. "Not at all," she replies. "He doesn't crush me with rules or try to control my life. On the contrary, His love is liberating. Over the last two years, Jesus has been freeing me from my obsession with food. Through him, I've learned that focusing on the addictions in life—whatever they might be—and trying to will my way to victory is impossible.

"Instead, I've discovered that I must seek something more compelling than food. Then I'm eventually able to forget my food obsession since I'm relating to something far better. For me, that's Jesus. I practice His presence in my heart instead of compulsively interacting with food."

"Jesus is like your focus for meditation," Julianna suggests.

"Yes and no," Rachel answers. "No, in that He isn't just a positive thought that I meditate on like some mantra. But yes, in the sense that when I fix my eyes on Him, I experience peace and joy, and purpose. He isn't just a cognitive distraction, however. He's a real person who lives in my heart."

Julianna stares at Rachel, and her face contorts in disgust. "How strange," she says. "You say he lives inside of you? Sounds like one of those alien movies I watched as a teenager when I wanted an emotional arousal to distract me from Harley's torture."

"Jesus doesn't literally live in my body like some physical parasite," Rachel clarifies. "God is spirit. As a spiritual being, he lives inside my spiritual self—inside my heart. My heart is his temple, so to speak. His home."

"But you said He doesn't control you like some dictator," Harley Hawkstern's daughter says as she tilts her head and raises one eyebrow.

"No, he doesn't," Rachel replies. "He woos me. He invites me to come to Him and obey Him. There's no heavy-handedness with God. He said that He wants us to experience His love first and only then obey Him instead of obeying Him first and then earning His love. He never wants our motivation to be *shoulds* because then we're obeying Him for all the wrong reasons. A relationship that begins and continues with love is always primary with Jesus."

Julianna shakes her severe head again, and her sharp brown hair slides back and forth like dangling paring knives. "Sounds *so* nice," she says with a crooked smile. "Like magic. Believe in Jesus and—*abracadabra*—suddenly you're loved, and you live happily ever after! And here I thought magic wands were merely fictional devices created by children who wish for quick and easy fixes for life's problems."

Rachel had anticipated the woman's words. "You're right, Julianna," she says with a conviction that surprises herself. "There are no magic wands in this world—as much as we wish there were. And yes, I agree that the fictional ones are reserved for children and maybe some adults who have no other solution to life's problems except to escape to wishful thinking.

"If there's one thing I've learned at the Academy, it's that in this world, we're born into a war. Every day is a battle between light and darkness, heaven and hell. Everything good and holy, and right is opposed—especially God's love. Wielding magic wands in that battle would be like fighting dragons with blades of grass!"

The emaciated woman with the long face stares at Rachel and puts another French fry into her mouth. She appears completely unaware of what she is doing. Her full attention is on the energized woman across from her with the red hair and the field of freckles strewn over her nose and cheeks. She remains silent and seems momentarily receptive.

Encouraged, Rachel continues her explanation. "Believing in Jesus is the opposite of believing in magic. Jesus is found in the nonfiction section, whereas magic is fictional. Honestly, trusting Jesus is the best thing I've ever done, Julianna. But it's also the hardest thing I've ever done. Anyone who says that Christians are weak-minded people looking for easy answers to life's problems have no idea what they're talking about.

"Believe me," Rachel says with fire in her eyes, "following Jesus isn't some comic book version of life. On the contrary, it's a sledgehammer in a world of rock piles. It's a map for people lost in the middle of a terrifying forest. It's a bright light for those who realize they're trapped deep in the bowels of a cave and they're tired of living in endless darkness. It's about giving your life to God and dying to yourself and then beginning a life-long journey of growth toward the joy that comes from being increasingly like Jesus. Yes, it's all about surrender and growth. And growth is a thousand times harder than simply finding ways to feel good."

This time Rachel does not wait for her listener to reply. She keeps going. She is on a roll.

"Belief in God isn't a crutch for sick people," she asserts. "It's the antidote for dying people who have been sick all their lives but never could find a doctor who knew how to heal them. Maybe they tried the 'doctors' of street drugs, alcohol, sex, food, wealth, accumulated knowledge, fame, or even romance. The list is almost endless. But none of these 'physicians' could heal them of their terminal illness. Not one.

"Finally, in their despair, they turned to Jesus, the physician who said that He had come to heal those who admitted they were sick, not those who thought they were well.

"These 'sick' people pushed past all the spiritual opposition from the dark side that whispered so sweetly in their ears that Jesus was no more than a lunatic, a liar, or a legend, but certainly not the Lord of the universe. They ignored the shouting voices that accused them of being weak, irrational people who wandered down some abandoned rabbit trail in the woods when they could cruise down the eight-lane freeway with the rest of the world."

Rachel pauses and sweeps aside a strand of red hair that has fallen over her right cheek. "No, Julianna, living for Jesus isn't magical—and it certainly isn't easy. People who believe the material world is all there is and simply make up magical tales to satisfy their deep hunger for the metaphysical world won't have the bandwidth to trust Jesus. After all, faith in Jesus is about choosing to believe in someone you can't even see.

"But there's one thing about faith in Jesus that makes it the most logical choice in the whole universe: It's not some happily ever after fairy tale that offers you enough denial to make it through this meaningless world. The good news is true. It's a fact. Jesus changes lives. Millions and millions of people are witnesses to that truth."

Harley Hawstern's daughter continues to stare at Rachel. She slides a piece of chicken into her mouth and chews slowly.

"I have to admit," the woman finally says, "your Jesus is certainly different than the man who was involved in my conception. The problem for me is that I won't embrace atheism because it's Harley's faith, and I can't embrace Christianity because it involves a God who calls himself a father.

"Yes, as you can probably imagine, I've always struggled with any religion that portrays God as a Father. The impersonal faiths of Buddhism and Hinduism are easier for me to believe. Why do you think there's so many people out there who embrace an eastern religion after growing up in a Christian home with an authoritarian father? It's not an accident, you must know."

Julianna keeps chewing on her chicken and says, "Me, I've settled into being an agnostic. That way, I don't have to commit myself to any religion that might end up dictating my path. Besides, then I don't have to be an arrogant atheist—like Harley, once again—who believes she can rule out the existence of a god simply because I insist He doesn't exist."

Rachel nods her head and says, "I can see why agnosticism would be a safer option for you."

When Rachel chooses not to push her point any further, Julianna inquires, "So how exactly did Jesus help you with ED? Is He like the power of positive thinking? Does He fill your brain with good thoughts?"

"The renewal of our minds is part of it," Rachel admits thoughtfully, her eyes narrowing thoughtfully under the widely scattered freckles on her forehead. "But it's far more than that. Like I said earlier, when you believe that Jesus is the Son of God and that He has come to save you from your sins, He enters your heart and creates a new person inside of you who desires to obey Him. The old self is still a part of you, of course, but now there's a new creation in you as well. The new self wants to obey Jesus instead of obeying the desires of the old self that is committed to selfishness and autonomy."

"The old self—that sounds like Harley," Julianna announces bitterly, nodding her head and crinkling her nose. "Selfish. Yes, that's Harley Hawkstern."

"I was the same way before Jesus came into my heart," Rachel confesses. "I was very selfish and angry, and I took everything so personally. I still do at times. But Jesus has given me the power to not make everything about me but instead to trust that He'll take care of me even when humans don't."

"So, what about anorexia?" Julianna demands impatiently as she chews on one of her fries.

"Yeah, okay," Rachel says. "Jesus helped me with anorexia and later with bulimia by showing me that I don't have to be in control. He's in control. If He created the whole universe, I can trust such a huge God to take care of me and my world. I can let go of my control.

"And I don't have to be perfect, either," Rachel adds. "Of course, I can't be perfect even if I tried. But Jesus takes away all my sin because he paid for them with His death on the cross. And then on top of that gift, He then gives me His righteousness in exchange for my sin so that when God the Father looks at me, He sees perfection."

Rachel pauses and then clarifies, "God's love doesn't depend on me obeying Him perfectly. His love for me never changes or falters based on what I do or don't do. It's unconditional. His perfect love means I don't have to make myself perfect or work out seven to fourteen times a week to purge my imperfections."

Julianna takes another bite of her chicken filet and says, "Intriguing, but a bit confusing."

"Jesus is far more interested in the inside of us than our outside appearance," Rachel goes on to clarify. "In fact, He said that instead of cleaning the outside of the cup, we need to focus on cleaning the inside where our thoughts and attitudes, and desires live. He wants us to grow increasingly like Him in our character as we surrender to His love. He's opposed to people who try to make themselves look good on the outside while their hidden hearts are full of greed, bitterness, lust, and unforgiveness."

"Careful, Rachel," Julianna warns, narrowing her eyes. "You're stepping on some toes here."

"Sorry, Julianna. All I'm saying is that Jesus is more interested in your heart than in your body. I don't mean that we should be slobs or anything. He still wants us to exercise self-discipline even in relation to our bodies. It's just that He doesn't want us to be obsessed with what goes into our bodies and how we think we look. He doesn't want us to worship control and perfection and self-atoning behaviors but to run to Him as our source of goodness."

"Strike two," the gaunt woman says as she lifts her chin and stares at Rachel with icy eyes.

Rachel is going to add another thought but thinks better of it. She falls silent and chews on her lower lip as she contemplates what offended her listener.

Julianna presses a piece of chicken into her organized salt field and then looks up at Rachel. She asks pointedly, "Has your class talked to Harley about this Jesus person?"

"We eventually get there with him most class periods," Rachel responds. "Is it our intent to lead him to faith in Jesus? Maybe. But I think even more important is our desire to stand up for truth when Dr. Hawkstern runs rough shod over it."

"For crying out loud!" Julianna exclaims suddenly. Her eyes are wild with disgust, and both of her hands are pressed against her stomach. "I've eaten all the food!"

Rachel nods her head and smiles. "Yes, I watched you take every bite. You certainly accomplished your goal coming here today. You were even able to eat in front of me. I call that amazing!"

"I suddenly feel gross," the woman snarls at the air. "I feel nasty." She shakes her head and curses under her breath.

Rachel glances around the room before her eyes return to Julianna. She says, "I have an idea. Let's go for a brief walk—unless you have to get back to the university."

"You know, don't you. You know I'm going to purge," Julianna replies as she looks at Rachel with eyes narrowed by suspicion. "Of course, you do. You've been down that road yourself hundreds of times." Consistent with the woman's earlier demeanor, her eyes are hard, and her voice is cold.

Rachel shakes her head and says, "I wasn't thinking that you were going to purge. Yeah, I know you're probably tempted to do it. I would be, too, if I were in your shoes. But—" Rachel pauses when she looks down at Julianna's hands.

"Little Miss Marple, are we?" the daughter of Dr. Hawkstern remarks as a scowl twists her face. "You can tell by looking at my index finger that I've been purging."

"You read Agatha Christie?" Rachel asks partially out of genuine interest but mostly to derail the woman from her negative track. "I'm a fan, too. I've read her novels since I was like nine years old. I love her Miss Marple stories."

Julianna lifts her chin a bit and sits straighter in her chair. "Yes, of course I read Agatha Christie's murder mysteries," she replies. "After all, I teach twentieth-century lit at the University. But maybe that doesn't matter to you. In your eyes, I'm just a target for your gospel gun."

Rachel gets up from her chair and says, "Do you have a favorite Miss Marple novel? I've always liked *A Caribbean Mystery.*"

Julianna rises from her chair as well. A bit of the stiffness has returned to her lanky body. "I avoid identifying favorites since all Christie books have merit. Except maybe *At Bertram's Hotel.* I've never found that novel compelling."

The tall woman pauses and adds, "I suppose if you put my feet to the fire, I might confess to you that *The Murder at the Vicarage* is high on my list—probably because I've always believed that the first suspect in a murder case should always be a family member."

The daughter of Dr. Hawkstern laughs without mirth and then muses aloud to herself, "I suppose it's quite possible that *The Murder at the Vicarage* is my favorite because Harley is as odious to me as the despised Colonel

Lucius Protheroe was odious to those around him. Both men should be removed from the face of the earth. Unfortunately, only one of them has been extirpated at this point in time."

Soon the two women are outside. They are walking in the warming spring air that is saturated with sweet fragrances from the blossoms on the trees and bushes that explode with color around them. They talk about Agatha Christie novels—or, more accurately, Julianna talks about the novels—and then they move on to the topic of the woman's husband and her two children.

Julianna reveals that she dotes on her two sons. She gives them what her mother could never give her as a depressed and anxious woman living at the mercy of her husband's capricious appetites. Julianna admits that she has little time for her husband since he is a man and also because he has never been the father she had hoped her sons would have.

Rachel wonders if part of the woman's disgruntlement with her husband's fathering is due to the impossible standards she has set for him after the massive disappointment she experienced with Harley Hawkstern. She can only imagine that Julianna's cold demeanor and critical spirit would be very eroding to a spouse's spirit. In many ways, the daughter appears to have become very much like her father. Of course, Rachel has no plans to share these observations with Julianna.

After walking in silence for several minutes, the tall woman turns to Rachel and addresses her forehead. "I'm an intelligent, educated, twenty-nine-year-old woman who despises her father and can only recall painful things about him as far back as I can remember. So, tell me why I still seem to want something from the man. That seems idiotic, even borderline insane to me. Why would I want anything from someone who has only hurt me time and again? Why would I want water from a well that only yields poison?"

"I don't know for sure," Rachel replies as she reaches over and briefly touches Julianna's bony shoulder. "All I know is that no matter how he's hurt you, he's still your father. I think every child has an innate desire to receive love from her father—even when the child becomes an adult. Even if it's counter-intuitive."

Julianna stares at Rachel's forehead for a long time, then looks away. The two women walk for five more minutes without saying a word. They now have done two laps around a three-block area since they left the restaurant twenty minutes ago. Julianna walks at a fast pace that matches her frenetic personality.

"I need to get back," the daughter of Dr. Hawkstern announces abruptly. "My car is over there," she adds, nodding toward an SUV parked across the street.

"Understood," Rachel says with a smile. "I'm sorry if I've thrown a curve ball into your schedule today."

Julianna ignores Rachel's words. She demands more than asks, "Leave me with one more of your Jesus thoughts. I want to meditate on what you've said today while I do my daily ten-mile run later after yoga. I need one more nugget to examine. What can you give me, Rachel?" The woman's voice is not cold. Neither is it warm.

"Oh, okay," Rachel replies and immediately prays in her head for wisdom to know what to say to the alternately intimidating and pitiful woman beside her.

After a short pause, she stops walking and looks up at the angular woman who is at least six inches taller than her. "I can go straight to Jesus' love letter and tell you what he says." Rachel very intentionally does not mention that the words she is about to quote were written by an apostle of Jesus named Paul. She reasons that Hawkstern's daughter is angry enough at men that she does not need an allusion to another male authority figure that might further inflame her contempt.

Rachel quotes from the book of Ephesians: "'You have heard about Him and were taught in Him, as the truth is in Jesus, to put off your old self, which belongs to your former manner of life and is corrupt through deceitful desires, and to be renewed in the spirit of your minds, and to put on the new self, created after the likeness of God in true righteousness and holiness'" (4:21–24).

Rachel pauses before she adds anything further since she is afraid of eliciting strike three from Julianna, "As I said earlier, God wants to create a new self within you so He can live within you and commune with your spirit. Some people refer to it as being in union with Christ. Then you'll have power and strength beyond your own ability to say no to obsessing about things like food. To say it better, you won't even want to settle for obsessing about food and your body since you now have a better option. Jesus will fill you with love, joy, peace, patience, kindness, goodness, faithfulness, gentleness, and self-control."

Instead of announcing strike three, Julianna stares down the street and says with contempt in her voice, "Everything my father wasn't. Self-control—ha! Faithfulness—never! Good and kind—in your dreams!"

The professor falls silent for a long time. Then she mumbles to herself with wistfulness tempering her bitterness, "If only he had been those things. Everything would have been different. Everything!"

After another silence during which Julianna's face shape-shifts from resentment to sadness to hollowness and then back to resentment, she turns to Rachel and says, "Well, Miss Marple, our accidental meeting today was a revelation that I will ponder for days to come. After all, serendipitous moments can alter the future path of one's life forever," she says. This time she is looking directly into Rachel's eyes.

"Today was no accident," Rachel replies.

"What do you mean?" the woman inquires as her eyebrows rise and she turns hawkish eyes on the younger woman beside her.

"As I sat at that table in the restaurant today, I prayed that God would bring someone to me," Rachel explains. "He brought you. His fingerprints are all over this encounter."

"Seriously," Julianna says.

"Seriously," Rachel echoes.

Harley Hawkstern's daughter tilts her head and narrows her eyes at Rachel. Her short brown hair falls like sharp miniature tines over her carved skeletal jaws and concave cheeks. She compresses her thin lips together so tightly that they are bloodless.

Rachel is amazed at how much the woman looks like a statue chiseled out of alabaster.

"This indeed is a mystery to be solved," the lips of the statue say.

The way Julianna looks at her, Rachel believes that the woman is not speaking to her as much as to Agatha Christie's elderly spinster with the amazing deductive skills who moonlights as an amateur detective.

"Maybe not a murder mystery," the professor says, massaging her chin with her bony index finger. "But nonetheless, a mystery. A mystery that cries out to be solved."

Abruptly, the woman turns and, without saying goodbye, crosses the street and gets into her car. Seconds later, she pulls away from the curb and disappears into the flow of the afternoon traffic.

Rachel remains on the sidewalk, gazing in the direction of the literature professor's retreat. "Well, Lord, that was interesting," she says aloud. "I prayed, you answered, and along came Julianna Hawkstern, of all people in the world. Are your fingerprints all over the last three hours or what? Even the Miss Marple connection was well done, Jesus. Why settle for serendipity when you can have Divine providence?"

Rachel eventually walks back to her car. She knows she will be late for her class in the Aquarium. *There's nothing like descending that submarine ladder in the middle of class, hoping I don't fall flat on my face,* she thinks to herself. *Oh well, Dr. Greenlay will probably be later than me,* she reminds herself with a smile.

As she drives back to the Academy, she prays for Julianna. "Great and awesome Father, show yourself to this woman in such a lovingly gentle way that her mind and heart will be able to separate you from her earthly father. Open her eyes to see that her days in this world are all about knowing you. Nothing else matters if you are not first in her heart.

"Be her father, God. Be her daddy. I'm certain there's a little girl inside that controlled woman who is terrified to let go and trust someone beyond herself. Please remove every obstacle that stands between her and you. Then she will receive the joy you gave me when you adopted me into your family. And she will experience the same amazing, unconditional love that says, 'I will never leave you or forsake you.'"

Tears are rolling down Rachel's face when she turns into the Academy parking lot.

"The Dark One will not be pleased with this encounter," the demon called Starvation grumbles loudly. *"No, he will be incensed. How in all of Hades did*

she meet that obnoxious, meddling woman from the school who wasn't even loved by her own parents?" The voice is angry and very nervous.

"This rendezvous is potentially disastrous," the dark spiritual being grumbles to himself. "If this woman surrenders to Him, it will turn the trajectory of the whole family system upside down—a family that has been in our camp for two hundred years. No, this is not good. This is bad. This is awful.

"I must tell the legion lord that the ancient wall is crumbling! No, I mustn't tell the legion lord. He will threaten me with the abyss. But the rumor is that the dark lord does not have either the authority or the power to throw me into the abyss. Only the One can do that. What shall I do?

I will flee and hide. Maybe he will forget about me in the carnage of the coming battle. Yes, I will flee.

Starvation stands paralyzed, shuddering with fear. Then, abruptly, he disappears into oblivion.

CHAPTER 7

———

EMBEE AND EMILY

———

Emily and Dr. Livingstone, a.k.a. Embee, slip out of their shoes and socks and ford the knee-high-deep river that runs through Lighthouse Farm near Fox Hollow. The air is warm on this February day, but the water feels like runoff from a glacier.

Both women cry out in discomfort as they wade through the liquid ice. They also laugh like two schoolgirls at their derring-do to endure the physical pain and master the challenge of a rushing river-like pioneer woman on the Oregon Trail. When they reach the far bank, they pause to wipe their feet with the towel Embee brought for that express purpose. Then they pull on their socks and step back into their shoes.

They walk up the hill past the wooden statue of Summer and across the field that, according to Embee, Sunny plants most years with soybeans. Soon, they reach the woods on the far side where the beloved but disobedient dog disappeared years ago. Embee leads the way through barren trees and bushes to a small clearing two hundred feet into the forest. There, beside a gurgling spring, she spreads out a blanket, and the two women sit down to talk and occasionally take a bite of their picnic lunch.

Embee swallows a bite of her chicken salad sandwich and comments, "I came to this woodland refuge every day after Abraham died. I swear that half the water flowing from this spring is the tears I shed that summer thirty years ago. I walked for miles on the country roads around our farm and then ended up here—even in the winter."

"Life isn't fair," Emily declares abruptly, more to herself than to the other woman.

Embee shakes her head slowly and gazes into the young woman's eyes. She says, "You're right, Emily, it's not. Not at all. Wise is the woman who assumes that life will not be fair instead of beginning with the belief that life should be fair and then being crushed by subsequent disappointment. But God is good.

"After Abraham's death, I was angry with Him," Embee continues as she brushes away a strand of silver hair from her cheek. "I pleaded with Him, I cried out to Him. I rejected Him. But He never sent me away. Instead, He invited me to come to Him with all my sorrows and fears—even my rage. Decades later, I can confidently say that He has never failed me even in the darkest valleys of this fallen world."

There is a brief silence, and then Emily says, "I can't imagine what it must have been like for you to lose your little boy. I simply can't imagine." To herself, she thinks, *I don't like talking about Abraham because then I think about...other babies.*

"I certainly wasn't prepared for his death," Embee replies. "I was fortunate to have had several strong friends in my life who walked with me through that darkest of valleys."

"Was your mother there for you?" Emily inquires.

The professor sighs and takes a swallow from her water bottle. "She was not," she confides to her student. "She was too entangled in all of the 'causes' she was so zealously pursuing. She thought she was making the world a better place—and maybe she was—but I think her driving motivation was trying to find a purpose to live. She was pretty strung out on drugs and alcohol."

"My mother would be there for me in a heartbeat," Emily volunteers. "She would drop everything and come to help at a second's notice. But my mom and I are two very different people, I've come to realize. I don't connect with her—not deeply—and that creates a distance between us. I don't know if she sees that or not. I don't think she does."

"What about your father?" Embee asks as she pulls her long silver hair over her right shoulder.

The young woman pats the headband that, like a mini hijab, covers a wide swath of her golden hair and replies, "He thinks he knows me. In some ways, he does, sometimes even more than I know myself. I can't keep everything from him. He just knows. In that way, he's dangerous. Sometimes it's better to have parents who don't see beyond the surface of things."

"If you want to *hide* things," Embee interjects off-handedly.

Emily gives her professor one of her colder looks, but it fades quickly from her oval, fair-skinned face with its slightly upturned nose. She looks down and plays with her food.

"Do you know what's more dangerous than a father or mother who sees past your false self?" Embee asks.

Emily's eyes roll on the way up to meet Embee's eyes. "What?" she says disgustedly, even though her heart is not deeply invested in her emotion. "Sin?"

"Well, of course," the mentor agrees. "But I was thinking about secrets. Did you know that secrets have a unique power to destroy you from the inside out? The longer you barricade secrets inside your heart, the more they distance you from yourself, others, and God. You see, secrets are about hiding, Emily, and hiding is almost always about preventing others from seeing something inside of you that you feel ashamed of."

Embee takes a swallow of the sweet tea in her water bottle and then explains, "But hiding is often about another factor, too—not wanting to let go of something that has the power of an addiction. If you were willing to give it up, you would tell someone about it just to get it out in the open, where it would lose its irresistible pull."

There is a long silence between the two women. Embee continues to eat her sandwich while Emily sets hers aside. The gentle gurgling of the spring becomes a backdrop for the bright songs of chickadees and sparrows, along with the furious chattering of several squirrels. The intermittent echoing sound of a red-headed woodpecker jackhammering a nearby tree also floats on the afternoon air. A lazy yellow jacket born too soon buzzes through the clearing, searching for flowers it will never find.

Realizing she needs to break the silence this time, the professor finally asks, "Do you wish to share your secret with me?"

This time the young women is highly invested in her emotion. "Why do you think there's more?" she cries out with sudden anger. "Just because I confessed to you the boys, my alcohol abuse, the drugs, and the abortions, must you assume I'm hiding other secrets?"

Embee sighs and shakes her head slowly. "I'm not on a witch hunt, Emily," she explains. "I'm not trying to shame you or condemn you. You know me better than that. I simply want to know you if you will only allow it."

The young woman looks at her mentor and tilts her head. "Did my parents call you?" she asks slowly, her eyes narrowing.

"No, your parents didn't call me," Embee says quietly. "You're just so guarded, Emily," the older woman remarks, "and not even primarily from others. More from yourself, I think. It's like you really don't like yourself deep inside, and you're trying not to be you or even know you."

"Now you sound like a shrink," Emily says reproachfully.

Embee holds up her hands and says, "Okay, okay. Guilty as charged. I'm sorry. I don't want to sound like I'm analyzing you."

The younger woman looks up at the silver-haired woman. "Thanks," she says, relenting a bit in her anger, "I appreciate it when people admit they're playing shrink or the Holy Spirit—trying to be God's condemning voice in my life."

There is another silence, but this one does not last long. Emily is the one who breaks it this time. She looks over at her mentor and says with a speculative tone in her voice, "Tell me, what's a girl to do when somewhere deep inside she *might* know that what she's doing *might* be wrong—whatever that means these days—but she *might* not have that awareness very often, if at all, for long periods of time. And, she *might* not desire to ever have that awareness in the first place."

Embee leans back on the palms of her hands and arches her back as she looks at her mentee. "Tell me why the girl doesn't want to have that awareness."

Emily leans back on her hands as well and looks up into the barren branches above her head. "Let's say because then she *might* feel guilty and think she should give up the desire in question."

"So, the girl in question does admit in her more lucid moments that what she is pursuing might be unwise," Embee says.

"Maybe," Emily admits, dividing the word into two long syllables. "Sometimes. Rarely."

"But the desire feels so good to her that she has to believe it must be right," the mentor says.

"True," the younger woman says with a nod of her head as she continues to gaze upward.

"And she can't imagine living without this...behavior or desire."

"Right, again," the younger woman admits slowly.

"It doesn't seem possible to the girl that obeying God will ever give her the same love and good feeling that she gets from this other affection," the silver woman says, probing carefully.

"I suppose," Emily admits after a brief hesitation.

"But most days, she doesn't even believe that what she's doing is wrong. After all, it's who she is, what she's made for—maybe even her core identity," Embee says, sitting up and leaning toward her listener.

When her student does not respond, Embee continues, "If the culture tells her it's okay, if her own feelings convince her that it's true love, if Hollywood celebrates it as a wonderful thing, and if even many churches view it as a normal alternative way of life, then how can anyone dare to question it?"

Emily sighs and looks down from the sky. "You do know, don't you," she says, her face flushed with an emotion that resides between shame and anger.

The professor nods her head.

"How long?" the golden girl asks.

"A long time," the silver woman says, "but that doesn't matter. What matters is that we're talking about it now. No more secrets between us."

Emily sits up straight and looks at Embee. "So," she says.

Embee looks at her student and says, "So...so now that you know that I know, how are you doing?"

"I'm okay," Emily answers with a shrug of her shoulders. "In one sense, it's a relief to me that you've known all along and that you still treated me like you treated everyone else. Not all Christians would do that. Some would even say I'm possessed by a demon."

"None of us are called by God to judge others," the professor says. "In fact, God strongly commands us not to judge one another."

"Tell that to some people I know," Emily says bitterly. "They seem to think they're expressly called by God to judge people like me."

"Well, they're wrong," Embee replies with conviction. "Jesus called us to love, not to judge."

"But you believe that being gay is wrong," Emily states slowly as she tilts her head and narrows her eyes.

"Let me start with this thought," the professor says, "and build from there." She pauses and then carefully wades into the spiritual vortex while she prays in her head. "I'll be honest with you, Emily. I don't believe that same-sex attraction is a sin."

"What?" Emily exclaims, wide-eyed. "You're okay with me being gay?"

"Not so fast," the professor says, raising a hand. "What I mean by that statement is that I don't believe it's a sin to feel attracted to a person of the same gender or experience the temptation to want to touch or be with that person. The desire itself might be part of the fallen world, I suppose, but it's not like a transgression where you willfully cross a line in disobedience. But for sure, if you *act* on that attraction, if you give in to the temptation and start to behave sexually with her in your mind or in the outside world, that's where it becomes sin."

"Okay, I get it," Emily replies with disappointment in her voice. "I've heard that explanation before—from my father—surprise, surprise. You stoked my hopes there for a second, Dr. Livingstone. Then you dashed them."

Embee pulls her abundant hair together in front of her and twists it into a rope. Then she begins to stroke it with her hands.

"We're all tempted by something," the professor reflects. "We can be tempted by everything from sexual sin to financial sin, from sin based on anger to sin flowing out of envy and jealousy and judgment. I don't believe the temptation itself is sin, although it does arise from our sinful nature. We must make a conscious, intentional choice to actually do it or practice it before it becomes willful sin. That applies to same-sex attraction, opposite-sex attraction, alcohol abuse or dependence, the love of money, judgment of others, stealing, murder, religious abuse, you name it."

"I know all about that," Emily says. "You'll tell me that it's not wrong if I'm tempted to steal your car. Only if I actually take it does it become sin."

"I suppose that's true," Embee admits, "unless you fantasize in your head about stealing my car. That's when Jesus tells us that even thinking about another person sexually in our imagination is as much a sin as actually doing it in the flesh."

Emily grits her teeth in disgust and then snaps, "What is sin, anyway? And who gets to decide what is sin and what isn't?"

"Now, those are excellent questions," Embee says as she works her hair into a bun to get it off her neck, which is warm from the afternoon sun.

"I think sin is several things," Embee continues. "Simply said, I believe sin is disobeying what Jesus instructs you to do and making yourself the authority instead. It's placing yourself on the throne of your life and doing what you want to do instead of doing what pleases Him.

"But if you choose to see God's commandments not as prison walls meant to confine you but as guardrails lovingly designed to protect you from driving off the cliff, then you'll want to obey God and avoid sin. As you obey Him, you'll experience the love, joy, peace, true identity, and pleasure found only by those who are in relationship with Him. There's a myriad of wonderful things you'll never experience until you surrender to Him."

Emily sighs and asks, "What if I believe that being gay is God's will for me, that He made me this way?"

Embee looks at her mentee and replies, "Emily, you've been raised in a home where your parents believed in Jesus. You've gone to church all your life, participated in short-term mission trips, spent weeks at summer camps, and even attended a private Christian college. Your heart knows what's true. You're just deciding not to obey it at this time in your life.

"Like any other human being in this world, you can make the Bible say what you want it to say and approve of whoever you want to be. That's what sin is, after all: exchanging God's commands for your own desires. Then you don't have to be under His authority. He's not God anymore—you are."

Embee begins packing up the leftovers from their lunch, placing them in the small wicker picnic basket. She glances over at Emily and says, "Sorry, I have that late afternoon class I told you I have to get back for."

She takes a final swallow of her tea and then says, "I'd like to leave you with one last thought, however: If the Bible is right about what it says about sin in general and same-sex behavior in specific, then the day will come, if it hasn't already, when you'll experience emptiness and shame inside your heart, but you'll find a way to deny or numb those things."

The professor closes the lid of the basket and looks over at Emily. "Sinning is like eating cotton candy," she explains. "The sweet confectionary tastes delightful for a time, but if you make it your go-to staple and consume it for breakfast, lunch, and supper day in and day out, you'll eventually get sick of it.

"The same is true of sin. It does offer a sweet taste, or you'd never choose to eat it in the first place. But when you consume it repeatedly and try to fill your heart with it, you'll eventually get sick, and you'll experience a profound emptiness that can lead to anxiety and depression. Sin simply won't satisfy us. We weren't designed for sin even though many of us settle for it and defend our right to practice it."

The two women fold up the blanket, and Embee concludes her thoughts by saying, "My prayer for you, Emily, is that one day, hopefully soon, you'll recognize the emptiness and shame you experience from sin and turn back to Jesus for joy."

Emily is silent. Her face is expressionless.

Embee glances over at her student and adds, "It all comes down to trusting that He has the best for you. That's the only reason you'd choose to obey Him—if you know He wants the best for you. But if you choose to do what you want to do, then you're trusting yourself above the God of the universe."

The two women make their way through the forest that is groaning with desire to be clothed with the greenery of spring. When they arrive at Sunny's bean field, Emily stops and observes flatly, "This is the place where Summer was seen for the last time."

Embee adjusts the blanket under her arm and nods her head. "This is the place," she confirms.

Emily is silent for a while, then begins to walk across the unplanted field. Embee catches up to her, and they walk toward the river. Neither woman speaks.

A few minutes later, they take off their shoes and socks again and roll up the legs of their pants. For a second time, they wade through the bracing water, but this time without girlish excitement. Like a cold rain, something almost tangible has dampened their interactions.

As they walk up the hill toward the farmhouse, Emily speaks to her mentor without turning to look at her. "I believe I was born gay and that I'm happiest when I'm in a relationship with a woman."

Embee sighs and glances heavenward. Oh, Jesus, she prays inside her heart, *I place this beautiful young woman into your hands. I know I can't change her heart, so I'm not even going to try. Besides, I remember how I felt when I was young and someone tried to convince me of something against my will. I just resisted even more. So, Holy Spirit, speak to her heart in a way that I can't.*

The silver woman stops praying and then confesses, *Sometimes I wonder, Jesus, why you ever brought Emily to the Academy. I don't see the purpose for it—at least not at this moment.*

The professor walks her student to the black Jeep that is parked at the top of the driveway next to the barn.

"Thanks for lunch," Emily says with a wan smile that masks a grimace.

"My pleasure," Embee says with a forced, tired smile of her own. Defeat drifts over her like a steel cloud.

When the jaded golden girl climbs into the vehicle, still wearing her white hijab, Embee says, "There's someone I'd like you to meet, if you're willing. She's a much wiser person to speak to about SSA and identifying as a lesbian. I think you'd find her very interesting."

"I'll think about it," Emily replies, her cool voice a study in resistance.

"That's all I can ask," the mentor says. "I'll see you in class tomorrow."

Emily closes the door and glances at her professor through the driver's side window that frames her face in a dreary mug shot. Her beautiful eyes are lifeless, and her face is blank. The joy that used to splash rapturously in the brilliant green pools of her eyes and the peace that in another lifetime would swim in the radiant oval lake of her face are now gone. The rumors of their past existence fade away further and further every day as she follows Summer deeper into the woods. The once-vibrant life has been forfeited, exchanged for the dark fruits that always accompany rebellion against the Creator.

Oh, what a costly price is paid for pursuing one's own road instead of trusting the ancient path of the map-maker.

It is an inviolable truth that when someone turns her back to the Light, dark shadows will be her path, settling for less her modus operandi; emptiness her harvest; and death her end. Not always immediate physical death, but certainly the death of the divine purpose in a life intended for ever-deepening glory until its full realization on that magnificent Resurrection Day.

As Emily navigates the Jeep down the Lighthouse Farm driveway, Embee waves and then smiles.

Her abiding consolation is knowing that Jesus loves Emily even more than she does, and He is never without a plan.

CHAPTER 8

———

Draegan Omar Atticus DaFoe

———

The enormous man climbs out of his Range Rover SV Autobiography Dynamic and slams the door. He savors the moment of the heavy portal merging with perfect precision into the door frame of the luxury vehicle. He clucks his tongue in symphony with the beautiful sound. How he loves exactness!

He pauses next to the $200,000 SUV with the 557-horsepower Supercharged V8 engine and adjusts his Giorgio Armani tailor-made Wall Street Wool suit. The jacket and trousers ensemble is considerably more expensive than what most men would pay because the material required to produce it is massive due to the man's corpulence.

His body size is visible evidence of the expansiveness of his desires. He is a rapacious man, dedicated to excess in every area of life that the imagination can visit. He is never satisfied. Always hungry. Empty and forever attempting to fill the great void inside with anything and everything he can possess. He always gets what he wants—at whatever expense to himself or to others.

Most often to others.

The forty-five-year-old man is six feet three inches tall with a broad frame that carries a massive amount of flesh, hiding deceptively strong muscles. His face is as broad as a field and is interrupted by a small mouth and even smaller eyes. Their disproportionate size makes it look like they have been placed in the wrong face. His nose is rosy and bulbous. His jowls sink into his shirt collar and give him the appearance of a hound dog. His thick hair is combed back and pasted to his skull with enough gel to grease the tracks of a tank. His ears are cauliflowers, the residual of twelve years of headlocks and cradle holds and other maneuvers by opponents seeking to gain an advantage over him on the wrestling mat.

The man's name is Draegan Omar Atticus DaFoe. He is the son of Lazarus DaFoe, who is the son of Steele DaFoe, who is the son of Romulus DaFoe, who is the son of Philip DaFoe.

Draegan's father, Lazarus, is the CEO and majority owner of a multi-billion-dollar IT company that ranks in the top one hundred on the Fortune 500 list. The big money-maker for the company is an innovative cloud division that has doubled revenue growth in the last two years. Draegan has been a consultant for the company ever since he graduated from Harvard with an MBA twenty years ago.

Consulting is Draegan's avocation. Serving as police commissioner of Hilton County is his vocation, a position that was carefully and strategically arranged. He was appointed to the position twelve years ago by the mayor, who "coincidentally" was a good friend of his father, Lazarus.

On paper, Draegan's job is to oversee the police department's accountability to the community it serves and to ensure that it responsibly enforces all laws and ordinances. In the real world, he leverages his position to ensure that the police department enables his primary desire in life, namely, to become as rich and powerful as possible. What makes Draegan singularly dangerous—whether pursuing his consulting work for DaFoe Technologies or his role as police commissioner—is his amoral heart married to his near-genius intelligence.

Draegan secures the two buttons on his single-breasted suitcoat and lumbers around his vehicle to the adjacent sidewalk. His personal bodyguards, who accompany him wherever he goes in a separate vehicle, are already waiting for him. The two men could not be more unalike.

The first bodyguard, Anthony, is built like an M1 Abrams tank. He looks like he belongs in the Cosa Nostra and has a habit of frequently quoting, "It's nothing personal. It's just business." His face is massive with a large, hooked nose and eyes that appear passive but miss nothing. He sports a crew cut and is dressed in a black button-down shirt beneath a gray suit coat. He always wears sunglasses, even indoors.

The second bodyguard simply goes by the name Chan. He is a reticent man. If he speaks more than one word at a time, he is considered talkative by his more loquacious peer, Anthony. Chan's left nostril is missing, and a wide, jagged scar runs from beneath his nose, over his lips, and down his chin. His black ponytail extends to the middle of his back. Even though he is two inches shorter and thirty pounds lighter than Anthony, he is still an imposing man. He is dressed similarly to Anthony, just without the sunglasses.

The two bodyguards have been in Draegan's employ for over ten years, ever since he became somebody of importance—and somebody people loved to hate.

In addition to his father, Lazarus, Draegan comes from a storied line of wealthy businessmen, all of whom have exerted notable influence in the political sphere. His great-great-grandfather Philip was a prominent railroad entrepreneur who dominated the lucrative market of transporting agricultural products around the country until he mysteriously disappeared in 1896. His body was never found. Draegan's great-grandfather, Romulus, was a war profiteer during the first world war, while his son, Steele, followed in his footsteps in the World War II arena.

Both men specialized in the production of machinery, artillery, and military vehicles. Steele, especially, became highly involved in the political realm via his vocal lobbying efforts and sizable campaign contributions. It was said that he significantly influenced at least two presidential elections in years past.

Besides being a highly successful businessman, Draegan's affluent progenitors all embraced secular philosophies. They all claimed to be materialists and atheists. Several of them, however, cheated a bit in their beliefs. Draegan's grandfather, Steele, notably denied the existence of God but simultaneously embraced the existence of a dark personality in the universe, who he referred to as Baal. He bowed down to this being and prayed to it for success and power.

While Steele worshipped Baal, Draegan worshipped his grandfather.

Since Draegan's father was preoccupied with international business that involved frequent travel, Steele took his grandson under his wing and inculcated into his young mind entrepreneurial wisdom, weapons expertise that led to hunting trips around the world, and his dark philosophy of Baal worship.

Since he was so close to Steele, Draegan was devastated when his grandfather was literally taken from him during a big game hunting trip in Africa. It happened on a day when grandfather and grandson were traveling down the Nile River in a smaller native watercraft. Seventy-year-old Steele, dressed in khaki shorts and wearing a wide-brim Boonie hat, was dozing in the afternoon sun, his arm extended three feet out of the boat above the murky waters of the 4,000-mile-long river. Eighteen-year-old Draegan was drifting in and out of sleep beside his grandfather.

Awakened by a bad dream, Draegan happened to be gazing at his grandfather when the waking nightmare occurred. The river exploded, and a mammoth crocodile launched itself out of the water, seizing Steele's arm in its massive jaws. The last thing Draegan saw—and he would never forget the image—was his grandfather's horrified face as he was violently torn from the boat and dragged into the depths of the Nile. His body was never recovered.

Not even a finger.

Young Draegan was never the same after the tragic loss of Grandfather Steele. Many people who knew Draegan whispered that he was possessed by evil not long after the tragedy in the Nile River basin. Rumors circulated that Draegan took extreme measures to raise his grandfather from the dead by calling on the dark power of Baal—all to no avail.

Even before the loss of Grandfather Steele, Draegan was not a typical child.

His elementary school teachers viewed him as a bully. They were wrong. Bullies are usually driven by deep insecurities to make themselves bigger than others around them through intimidation and posturing. Draegan was not insecure. On the contrary, he was confident and sadistic. His constitutional meanness was not driven by the need to protect a fragile inner self.

A desire to dominate and harm had been an ingredient in his character since early childhood, and it only increased as he grew older. Practicing evil makes one quite good at it.

Draegan was not content with frying ants with a magnifying glass. By the time he was eleven, he discovered that a screen removed from a rear projection television and adjusted to the correct angle relative to the sun would burn holes into bricks, melt pennies into molten messes, and even set his mother's garden lattice ablaze. He went so far as to inflict damage on squirrels and neighbors' pets with the instrument he referred to as his "Ra laser," named after the Egyptian sun god.

In early adolescence, he graduated to vandalism and theft. He began by stealing bicycles and eventually worked his way up to cars and, on one occasion, an eighteen-wheeler with a trailer full of cattle that he overturned in a ditch.

If anyone in Draegan's family had taken the time to pursue psychological help for the boy, he most certainly would have been diagnosed with ODD in his younger years and Conduct Disorder in his teen years. Anti-social Disorder was waiting on the horizon for him when he turned eighteen—impatiently waiting.

One quirk of fate was that Draegan was never apprehended perpetrating his abnormal and illegal behaviors—even the theft of the eighteen-wheeler. Accordingly, he never experienced consequences for his deviancy. He grew to believe that he was above the law.

As a high schooler, he prided himself in his ability to outsmart others, beginning with his mother and, later, with teachers, principals, store managers, and law enforcement personnel. His father, of course, was never present to discipline him for his aberrant conduct. Even if he had been present in Draegan's life, any correction he would have applied to his son would have been the pot calling the kettle black or, more appropriately, the devil calling a demon ungodly.

Lazarus DaFoe was an inveterate white-collar criminal who daily had to fend off the consequences of his illegal actions in the business world. He retained a small army of attorneys to defend the immoral machinations he employed to obtain the almighty dollar and to vanquish his foes by any means available. He was known as the most litigious CEO in the Midwest, infamous for how he used the small print in his IT sales documents to squeeze millions of dollars out of his customers during annual use audits.

Draegan was his father's son. His penchant for domination and harm spread like a toxic chemical into all his relationships—especially with women. He winsomely wooed and then ruthlessly manipulated them like inanimate objects, especially in the domain of romance.

As a teenager, Draegan was not particularly handsome, but his Herculean body, which he maintained in perfect condition as a heavy-weight wrestler, more than offset his pedestrian facial features. Girls were attracted to him like bees to honey, supporting the belief among Draegan's friends that many women fall not for the man who has integrity but for the one who will use and abuse them.

He quickly gained a reputation among his female peers. Many of them loved him. Just as many hated him. The ones who loved him had not yet encountered his utter disregard for the female gender. Rumor had it that he was not discriminating in his "affections" toward humans. Anyone could be a target of his legendary sexual appetite with its accompanying abuse.

During the year after his grandfather was killed by the offspring of Sobek—who, ironically, Steele had worshipped—the curtain lifted on Draegan's anti-social personality disorder, and he collided with the world. His manipulation of others for his own designs became legendary. His voracious appetite for food exploded, and he gained fifty pounds in three months. Despite his weight gain, he was a terror on the wrestling mat. He was as strong as a polar bear and not a bit less nasty. He did not simply compete to defeat his opponent. He wrestled to destroy them.

During his senior year of high school, he was banned from wrestling after he demonstrated a pattern of physical harm against other grapplers—every single one of his matches was suspended due to injury.

Draegan's physical sadism left several opponents with significant injuries ranging from shoulder separations to hyperextended knees. His final appearance on a wrestling mat was abruptly ended when he broke the neck of his opponent while placing him in a full nelson.

Draegan's most vicious and controversial act occurred at a frat party while attending the university. At the end of a night filled with alcohol and debauchery, a cocky recruit on the football team accused Draegan of inappropriate behavior toward his girlfriend. When the verbal confrontation became heated and spilled outside into the backyard, the other man called the young Draegan several demeaning names and then abruptly punched him in the face.

The poor freshman was from Texas. Tragically, he knew nothing of Draegan's reputation.

The accounts of what happened next varied greatly, certainly influenced by the level of inebriation in each eyewitness. The only fact that everyone at the party agreed on was that Draegan reacted to his aggressor's sucker punch with a single swift and vicious uppercut with the palm of his hand that crumpled his adversary's nose. Following the blow, the young man stood on his feet for a full five seconds. Then his eyes rolled back into his head, and he toppled like a felled tree.

Whether it was the blow from Draegan's hand or the man's head striking the ledge of a stone planter, the lethal result was a subdural hematoma. The young middle linebacker died in the early morning hours during emergency surgery to stop the bleeding in his brain.

Only a masterfully articulated argument of self-defense by a large legal team led by the leading criminal defense lawyer west of Chicago and bolstered by the eye-witness testimonies of many of his frat brothers kept Draegan out of prison.

Once again, Draegan had reason to believe that he was untouchable, that he could do whatever he pleased without fearing consequences.

From that night onward, he was referred to by the nickname, "DOA—Dead On Arrival" inspired partly by the initials of his name (Draegan Omar) but more so by the infamous event at the frat party. From that day forward, everyone feared him, even his friends. Especially his friends.

On this day, twenty-five years after his christening as DOA, Draegan enters the massive three-story house with the huge window set into the steeply sloping roof. Anthony and Chan are on his heels.

The huge police commissioner walks through the living room and then up the four flights of stairs to the top floor, where he is welcomed into the penthouse by a deferential bouncer. Despite his size, Draegan is not breathing hard. His two bodyguards, however, are struggling. They both hate the stairs, all ninety-six of them. Panting, they mop their foreheads with handkerchiefs.

The imposing man enters the 100'x100' room with its coal-black carpet and blood-red walls and strides toward the far side ponderously, not because he is clumsy but because of his enormous bulk. The clusters of people scattered throughout the room continue their conversations but in hushed tones as they rivet their eyes on Draegan.

Behind his back, some people refer to him as "the Dragon." He is every bit as intimidating as a dragon, except that he does not breathe fire through his nose. Instead, the fire pours forth from his small eyes whenever they are not twinkling with their beguiling charm.

When DOA reaches the massive U-shaped table that occupies much of the penthouse room, he sits down in the chair of honor where, like a king, he can survey his subjects as well as gaze up into the heavens through the huge skylight window cut into the roof above his head. Anthony and Chan sit in armchairs directly behind him, looking convincingly like the two bullies they are.

When Draegan has taken his cushioned throne, he clears his throat loudly. Immediately, the voices around him fall silent. The people scattered about the room promptly scurry to the horseshoe table and take their places in the red velvet chairs.

When his subjects are seated, Draegan's small, snake-like eyes dart over the members of Pandora's Lair who are in attendance. Among the familiar faces, he sees his cousins, Aamon and Damon DaFoe, Steve Slotter from the Silver Bay Lodge, Clare Tunstile, the county coroner, William George, the mayor of the city, and several partners at a large downtown law firm.

Also present are four board members from DaFoe Technologies as well as a handful of officers from other prominent businesses in the city. Two principals and a superintendent from public high schools in the area are sitting across from him while three dozen public school teachers are scattered around the table. A councilman and a newly elected female Senator are seated to his right.

At the top of one of the arms of the U-shaped table, rising head and shoulders above everyone else, Draegan sees the distinctive figure known as Dr. Harley Hawkstern, the human giant who undoubtedly descended from the wooly Mammoth.

Draegan DaFoe calls the meeting to order with a simple clarion pronouncement: "To thee, Baal, we submit the offerings of our time, our passions, and our bodies."

When everyone is attending to their lord, Dragan looks back and forth and up and down the long arms of the table that seats well over a hundred people and smiles. His eyes sparkle with a comingling of pride and condescension.

After a long silence, the monarch declares, "Welcome once again to Pandora's Lair. For those of you who are new to our gathering, in the spirit

150

of liberty and noncompliance to any authority, we adhere to no parliamentary procedures here. So, unhindered by enslavement to order and rules, I have chosen to bypass old business today and move directly to updates on new business. I don't want to be disappointed by lollygagging, sheer laziness, and mealy-mouthed reports. Deliver me good news, fellow citizens of the Lair. I insist."

After a brief silence, several people offer progress reports. Since the philosophy of the Lair is to advance secularization and impede the influence of religion on the values and identity of the culture, the first individual shares an update about the passing of a bill in a neighboring state that prohibits all therapy and ministry activity that in any way encourages the reversal of same-sex attraction whether it involves the exchange of money or not. The expressed hope is that a similar amendment will soon be introduced and passed in their state as well.

Another member of the Lair reports that a "family-friendly and pro-choice clinic" in the city has now been fully financed thanks to the Lair's fundraising efforts. In related news, several influential politicians are working to ban all protests within one block of the clinic.

A third person reports that key representatives from the city government are traveling to the nation's capital to join a special task force lobbying against the tax-exempt status of all religious, academic organizations unless they embrace progressive values and hire individuals who hold alternative "philosophies." Seven schools in the city will be impacted by this potential change, including the Teleios Academy.

The final individual to speak informs the members of Pandora's Lair that over the last two months, all books supporting creationism/intelligent design have been removed from the city's public libraries and from all other institutions that are wholly or partially supported by tax dollars. In addition, a small but vocal lobby has convinced the largest online retail company to remove all books from their cyber shelves that are pro-family in the traditional definition and/or not gay-affirming, trans-supportive, and pro-feminist.

Draegan DaFoe is especially pleased by the last speaker's information concerning the banning of books since the leader of the Pandora's Lair has a personal and deep disregard for the family system. He loathes the idea of being held accountable by the restrictive straight jacket of a marriage commitment and instead demands the freedom to graze where the grass is the greenest with no fences to limit his roaming appetite. Since pleasure is his god, morality simply cannot be allowed to restrain him. It must be eradicated. What does not exist cannot convict him of wrongdoing.

He also despises the traditional family system for another personal reason. He has nothing but scorn for his pathetic mother, whom he perceives as weak and unassertive. He also hates his father, who was absent from the home most of his life. On the rare occasion when Lazarus was present, he was prone to an unpredictable maniacal rage toward both his wife and son that terrified Draegan when he was very young but that later became his template for his own relationships.

The truth was that Lazarus had no affection or time for his family. His wife and son, at best, were inconveniences to him. At worst, they were balls and chains from which to seek release. No wonder Draegan grew up with such a bitter taste in his mouth for the traditional family. His distaste certainly was not conceived in a vacuum. On the far edges of his consciousness, he has a murky awareness that his aversive philosophies flow not so much from a dispassionate intellectual value system but from a seething emotional reaction to his childhood world.

When the new business has been discussed at length, Draegan clasps his large hands together and announces, "Ah, my children, we finally are gaining ascendency in our campaign against superstition and narrow-mindedness."

His eyes glint with pleasure as he adds, "We have impatiently endured so many decades when our culture was opposed to the philosophy of the eradication of God even when advanced thinkers like Nietzsche and Feuerbach showed us the way. But now, the world around us is falling into lockstep with our demand for secularization and materialism."

Dragan's small mouth smiles like a Cheshire cat, and he says, "Soon, no one will dictate to us what we can and cannot do. We will be a law unto ourselves. Anarchy will no longer be necessary, and revolution will be obsolete. We will be the plumb line by which the rest of the world measures itself!"

The men and women around the huge table smile and begin to clap loudly. Some utter words of gratitude to Baal; others, to good karma. A few pound their chests with a fist and then point at each other. One man who is particularly unaware announces, "Finally! Thank God!"

After the celebration subsides, the county coroner and adjunct medical school professor, Clare Tunstile, rises from her chair beside Draegan to read the weekly meditation from the Lair manual. Today's topic—*The Superfluousness of God*—was penned in the late 1800s by none other than Philip DaFoe himself, the founder of the original Devil's Lodge. Of course, in more recent years, the Lodge has changed its name to be more politically correct and...palatable.

A handful of individuals know that beneath the gentler name, there exists a darker meaning. Draegan himself has defined Pandora's Lair as a secret place full of mystery that initially appears innocuous but later proves to be accursed.

After ten minutes of reciting Philip's words, Clare ends the reading with the closing paragraph: *"In conclusion, we are confident in our assertion that the God of the Bible does not exist. The death of the divine renders his 'holy book' nothing but a human creation, along with* Les Misérables *and* The

153

Importance of Being Earnest. *Unfortunately, it's a creation that is destructive to the human spirit. How can we be so certain of this fact? Because we rest secure in the tested truth that life is a human-centric phenomenon. Life is not meant to be a denial of appetites; rather, we are here to satisfy every hunger during our brief sojourn on this planet that hurtles through the nothingness of space.*

"The human fiction known as the Bible strangles humanity with its stifling commandments and crushes the human spirit with condemnation. Any purported revelation that so robs men and women of their natural desires and instead offers them condemnation must be viewed as a construct designed by those who wish to kill the 'joie de vivre' that makes life endurable. To make matters worse, they replace freedom with Socratic shackles and chains.

"We have no choice but to reject this strangulating philosophy. No, we must rebel against it, even to the point of violence and bloodshed! After all, do we not live under the Darwinian decree that only the fittest will survive? And we all are counted among the fittest."

Not long after Clare concludes Philip Dafoe's meditation, Draegan dismisses himself from the Lair meeting and retreats to a private room on the second floor of the house. He is accompanied by his inner circle.

Aamon and Damon are in attendance, along with Steve Slotter and Clare Tunstile. Together, these individuals compose the Pandora's Lair Council of Five. Drinks and snacks are served by Anthony and Chan, who are never far from their employer. The five council members navigate more sensitive business, including where to invest a generous donation bequeathed to the Lair by a wealthy CEO.

After an hour of discussion, Draegan dismisses Steve and Clare from the room. Steve leaves obsequiously while Clare retreats with a scowl. Intimidating Anthony and silent Chan also exit the room and position themselves in the hallway outside the door. Now only the inner 'inner' circle is left, populated by Draegan and his two cousins. They are known as the Triumvirate.

Draegan, of course, has never stated the obvious truth to his two cousins, namely, that there is a final inner circle composed of only one individual—The Director.

There are some things that only he is privy to—such as the existence of his great, great grandfather's treasure that has been missing along with Philip for over a century. Of course, Draegan does not know the location of the treasure; neither does his father. His grandfather was unable to find it even though he dedicated many resources in search of it. Steele was aware of the Devil's Lodge cave system and searched it extensively, but maddeningly never found even one clue of the treasure.

Draegan is also the only member of the Triumvirate who knows of his private company committed to the development of a device known as the Deep-Penetrating Pulse Induction Probe-Drone that can locate precious metals beneath tons of rock as it hovers anywhere from twenty to fifty feet above the ground.

Draegan's personal nickname for the device is the Trouve Trove Deep Detector (TTDD), named after the 19th-century Parisian inventor who first developed a metal detector designed to locate bullets and shrapnel in the bodies of human patients. Draegan knows he has only two potential ways of finding Philip's treasure: successful application of the TTDD or by locating and reading Jacob Sutherington's journal for any clues. He knows of the existence of the journal through one of Jacob's relatives who lives in the area.

Draegan considers beginning the meeting of the Triumvirate by informing his two counterparts of a recent international mission known as Infiltration Al Quds. He fights off the fleeting temptation and instead begins with the comment, "Update me on the progress with JJ—Jacob's Journal."

The police commissioner has always been enamored of acronyms and precise titles, and discussion of the missing journal does not fall outside the purview of this pet habit. "I insist that you encourage me with good news," the grandson of Steele says with a sickeningly sweet smile that makes his round cheeks even rounder. His eyes convey a different message—disdain.

Damon, the larger of the two brothers, athletic and broad, still thinks that the leader of Pandora's Lair is looking for the journal so he can locate the Lady Libertys. He knows nothing about the treasure worth fifty times more than the coins. He says, "As you already know, the students at that religious school have been on winter break for the past six weeks and have only recently returned. We have constant surveillance in place and will soon know the location of the journal."

"Does your surveillance team still consist of Clyde Kildaire and Donnie Caruso?" the huge man asks with a snort.

Aamon sends a worried glance at his brother and then looks back at The Dragon. He nods his neckless head and replies, "Yes, the two cousins are tracking Jack Sutherington day and night. Sooner or later, he'll slip up and reveal the location of the journal. Clyde says he may also apply further pressure to the situation to speed up the process as needed."

Draegan snorts again, and the smile on his face degrades into a perturbed frown. "Pressure is not *needed*," he growls. "It is *imperative*. I may even need to grace this Jack Sutherington with a visit of my own. No hick kid from Colorado is going to throw a wrench in the DaFoe machine.

"Speaking of hicks, I'm losing patience with those bumbling dolts, Clyde and Donnie. I would send Anthony and Chan after this Jack if I didn't fear that they would handle him too roughly and kill the boy. But I'm growing very impatient. We began with soft persuasion, but now we need to graduate to cruel coercion. It must be impressed on Jack Sutherington how serious we are about taking possession of that journal."

"I understand," Damon says as he rubs his flat nose that looks like it had been pummeled one too many times in the past and never recovered its normal appearance. "I will speak with the two men."

Draegan adjusts his mammoth body in his over-stuffed chair and remarks, "Remember, once we find those coins, you will receive a third of the proceeds. Of course, I trust that both of you will funnel some of the proceeds back to the Lair fund to serve the purposes of our underground movement."

The reptilian eyes of Damon dart toward his brother. His tongue flicks across his lips, and he nods his head. "Of course," he says. Then he adds, "The twenty-six ladies have our full attention. Right, Aamon?"

The smaller man nods his head at his brother. His protruding eyes are unblinking and flat, but his lips are twisted into a smile. "Full and unwavering," he comments.

Draegan stares at the two brothers for a long time. His face is pensive, and his intelligent mind is thumbing through various scenarios like they are pages in a book.

Finally, the huge man leans forward in his oversized chair and announces agreeably, "I will personally go and meet with this Jack Sutherington. I will stir the pot and incite fear in his pathetic heart. Then we'll send in Clyde and Donnie to exert a bit more muscle and secure the journal. Very soon, we'll locate the whereabouts of Philip's wife and the other Ladies."

As Draegan smiles at the two cousins who are merely lapdogs to him, he thinks, *The journal will also lead me to my great, great grandfather. If I*

157

find him, I find the trove accumulated by Philip and his father before him that will make the Lady Libertys look like gift-shop baubles.

Then I will have the cultural and financial capital to embrace my destiny as the Supreme King and to advance my agenda unhindered.

CHAPTER 9

——

Jack's Siren

The young woman's name is Heather. She is brunette and beautiful. Her body has curves in all the right places. Her legs are long, silky, and slender. She walks with a sensual motion that uniquely captures the male eye. Chronologically, she is twenty-two years old.

Emotionally, she is seven.

Heather's fingers delicately hold the rim of her large sun hat before a breeze that gusts occasionally on this hot April day. Her sky-blue bikini that minimally obscures her tantalizing body peeks out seductively through the sheer fabric of her cover-up that does not reveal too much, but neither does it reveal too little. "Enticing" is the appropriate word to describe the premeditated balance of seen and imagined.

Heather knows exactly what she is doing. She wants to be seen. She is aroused by the satisfaction that male eyes are watching her, wanting her.

Beyond the desire to be seen and wanted by men, she has little to no conscious appreciation of her inner world. For instance, she is not aware that her experience as the only child of an alcoholic father and an adulterous mother has left her with a debilitating fear of abandonment.

When she was five years old, her parents' tumultuous marriage ended bitterly. From that point on, Heather divided her time between her mother and her father.

When she was with her father, he would drink every night until he passed out, leaving little Heather alone in the dark trailer that was his home. His physical body was present with her on the bed or the floor or the couch, but in every other way, he was totally absent. Occasionally, the little girl would fear that her father had died. On those nights, she would weep herself to sleep, feeling abandoned by the man who was supposed to see her and protect her.

When it was her mother's turn to have her, the emotionally volatile woman was absent to Heather in a different manner than her father but no less devastating. She drove her daughter away with her unpredictable rage, or she abandoned her whenever she sank into a deep depression and retreated to her room for days at a time.

Physically, Heather's mother frequently left her daughter alone in the apartment while she went to a bar or club, seeking male attention. It was not uncommon for her to be gone all night during some of her evening escapades. On other occasions, her mother brought strange man home, and Heather would witness by sight or sound the disturbing sexual engagement of the two adults.

At these times, it was never clear to Heather if her mother was happy or terrified, if she welcomed what was happening to her or if she was being dominated against her will by the bad man on top of her.

Initially, the little girl believed that her mother chose the intruders over her. In the end, it was much less painful for Heather to believe that the strange men took her mother away from her. She came to despise their presence in her home.

So it was that Heather grew up at the mercy of other people's moods, physical unavailability, and emotional deficits. She lived with the constant unpredictability of fleeting presence or total absence—most often the latter. She came to hate the rejection she felt when her mother's attention was diverted to the bad men or when her father abandoned her for the bottle he so readily chose over her.

On the good days, Heather felt elation when her mother was home with her alone or when her father was awake and alert, looking into her eyes and listening to what she was saying. This rollercoaster of absence and presence, hatred, and happiness made the young girl feel crazy and sowed the seeds of bipolar mood disorder inside her soul.

This, then, was the narrative of her internal world: love and hate. She loved her mother, and she hated her. She loved her father, and she hated him. She loved other humans, and she hated them. The strong emotions in her heart and the powerful obsessions in her mind were fueled by this ever-present ambivalence as she grew into a teenager.

As an adult, Heather hates the familiar experience of needing others more than they need her. How she despises her mind's obsessive preoccupation, anticipating how long it will be before her current boyfriend, whom she desperately loves, will abandon her like all the others. True to the poor development of a self, she is in touch with only a few of the many roiling emotions that inhabit her heart, like secrets hidden in a diary.

What she does know is that she hates the little girl inside who is scared, clingy, and weak.

Beyond her awareness, Heather is divided into two people, psychologically speaking, that is. She is the dependent five-year-old girl who, incidentally, she attempts to eradicate, and she is the twenty-four-year-old woman who needs no one.

The adult woman is strong and lusts for power. She is a false self that functions as a mask to negotiate interactions with people she perceives are all far ahead of her in emotional maturity. Her true self—the young girl—is needy and insecure in the relational world. It is no surprise, then, that she imprisons the pathetic young self in some inaccessible dungeon, albeit at the high price of divorcing her own soul, and then interacts with others through the faux adult.

The primary way the adult woman wields power is through her body.

Heather is almost entirely clueless about what motivates her interactions with other adults. Someday in therapy, she will learn that her relationships are driven by a singular currency: the dynamic of power.

Love has nothing to do with it.

As an adult, Heather exerts her power over any man who notices her. And it is a formidable power. She has detached from the needy girl who is at the mercy of men and now manipulates men to be at her mercy.

She is practiced at making men want her. Living out of her false seductive self, Heather never has to fear rejection again. The tables are now turned. She has the power to lure a pathetic man to her with her goddess-like body and transform him into a puppy salivating for a treat. Even a longer gaze with her hungry eyes is enough to draw a man to her like a bee to honey. Then, whenever she chooses—which is always at the highest peak of arousal—she will reject him. She might even make him watch and squirm helplessly as she seduces another man right before his jealous eyes.

Men are such pathetic pawns—objects to be manipulated, so willing to surrender their power before her irresistible sensuality. She is a modern-day Delilah seducing Samson.

No, it has never been about love for Heather. Rather, it is about power, control, manipulation, and, when possible, torture. She experiences a deep, twisted satisfaction in knowing that she can make others feel how she once felt—rejected—when she was the helpless and wretched little girl. Oh, the broken road of fractured relationships; the perilous path potholed with rejection, abandonment, loneliness, rage, and the protection of the private dungeon that is the first step into the hell of emotional isolation.

If there is anything that can be said in Heather's defense, it is that she is largely unaware of her behavior and, even more so, her motives. Nonetheless, she is not a creature enslaved by destiny; she is at least partially a free agent whose chosen and rehearsed coping skill is to sadistically manipulate others. On some level, she is accountable for her actions.

Today, she is "strolling" along the path that follows the shoreline of Silver Bay Lake from the hotel to the public beach that will soon open for the summer season. Three delicate fingers are attached to her chiffon sun hat. She is wearing no sunglasses. Her eyes are very powerful instruments—like strong magnets—and she wants to showcase them to their full potential.

She is aware that she is being watched. She smiles inside. She is most pleased. Later, she will go back to her room at the university and daydream for hours, if time permits, about being seen and wanted. The eyes of men tell her that she is desired. Always the eyes.

———

Jack is taking his daily run this Friday afternoon. His typical course takes him along the lake, up the hill, through the forest, and past the cemetery. He almost always runs in the early morning hours. Today is different. He changed things up—the timing and location of his run—because he slept in after a late night preparing for his koine Greek exam. A classmate in the dorm then convinced him to play a new jungle combat video game that made two hours slip by like two minutes. The undisciplined decision threw his whole schedule off.

As Jack jogs around a copse of trees next to the lake, he sees a young woman gliding toward him on the path. Jack may be particularly vulnerable on this day due to physical exhaustion; or maybe because he feels an emotional relief after completing his Greek exam; or maybe because the young woman is so stunningly beautiful; or maybe because he is caught off guard at the sight of a woman so provocatively dressed for the beach when summer is still weeks away. Whatever the case may be, his eyes behold the woman and fix on her like a heat-seeking missile fixed on a target.

When her large brown eyes shift from the lake toward him, Jack looks straight ahead, pretending not to notice her. He wonders if she saw him looking at her. He watches her out of the corner of his eyes as he approaches her. Her high cheekbones are elegant, her nose is delicate and perfect, and her lips are full. They are slightly separated.

Heather sees the runner emerge from behind the trees on the path ahead of her. Even though she is gazing at the lake as she strolls, her excellent peripheral vision is taking in everything around her. The running man is tall and muscular in an attractive way. He is not one of those vain bodybuilders her mother would bring home who look grotesquely sculpted. His pectoral muscles are visible under his tight sleeveless T-shirt that says, "D-II Champions." His blonde hair stops just short of his shoulders. He is not unhandsome. He is a candidate. His strides are long and confident. From the corner of her eyes, she sees him looking at her.

She glides her gaze from the lake toward the runner, and he looks away. But she can tell that he is still watching her with his peripheral vision. She discerns that he is not the type who will hit on her directly. He is too careful, or shy, or—committed.

Just before they pass each other, the runner's eyes glance at her. Heather smiles sensually and turns her head toward him slightly. Not too invitingly, though. Just enough to incite interest.

Even as he runs, Jack fills his cheeks with air and lets it out quickly after he passes the woman. It is a sigh of relief. There are women in the world who are attractive. And then there are women who are mirages. This woman is the latter—at least to Jack's evaluative eyes. He has lived long enough in the world, especially at the university, to know that mirage women usually communicate their magical aura intentionally. It is manufactured. There is a specific objective in mind. But knowing that the woman is intentionally attempting to attract attention does not necessarily reduce the seductive power of her presence.

Intentionality only serves to increase the attraction.

Jack continues his run around the glistening lake past the public beach and toward the Silver Bay Lodge. Ten minutes later, after checking his time and pulse on the device attached to his wrist, he turns around and heads back the way he came. He has not forgotten the mirage despite his best efforts to shut the image out of his mind.

He runs past the beach and follows the asphalt-paved trail back toward the Academy. He is five minutes away from the campus when the mirage appears for a second time. She is a hundred feet away, walking toward him. She is no less striking than the first time he saw her. Jack feels something stir in his body that he identifies immediately: Desire is the euphemism that describes it. Lust is the more honest term.

"Excuse me," the young woman says pleasantly as Jack draws close to her. "Are you from around here?"

Jack slows to a walk and then stops beside the young woman. There is nowhere he can settle his eyes without experiencing a strong stirring in his body. A gentle breeze lifts the woman's cover-up, and it touches Jack's leg.

Jack shakes his head. "Not from around here," he says, breathing hard from his run. "I'm from Colorado but here for school."

"Oh, okay," the mirage says. "I'm not from around here either," she lies.

"I'm here with my cousin for a few days to visit my aunt. I was wondering if you know somewhere to get good food in town. I can locate the restaurant using GPS, of course, but I need to know the name of a specific place before I search for it."

"Are you talking downtown?" Jack asks as he runs his hands through his straw hair.

"Whatever you think is best," the young woman says coyly as she gazes at Jack. Her large eyes communicate desire.

Jack knows bait when he sees it, and he swallows hard. Some bait is almost irresistible. The first random thought that travels through his muddled brain is, *Don't be the sucker fish that bites on the hook.* His second thought is, *This is nothing but innocent fun and—it feels really good.*

"I'd recommend two restaurants," Jack replies after a pause. "A.J.'s downtown for more traditional food and Fai Sai just a mile away from here on Grand Avenue if you like genuine Thai cuisine. Both are amazing."

The young woman smiles invitingly and says, "Thanks for the recommendations. How can I ever repay you?"

Jack returns her smile and says, "Not a problem."

The mirage extends her hand toward Jack and says, "My name is Heather, by the way."

Jack reaches out and gently takes her hand in his. Her skin is soft, warm.

When he pulls his hand away, she holds onto his a second longer and then slides her fingers over the palm of his hand as she withdraws hers.

Loud alarms go off in Jack's head. He swallows hard again as desire rises—if possible—to an even higher level of intensity in his body. Something inside him wants this woman. He is standing on the proverbial line of no return, ready to cross. As he gazes back at Heather, he knows that his eyes must look as hungry as hers. He does not even think about God at this moment. He has forgotten God. Physical desire has taken control of his body and hijacked his neurotransmitters. He wants to hold this woman close to his own body.

As he stares into the woman's enticing eyes that remain unblinkingly locked on his, her hand searches for something in the pocket of her cover-up. Then she reaches out to hold Jack's hand again. Before Jack can protest—not that he would have done so were he given the chance—Heather writes something on the palm of his hand with the pen she extracted from her pocket.

"My cell number," she says, tilting her head playfully to one side as her eyes continue to gaze at Jack. "Call me sometime. I'll be in town until Sunday night. Maybe we could hang out for a while." Her voice is enchanting, and Jack's brain becomes further muddled.

Jack realizes that the young woman is still holding his hand. "I would like that," he hears himself say.

"Cool," Heather replies. "It's a plan, then. I'll wait for your call."

She releases his hand in her provocative manner and smiles at him one last time from beneath her wide-brimmed sun hat. Then she turns and begins to walk away like a fairy tale sprite tiptoeing magically over lily pads. When she is not even ten feet away, she stops and looks back at Jack one last time. Her hand, with the soft, sensuous fingers, waves at him before she turns and glides away.

Jack watches the young woman for a long time before he eventually wills himself to turn around and look straight ahead toward the Teleios Academy. His heart is beating fast and not from physical exertion. He runs his tongue over his lips and takes a deep breath. He raises his hand up toward his face and looks at the phone number written on his palm. Below the number are the words, "In your dreams tonight." He has a difficult time remembering the last time he felt so...aroused. Wisely, he drops his hand to his side.

As he stands there on the path beside the lake, a battle begins to rage within him. Part of him wants to look at his hand again and memorize the phone number. Another part of him is afraid that he will look at the number and never forget it. He keeps the hand with the dangerous inscription at his side as he begins to run toward the citadel. He runs hard. He pushes himself into a sprint for the last half mile. It is not until he has run for several minutes that he cries out in his head, "God, please help me!"

Meanwhile, Heather walks past the beach area. She straightens her back and sucks in her tummy. She feels several sets of new eyes on her, and a wonderful rush flows through her body like whitewater. Even if no other man stops to speak with her, her mission has been accomplished. She has captured a man's attention—completely. She will return to her room and lay on her bed, and relive the experience. She will reconstruct every moment, including the huskiness of the man's voice, the touch of his hand, the hunger in his eyes, and the fact that he will go home and make love to her in his imagination. She will repeat the encounter for hours until it is so well rehearsed that she has it memorized. She will then "feed" off the memories for days. Here is the pleasure component for Heather.

Then there is the power component: the power of her beauty and the power of her rejection. Oh, how exhilarating to experience someone needing her so desperately when she needs him, not at all. She only desires the experience of him wanting her. She does not want the man himself. She did not even ask him his name, after all. And she gave him a random set of numbers that are certainly not her phone number.

The man is not a person to her. He is a mere object to be used and then forgotten. She has never made love to a man. That would mean giving her power to another or admitting that she needs something from him. She will never allow that to happen. She is above needing. She will never again put herself in a position to be rejected by someone ever again. Truth be told, she despises the man she just seduced because he is pathetically weak and needy—just like five-year-old Heather.

Jack slows down to a run and then a jog, and finally, a walk. He is panting. The massive castle with its towering turret looms ahead of him. Off to his right are the dark March waters of the lake that are churned by the gusting wind.

He stops and stands at the end of the trail. He is trying to engage his brain. He is remembering. He is in conflict. He begins to lift his hand up toward his face.

He hesitates in the middle of the movement. Out of nowhere, he remembers Joseph's experience with Potiphar's wife. Joseph has always been one of his heroes on his journey of faith. He recalls how the young man in Egypt resisted sexual temptation even when it presented itself to him repeatedly. Even when it pursued him. He was obedient to God even to the point of imprisonment.

Abruptly, Jack turns and walks down to the lake. He gets on his knees and vigorously scrubs the palm of his right hand in the cold water. He scrubs it for several minutes until none of the numbers are legible.

Jack sighs deeply and looks up into the bright blue sky above him, and begins to remember God again. Then he turns toward the four-story edifice that is attached to the castle and strides toward it like a man on a mission. He knows where he is going. He knows what he must do.

CHAPTER 10

RUNNING LIKE JOSEPH

Jack is breathing heavily—the consequence of sprinting up six flights of stairs up to the fourth floor—when he arrives at the office door. He hesitates briefly, his fisted hand inches away from the dark-stained wooden door, then knocks loudly. He glances up impatiently at the tall ceiling with its shiny Venetian plaster and mahogany crown molding. He is about to knock again when the door opens. He finds himself face to face with the bearded Dr. McNeely.

"What a surprise, Jack," the professor utters in his bass voice. "I was just praying for you a few minutes ago—but not to show up at my office," he says with a smile that parts his brown mustache and beard. "Why are you breathing so hard?"

Ignoring the man's question, he asks one of his own. "Why were you praying for me?"

The president of the Teleios Academy tilts his head downward and examines Jack's face over his reading glasses. "Why don't you come in," he says slowly with a knowing look. "Something tells me you have a lot on your mind."

Jack nods his head in agreement and says, "Yeah, I was hoping you'd have time to talk."

The student enters the familiar office that is chock-full of tomes, stacked periodicals, maps, and artifacts. There are so many of these four items that if they were people, the office would be deemed overpopulated. Jack does not collapse into the old leather chair, as is his custom. Instead, he sits on the threadbare oriental rug in front of the professor's squeaky chair. "I just got done with a run," Jack explains. "I'm still sweaty, so I'll just sit on the floor."

"Works for me," the middle-aged man says as he walks over to his chair. As he collapses into it, the old piece of furniture emits its usual tortured cry.

Even before the man is fully situated, Jack asks again, "Why did you pray for me a few minutes ago?"

The professor adjusts himself on his wooden mount that tilts noticeably to the man's right. Finally satisfied with the fit of his saddle, the man's eyes look out at Jack from beneath his overhanging forehead, and he replies, "I prayed that the Holy Spirit would give you strength to stand up against the attack of the enemy."

"Do you always pray for me randomly like that?" Jack inquires.

"It wasn't random, Jack," the man explains as he folds his tortoiseshell reading glasses and places them in his shirt pocket. "Every day, the Holy Spirit nudges me to pray for different people. Today, he brought you to my mind, and so I prayed for you."

"Well, thank God that he nudges and that you obey," Jack says as he sits cross-legged on the ancient rug that covers a 10x10 section of the office floor. "And thank God that He answers your prayers."

The professor considers his student for a while as he runs his index finger back and forth over his lips. Then he asks, "What is this all about, Jack?"

"Normally, I wouldn't be here," Jack admits. "But ever since the end of last semester, you've been beating me up about not being so stubbornly self-sufficient. So here I am, taking your advice. I'm trying not to fly solo."

"I like what I'm hearing," Dr. McNeely says as he continues to massage his lower lip. When Jack does not immediately reply, the professor asks, "So what happened? Why was it so important that I prayed for you today?"

Jack leans back on his hands and confides, "This isn't easy for me to talk about."

"No, I suppose not," his mentor says slowly. "At least not for you who is accustomed to being as private as a pocket gopher in its burrow."

"You do know me, don't you," Jack replies. "Increasingly," the professor replies with a smile.

Jack glances at a drawing of King Herod's palace in Jericho with its large swimming pool, aqueduct, and opus reticulatum wall construction. Then he looks back at his listener. "You most likely prayed for me today during a moment of strong temptation—huge sexual temptation."

The professor says nothing but looks at Jack and nods his head slowly.

Jack explains the encounter with Heather that occurred only minutes earlier. He leaves nothing out. He concludes his account by saying, "I can't believe how strong the temptation was. It was like being summoned by an irresistible force. I honestly believe your prayer saved me from falling."

Dr. McNeely looks at his mentee with intense eyes that are miniature cannons peering out from pillboxes. He says nothing for a long time.

Eventually, he clears his throat and comments, "You called her a mirage, Jack—a woman who was especially tempting for you." The president of the Academy pauses and lifts his chin slightly as he continues to look at the young man at his feet. Then he asks, "So why in the name of Him who is holy did you stop and talk to her?"

Jack opens his mouth to explain that he was simply being helpful to the young woman, but he stops himself. He looks down at his running shoes and admits, "I wanted to see her more closely. I wanted to hear her voice. If I'm honest, at a level I never go to, I...I was hoping something would come of it. At least part of me wanted that."

"I do commend you for speaking the truth, Jack," the mentor says, dipping his head slightly. "But...I also must call out your foolishness. By stopping on that running trail today, you were creating an opportunity for your flesh to have what it wanted. You knew this woman was especially tempting to your eyes, and still, you stopped and spoke with her. If Odysseus had done the same with the Sirens in the Odyssey, he would have been lured to his death."

"Ouch," Jack says testily. "Not many people have called me out as foolish. In fact, you're the first one."

"Do you remember Homer's Odyssey, Jack?" the professor asks. The mentee nods his head and replies, "Maybe. Why?"

"Do you remember that Circe warned Odysseus that the Sirens would beguile them and kill them and that he and his men needed to take precautions to prevent that from happening?"

"Vaguely," Jack replies.

"I'll refresh your memory," Dr. McNeely says. "Odysseus was warned about two mermaid-like creatures called sirens that lured sailors to their beautiful green island as ships sailed past. Apparently, it wasn't the physical beauty of these two sirens that was so tempting. It was their intoxicating voices as they were lifted in song. Sailors were so drawn to the seductive voices that they failed to notice the human bones piled up all around the sirens.

"Seduction is a powerful potion, Jack," the professor says gravely. "Just as those two sirens appealed to a hunger in the hearts of the sailors, so today Heather appealed to a hunger in your heart. I'm not saying that giving in to lust and pursuing sexual sin is always going to kill you the way those sailors were killed—only sometimes—but rest assured, sexual sin will impact you every time you surrender to it. In the end, we always reap what we sow in this world."

"Yeah, I don't disagree with that," Jack comments.

"Do you remember how Odysseus and his men resisted the sensual voices of the sirens?" the professor asks.

When Jack shakes his head, his mentor says, "Odysseus placed softened wax into the ears of his deck hands so they couldn't hear the seductive siren song. Then, Odysseus had his men tie his hands and feet to the mast so he could listen to the sensual voices but be restrained from jumping into the sea and swimming toward the creatures.

"When they finally arrived at the island, and the beguiling voices of the sirens were heard, Odysseus' temptation was so strong that he gestured repeatedly to his men to untie him. Instead of obeying his gestures, however, his men wisely restrained him with more ropes."

"That story reminds me of Samson and Delilah," Jack muses aloud. "Both stories have lusting men, ropes, and seductive women. I guess Odysseus was smarter than Samson, though. He found a way to have himself restrained while Samson freely gave himself to Delilah."

Dr. McNeely nods his hands and asks, "Do you see a similar wisdom being communicated in these two stories, Jack, even though the Odyssey is only a legend?"

"For sure," the mentee says as he runs his hands through his hair. "Be careful what situations you place yourself in as a man—maybe as a woman, too. Some temptation can be almost irresistible once you're in it, so it's best not to walk into harm's way in the first place."

"Exactly," Dr. McNeely replies. "God's Word says the same thing: 'Make no provision for the flesh.' Like you were getting at, Jack, wise is the man who does not foolishly put himself in a position where he'll be tempted beyond his ability to resist."

The professor crosses his legs, and the obnoxious squealing of his chair fills the office. Then he says, "You are living in a world where many people will think you're some type of prude or religious fanatic for saying no to gratuitous sex, Jack. And they'll perceive that you're judging them if you try to convince them to do the same.

"But trust me, the day will come when most of those individuals—both men and women—will see the pile of bones they've collected over the years due to their surrender to unbridled desire. I'm not even talking primarily about diseases and pregnancies, but about broken marriages, depressed and anxious children, unrestrained sexual appetite, pornography, jaded hearts, and the increasingly common phenomenon of sex reduced to physical lust with no love in it whatsoever.

"Yes, sex is reduced to a mere biological act like eating and drinking and toileting—a bodily function with no heart in it. Some people may convince themselves they're fine with that since they view themselves not as image bearers but as accidental animals, but it goes completely against what they're made for. All it does is cheapen them—bars of gold used for bathroom door stops."

"I know what you mean about the puritanical part," Jack replies. "I ran into that when I was doing my undergrad at the university. I made a vow, along with a bunch of other guys in a campus ministry, to save ourselves sexually for our future wives. After I played on the football team that won the D II championship, temptation grew like twenty times in intensity. I was idealized by a lot of girls on campus simply for throwing a cow skin ball around. It was difficult to keep my vow, especially when some girls made it very clear that they were available to me at any time and in any capacity.

"To be honest, it became a daily struggle for me," Jack admits as his shoulders slump. "I could relate to what we always said about our defense on the football team: 'Bend, bend, but don't break.' I bent more than I wanted to in my thought life. Pornography wasn't usually a huge issue for me, but only because I was accountable to the other guys in the ministry. If I ever started down that road, I knew I could view pornography for hours at a time. If there's any good news to my story, it's that I didn't break."

Dr. McNeely leans back in his chair and studies the ceiling for a while. Then he looks back down at Jack and says, "I like what you said about 'starting down that road.' It's a universal law that once you let yourself taste sexual temptation, it's very difficult to stop. When a man crosses the line of no return, he's hooked. That's why I tell young men to practice the five-second rule."

"What's that?" Jack inquires as he pulls his knees up to his chest and arches his back.

The president of the Academy replies, "*The five-second rule* simply says that once you encounter sexual temptation, you have five seconds to say no. If you hesitate any longer, odds are you won't resist. You'll experience that *summoning* you spoke of earlier and wander into sexual quicksand. Lingering leads to lust."

The professor pauses and then says, "That's why I believe there are situations when a man simply must do one thing: run. Don't wait. Don't rationalize. Don't think you have to be nice or worry about hurting the woman. Just run.

"Yes, sexual desire can be so strong that a wise man simply must flee. Men are such visual creatures that if they stay and look and stare and imagine, they'll be ensnared by desire. And the woman is not to blame. The man is totally responsible for managing his own appetite."

"But there are times when the woman is trying to light the man's fire," Jack counters.

Dr. McNeely nods and replies, "Yes, there are times when that's true. Certainly, from everything you've told me, Heather was a woman on a mission today. But remember, many times, a woman isn't looking for sex but for affection. The deepest desire of her heart is to be loved, and to get that love, some women are programmed to believe they must sacrifice their bodies on the altar of a man's lust.

"Some men will even tell their girlfriends that if they really love them, they must prove it by having sex. How manipulative is that?" the professor comments. "Love is simply a pig dressed up in nice clothing.

"But more to your point, Jack, Proverbs 5 does refer to the adulteress who pursues other men when her husband is out of town on business," Dr. McNeely comments. "These women are dangerous to a man who wishes to keep himself pure and faithful. They intentionally present themselves in a sensual way to a man to capture his attention and possibly woo him into a sexual encounter. Many a man has fallen because one of these women—a true siren—has lured the man with her hungry eyes, sensual body, and flattering words. I know even some pastors who have fallen to this type of woman.

"Things get dangerous when women use their bodies to tempt men and when men use feigned affection to control women. Both behaviors are manipulative. Both are about selfish desires. Both treat the other person as an object instead of a precious human being made in the image of God. Sadly, and I suppose, predictably, it's what happens when people settle for fleeting pleasure as the goal of existence instead of choosing to love God and others."

Jack leans toward the professor and says, "Your words remind me of something Dr. Livingstone told us. She said that desire, like a river, is a beautiful thing when it stays within its banks. But when it overflows and floods the land, it ceases to be beautiful. It causes widespread damage and even destroys lives. Many people allow their desire to flow wherever it may take them, even if it overflows its banks. They believe that if you desire something, you deserve it, and if it feels good, just do it."

Dr. McNeely rests a fisted hand under his chin and nods his head. "You're right, Jack. But also remember, as I mentioned last semester, that life isn't about desiring less. God wants you to desire more. He doesn't want you to seek sexual pleasure as your chief end, of course. Instead, He wants you to desire the best thing in the universe, namely, Himself. He wants you to desire Him above all created things.

"If you seek the most beautiful Being in the universe first, then everything else falls into its proper place. When you are filled with God Himself, you will view others as God views them—eternal beings bearing God's image who are not meant to be used for selfish pleasure but loved as God Himself. In short, the best sex comes when God is loved first."

"Sometimes it's easy to forget that the unseen things in the universe need to come first," Jack says. "They seem so unattainable and even unreal at times. It's easier to focus on the immediate pleasures that are so easily seen and touched."

"I can't disagree with you, Jack," the professor replies. "We must never forget that there is a terrible adversary in this universe. This enemy hates it when God's image-bearers love things in the proper order—the Creator first and then the creatures. So, he attempts to disrupt that love. His wicked scheme is to manipulate us to exchange God for idols and then to hate the loving Father when He takes away our mud pies all because He wants to give us a banquet in the palace."

Jack nods his head and says, "I'm more aware of the adversary every day and his campaign to make me forget the unseen things."

The professor rubs the back of his hand over his beard and says, "Two final thoughts about sexual temptation, Jack, is that it's difficult to fight alone, and frontal attacks are often futile. What I mean, first, is that you need to be in a community with other men you can share your deepest secrets and struggles with because the destructive power of addiction lies in isolation. Never try to fight the battle alone, which we know is your default position, Jack. We all need someone to have our back.

"Secondly, instead of white-knuckling your way through temptation—focusing all your energy on trying not to do what the fallen part of you wants—a better strategy is to love something more than the sin that tempts you. In Star Trek terms, you must redirect energy from the photon torpedoes toward strengthening the structural integrity of the Enterprise. Make the hull stronger. As you dedicate more time and energy to being with God and growing to love Him, you'll desire creatures less and the Creator more."

"I grew up on Star Wars, not Star Trek, but I get what you're saying," Jack replies as he gets to his feet. "Growing my affection for God instead of simply trying to fight off sin head-to-head is the way to go.

"Thanks, Dr. McNeely," Jack says as he stretches down and touches the toes of his running shoes. "Sorry to take off so abruptly. I've got to get to Hebrew class with Silverstein. I appreciate you making time for me. I'm slowly learning not to be alone. Needing God and others is not weakness but wisdom."

"Well said, Jack!" the professor exclaims in a loud voice that reverberates among the books and the stacks of papers, and the maps on the wall.

"I'm going to be like Joseph," Jack says as he opens the office door. "I'm going to remember that there are times in life when the wisest thing to do is run, maybe not mostly from the other person but from my own disordered desires. After all, I want to be known as a man who loves women, not one who manipulates and uses them."

The Academy president gets to his feet and says, "One last thing, Jack." He walks over to his student and says, "Just remember that sexuality is a wonderful gift. God created it for us to enjoy within a human covenant relationship that reflects our covenant relationship with Him. My belief is that the intense and pure intimacy experienced during loving sex with your spouse is a small foreshadowing of the pleasure we'll have in God's presence one day. You'll never find that in lust.

"So, always remember, Jack—Christians *should* have the best sex in the world. I think there's even some research out there to support that."

Jack smiles broadly at Dr. McNeely and comments, "Thanks for the great news. I look forward to giving and receiving that gift in my future marriage."

Jack is almost out the door when his spelunking guide comments, "If I was hard on you today, just remember what Proverbs 9:8 says: 'Do not reprove a scoffer, or he will hate you; reprove a wise man, and he will love you.' I know you're striving to be a wise man, Jack. I called you out because I know you'll take it and learn from it."

The man's eyes shine with confidence as he announces, "An individual like you is uncommon these days, Jack—a man who wants to serve others instead of using them. A humble, teachable man like you will be a faithful husband for that future wife of yours, and an amazing father, your kids will be able to trust and respect. I have no doubt about that, Jack. Never forget my words because you will be tested repeatedly by the enemy in the days ahead."

The professor nods his head slowly as he says, "Satan will fight to distract you from Jesus' love and will even attempt to erase God's identity within you."

Jack nods his head, then turns and walks out of the office. He does not reply to his mentor because the words are stuck in his throat. Rarely has a man spoken so highly of him. He has just received "the blessing" that every son desires from his father.

As he walks down the hallway, Jack's stride is a little longer, and he holds his head up a bit higher.

CHAPTER 11

DEAD ON ARRIVAL

Emily agrees, but not without significant initial resistance, to accompany Jack to a park twenty minutes from the Academy. He has asked her to speak about her winter break since she has remained entirely reticent about the topic since her return from Florida. After Jack kills the engine, the two Academy students get out of the Jeep and walk over to an open area next to a large pavilion. Although there is no snow on the ground, the air is chilled by a cruel mid-February breeze. The park is entirely deserted.

Jack feels depression settle over him like a heavy, black shroud. The most frustrating thing about it is that he has no idea why he is feeling so dark. He takes a deep breath as he tries to shake it off.

They toss a football around for fifteen minutes. Although the ball is as hard as a rock, Emily does not complain. Jack has previously discovered that the young woman is an amazing athlete who has played multiple sports, including soccer, basketball, golf, and softball. Today, she throws perfect spirals most of the time, and some of her catches are impressive.

When they have had enough of the toss and catch, they walk over to a bench beneath a leafless tree adjacent to a small pond. They sit down and engage in some preliminary small talk as they gaze at the small forest of cold giants that rise naked into the pewter canopy of winter. Eventually, Jack turns to look at Emily.

The young woman's oval face, framed by her long blonde hair, is roused to color by the cold air. Her eyes communicate an attitude somewhere between resolute and intransigent. Her arms are folded over her chest, and her body leans away from the young man seated next to her. Jack opens his mouth to ask a well-rehearsed question calculated to penetrate Emily's defenses. But before he can say a word, a higher-pitched male voice interrupts him.

"Ah, what a magnificent day for romance!" the voice announces pleasantly.

Surprised, Jack and Emily look up to see a man about Jack's height but at least twice his breadth. His small mouth is smiling, and his eyes are sparkling. Above his blue suit, red tie, and the large jowls of his face, his hair is slicked down severely. His hands are clasped quaintly in front of him like a child standing in the front row of the choir.

"Do we know you?" Jack inquires, at a loss for any other response.

"That is the question, isn't it?" the obese man says, nodding his head. "No, I don't believe that you know me. However, I know both of you," he says with a chuckle.

"How—" Jack begins to ask before the huge man raises a hand to silence the young man.

"I'm most interested in you, Jack," the undesirable guest says, bending slightly forward at his massive waist. "Although I must confess that I'm always interested in someone as beautiful as you, sweet Emily," he adds as his eyes twinkle brightly and his eyebrows arch devilishly.

Jack sits forward on the bench and begins to protest the stranger's words. Once again, he is interrupted, this time by a gentle hushing sound from the man who has raised a finger to his lips.

184

"How dare you judge my lust for this young woman when you're as guilty as me?" the corpulent man comments in his obnoxiously pleasant manner. "You desire her as well, do you not? Now, don't try to lie to me, Jack. I know what's in you. After all, didn't I observe you at the beach several weeks ago touching an exquisite young creature? Is that an infrequent habit, or do you often flirt with women you've never met before?" A smile plays on the huge man's small lips that are as pink as a sow's nose.

Jack feels Emily's eyes on him as he hesitates and then stammers defensively, "I didn't touch her. She touched me."

"Ah, defensive, are we?" the man comments with another irritating chuckle. "You wanted her to touch you, though, didn't you, Jack? You stopped and spoke with her when you could have kept running. You were hoping to sleep with her since you couldn't have sweet Emily here."

Jack abruptly rises to his feet, his eyes flashing. "I don't know who you are or why you interrupted us, but it's obvious you need to leave," he demands sternly.

"Ah, so you are capable of engaging me man to man. I am pleased with you, after all, Jack. You have my sincerest apology for judging you in my heart as an emasculated juvenile who hides behind young women." The mouth smiles again, and the fleshy cheeks bloat with what Jack can only interpret as condescension.

Jack stares at the interloper in front of him. He watches as the man's small eyes slowly drift over his shoulder and travel down to look at Emily. Jack moves his body so that the intruder's view is obstructed.

"Like I said, it's time for you to leave," Jack announces. He looks into the man's eyes and sees a lengthening shadow spread over their sparkling surface.

"I will take my leave soon enough," the man replies in his pseudo-soothing voice. "But first, I have an offer to extend to you, Jack."

"Consider me uninterested," Jack replies with a mirthless laugh.

The fleshy man's small mouth contorts, and he sighs deeply. "Jack, Jack," he chides, "you will listen to what I have to say, and you will do what I ask. No wise man ever refuses Draegan DaFoe—at least no wise living man."

Jack discerns that the man across from him is watching him closely for a reaction. Distracted only for a moment, Jack registers the DaFoe surname, and a chill rushes through his body. He realizes that he is looking at none other than the infamous police commissioner that Louis Fagani has spoken of to the micro-cohort. This man standing before him is the descendent of Philip DaFoe, killer of women and children.

While Jack examines the eyes that are examining him, the big man raises his hand to his face to scratch his cheek, and Jack spots the large gold ring with the inverted cross on his thick finger. Jack's mind races to remember where he has seen the ring before ...

"As I was saying," the big man continues, "I have an offer for you, Jack. I want you to find the body of my great-great grandfather, Philip. You know who I'm talking about," the man says, secretly guessing but speaking with a tone of certainty. "You find Philip, and I'll let you keep the ladies—I don't mean the ones you lust after, Jack. Although, maybe your greed for the silver ladies could be deemed a type of lust as well." Draegan's bright eyes continue to survey Jack as the mammoth man tilts his head coyly.

When Jack does not immediately respond, the man says, "I know you, Jack. We're much alike, you and me. Neither one of us will rest until we get what we want. I know you're at the Academy to find what you believe belongs to your family, and I'm only trying to find what belongs to my family."

This time Jack does not hesitate. He announces with confidence, "You're absolutely wrong about that, Draegan DaFoe. You don't know me. If you did, you would know we're two totally *different* men. You're in love with the material world, while I'm in love with the unseen rewards found in Jesus. You look to what you can see while I see Him who is invisible."

Even as the words are still ringing in the air, Jack knows he would not have spoken so boldly before his adventure with Armando in the barrio or before his recent experience in the Cave of Dread. He is a man of greater courage now, thanks to Jesus, Jim Elliot, Armando, Violet's dream, and the challenges and encouragement of Isaiah Windsor and Milner McNeely.

Draegan smiles again, and his eyes burn with something between impatience and malice. "You don't want to be like your pathetic father, do you, Jack?" the huge man inquires smugly. "He was a coward who encountered a most dreadful accident while fleeing the scene of a house fire that he should have been extinguishing."

Jack is shocked. He has no idea where Draegan DaFoe acquired his information, but it appears that he knows just enough to be dangerous.

"My father was not fleeing," he insists. He hates it that his voice quavers as he speaks. "He was a fireman rushing a pregnant woman to the hospital who had been injured in the fire!"

"Is that your mother's narrative, my dear Jack?" the man inquires softly with his infuriating chuckle. His voice is taunting in a smooth, sickening way. "Okay, have it your way. Your father was rushing to the hospital with his lover who was carrying his unborn child. Didn't your poor mother ever wonder aloud where your father was all those nights after work?"

Jack feels a rare emotion building inside of him—rage. The only thing that derails him from physically attacking the man is counsel from the Spirit

187

that somehow elbows past his intense emotion and achieves a tenuous foothold: "Be angry, but in your anger do not sin." A moment later, other words run the gauntlet of his emotions and establish a beachhead of wisdom in his brain: "Do not fret because of those who are evil or be envious of those who do wrong; for like the grass, they will soon wither, like green plants they will soon die away."

As the blood vessels of his forehead begin to throb less violently, he has enough space outside his aroused amygdala to recall a verse from Psalm 119 he had read just that morning: "I have hidden your word in my heart that I might not sin against you."

Jack takes a deep breath and looks at the heavy man with a renewed calm in his spirit. "As I said earlier, it's time for you to be on your way, Mr. DaFoe. I don't make alliances with men who twist truth."

Draegan lifts his fleshy chin and replies, "Ah, truth. What is truth, Jack? Your truth? My truth? Whose version? It's all relative, my dear young man," he comments in a calm, unruffled voice that reeks with condescension.

"You don't believe in absolute truth," Jack states.

"There is no such entity," the man says with his sparkling eyes. "We're all a truth unto ourselves."

"Interesting," Jack comments and then stops.

There is a long pause while both men stare at each other without blinking. Finally, Draegan chuckles and says, "Okay, Jack, I'll take the bait. What's so interesting, my young friend?"

"You said there's no absolute truth," Jack observes.

The big man smiles and pauses, sensing that he is about to walk into a trap. "Yes, those were my words," he says slowly.

Now it is Jack's turn to smile. "You just contradicted yourself, Mr.

DaFoe. You made the absolute statement that there is no absolute truth. You can't have it both ways. Unless...unless you like to cheat."

The obese man stands quietly beneath the naked tree, whose branches spread out over the bench and the pond. His jowls sag into his collar, and his triple chin spills down the front of his shirt. He stares at Jack with eyes that eviscerate their object. The sparkle is gone for the moment, replaced by something that appears two shades darker than hatred.

"I discern you are a philosopher, Jack," he finally says in his irritating tone. "I never deemed you capable of such deep reflection since you attend that primitive school that peddles ignorance and superstition."

Jack clenches his fists but otherwise does not react to the man's words that are undoubtedly uttered to incite. In fact, everything about the man seems designed to whip others into a rage. Jack wonders how many men have physically attacked the police commissioner in the past, only to find themselves in jail or the hospital or even at the bottom of the river wearing concrete shoes.

After the two men have stared at each other for a long time, Draegan finally says, "So we have an understanding then, Jack. You find the body of my great-great-grandfather, and I'll walk away from the Lady Libertys."

"As I said earlier," Jack repeats, "I don't make deals with a man who manipulates reality to his liking and who treats women like they're entrees on a menu. So, no, we don't have an understanding."

The large man nods his head slowly, and his eyes narrow to slits. "You should know, Jack, that I don't take no for an answer. Ever. There will be— how do I explain it to a lesser intellect—consequences. Yes, there will be consequences for your refusal. These consequences can reach as far as, let's say, as far as sweet Emily here," he says, leaning to his left so he can smile down at the young woman and observe her with his small, hungry eyes.

189

The man hesitates as if deciding what to say next, then adds enigmatically, "My consequences have the power to reach as nearby as the campus of your diminutive academy or as far away as the homeland of your mythical Messiah." The huge man's eyes again survey Jack's face as if awaiting a reaction.

Jack pauses for a moment as he registers the meaning of Draegan's comment. When realization dawns in his mind, he inquires with incredulity in his voice, "Is that a confession? Are you admitting that you're responsible for the attack on our friends in Jerusalem?" Like the scalding water of a geyser, he feels rage rise within him again. He senses that Emily has risen from the bench and is standing just behind his right shoulder.

The man shakes his head in a scolding fashion and clucks his tongue. Then he replies in a condescending tone, "Jack, Jack. I said no such thing, and I have no idea what you are alluding to. You are so quick to rush headlong to unfounded conclusions. And here I thought you were more disciplined than that. Once again, I have overestimated you. How disappointing."

Jack pauses as he again seeks God's Word to comfort him in the face of DaFoe's condescension. Finally, he decides to go in a different direction.

"Okay, Draegan," he says, "listen to this. I think you're willing to give up the silver ladies because you're after something bigger. You know that Philip's body will lead you to an even greater treasure than the coins."

The man smiles and replies, "Well, of course, Jack. What you're stating as some type of epiphany is a fact obvious even to the mind of a child. I concern myself with a search for something more precious, let us say, to the DaFoe family."

The police commissioner clears his throat loudly and spits on the sidewalk at Jack's feet. "If you remain unwilling to cooperate with me in my endeavors," he warns, "I have no other choice but to commit all my resources to shadow you wherever you go. Every second of your waking hours will be observed by my people. And my people are everywhere," the mammoth Draegan announces, "even at your right elbow."

The man pauses and straightens his fleshy body to its full height. He looks over Jack's shoulder and addresses Emily one more time. "And as for you, my sweet lily, how sad that you settle for Jack, a person who can only play at being a man. If he ever speaks to you of courage, do not listen to him. He does not even know what courage is." His dark eyes flash as they rivet themselves to Emily's face.

Draegan's small eyes eventually slither back to Jack and search his face one last time like a vulture contemplating which eyeball to rip out of its socket first. Jack has undergone surgeries that feel less invasive than the penetrating gaze.

The descendent of Philip DaFoe opens his small mouth and intones quietly, "You honestly are the weakest man I have ever encountered in all my years, Jack Sutherington. I thank the stars you're not my son, because you would arouse deep embarrassment in me if you were my offspring. Your own father no doubt welcomed death as an opportunity to be liberated from your pathetic presence. One day soon, the earth will rejoice at your passing."

The mammoth form turns to leave but hesitates and then looks back at Jack. "We will see each other again, Jack, just under more unpleasant circumstances." He pauses and then adds with a smile, "You have my word on that."

Jack watches the giant man ponderously walk away until he disappears behind the park's pavilion.

When Draegan is finally out of sight, Jack turns and looks at Emily, who is standing just behind him. Her face is pale, and her chin is quivering. Wordlessly, he steps toward her and gently embraces her. She does not resist, but neither does she return his affection. He holds her for a long time.

Before Jack releases her, he speaks soothingly into her ear: "Don't be afraid, Emily, I will protect you with my life just as Jesus has protected me with His. Just wait and see. Everything will be okay."

After he has spoken the words, he is almost certain that he believes them.

"Take me back to the Academy," is Emily's only response.

Jack observes that the young woman is shivering, and not from the cold. Her eyes are intense with emotion. Jack nods, and the two students walk back to the parking lot.

After they get into the Jeep, Jack starts the engine and looks over at Emily. "Are you okay?" he inquires.

"What do you think, Jack?" she retorts with flashing eyes. "A man just abused me with his eyes. Do you really think I'm going to be okay?"

"No, of course not," Jack replies. "My bad for asking a stupid question." He watches Emily for a while but is at a loss for words. Finally, he backs the vehicle out of the parking spot and drives out into the street.

"How do people become so evil?" Emily eventually mumbles as she stares out the passenger window. "I consider myself an open-minded person, but I simply can't wrap my head around the belief that people are basically good—especially men."

Jack is not sure if the question is rhetorical or if Emily is expecting an answer from him. He is silent for a long time as he gazes steadily at the road in front of him.

Eventually, he proffers, "I think you have to practice for a long time to become as evil as that man. Yeah, I think it's all about practice. The more we do anything, the more it becomes us. My coach back at the university used to always say that 'practice makes permanent.' Obviously, Draegan DaFoe has practiced evil for such a long time that it's now a permanent part of him."

After another silence, Jack comments while still staring straight ahead, "But there's more to it than practice. I think everyone comes into life with two paths set before them. Every decision we make either takes us toward the straight path of light and truth, or it takes us away from it into crookedness and darkness. After forty years of making crooked choices, a person ends up so far off the straight path that he can't see it anymore—even with binoculars."

Jack pauses and then adds, "By that time, the person who has wandered so far from the path of light doesn't even want to go back. Isn't John the one who writes that everyone who does evil hates the light? They've become so practiced at loving darkness. Besides, they know that the light exposes things, so why would they ever want to move toward it and have their dark deeds outed? It's a sad thing when someone comes to hate the light just because they've learned to love darkness."

Jack glances over at Emily. She is still looking out the window, hiding her face. Eventually, she muses out loud, "I wonder what God will do with that man. I know the Bible says that mercy triumphs over judgment. Maybe God will have mercy on him."

Jack looks at the road and then back at Emily. "A minute ago, you hated the man," he observes as frustration rises within him. "Now it sounds like you're hoping God will spare him."

There is a pause. "I'm just thinking that God is a merciful God who maybe overlooks sin," Emily comments toward the window.

Jack shakes his head and says, "Are you saying that a person can have their cake and eat it, too? That you can disobey God and expect Him to wink at your sin? You know that's not true, Em. You know God is pure and holy and can't wink at sin any more than a human can breathe under water."

When Emily does not respond, Jack says, "What would your earthly dad do if you were a teenager and you kept coming home from the mall with stolen clothes? Would he simply look the other way and do nothing?"

"Maybe," Emily replies coolly.

"Only if he didn't care about you," Jack argues. "A loving father would challenge your behavior, point out how it's wrong, and let you know that it could lead to serious consequences someday. If you didn't stop shoplifting, he'd give you a consequence, right? He'd take away the car keys or ground you or maybe take you to a counselor."

"What if I keep on shoplifting?" Emily responds. "What if I grow up to be an adult and continue shoplifting? What if I move out of the house and my father can't take away the keys or ground me anymore? I don't think he'd stop loving me or suddenly leave me. I'm his daughter, after all."

"That's true," Jack admits as he accelerates forward from a stop sign.

"So, wouldn't God the Father be the same way?" Emily says, finally turning away from the window and glancing at Jack.

"That's a tough question, Em," Jack replies. "It makes me think of the first chapter in Romans, where it describes how God responds to His children who keep on sinning even when they know that what they're doing is disobedient. It says three times in that passage that God gives these disobedient children over to their sin since they refuse to listen to Him."

Jack pauses to switch lanes and then says, "Romans isn't saying that God stops loving his disobedient children or turns His back on them.

But it is saying that since God's repeated correction has not changed their minds or altered their behaviors, He's taking the final step of letting them go to do what they so stubbornly want to do. He knows that sooner or later, these disobedient children will discover for themselves that sin is empty and unsatisfying. Then maybe they'll turn away from their idols and turn back to Him."

"I've heard all that before," Emily says with a hard edge in her voice.

Jack sends a sidelong glance at his passenger and then looks back at the road. After a short silence, he says, "Have you heard the old saying that 'you can lead a horse to water, but you can't make it drink?'"

"Of course, Jack," Emily says impatiently as she stares out the passenger door window again. "I do realize people can be like a stubborn horse."

"Well," Jack replies, "there's another version of that old adage. It says, 'You can lead a horse to water, but you can't make it drink. But you can salt its oats.' That proverb helps me understand the Romans passage. I believe that when God gives us over to our sin, it's like salting the horses' oats. As He gives us free rein to pursue whatever evil choices we refuse to give up, our sin will eventually become so salty and make us so thirsty that we'll run back to God and ask Him for the living water that can satisfy our thirsting hearts."

"I've never heard that version of the old adage before," Emily comments woodenly. "Are you saying that Draegan DaFoe's oats haven't been salted enough?"

"Maybe, or that he's so set on doing things his way that he'll never choose to obey God," Jack offers. "After all, sin isn't just about seeking fleeting pleasures. It's also about being in a state of rebellion against God."

Emily squirms in her seat and closes her eyes. They remain closed when Jack says, "Even if I hate what that man does, I don't judge Draegan. I'm a sinner just like him, so I can't throw any stones at him. And I certainly don't judge you, Emily."

"Why would you judge me?" Emily retorts as she sits up stiffly and turns glaring green emerald eyes toward him. "What have I done that would warrant your judgment?"

Jack glances over at his agitated passenger and replies, "Hey, cool it, Em. I said I don't judge you. Besides, I don't know you well enough to decide what I'd judge about you even if I wanted to. You keep yourself so well hidden."

"Well, good," she snaps. "That's the way I want to keep it!"

Jack does not respond as he pulls into the parking lot at the Academy. He shakes his head in frustration and shifts the Jeep into park. As Emily opens the door and gets out of the vehicle, he finally says testily, "I don't know why you won't let me in, Em. I'm your biggest fan around here."

The only response he gets is the slam of the vehicle door.

As he watches Emily walk away, he says with exasperation in his voice, "God, what's up with that woman? Sometimes she acts like I'm the vilest person on the planet. No, let me amend that. She *rejects* me like I'm the vilest *man* on the planet. Lord, what is it about Emily and men? And why in the world am I still attracted to her? Yes, she's physically beautiful in my eyes, but there's something deeper in her that is also attractive even if it is guarded with quills."

Jack leans back in his seat and rests his head against the headrest. He sighs loudly and says, "Okay, God. If I'm going to keep pursuing that woman, I'm going to need your help. She's a clam with an attitude, and I don't have a crowbar big enough to pry her open."

Jack stares out the window and sighs again. "Jesus, why is she so afraid of judgment from you and from me?"

As if in answer to his question, a thought enters his mind: *The more darkness people are hiding, the more they fear the light that will expose their darkness; and the more they fear the light that will expose their darkness, the more they will attack the light or hide from it.*

Jack decides Emily is hiding something, and it is not small.

CHAPTER 12

ANOTHER JAZZ ENCOUNTER

Dr. Isaiah Windsor parks the van in the tall grass just off the crumbling asphalt road and kills the engine. "Well, people, here we are—at the Bridge," he says, glancing at Jack and Rachel in the back seat. Then he turns to Armando in the front seat and asks, "Will you pray for us before we get the mess hall set up?"

"Yes, Colonel," Armando replies with a smile.

"Jesus, be with us today," the young man begins his prayer. "May your love flow through us to all the homeless people we meet today. We thank you that you showed us how to love the poor and the disadvantaged and not to look down on them as less than others. You came into this world as a servant and died for all of us, and so we are here today as your servants for your people. Thank you for this opportunity to love those who you designed so wonderfully. Also, please help us to connect with Jazz again today. Amen."

"Okay, let's get this show on the road," Dr. Windsor says as he opens his door.

The professor and the three students climb out of the van and begin to unload the supplies from the back. They remove four collapsible tables, four camp stoves, and boxes of food, clothing, toilet paper, sleeping bags, flashlights, batteries, wet wipes, and medical supplies, including syringes, insulin, anti-bacterial creams, and knee braces. They carry everything to a spot beneath the six-lane bridge that serves as a shelter for the homeless. The "roof" above hums with the sound of speeding tires as cars and trucks whiz over it, completely ignorant of the world that ekes out a hard-scrabble existence beneath them.

Dr. Windsor and the students set up the 6' tables under the bridge along with the four camping stoves. Within an hour, a meal of chicken alfredo, French bread, fresh fruit, and chocolate chip cookies is ready. On this Tuesday, forty-six people file through the line to enjoy the meal served weekly by Academy students and professors.

While people are eating, Dr. Windsor and the students sit on the concrete ramp under the bridge among the men, women, and children. As they converse with the people, they inquire about special needs or concerns they may have—physical, mental, or spiritual. An hour from now, a nurse or a physician assistant will arrive from a local clinic to attend to any medical needs that have been identified by Dr. Windsor. This afternoon, for instance, there is a child with a high fever, a teenager with an infected toe, and a fifty-eight-year-old man with what looks like an early outbreak of shingles.

When everyone has eaten their fill—there rarely is any food left over on these nights—Dr. Windsor stands under the bridge and speaks to the people over the whine of tires. His topic today is how a good God can exist in an evil world. Shortly after the professor begins speaking, Jazz appears and sits down halfway up the ramp.

Fifteen minutes later, the professor—who is dressed in his usual khaki pants and long-sleeved button-down shirt—concludes his message with words from Habakkuk 3: "Though the fig tree should not blossom, nor fruit be on the vines, the produce of the olive fail and the fields yield no food, the flock be cut off from the fold, and there be no herd in the stalls, yet I will rejoice in the LORD; I will take joy in the God of my salvation. GOD, the Lord, is my strength; he makes my feet like the deer's; he makes me tread on my high places."

Jack is always surprised by the number of voices that utter an affirming amen at the end of the weekly meditation. Tonight is no exception. Even though these people own nothing except for the clothes on their backs and any items they can load into a shopping cart, old backpack, or moldy suitcase, many of them are amazingly positive and grateful. Just in the last eight months, he has learned so much from these people who are not distracted by the pursuit of wealth and entertainment.

Under the bridge, Jack speaks at length with Freddie Williams and Junior. Later, he plays football with the two older Ramirez brothers. Lastly, he visits Sophie Jackson, the young mother who has a toddler and another baby on the way. Her health has been more stable since getting out of the hospital a week ago. She reports that she will likely have some Section Eight housing options available next month after being buried on the waiting list for over two years.

Unlike Sophie, some of the people gathered under the bridge have no desire to live anywhere other than outside, under the open sky, or under the bridge.

When Jack walks back to the tables to begin cleanup, he observes a conversation already in progress between Armando, Dr. Windsor, and Jazz. The young ebony-skinned woman who had sported an impressive Afro the last time Jack saw her three months ago now has buzzed her hair to within an inch of her skull. She looks scary-thin, and her beautiful face is even more haggard than the last time he saw her.

When Jack walks up to the professor, his roommate, and the "girl-in-a-bind" as he has come to think of Jazz after their first encounter, the young woman turns her head so slowly that Jack is convinced she is ill or shooting up.

"Yo, Jack," she says in a subdued voice. "Or should I call you Juan? Where are those dope wheels you drove last time?"

Jack laughs and says, "Back at school. Today, we drove the soccer mom vehicle."

Jazz nods her head and says, "Yes, I see, the good doctor's van—the man who provides living proof that your parochial academy is surprisingly integrated, albeit in a token sense only. You can park those wheels here all night, and nobody's gonna touch it—except maybe to sleep in it. Not like that Jeep of yours that would be sitting on cinder blocks and stripped to the bone in a New York minute."

"What happened to your hair?" Jack asks in a diplomatic tone.

The young woman with full lips and high cheekbones smiles grimly and sighs. "I was telling Armando and the professor that my life has been in the toilet lately." She sighs again. "My 'coiffure,' as my grand-mammy calls it, has always communicated my lot in life. So, I cut my hair to reflect my current status. Three weeks ago, my head was as shiny as a cue ball down at Billy's Billiards. Only it was black, of course," she says with an enigmatic glance.

"Sounds like you've hit rock bottom," Jack observes.

Jazz compresses her lips, then nods her head and looks down at the ground. It is clear to Jack that the ivy-league-student-become-street-person is broken.

"We were just checking with this young lady to see if there's anything she needs today," Isaiah Windsor says as he runs his fingers over his hair that is the same length as Jazz'. Jack notices that small patches of snow have

202

crept into the professor's scalp around his temples and ears. He is convinced that the white invasion has appeared in the four months since Violet died.

"Do you need something to eat?" Jack inquires of Jazz. He glances at Armando, and the two men immediately look away to hide their smiles. They both know what the other is thinking: Jazz ate four muffins the last time they were together. Jazz, usually as vigilant as a hawk, does not seem to notice.

"I'm not hungry," the woman says quietly.

"What's going on, Jazz?" Jack asks. He notices that the young woman's Susan B. Anthony sweatshirt has been replaced by a dingy brown shirt that hangs loosely from her body.

Jazz does not answer his question but shakes her head as if trying to wake herself up. Finally, she says on a totally different tangent, "Oh, by the way, I spoke with my granny, Ida. She told me some interesting anecdotes about her grandmother back in the late 1800s."

"You mean about her experiences with the Sutherington family?" Jack asks.

The young woman closes her eyes and replies, "Actually, no. I got it wrong. Lydia Marie didn't work for the Sutherington family. She was employed by the DaFoe's—Philip and Madeline."

Just then, Rachel walks up to the group of four and says with a chuckle, "Did I hear someone mention Philip DaFoe?"

Armando begins to introduce Jazz when Rachel interrupts and says, "Oh, we met earlier, just after Dr. Windsor's message."

Jazz looks at Rachel and says, "Yeah, I was just talking about my great-great-grandmother, Lydia, who was a domestic worker for the DaFoe family." She pauses, sighs, and then says, "Over Christmas, my grandmother, Ida, told me some intriguing stories about Lydia's experiences at their home."

"I can only imagine," Armando interjects in a sarcastic voice as he rubs the back of his fingers over his goatee. "I suppose she claimed that Philip had a secret torture chamber in his backyard shed?"

The young woman with the skull cap of hair narrows her eyes at Armando and tilts her head. "How did you know?" she asks. "You been talking to my granny?"

"Are you playing me, Shorty?" Armando asks with a laugh.

"The question is, are you playing me?" Jazz responds.

"You're serious, then," Armando says. "Dead Lydia told her granddaughter, Ida, that Philip had a torture chamber in the backyard shed."

"Maybe not a torture chamber," Jazz clarifies, blinking her eyes as if the dim light under the bridge is too bright. "Lydia told Ida that there was an old shed with a root cellar in the back. She said it was like 100 feet from the house and next to the edge of the woods. Apparently, Philip spent many evenings out there when he wasn't away from the house for business or personal reasons. But that's not the strangest thing," the young woman says, her large brown eyes even bigger than usual. Jack notices that they are also red and watery.

"What was the strangest thing?" Rachel inquires in her Boston accent and then stops breathing as she waits for Jazz' reply.

"Ida told me her grandmother occasionally saw Philip head off into the forest at night with a lantern, an old wooden cart, and a shovel," Jazz says as she closes her eyes and rubs her forehead with both hands.

"Seriously?" Rachel says. "That sounds creepy. What was in the cart?"

"Lydia never saw anything because it was too far away and too dark," the haggard young woman says. "But there's more."

"What do you mean there's more?" Rachel asks, leaning closer to Jazz.

"Lydia told my granny that she occasionally heard the man chanting in his study," Jazz replies, "and that he would have secret meetings there with different VIPs from the city—big wigs they called them back in the day."

"We know some things about Philip DaFoe, too," Jack informs Jazz. "Since we last spoke with you, we've been reading a journal written by a man named Jacob Sutherington. Turns out, he's a relative of mine. Who would've ever thought that I'd come out here to the Midwest only to discover that my roots can be traced back to this city? Jacob repeatedly mentions Philip in his journal. From everything we've read, it appears that Philip was a very evil man. It sounds like your great-great-grandmother might have been aware of that."

"She thought he was an eccentric man," Jazz counters.

"I wonder what Philip was doing out in the woods," Rachel muses aloud as she looks up at the concrete ceiling above them.

Dr. Windsor looks at Rachel and responds, "Well, it seems obvious. He was either burying something or digging something up. Either activity would be highly suspicious in the middle of the night."

The professor glances from Rachel to Armando to Jack and says in a stern voice, "Sounds like you three have some explaining to do."

"You mean about Jacob Sutherington?" Jack says, "Yes, we do. We just haven't known how much to tell you over the last few months. We didn't want to bother you after...after Violet died."

"Violet?" Jazz says, suddenly a bit more engaged. "Who's Violet?"

Isaiah Windsor looks at the young woman and swallows. "Violet was— is—my wife," he says evenly. "She passed last December. Cancer."

"I'm sorry," the young woman says in a soft tone that is far removed from the harsh voice she used in her first encounter at the Bridge with the Screaming Eagles the previous autumn. "I—" she begins but then falls silent.

"What is it?" Rachel inquires as she dares to reach out and touch the woman's shoulder. "What's wrong?"

Jazz licks her lips and says, "My father died two months ago. He had a massive heart attack while preaching on a Sunday morning. Go figure, right. People say he was dead before he hit the floor."

Jack and Armando feel like they know the young woman's father. Jazz had told them—and Aly—all about the man she had been rebelling against since she was in middle school. Rachel had not been with her classmates when they had learned about Jazz' struggles with her father. However, Jack, Armando, and Aly had informed her, along with Emily and Stewart, about their encounter with the young woman at the Bridge.

Before anyone can reply, the young woman looks over Rachel's shoulder and interjects, "If you're wondering if I reconciled with my father, the answer is no. I haven't seen him since I spoke with you the last time."

"You didn't attend the funeral," Armando states more than asks. The emaciated woman looks at him and shakes her head.

"You didn't find the middle ground, then," Jack says as he runs his hand through his flaxen hair that is getting longer again since his return from LA. "You're settling for the Pyrrhic victories."

"Some things are different," she says. Her voice has an edge to it. Turning to Armando, she comments, "Your question last time about if I considered my father evil or ignorant was helpful. I decided that as much as I hated the way he treated me, my father wasn't trying to annihilate me. He wasn't an evil man. It helped me to see him as ignorant. I'm not as bitter as in the past.

"However," she says, looking over at Jack, "I'm still stuck. If I do what I know he would want me to do. I feel like he's controlling me—only now from the grave. If I intentionally do the opposite of what I know he would want me to do. I'm at the mercy of my rebellious heart. Either way, I still can't be me. I'm in that bind we talked about. I can't let myself obey him, and I can't let myself be me."

Dr. Windsor clears his throat, and the three students from the Academy know that the expert in munitions is about to drop a bomb. A good-intentioned bomb, but nonetheless, a bunker-busting bomb that is designed to expose a person to the truth about herself.

"Young lady," the professor begins, "in life, it's not what happens to you that's ultimately important. Of far greater impact is how you choose to respond to what comes at you."

Jack sees the young woman's jaw tense. "Are you saying that what the victimizer and the perpetrator and the oppressor do is immaterial, even defensible?" Jazz parries, switching to her ivy school persona, who can generate a compelling intellectual defense against the fiercest foe. "That's like saying the rapist walks, but my response to the rapist is the perp that's on trial," she remarks, suddenly energized for battle.

"Young lady, you know that's not what I'm saying," the retired colonel says firmly with no change in his tone or his face. His eyes hold Rachel's not defensively but with strength. Jack has always been impressed that Dr. Windsor can be challenged and even attacked and not take it personally.

He's got thick body armor, Jack thinks to himself, *not thin skin.*

"The way I encourage you to look at it is like this," the professor continues. "The one who sins against you is always culpable for what he did and deserves consequences commensurate with the crime. That part of the equation is assumed. But even more important is how you respond to being sinned against. You can choose—note my emphasis on your agency in this equation—to adopt the role of being the victim as your identity, or you can forgive after confronting the offense.

"If you choose the identity and *attitude* of the victim, you will blame the other person and rehearse anger in your heart over and over until you are consumed by bitterness and hatred. You will never know freedom if you choose to react this way. The other option is to adopt the attitude of Jesus, who said, 'Father, forgive them, for they don't know what they are doing.' This forgiving attitude empowers you instead of rendering you powerless to the perpetrator's actions and to your own resentment. Of course, it might take significant time to get to the place of forgiveness."

"So, you want me to be nice, just like my father insisted," Jazz retorts as she crosses her arms and lifts her chin. "Be good. Don't color outside the lines. Let people walk all over you and use you at their whim and fancy."

"You're still not hearing what I'm saying," Dr. Windsor remarks as he shakes his head. "You're hearing what you want to hear, young lady. In a very real sense, you're manipulating the world around you to say what you want it to say so you can then react to it with rehearsed defenses and memorized lines. You see the world as the adversary and so justify your identity as the victim."

The professor pauses and then says, "You're creating your own reality, young lady."

"Stop calling me a 'young lady,'" the Afro-less Jazz snaps. "It's demeaning! If you weren't from my tribe, I'd wonder if it was a latent expression of racism. For sure, it betrays total gender insensitivity!"

The colonel is unphased by Jazz' anger. "I know your father hurt you," he says with raised eyebrows and sad eyes. "Again, that truth is not in question. I'm sorry that he didn't know how to love you. Your wound is deep and, I fear, close to being fatal."

Dr. Windsor sighs and pinches the end of his nose. "You remind me of a soldier in my battalion who was injured by shrapnel from an IED. Do you know what her reaction was as she's bleeding out?" the professor inquires of Jazz.

The expression of disgust on the young woman's face with the severely short hair does not alter. She crushes her lips together and stares at the man across from her. A spear would not be sharper than her glare.

"Her first reaction was to look at the wound and think that she's going to die," Dr. Windsor says. "And if she had continued to focus on the wound, she would have panicked, and all her vitals would have reacted accordingly. Then she would have been nearly impossible to treat. She might have even fought with the medic and interfered with life-saving interventions. No, focusing on the wound was not helpful.

"That day on the side of the road in Afghanistan, I commanded that soldier to listen to me. I insisted that she look at me, not her wound. She had to trust me in that moment. After much struggling, she finally did obey my command and focused on my face. She calmed down quickly. A few minutes later, the medic showed up and treated her wounds. She survived."

The colonel pauses, and his gaze locks onto the young woman's narrowed eyes. "Look at me, Jazz," he insists as he stands straight and tall in front of the woman. "You're going to live if you stop focusing on the wound. I know your father undermined your ability to trust any man, but you must look at the medic when you're wounded. You must look at me and the Great Physician, Jesus. We're here for you, Jazz. Healing is available to anyone who fixes her eyes trustingly on Him."

All three students are relieved when the professor does not refer to Jazz as a "young lady" again.

"And," the professor adds, "Jesus is the One who tears down the dividing wall between black and white, rich and poor, uneducated and educated. He loves us all without partiality. He calls us to a brotherhood and sisterhood of believers whose love for one another is even stronger than for blood family."

There is a brief silence under the bridge. The sun has set, and it is becoming dusky and cold. The obnoxious hum of tires on the roof above has been reduced to an intermittent whine. A chorus of unseen frogs begins to sing in a nearby pond.

In the small huddle of five people, four are praying while one is on fire inside with bitterness and rage. Jazz is still glaring at the man in front of her, who reminds her so much of her father but who is also threatening to penetrate the ancient wall that has stood impregnable for twelve years.

She must not listen to this man. She must not allow any man authority over her heart.

Out of nowhere, something rumbles inside the young woman. The two extreme personas—the compliant one and the rebel—that have created the enslaving bind inside her and rendered her a house divided against itself, teeter back and forth momentarily like flimsy walls. Then they crash into the middle.

Jazz has a brief image of seeing Jesus—not her father—standing amidst the billowing dust generated by the collapsed extremes. Then her eyes roll up into her head, and she crumples to the ground.

Dr. Windsor is visibly upset at how long it takes the ambulance to arrive at the bridge. He mutters something to himself about favoritism to the higher

SES and mumbles about where his tax dollars go. Then he refocuses on the very God he had challenged Jazz to trust a few minutes earlier, and he prays to Jesus.

Although unconscious, the young woman's heartbeat remains strong albeit elevated, so no one panics.

Ten minutes later, the ambulance finally arrives. The EMTs confirm that Jazz is stable but determine that she needs medical attention beyond what they can offer her in the field. Quickly, they strap her to a stretcher and load her into the back of the emergency vehicle. The professor volunteers to ride with the "young lady" to the hospital. The students will drive the van back to the Academy.

As the emergency vehicle pulls away with lights flashing, Armando turns to Jack and Rachel and says, "I'm convinced Dr. Windsor has the power to hypnotize people. As I was looking into his eyes when he was talking to Jazz, I knew I should be forgiving someone, I just didn't know who."

Rachel laughs and replies, "I felt the same way. He's very charismatic. He must have been some amazing leader in battle."

Jack smiles but says nothing. A heaviness has settled on his chest, and he knows that the powers of darkness are in their midst. He closes his eyes and asks Jesus to show up in a powerful way.

He is reminded of a passage he had read that morning in 2 Corinthians 10: *For though we live in the world, we do not wage war as the world does. The weapons we fight with are not the weapons of the world. On the contrary, they have divine power to demolish strongholds. We demolish arguments and every pretension that sets itself up against the knowledge of God, and we take captive every thought to make it obedient to Christ.*

"I hope Jazz will be okay," Rachel comments as they begin to load up the van.

"I do, too," Jack says with a grim smile. "The hospital is probably the best place she can be right now."

Armando nods his head and then remarks, "Now we have to dig up a grave, excavate a cave, and look for buried bodies in the woods behind Philip DaFoe's house."

"He lived there over a hundred years ago," Rachel counters. "There must be a mall parking lot built over it by now."

"Not necessarily," Jack offers. "If the house was out in the country, where I can imagine someone like Philip would have wanted to live, the woods might be undisturbed."

"Sounds like a job for Stewart," Armando states. "He can do some research to locate the house address and let us know if there's some technology that might help us locate and recover all those buried bodies."

Rachel places a box in the back of the van and then turns to face Jack and Armando. "I like adventures, guys, but I feel like we're getting in pretty deep here. Shouldn't we be calling the police at this point?"

"Rach," Jack says as he places a hand on his friend's shoulder, "we've been through this before. You know why we're not contacting law enforcement—especially after my encounter with the police commissioner."

"I remember," she says with some impatience. "But didn't someone say that Dr. Greenlay has a brother-in-law with the state police?"

"His brother-in-law is with the highway patrol, yes," Jack says. "We could contact him. But first, let's do what Dr. Windsor said earlier."

"Yeah, Juan," Armando agrees, "like Desi used to tell Lucy, 'You've got some 'splaining to do!'"

The three students laugh, and then Jack slams the back gate of the van. "Yes, it's about time for the Screaming Eagles to have a meeting with the professors."

CHAPTER 13

JACK IN THE CAVE OF DREAD

The day of Jack's sojourn in the Cave of Dread finally arrives. Privately, he has deep misgivings about being alone in the darkness for eighteen hours but knows that it is his turn to receive what God wants to say to him in the place of darkness and intimacy. Exhausted from many late nights of studying, Jack falls asleep in the pitch-black cavern not long after his mini-cohort members and professors pray for him and leave.

When he wakes up, he does not initially know where he is. The darkness is so complete that he cannot see his hand even when he holds it inches away from his face. He begins to panic.

Just when he is ready to cry out, a quiet voice speaks in his mind, reminding him where he is. Immediately, his body relaxes. He takes a deep breath and lets it out slowly. Without a watch or phone to tell him the time, he guesses that he has been asleep for an hour at most. Unfortunately, he senses the familiar sinister presence that always makes him feel like he is being watched.

He sits up on the small mattress and begins to grope around for the candle. Then he stops himself. He decides that he must face his sojourn in the darkness without material light and only rely on The Light of the world.

Reflexively, he begins to sing a favorite song he learned in the early days of his new faith in Jesus. It has always been a ready source of comfort to him. Here in the Cave of Dread, however, it feels empty. It generates no soothing. He stops singing. He begins to pray instead. But his prayers rise no higher than the rock ceiling of the cave that he cannot even see. They do not seem to be reaching God. He stops praying.

He sits quietly on the dank mattress for a long time. He hears nothing. Absolutely nothing.

Finally, he gets up and walks toward the center of the cave. He cannot see a thing, but he knows he can walk maybe thirty steps before he gets anywhere near the other side of the cave. The presence remains, and his skin crawls. His imagination convinces him that something—or someone—is going to reach out of the darkness and grab him.

He remembers something he had forgotten. He remembers that he has never liked the dark. As a boy, he would often go down into the unfinished basement of his parents' house to retrieve something from the storage room for his mother. The full basement had a feature he always hated—the lights could only be turned on by walking to the center of each of the four large rooms and then groping around in the darkness for a string hanging from the ceiling. When he finally located the string, he would pull down on it, and the single bulb would come on.

When he was only six years old, he had to stand on his tip toes to try to locate the string with the little silver thingy attached to the end of it that resembled a miniature silver lampshade. When reaching up into the darkness, he always felt exposed and vulnerable. He feared that he would bump into something before he located the string or that when he finally turned it on, he would find himself nose to nose with a hideous monster.

Frankenstein was the monster that appeared most often in his imagination. (It was not until he was an adult that Jack discovered that Frankenstein was not the name of the freakish oddity but that of the monster's "builder.") Jack had frequent nightmares about the huge monster-man clomping slowly, mechanically, up the stairs from the basement and toward his bedroom. He often woke up in the night and waited, terrified, for the creature to appear in the doorway of his bedroom.

Fortunately, the eight-foot-tall, terrifying creature with yellowish skin and sinister black lips never did make it to his room. The closest it ever ventured was several feet from his door. It might have helped calm little Jack if he had known that the creature was sensitive and only looking for friendship—in the beginning, at least.

And then there was the witch with the long, curved fingernails who lived under his bed ...

The room in the basement furthest from the stairs was the scariest for Jack. It contained a large tank of heating oil for the furnace that sat adjacent to it. The tank and the furnace were especially terrifying for young Jack because of what he thought must lurk behind them. He rarely put a name or face to these macabre beings who were hiding in the dark. He just knew they were there. He was convinced that evil beings, even worse than Frankenstein, existed beyond the world of ordinary sight and that darkness was their domain.

As twenty-four-year-old Jack walks slowly toward the middle of the pitch-black cave with his arms stretched out before him (which reminds him of Frankenstein's nightly inexorable march toward his bedroom), he feels the same sensations the six-year-old boy experienced when he was in the basement. A tingling wave runs up his spine, and goosebumps erupt on his arms and legs. A crackling energy runs through his body, and he wants to cry out. He keeps moving forward.

The scariest moment in the basement occurred when he was leaving a room and had to pull the string to turn off the naked bulb. As he dashed out of each suddenly darkened room toward the inviting light of the adjoining room, he always sensed that something was pursuing him. He wanted to turn and look over his shoulder but never dared to do so for fear of what he might see. He would just pull the string and rush into the next room, trying to outrun the darkness.

The last string was the most terrifying to pull. When he did so, the whole basement was swallowed up by ink—the blackest of ink that flooded everything with darkness. It was then that he had to run as fast as he could to the stairway and get up the steps before anything could grab him from behind and drag him into eternal darkness.

The best nights were when his father accompanied him into the basement and walked with him from room to room. Since his father feared nothing, Jack felt unafraid when he was with him—almost.

Tonight, in the cave, no one is with him, except for the Frankensteinian presence that is growing larger in the cavern by the minute.

His father...Jack does not want to remember his father. Not here. Not when he is all alone.

He comes to a stop in the utter darkness and stands unmoving for a long time. He is remembering another dark place in his past.

His mother awakens him. She touches his shoulder with an ice-cold hand and repeats, "Jacky, Jacky." Even though he has been torn from a deep sleep, Jack immediately hears the high-pitched panic in her voice. He opens his eyes and sees that her face is frantic. Her eyes are wide with fear. He is seven years old.

He will never forget his mother's words. They are forever engraved in his memory. "Your father was in a terrible accident, and he's going to die," she moans. If a single sentence could rock Jack's world, this was the one.

They enter the hospital in Denver an hour after his father arrived by ambulance. Jack and his mother follow the nurse down a dimly lit, deserted hallway past a sign that has the letters ICU on it. When he looks back on that long walk in the hospital, he remembers that he is pulling his mother forward. She is resistant, afraid. Jack knows she does not want to be there.

When they arrive at the room of nightmares, his mother hesitates at the doorway. Jack releases his grip on her cold hand and has to tug his hand out of hers.

He walks to the foot of the unusual bed. The end board is almost as tall as him. The bed has railings on both sides, like his loft back at home, except that these are silver like the fenders on his old bicycle. Why would his dad need railings?

The walls of the room are with outlets, weird cords, buttons, and a screen with wavy, colored lines. Several tall, skinny poles—cold and sinister sentinels—stand next to his father's bed with plastic bags dangling from them like colorless water balloons.

After he has scanned the room—his eyes large with curiosity and his stomach aching from an unknown sensation—Jack walks over to the side of the bed and looks at the figure who is lying there. It is not his father. It is some strange person with a big head and a mangled face. It looks more like Frankenstein, especially with the weird metal rods running out of both sides of his head. The nurse tells his mother it is a halo. Jack also hears the nurse say that her husband did not want to be intubated, whatever that means.

Jack walks back to his mother and takes her hand. "We're in the wrong room," he announces. "That's not Daddy."

His mother looks down at him with a hand over her mouth. Is she sick? Jack wonders. Is she going to throw up? Then she starts to weep and moan and sob.

She cannot speak. Her knees buckle.

His mother has never been a strong woman.

The nurse whispers something to his mother and leads her out of the room with her hand around her waist. Jack is alone. He stares at the man in the bed.

His eyes open wide when he hears a voice from the bed gargle his name. When the creature repeats his name, again and again, Jack becomes angry. Finally, he demands in a quavering voice, "What do you want, Frankenstein?"

"Come," the monster gurgles in a volume not much more than a whisper. Only his lips move. No other part of his body even twitches. "It's—me. Daddy."

Jack swallows hard and walks forward several steps. He stops five feet from the bed. He is not angry anymore. He is scared.

"Sorry," the alien voice that sounds weirdly like his father's, rasps. "Sorry to scare you." There is a long pause, then the voice growls, "Love you... buddy." Now Jack knows the monster is his father. "Take care of your mother and—"

Silence fills the room except for scary sounds that come from the monster, who is his father. Jack does not like the sound. He wants to leave the room. He stays.

Eventually, the breathing changes to the sound his straw makes when he is sucking up the last of his milkshake. Then the room is totally silent. The voice from the oversized Frankenstein head speaks no more.

Jack is standing next to the hospital bed when a shrill beeping noise fills the room. Soon, a small army of people rush into the room and surround the bed.

Jack's body begins to shake, and he cannot move his feet. Eventually, a woman dressed in blue pajamas takes Jack by the hand and leads him out into the hallway. Her hand is warmer than his mother's, and her voice is calm and strong. She hugs him. Her face against his cheek feels warm and safe. Something powerful stirs within his chest. In an instant, he attaches to the strange woman who he never wants to leave but who he will never see again.

Jack is on his knees in the cave. He is young. His father's last words to him were to take care of his mother. He hears more than what his father said.

Yes, he hears that he is supposed to be strong for his mother. But like children often do, he also hears more. He hears that he is not supposed to need anything from his mother. He must be strong. To need is to be weak. He must make his father proud. He will protect his mother. He will be vigilant to her needs and to those of his sisters. In fact, he will be aware of the needs of every woman in his life. He will be a nice boy who takes care of girls and women instead of hurting them and making them cry. Even when he is scared, he will be strong. And...he will fight off the strong urge for a woman to hold him and comfort him because his job is to take care of her. His father told him.

He will even go down into the basement and try not to be afraid.

Jack opens his eyes. The basement is as black as a cave. No, he is not in the basement. He is in the Cave of Dread. He is all alone.

Most of his life, he did not even know he was alone because he thought it was normal to feel this way. Then Jesus found him, and he discovered for the first time that he had been alone since the day his father died. But even after Jesus loved him and sent the Holy Spirit to live in his heart, he still thought he was supposed to be strong. In fact, the day he had believed in Jesus, he told himself, "I'll make God proud of me. He'll be pleased with me."

So it was that when he trusted in the Almighty God who created the universe and everything in it, Jack still held on to the belief that he had to be strong. He had a dim awareness that trying to be strong for God was like a sparrow being strong for a Boeing 747 Dreamlifter, but he could not fully challenge the belief in his head that he was supposed to be the big one, the unshakable one. He believed in God as the One who saved him from sin but not the One who would take care of him.

God was his savior but not his father. How could he fully trust God to take care of him? After all, even fathers go away.

So, Jack had never let himself need God. Needing was for weaker people. Needing meant that he had to lean on others, and that was not the way things worked. He was supposed to be strong for others, not the other way around. It was a one-way street. So, he lived with a deep lie implanted in his brain like a massive tumor. It destroyed the part of his brain that taught him to trust others; and it even separated him from God in a twisted way. The enemy had found a way to perpetrate the devious lie that being separate and alone was what men do.

Strong and alone—Jack's life story.

Jack is still on his knees. The darkness of the cave unnerves him. He looks to the left and then to the right but can see nothing but the black ink—the same ink that flooded his basement as a boy. No, he can see nothing, but he does feel the presence watching and waiting. He thinks of Frankenstein and then of the witch that lived under his bed.

"Be strong, Jack," he counsels himself aloud. Then he says to his God, "Jesus, you promised to never leave me or forsake me. I claim that promise right now."

He is facing his nemesis, namely, being alone, and even more than that, being alone in the darkness.

On some level, he has always hated being alone. But is not the cost of strength that is rooted in self-sufficiency, aloneness, and is not the cost of aloneness, fear, and anxiety? His father commanded him with his last breath to be strong and not need anyone, did he not? Or did he simply ask him to take care of his emotionally fragile mother?

Whatever the intent of his father's final words, the message is the same to Jack: Do not burden others with your needs, not even God. Besides, who can he trust to be there for him? His father left him, and his mother needed someone to take care of her. Who would be there to parent him? Who would hold his hand and encourage him? It has never been wise to depend on someone else to be strong for him. As the years went by, he found it increasingly unnecessary, even undesirable.

He hears something. He stops breathing and listens. He swallows hard. He hears the ugly sound that came from Frankenstein's throat in the hospital when the creature was trying to breathe. It is a gurgling, sucking sound, like water going down the bathtub drain. It has appeared in many of Jack's nightmares.

Of course, he has never told anybody what happened in the hospital room during his father's dying moments. It has always been his terrifying memory to carry alone. He could never tell his mother—one would never expect a Shetland pony to pull a wagon that only a Clydesdale could budge. Besides, she never asked him about it. He has always believed she did not want to know.

A shiver ripples through his body. He closes his eyes and touches the cold floor with his forehead. Be strong, Jack.

The suffocating sound slowly morphs into something else. Strangely, dreadfully, he hears chanting—deep voices mumbling something in the dark. At first, he cannot make out what is being said. He listens more closely. Finally, he discerns the words, "Jack, you lack. Jack, you sack. Jack is a lacker and a slacker. Jack is a whack and a hack." The voices sound far away.

Until he hears the one directly behind him.

He jumps to his feet and whirls around. He reaches his arms out as he did in the ancient basement, hoping his fingers will not touch anything. They do not. He blinks his eyes hard and opens them as wide as they will go but still sees nothing. He does not bother asking who is there because he knows the voice is not coming from a material being.

He is seven years old and in the basement. All the lights are off. Whatever was in the furnace room is now in the cave with him. But this time it is not a product of his imagination. Something unseen but very real lurks in the darkness just beyond the edge of material reality. A presence is inhabiting the same space he is in but in a different dimension.

His heart is racing. He wills himself to stride across the cavern and light the candle, but his feet are frozen. He wants to run out of the basement, but he is too afraid to move. He is also too afraid to stay where he is. Torn. Powerless. Stuck. His whole body is crushed by fear. It is too much for him—the cave, the basement, the hospital room with his father. He cannot remain with his body. He must leave somehow—flee from what his body is feeling. But he cannot escape. He has lost the power to leave his body as he could when he was a child.

The chanting voice begins again. This time it sounds like it is speaking into his ear.

"Jack," the breathy voice says. "Jack. You are alone in this place, and you always have been always. There is no one besides you. He does not exist, does not. You created him to comfort yourself when you were but a child but a child. You know that children have amazing power to survive in the darkness of the world. You found a way, a way to endure. It was all you."

The voice is almost comforting—tempting to believe. Jack stands motionless in the black night that rumbles with dread. He closes his eyes tightly and tries to shut everything out—just as he did when he was a boy.

"Jack," the voice continues persuasively, "the truth is that everyone is alone. You are not asked to bear a burden heavier than anyone else a burden. Courage is realizing you are alone in the universe and then living your days all your days with resolve and self-generated happiness. Dying alone is the ultimate act of bravery ultimate act. It resonates with mythological grit. In this cave, you have a foretaste of that event in this place. Just as your father died alone and alone slipped into nothingness, so you will die alone. Embrace it, Jack Jack."

"Jesus!" Jack cries out in his head, and the whispering voice immediately falls silent.

A moment later, words flow through his mind like a refreshing brook through a desert land: "Jack, be strong and courageous. Do not be afraid or terrified because of them, for the Lord your God goes with you; He will never leave you nor forsake you."

There is a brief silence before the other voice speaks again, this time with a hint of impatience.

"Jack, Jack," it says with chiding persistence. "It is only natural to seek comfort in your imagination at a scary time like this. Every child escapes into the world of fantasy to deal with the things that go bump in the night. But as a grown man, recognize it for what it is, Jack, Jack. It is nothing but the construction of your own mind nothing but your own mind. You are all alone in this universe alone."

Jack shakes his head and keeps his eyes shut. He says aloud this time,

"Help me, Jesus." The words do not roll easily off his self-sufficient lips.

Even before he finishes speaking the name, a voice in his head as large as a mountain says, "For I am sure that neither death nor life, nor angels nor rulers, nor things present nor things to come, nor powers, nor height nor depth, nor anything else in all creation, will be able to separate us from the love of God in Christ Jesus our Lord."

Jack's racing heart begins to slow, and he is able to take a deeper breath. But the relentless voice is not through with him yet. This time when it speaks, it sounds exasperated.

"Jack, you're a sack of bones, skin wrapped over dust wrapped over," it accuses. "You are nothing. You came from nothing, and soon enough, you will return to nothing, nothing. You are nothing but a putrid weakling just like your father, who was also a weakling and an adulterer your father. You are alone, Jack, Jack. You were alone as a boy, and you are alone now; you are alone. It is your destiny to be alone."

Jack shudders with the same fear he felt in the hospital room so many years ago. For the third time, he defies the ancient code of self-sufficiency that so predictably births aloneness and anxiety and yells out, "Jesus, I need you right now!"

A moment later, he shivers because he senses a new presence. His eyes are still closed. He is back in the dreaded hospital. An illumination appears above his father's hospital bed and flows gently through the room in the ICU like liquid candlelight.

Then, in an instant, he is transported to the Stygian basement of his childhood home. He is standing in the furnace room beside the grotesque, eerie oil tank. A bright light appears behind the sinister container and rushes into every dark corner of the terrifying room, driving out all darkness.

Then the voice that is as large and majestic as a mountain speaks again.

"Where shall I go from your Spirit?" it says. "Or where shall I flee from your presence? If I ascend to heaven, you are there! If I make my bed in Sheol, you are there! If I take the wings of the morning and dwell in the uttermost parts of the sea, even there, your hand shall lead me, and your right hand shall hold me. If I say, 'Surely the darkness shall cover me, and the light about me be night,' even the darkness is not dark to you; the night is bright as the day, for darkness is as light with you."

Jack opens his eyes just in time to see the large cavern explode with light as if someone had flicked on a switch connected to ten-thousand bulbs. An instant later, a loud agonizing scream rends the room and echoes off the thirty-foot ceiling and the walls of the 40 X 40 room.

Jack closes his eyes to the brilliance of the bright light and then opens them again. The darkness is back, but the malicious voice that had lied to his heart so convincingly and so accusingly is gone. He is not alone in the utter blackness, however. A presence remains.

A voice begins speaking. It is not simply one voice. It is more like an orchestra with many different instruments playing in symphony to produce a beautiful melody. It plays the words, "You were born into a conflict, Jack—a world at war. Some of the conflict is seen, most of it is not. Children are not spared from the fallenness of the world. The sharp edges of its brokenness pierce even their small bodies and hearts.

"So it was that you were not spared as a boy. Fear, death, grief, and aloneness besieged your safe hiding place and scaled its walls like marauders. They pillaged your heart. But The Majestic One uses it all for good—even the darkest evil. His plan permeates all reality.

"Some rage against the Father who allows such pain and suffering even to the innocents. They demand that life should be and must be fair, comfortable, safe. They complain and grumble and raise their fists against their

225

Creator. These men and women who rail against their king leave themselves vulnerable to the murderer of their hearts. They unknowingly allow the dark one to enter, the one who delights in the deflection of human affection away from God and toward the pursuit of idols available in a thousand different forms.

"Let it be known, Jack, that it is not their questions or their doubt that open the door to darkness. Rather, it is their growing disaffection. When they forsake The Light, the dark naturally creeps in, for it is the default position. It is all that remains when they turn their back on Him."

There is a brief silence in the cave as the echo of the voice fades to nothing. Jack is now on his knees with his head bowed.

"Life is like a puzzle," the voice speaks, sounding now like a thousand trilling woodwinds. "Some people view the first ten pieces of the puzzle and abruptly judge the end from the beginning. They abhor the injustice of these early pieces of their lives that contain pain and suffering. They loudly raise their voices in angry protest.

"But they have it all backward, Jack. Life is not about judging the end from the beginning but about interpreting the beginning from the end. God has a plan if humans will trust Him even in times of utter darkness instead of insisting that they know better. Ten pieces do not make a one-hundred-thousand-piece puzzle. Life is a marathon, but people who do not trust their Father insist that it is a sprint.

"Then there are those who know the world is fallen and accept it as a tragic truth," the woodwinds voice continues except an octave higher. "They realize that lamenting or grumbling against this present darkness is wasted energy and will only lead to bitterness and stonewalling of the heart against God. They recognize that the fallen world will always be marked by suffering and death and pain and separation from love.

226

"They know, more than anything else, that God Himself entered this world that is full of so many fractured pieces. He came to wear their skin, walk in their shoes, and die for them so that He might deliver them from forever darkness. He came carrying within Himself the light of hope into this world that, for those who have eyes to see, has always been a starless and moonless night."

"Indeed, He Himself is the Light of the world."

The voice begins to crescendo in volume, the woodwinds now joined by stringed instruments that sound as graceful and elegant as eagles floating on updrafts of warm air. The majestic sound is around Jack, above him, inside of him.

"Those who weep and mourn do not set themselves against the Deliverer but invite Him close," the voice intones. "They welcome God into their hearts as a faithful ally in their battle against suffering and darkness. This night, Jack, you have welcomed the Savior of the world into your darkness, and your cry has come to the ears of God. Instead of stubbornly relying on yourself, you have acknowledged your need for His presence. You have cried out to the One who makes His strength perfect in weakness, for He Himself tasted suffering and death in this world.

"Dark times lie ahead," the celestial voice says in full instrumentation, joined now by the bold sounds of brass instruments that make the cave tangibly reverberate. The symphonic voice is loud and moves at an energetic pace. "You will face fierce opposition, Jack. You know this. You have known this since you were a child. But Jesus will turn your darkness into light. You know this as well. You experienced it only several months ago. He will give you strength to advance against a troop and to scale a wall. He will be your shield and your rock. He will arm you with strength to stand against the foe, for He takes great delight in you."

There is a brief silence, and then the strident voice slows and softens into the sound of a broad, flower-filled meadow basking in sunlight. It sings, "You are no longer a youth, Jack. You are a warrior called to pursue those who have been taken hostage by Satan and even now are wasting away, captives in the enemy's prisoner of war camp. You are called to love them and speak the message of life to them.

"Be their servant, Jack," the full orchestra sings in such a beautiful unison that Jack begins to weep. "Be their friend so they might desire the great Lover whose love flows from you to them. Be a window through which they might view the very heart of God and a door of truth through which they might escape their prison."

When the two professors and the five Screaming Eagles enter the darkness of the Cave of Dread at the appointed time, flashlights in hand, they find Jack on the floor in the middle of the cavern. They all gather around the spread-eagled young man and shine their lights on him.

"Talk about sleeping like a baby," Rachel comments, shaking her head.

"Yeah," Armando adds, "Waking up every two hours and screaming. We just caught him between feedings."

Emily looks envious. Stewart adjusts his glasses but reveals nothing.

"He appears to have encountered the peace of God," Aly comments with a smile on her heart face.

"But not without some fierce wrestling first," Dr. McNeely says as if he somehow knows some inside information.

Embee gazes around at the shadowed faces of the others and says, "He has been in the presence of his Father who says, 'For the mountains may depart, and the hills be removed, but my steadfast love shall not depart from you, and my covenant of peace shall not be removed,' says the LORD, who has compassion on you" (Isaiah 54:10).

After a long silence, Armando kneels on the damp floor and shakes his roommate's shoulder with his hand. "Time to wake up, Juan," he says. "*Siesta* is over, *hermano*."

Jack does not want to wake up. He does not want to leave the hospital room where two fathers are present. One is embracing him tightly. Never has Jack felt such peace.

Never has he felt less alone.

CHAPTER 14

ABRAMOVICH AND THE
FOURTH ASSAILANT

A single naked bulb burns at the end of an electrical cord dangling from the ceiling. The cramped cinder-block bunker contains only a compact desk and two chairs—just the way he likes it. Both chairs are occupied. If the face-to-face encounter between the two men was a chess game, it would be called the Fool's Mate. White has committed an irreversible blunder opening the door for Black to achieve the rare two-move checkmate. Black queen has moved to h4, and White's vacated pawns leave no option for the defense of the White king.

The only difference between the engagement at the small desk and the Fool's Mate chess game is that it is not the Black queen that is on the attack but the Israeli Colonel. Colonel Abramovich, that is, the king of interrogation.

The major blunder by White, otherwise known as Mustafa Zarkan, is that his whole body is screaming out that he is guilty. He is perspiring profusely. His eyes refuse to meet the Colonel's hard gaze. He fidgets in the chair as if there is an ant farm thriving in his pants. His tongue darts back and forth over lips that are getting drier by the second. He is breathing so rapidly it appears that he is panting. He is squeezing his hands together as if attempting to snuff out a fire on his palms.

Mustafa's panic (guilt-induced) has made his heart totally vulnerable to the withering scrutiny of Moshe Abramovich. He is defenseless, and checkmate is imminent.

The brawny Israeli security officer taps the screen on his laptop computer with one of his husky fingers and remarks, "According to my information, Mr. Zarkan, you are a mercenary. Faithful to no one, bought by anyone—for the right price. You have been linked to two of the other 'terrorists'—I hesitate to call you that because you are nothing but a hired assassin—who were involved in the King David Hotel attack on January 11th."

The colonel pauses, and his small eyes narrow. He says, "You should know that the only person more reprehensible to me than a terrorist is a mercenary. You do not kill on principle or out of allegiance to your faith. You kill solely for money in your pocket. Such a man is the lowest of the low. I despise such men. You are less than a snake to me."

When the man with five days of stubble on his face does not answer, the Shin Bet officer says, "Few men I have 'interviewed' over the years have appeared as guilty as you, Mr. Zarkan. Maybe none."

The forefinger of the colonel's right hand seeks out the mole that rises impressively above the craters on his face. When he has found it, he massages the protruding nodule thoughtfully. Not for a second does he take his eyes off the face of the man across from him.

"You and two of the deceased gunmen were detained in Rome several years ago after the bombing near the Victor Emanuel monument," the officer intones. "Released for lack of evidence, but nonetheless guilty, I am certain."

The man across the table squirms, and his face twitches as if a pin ball is zipping around beneath his pale skin. The ball hits the flipper that is his left cheek and is propelled across his lips to the other side of his face.

The fingers of Moshe Abramovich's left hand pound out a loud rhythm on the wooden desk. The thrumming is ominous, like the sound of drums before an execution. "This time," the colonel announces, "you have played at mercenary in the wrong country, Mustafa."

The officer's voice is even but foreboding as he declares, "I will personally ensure that you never again see the light of day, Mr. Zarkan. The only decision that remains in the balance is whether we execute you tonight or lock you away for life."

The colonel's bald head glares under the single bulb overhead as he tilts it to one side. "Taking the life of three Israeli soldiers on their mother soil is anathema to me and every citizen in this country," he states. "This reprehensible crime demands quick and severe retribution."

The man who is built like an IDF Merkava tank pauses and then adds slowly in a low voice, "It only makes matters worse that one of the men you murdered was the best friend of my son."

Mustafa Zarkan's eyes furtively glance at the one-way mirror behind the battle tank. For the third time during the interrogation, the man demands to speak with a lawyer.

The colonel stares at the man in disbelief. Eventually, he snorts loudly and says, "This is not a civil court in Switzerland. This is an interrogation conducted by the Israeli Security Agency inside the bowels of a Shin Bet bunker in the city of Jerusalem with a man who has assassinated three Israeli soldiers in a civilian zone. You have no cards to play in this game, Mr. Zarkan. There is no phone call, no lawyer, no bail—not even a trial. You have been caught in the mouse trap with the cheese in your mouth. Those who are guilty beyond a doubt receive quick justice in this courtroom."

The colonel is not done. He pauses long enough to draw a deep breath and announces with growing volume, "There will be no change of venue for you. No postponements. No retrials. No escaping justice due to some flimsy appeal to a questionable precedent. No stay of execution. You have been found guilty and will be sentenced before you leave this room."

The cornered man sitting across from his intimidating interrogator groans loudly as if in pain. Then, abruptly, the dam breaks. "My gun jammed!" Mustafa Zarkan cries out as he slaps the table with an open hand. "I did not even fire a round! I turned and fled before I got within seventy feet of the hotel. I am not guilty of murdering anyone!"

"Why did your gun jam?" the colonel asks flatly as his steely pellet eyes penetrate the assailant's face.

The mercenary throws his hands into the air and replies, "How do I know what caused it to jam. Maybe a round—"

Moshe Abramovich interrupts the gunman. "No, no, no. That is not what I mean. I am asking you what you did that caused your AK to malfunction."

The man's eyes finally look at the colonel. He is stupefied. "I pulled the trigger, of course," he remarks slowly, stating the obvious. Even before the last word is a second removed from his mouth, Mustafa's body freezes. He begins to speak again but stops.

"Yes, you pulled the trigger," Moshe says grimly as he points a finger at the mercenary. "That is your guilt: You depressed the trigger. Your Kalashnikov Model 1947 may not have discharged, but your clear intent was to fire your weapon at innocent noncombatants as well as soldiers to riddle them with 39-millimeter bullets designed to penetrate their bodies and explode their organs. In short, you were there to take lives, Mr. Zarkan.

"In a court of law, you are as guilty as your three international murdering friends who are no longer here to lie on your behalf. You alone will bear the full weight of the heinous actions perpetrated by your band of cowardly mercenaries."

The colonel's large fingers drum the table again as he says gravely, "Now that the genie is out of the bottle, it cannot be put back."

"I was not the leader," Mustafa blurts out. "I—"

"It makes no difference," Moshe interjects with a wave of his beefy hand.

"I did not know we had live rounds," the man cries frantically. "I thought we were functioning only as a distraction, so—"

"That is a blatant lie," the colonel replies as his eyes rake the man's face. "You are walking out onto quicksand, and it is pulling you under."

"I—"

"That is a lie, too," the officer interrupts.

"I will tell you what I know!" Mustafa cries out.

The colonel's chin lifts slowly, and the lunar face rises higher in the air. His eyes flicker with mild interest.

"I will tell you everything I know!" he shouts.

The Shin Bet officer looks down his substantial nose at the mercenary and says, "Tell me just one thing I do not already know."

"If I tell you, will you let me live?" Mustafa inquires with wild eyes as he mops perspiration from his forehead with the sleeve of his shirt.

Moshe Abramovich does not move or blink. He simply stares at the man wriggling before him like a worm impaled on a hook—a hook of his own making.

The man's eyes hold the interrogator's glare for several seconds, then they plummet to his writhing hands. His shoulders slump. His eyes are still focused on his hands as he says quietly, "I will tell you what you want to know. All I can ask—plead—in return is that you will spare my life."

The man falls silent for a while. His troubled face betrays that he is trying to present the truth in a manner that puts himself in the best possible light.

Eventually, he begins with, "As I said, I was not the leader of the mission. Just a private, as usual. Nothing but a private. My life calling. It was Butros who communicated with the 'author' of the operation."

The mercenary sighs and looks down at the scratched and pitted wooden table that looks like it may have been abandoned by the British in 1948 when they suddenly left the country.

"I never heard him say the man's name," Mustafa insists, "but I do know he was an American. He ordered Butros to target the Muslims from the United States. Not the one with the beard but the clean-shaven one who came to the conference with his sister. None of us knew why he wanted the Muslim dead."

"The man was not a Muslim," Moshe finds himself saying. "He was a believer in Jesus, a new convert."

Mustafa's eyes dart up at the colonel for a moment, then look away.

"What else can you tell me?" the colonel demands impatiently.

"The man from America was wealthy," the mercenary replies. "He paid us more than we usually receive for such an operation."

The Shin Bet officer pounds out the drum roll on the desk with the fingers of both hands this time. "Of course, he was wealthy. How else could he afford to finance an international attack? What else?" he growls. "You need to give me more. Nothing you have said comes close to sparing you from death."

Mustafa looks over his interrogator's shoulder at the one-way mirror and shakes his head slowly. He says nothing for a long time.

Finally, he shrugs his shoulders and says, "I do not know if it is important or not, but Butros had one brief communication with our employer that was not usual. Butros thinks the man was unaware that he was on live visual feed until ten, fifteen seconds into the conversation. When he realized he was being seen, he ended the call immediately.

"Before the man hung up, Butros noticed two things. The man was big—very obese. And there was an old sign or poster on the wall behind him that said, 'Devil's Lodge.'"

Colonel Abramovich stares at the mercenary and then bellows, "That is all you can give me? You do not seem to value your life."

The man licks his lips and glances up at the officer. He says almost apologetically, "If I remember anything else, I will most certainly tell you."

Moshe scrutinizes the man's face a while longer before he rises abruptly from his chair. As he turns to leave, the mercenary yells, "I have told you everything I know! What are you going to do with me?" His face is contorted by fear, and his voice is pleading.

Abramovich pauses at the door and then turns to face Mustafa. "You may or may not be executed before a firing squad. But certainly, you will never leave this place. I am going to lock you up and throw away the key."

The colonel hears the panicked man cry out behind him, "But you—." Then he slams the door and walks down the hallway to the first door on the left. He opens it and walks into the room that is on the other side of the one-way mirror. He sees Mustafa sitting at the table on the other side of the mirror, his face in his hands. Moshe's son, David, and two other Mossad agents are in the small room where they have been watching the interrogation. Electronic devices fill the small room, including a video camera trained on the distraught mercenary.

"Observations?" the large man asks of the three men.

"We all agree he's telling the truth," David Abramovich says, glancing at the two other agents. All three men are dressed in suits with their ties loose around their necks.

"That's the difference between a terrorist and a mercenary," the Mossad agent observes. "A terrorist will resist to the point of shedding blood and still will not give up a thing. A mercenary, on the other hand, will soon sweat and then sing like a love-crazed hoopoe. Yes, this man has told us everything he knows."

The colonel begins to speak again, but David interrupts his father. "There's been a development."

"A development?" Moshe inquires. "In this case? What is it?"

"While you were interviewing Mr. Zarkan, I received a call from Aliyah Ahmed."

The colonel's round, lunar face uncharacteristically brightens, and he asks in a softer tone, "How is she, David? Is she healing well?"

David nods his head and says, "She's healing wonderfully from what she says. But that's not why she called—to tell me about her health. She called to inform me that a friend of hers named Jack Sutherington had an encounter with a man in a park near her school. During their conversation, this man vaguely admitted culpability in the bombing at the King David."

Moshe's small eyes narrow, and he says, "This man admitted responsibility for the attack? By chance, did Aliyah say if he was a large man? Excessively overweight?"

"No, Aliyah didn't give me a description of the man," David replies. "She did inform me that when he was making a threat against her friend, he boasted that his ability to deliver consequences to those who oppose him

238

had already extended to the country of Israel."

The colonel shifts his weight from his left foot to his right as he considers his son's words. His lips flail on his face like a fish out of water as he stares at his son's tie, deep in thought. It does not take long before he concludes, "This man might have learned of the attack through the news but certainly via social media. After all, this event did not happen in a corner. There were many guests in the hotel that evening who posted accounts and videos of what occurred."

The bulky man looks up from the blood-red tie and into his son's eyes. "However, how would this man in America know that Aliyah's friend, Jack, was somehow connected to this bad nightmare unless he possessed inside information the average person could not know?"

"My thoughts exactly, father," the younger Abramovich agrees, who received the comeliness of his mother and the relentless tenacity of his father.

"Come with me—only you," Moshe says to his son without hesitation. The Shin Bet officer exits the observation room and walks down the hallway to another door. He enters with his son on his heels. The room is a deserted lounge and has several comfortable chairs and a couch, but neither man sits down. They are as restless as two hounds that have picked up the scent. Like father like son.

"You must go to America," the colonel announces as he turns to face his son. "As soon as possible. This man was brazen enough to hire mercenaries far from his home for an attack in Israel, of all countries. He is dangerous. Aliyah and her friends are under dire threat, while this man is free to conduct his sorties without consequence. He must be stopped. By us."

"Do we need to contact the CIA?" David inquires.

"Not at this time," Moshe replies after a moment's thought. "As an agent of the Mossad Collections Department, it is advisable for you to go alone in an unofficial role. I will speak with Golda in the Political Action and Liaison Department to inform her of your travel plans. I will also speak with the Prime Minister. I think he will agree that if you are detained, and your presence is questioned, we will all stand behind the rationale that you are in America in a research capacity tasked with gathering intelligence relative to the King David attack. IDF will not be involved."

"It might be helpful to contact our operatives in Chicago," David offers.

The man with the large, square body and the round hairless head replies, "I have already directed you too much, my son. I might apologize for that were I not directly responsible for the internal safety of my country and its citizens. You will need to decide for yourself what to do about our people in America. Just be as discrete as possible. We want to fly under the radar until we have facts."

"I will fulfill my duty in wise fashion," David says resolutely, speaking not just to a father but to a superior officer.

The younger Abramovich turns to go but hesitates when his father remarks, "You will need to let Aliyah know you are coming."

"Of course," the Mossad agent says with a nod of his head.

There is a moment of silence before the colonel adds, "You were always pleased to see her when she visited you in the hospital." His comment is designed as a probe seeking information.

"If you're wondering if I still think about her," the Mossad agent says carefully, "I do. She's the only woman who visited me while I was in the hospital since Mother wasn't here to see me. However, I haven't spoken to you openly about Aliyah because I know you are bothered that she formerly was a radical Muslim, and her father is a Saudi espousing the Sunni sect. Also, I know her brother's past reputation was despicable to you."

Moshe gazes at his son with softer eyes. "Yes, if your mother had been alive, she would have stayed at the hospital until you were better," he muses thoughtfully.

"She would have slept in my room," David says with a smile.

The colonel smiles grimly and nods his head. He pauses as if uncertain whether to speak his next thought. In the end, he decides that life is too short, and he errs on the side of vulnerability.

"Aliyah reminded me of your mother," he confides.

David's face floods with surprise. He opens his mouth to reply, but his father is already speaking again.

"Not so much her appearance," Moshe clarifies. "Certainly not her height or her face. It is her eyes And her spirit. Like Deborah, she is strong and very determined."

David is smiling, albeit with sadness in his eyes. "I never thought I'd witness the day when you told me that a Muslim woman reminded you of your sweet Jewish wife."

"I surprise myself," the colonel says as he shakes his shiny head. "And I would only share this thought with you, David. Do you understand?"

"I understand, yes," the younger Abramovich says. "I will treat what you have told me as confidential information—for my ears only."

David pauses and then adds, "She did save her brother and me."

The Shin Bet officer frowns and tilts his lunar face. "How so?" he asks.

"She stopped us when we were leaving the King David that night," David replies. "She detained us just long enough that we were spared the worst of the bomb."

"She saw something?" Moshe inquires as he bends at the waist and leans toward his son.

David shakes his head. "You're going to find this difficult to embrace, my non-believing father," he announces. "Aliyah told me in the hospital after the attack that as we came out of the hotel, she remembered something a woman at her school in America told her months ago. This woman was a prophetess, no less, like Deborah in the Old Testament. You would appreciate that fact if you weren't an atheist. The prophetess told Aliyah not to hurry away from King David."

The large man stares at his son, attempting to absorb his words. "From King David or from the King David Hotel?"

"I'm not certain the exact words matter," David replies. "What does matter is that Aliyah understood what they meant at the right time and in the right context. When she remembered the prophesy and heeded the woman's words, she saved our lives."

The colonel massages his large lips with thick fingers and gives David a sidelong glance. "Are you telling me that on that night at the King David, both the son and the daughter of a Sunni Muslim man who would undoubtedly love to see me dead saved the life of my only son?"

David nods his head and smiles as he pulls at the knot of his red tie. "Yes, my father. Isn't that enough evidence to convince you of the love of Jesus?"

The big man with thick arms snorts and replies, "Almost, because I cannot deny the good I've seen in Daniel, Aliyah, Kameel, Mahmoud-become-Moussa, and, most of all, yourself. But not quite. Not quite. After all, the universe is full of serendipity and fate."

The colonel pauses and then says begrudgingly, "I do vaguely sense your Jesus is backing me into a corner, however. And my suspicion is that you will tell me there is only one way out of that corner."

David smiles broadly and laughs. "There's no doubt the Good Shepherd is leaving the ninety-nine sheep and pursuing you," he announces.

"What does that mean?" the colonel demands, sliding back into his usual gruff persona.

"It means that your corner is only going to get smaller every day," the Mossad agent remarks.

David stares at his father for a long time as he prays for Jesus to plant more seeds in the soil of his father's hard heart. Then he says, "Well, father, I'm going to leave your esteemed company and plan my travel itinerary. I hope to be in America no later than early next week."

The senior Abramovich nods his head and grunts. "Just be careful, my son. Deborah would never forgive me if anything happened to you. We came way too close only months ago."

"I'll be wise," David says, "and Jesus will keep me safe."

"The same Jesus who died on the cross?" the colonel inquires with sarcasm in his voice. "The same savior who couldn't protect Daniel? If he cannot even save his own life or Daniel's, how can you believe he will save yours?"

As David backs toward the door, he says, "You are alluding to the good news of God's grace, my father. When Jesus died on the cross, He gave His life for us so that He might save us from the second death—spiritual death. Because of Jesus, I will only die once since I have now been born twice."

"Yes, yes," the older man grumbles. "I know. I know. And you will no doubt tell me that I will only be born once and die twice."

"Not if I can help it," David says with a smile. "Like I said, the Good Shepherd is seeking you out. He'll pursue you wherever you run."

"You make me sound like Eichmann eluding Mossad," the colonel growls.

"No, father, never like that," David says softly. "Just a stubborn sinner loved by his relentless savior."

"Relentless," the Shin Bet agent grunts. "We'll see about that."

CHAPTER 15

THE UNIVERSITY DEBATE

The semi-annual debate takes place on a Saturday afternoon in a lecture hall at the university, several miles from the Teleios Academy. The hall is much larger than a classroom but smaller than an auditorium. It accommodates five hundred people and boasts a faux gold-tiled ceiling, impressive chandeliers, and is pitched in the stadium seating style like many movie theaters. The chairs are cushy and equipped with fold-away desktops for taking notes on laptops or, for a few dinosaurs, with pens and legal pads. The students and professors in attendance fill most of the room, leaving only several dozen scattered seats unoccupied. At the front of the hall, a platform rises five feet above the tiered seating.

On the platform, two tables are situated at a forty-five-degree angle resembling a "V." They partially face each other and partially face the audience. Two people sit at each table. Sitting at the table on the left from the spectators' perspective is the familiar gigantic person of Dr. Harley Hawkstern. Beside him is a woman dressed in a navy suit with a white blouse. Her name is Aspen Woods.

Sitting at the other table are the vibrant Dr. Greenlay and his wife, Nancy.

The spectators in the hall observe that the wife is noticeably taller than her husband. The only other person on the stage is the moderator of the debate, a young female from the university. Her name is Heather. Jack immediately recognizes her as the young woman he encountered beside the lake only weeks earlier. When he sees her, the first thought that enters his head is pretty little liar.

The Screaming Eagles are seated together in the middle of the lecture hall. Fifty other students from the Teleios Academy are seated in the same general area. The other four-hundred seats are occupied by university students and professors from the two schools. The room is buzzing with conversation and laughter. Everyone in the audience notes the difference in size between the gigantic Dr. Hawkstern and the diminutive Dr. Greenlay even while they are seated at their respective tables.

Armando leans toward Jack and quips, "Considering we're all descended from apes, there's a lot of beautiful women here. I'm just glad they're not as hairy as their ancient predecessors."

Rachel turns to the young man from La Puente and says, "I heard that. Should I take that as a compliment or an insult? Either way, I want to slap you."

Jack leans forward and looks past his roommate at Rachel. "Can you tell that Manny's pumped up for this debate on evolution? I think he should be seated up on the platform to assist Dr. Greenlay and Nancy. He could field all the questions about strange mutations due to his personal experience."

"Hey," Armando says with feigned disgust, "I resemble that. I mean, I resent that."

Emily, who is sitting next to Jack, groans and says in a rare demonstration of humor, "You're the only one who's going ape here. The rest of us are one hundred percent human."

"What does that saying mean—going ape?" Aly asks with a quizzical look on her face.

Stewart begins to answer Aly but stops when he sees Heather approaching the podium on the left side of the platform. When she reaches the microphone, she waves a hand at the table adjacent to her and announces, "Welcome, women and men! Welcome to this afternoon's debate entitled *Natural Selection or Divine Production.*

"Presenting the case for the science of evolution, we have Dr. Hawkstern, who teaches philosophy as a professor here at the university. He also serves as an adjunct at the Teleios Academy. His partner in the defense of the pro-evolution position is Dr. Aspen Woods, who is also a professor here on campus. She is the esteemed chair of the Humanities Department and has recently published a book entitled *God Isn't Sleeping—He's Dead: Why I'm an Atheist and Not an Agnostic.*

The sound of scattered applause ripples through the lecture hall and crescendos into a loud wave of clapping. A few screams are heard among the spectators.

"We're surrounded and outnumbered," Armando observes in a hushed voice.

Emily turns and comments, "I try not to see it as 'us versus them.' We're all in this together. We're all trying to find our way through this world."

"Not a bad point," Jack interjects as he nods his head. "The ground is level at the foot of the cross."

Up on the platform, Heather tilts her head at the other table and says, "Seated at the far table, we have the wife and husband team of Nancy Greenlay and her husband, Alan Greenlay. Ms. Greenlay is a writer of theological books for women, while Alan is a professor at the Teleios Academy. They are here to defend the anti-evolution position from a religious perspective."

Jack groans and shakes his head. "Are you serious?" he says in frustration. "Before the debate even begins, we have bias. 'Pro' sounds so positive, while 'anti' sounds so blamed negative. Why didn't she just say it's a debate between those who support evolution and those who support divine design?"

"Jack," Emily says impatiently, "that's how debates are structured. One side is 'for,' or 'pro,' and the other side is 'opposed' or 'con.'"

After Emily's comment, Jack hears a voice whisper in his head, *You're just being negative toward Heather because you feel guilty for lusting after her by the lake. You're projecting your guilt and anger onto that innocent woman instead of owning up to your sin. Keep your mouth shut, and stop being so judgmental. Your objectification of poor Heather effectively disqualifies you from voicing any opinion today.*

Jack looks down at his hands and silently prays. *Jesus,* he says, *give me clarity. I don't want to judge that woman, but neither do I want to be silenced by accusations. I want to know truth and be a voice for truth. I'm sorry for how I've sinned against Heather. Period. No excuses. I also need you to defend my heart so I'm not neutralized by the voice of the enemy and by shame.*

"We're going to begin today's debate with prefatory comments from both positions," Heather announces in a silky voice that has the power to mesmerize Jack. "We'll begin with the scientific position."

Jack groans again inside and thinks, *Yet another example of arguing for the separation of science and faith as if the two address totally different realms. One is presented as fact, and the other as myth and fantasy.*

Dr. Woods adjusts the microphone on her lapel and then begins. "Good afternoon. I and my esteemed colleague, Dr. Hawkstern, propose that everything that exists in the universe is here by natural selection working through variations. In other words, we support the clear and obvious evidence that points to a fully naturalistic evolutionary process first proposed by Dr. Charles Darwin in his book, *The Origin of Species.* This process tells us that life originated from non-living matter and then evolved over countless millennia into all the species we encounter in today's world."

Dr. Woods pauses and massages her forehead briefly. "Naturalistic evolution explains the existence of life simply and clearly without the excess baggage of religion," she announces confidently, her eyes scanning the lecture hall before her. "It says that because of the limited supply of food in the world, the members of a species that experience certain chance mutations that give them an advantage over their disadvantaged counterparts will survive. The other members of the species that do not experience these fortuitous variations will eventually succumb, leaving only the fitter, stronger members to carry on.

"By this vehicle of natural selection, the species continue to evolve upward into a more virulent organism that will progressively become more fit for survival as the generations pass.

"Clear examples of these random mutations or variations are witnessed in the beaks of finches, the color of moths, and the adjustments by bacteria to resist antibiotics. But evolution instructs us that over time, not only do species experience mutations that lead to a fish, for example, becoming a better fish, but that through repeated, steady, infinitesimally small mutations occurring over millions and millions of years, a fish eventually evolves into an amphibian and then a reptile and then a bird and finally a human being. Thus, we observe not only variations within species but eventually mutations that lead to the development of other species."

Dr. Woods adjusts the collar of her white blouse and clarifies, "I need to emphasize most adamantly that this scientific process of repeated mutations by which all life emerges from a single common ancestor is not guided by intelligence. Evolution is accidental, blind, and occurs by chance.

"We're all sitting here today because totally 'natural' processes in the universe led to a dynamic selection that produced higher and higher levels of animals over time until we later evolved animals finally came on the scene. We can thank Darwin for paving the way with scientific discoveries that permit us to be intellectually fulfilled atheists."

Loud clapping fills the lecture hall. Several whoops are heard, along with shrill whistles. As Jack had anticipated, the room is decidedly sympathetic to the evolutionary position.

"Thank you, thank you!" Heather says enthusiastically as she claps into the microphone. "Thank you, Dr. Woods!"

Jack shakes his head at the blatant bias of the moderator.

After the furor in the hall has quieted, the moderator nods her head at the "anti" table.

Dr. Greenlay clears his throat. A smile spreads over the face of the professor's wife and over the faces of the Academy students. They know what is coming from the unique man. The diminutive professor always begins his lectures with some type of humorous prologue. Today will be no exception.

"Someone once said," Dr. Greenlay begins, "that humanity's number one fear is public speaking. Number two is the fear of death. Does that sound correct to all of you? That means that if you go to a funeral, you're better off being the stiff in the casket than delivering the eulogy."

A smattering of laughter fills the hall, along with some loud groaning. A few boos are also heard.

The professor is not done with his introduction. "Someone told me once if I felt nervous in front of a crowd," he continues, "I should imagine all my listeners sitting in their pajamas. The problem with that suggestion was that when I attempted it, I started to get sleepy and forgot what I was going to say. So instead of imagining you in your PJs today, I'm going to picture all of you as mutations of sea anemones. I've never been nervous around sea anemones."

There are a few more random laughs. The loudest comes from Armando, who always finds the professor's humor prime entertainment.

"All seriousness aside," Dr. Greenlay announces with twinkling eyes, "my wonderful wife, Nancy, and I are here to advance the 'anti-evolution' position, as our moderator refers to it. Our position posits that there is an intelligent designer in the universe behind everything, and so the amazing complexity in nature is best explained not as the product of countless accidents but as a masterpiece reflecting the careful, beautiful brush strokes of a master painter.

"That means that all of you human beings sitting out there in the audience are not here by luck but by creation and therefore are amazing beings designed for a purpose instead of for nothing. So much for my strategy to imagine all of you as sea anemones."

When Dr. Greenlay pauses, Armando whistles loudly and claps. A few other students from the Academy join in with some reluctance.

"The second point that Nancy and I propose is that the presence of a divine designer is the simplest explanation for the existence of the universe," the professor explains. "In the tradition of the principle of Occam's razor, we believe that just as the existence of everything around us in this room—chairs, carpet, lights, projector, tables—are best and most simply explained as the creation of a designer, so we believe that the natural world around us—including all of you—is also best and most simply accounted for by the involvement of a designer instead of by millions of years of blind accidents."

"Thirdly," Dr. Greenlay says as he begins to speak faster and faster, energized by the thoughts pounding against his skull like a rushing river against a waterwheel, "we assert that when any theory about the existence of the universe begins with the assumption of materialism—the belief that only physical matter can exist—then the possibility of God's existence and His role in the formation of the universe is automatically ruled out without considering the evidence. The supernatural is excluded simply by human pronouncement."

The professor adjusts himself in his chair and scans back and forth across the audience as if his head is on a swivel. "My question to those who support such a presupposition is this: How do you know that it is absolutely certain that there is no supernatural world? Are you a god who knows everything? Are you omniscient? How can you dismiss the possibility of other dynamics in the universe besides what you can see and touch, a dismissal not based on fact but on prejudice? I humbly submit to all of you that such an assertion borders on arrogance and leads, in the end, to an existence of a god after all—namely, you.

"Lastly, if you insist that the material world is all there is, then the only explanation left for the existence of the universe must, by necessity, be a natural one, and the only marginally plausible natural explanation available at this time is Darwinism. Thus, if an intelligent designer is excluded at the beginning, then the variations of the finches' beaks that you mentioned earlier must be viewed as amazing confirmation of a godless evolutionary process.

"However, if God is left in the equation, a totally naturalistic evolution doesn't have to be true. Then the variation in beaks is simply seen as two finches with slightly different beak sizes."

When the professor is done speaking, there is more applause this time. Dr. Greenlay sits back in his chair and squirms like a second grader waiting for recess.

Armando says loudly enough for Jack and Rachel to hear, "Any bets on how long he'll stay in that chair? My wager is no more than fifteen minutes."

Rachel does not turn to look at her classmate but smiles and says, "No way. He'll only make thirteen, tops."

A minute later, the debate is off and running. Dr. Hawkstern begins by speaking at length about "descent with modification," arguing that species are not immutable but that new species have "occurred" over long periods of time due to thousands upon thousands of generational mutations.

Nancy Greenlay, clearly more of a sedate personality than her husband, nonetheless exhibits formidable explanatory power in her comments. After outlining some of her findings in her study of fossils, she pauses to ask Dr. Hawkstern if he believes in the philosophical doctrine of verificationism.

The large man smiles through his beard like a cat with a bird in its mouth and replies, "Of course. Only statements that are empirically verifiable—provable through the physical senses—are meaningful. Anything that cannot be proved empirically is meaningless. Accordingly, we can entirely dismiss as unverifiable—and therefore irrational—whole fields of study such as theology, spirituality, and metaphysics.

None of these can be considered credible sources of truth."

Before the confidently condescending man is done speaking, Nancy inquires, "Well, then, Dr. Hawkstern, since you are such a staunch believer in verificationism, give me one example of a change in kind, or a change in species such as you claim occurs in evolution, that can be verified by the physical senses."

The man snorts and replies, "Have you been listening? As was mentioned earlier, the beaks of finches have mutated over time, resulting in—"

"I've already heard about the birds and the beaks," Nancy says. "I'm not asking to hear any more about the finches. What I'm asking you to do for all of us is to identify one example of naturalistic evolution that can be verified by our senses."

The titan of a man shifts in his chair, begins to speak, and then stops. Eventually, he rolls his beady eyes toward his associate, who replies scoldingly, "Evolution is a process that occurs over millions and millions of years, Ms. Greenlay. One cannot simply pull an observable rabbit out of one's proverbial hat on demand."

"Fine," Nancy says. "Just don't claim, then, that evolution can be verified like I can verify that my car is out in the parking lot. Evolution is *not* verifiable. Proving that God does not exist is also not verifiable. I propose that believing in natural selection is a hypothesis that requires faith, just as believing in God requires faith. Evolution is not a *verifiable* fact. In a very real sense, it is not a science but a religion."

Dr. Hawkstern's face reddens, and he stammers, "Evolution is not a hypothesis. It's a proven fact. It's taught in our schools as a fact. It's based on science, and science is a fact. Your weak-minded alternative of supernatural creationism is a religion. Science is truth, while religion is based on mythology. Your beliefs are totally incapable of being verified."

"Not true, Dr. Hawkstern," Nancy replies. "God's Word tells me that 'The heavens declare the glory of God, and the sky above proclaims his handiwork. Day to day pours out speech, and night to night reveals knowledge. There is no speech, nor are there words, whose voice is not heard. Their voice goes out through all the earth, and their words to the end of the world.'"

Nancy smiles pleasantly and adds, "You look at the world of nature and see a mindless accident. I look at nature and see the masterpiece my husband mentioned earlier—a wonderful, beautiful creation designed by an intelligent artist. Both positions require faith."

Dr. Woods parries Nancy's words with the example of the long-term evolution experiment conducted by Dr. Lenski with E. coli bacteria that was initiated in 1988. She explains that after more than 50,000 generations of bacteria, observable mutations have resulted in a new organism notably different from the parent bacterium. She argues that these results are an amazing example of evolution in real-time and prove that in a laboratory setting, verifiable evidence of ongoing natural selection can be observed and that such changes can be extrapolated to validate the history of evolution over the eons.

Like a jack-in-the-box, Dr. Greenlay pops out of his chair, and the students from the Academy smile in unison. Rachel glances down at her phone and smiles the biggest smile—twelve minutes. She glances down at her phone a second time when it vibrates and sees that she has a new voicemail from Drew.

The Academy professor ambles as fast as he can with his short legs toward the other table where the two pro-evolution professors are sitting. Then he turns and walks back in the other direction with short, brisk steps that cause him to toddle from side to side. Dr. Hawkstern, apparently familiar with the antics of the small professor, sighs and shields his eyes with one of his huge hands.

Armando mumbles to Jack, "We definitely know what species Dr. Greenlay descended from—the penguin."

"We have discovered that the preponderance of mutations in nature are harmful, and the experiment with the E. coli is no exception," the Academy professor asserts, spewing words out faster than most people's lips can move. "Observations up to this point have revealed that the few beneficial variations in the E. coli bacteria will actually break genes and even throw other good ones away. If this long-term experiment is an example of natural evolution, Darwin's theory is not only suspect but dismissible out of hand."

A few minutes later, the debate shifts away from E. coli bacteria to the weakness of the natural selection argument. Nancy observes that Darwin could not generate any impressive examples of the evolutionary process. Dr. Hawkstern counters with the argument that Darwin appealed to present-day analogies as convincing evidence for evolution. Dr. Woods looks down and shakes her head as if incredulous at her partner's defense. Then she looks up and warns quietly, "Don't go there, Harley."

Ignoring his co-combatant's visual and verbal frustration, the mammoth man adjusts his giant-sized, iron-framed glasses and lumbers forward. He argues that professional breeders have been able to alter both plants and animals significantly by introducing mutations. These examples of selection have produced woolier sheep, more fertile cattle, better fruit, and hardier plants. He goes on to argue that Darwin pointed to these examples in the world of breeding to prove that evolution occurs today and did occur in the ancient past.

"There's only one problem, Harley," Nancy states flatly as Dr. Woods rolls her eyes and throws her hands into the air.

The man's billowy eyebrows writhe above his small eyes as he stares back at his debate opponent. He says nothing, apparently sensing a trap.

"All these analogies that you and Darwin claim are evidence of natural selection are actually examples of artificial selection," Nancy observes. "Have you paused to consider that all these 'mutations' you've cited require an intelligent 'designer' with knowledge and feedback gleaned from previous experimentation to produce the significant results you refer to? These analogies are all diametrically the opposite of Darwin's selection which occurs by natural, blindly stupid mutations. You're juxtaposing examples of purposeful planning with dumb luck and then saying that good things come from dumb luck because good things come from purposeful planning."

The giant's eyes drift down from a spot above Nancy's head and retreat to the shelter of his notes. He does not say a word. Never have the Screaming Eagles seen the professor so cowed.

"And I'm not done," Nancy says as she pushes strands of her brown hair behind her right ear. "I want to add that your examples of artificial intelligence actually reveal that breeders encounter clear limits regarding the degree of variation they can attain in their efforts to produce beneficial 'mutations.' Breeders have discovered that they simply *cannot* produce new species through their efforts. In addition, many scientists have deduced from these 'analogies' that natural selection functions to actually *prevent* the extreme changes in an organism that intelligent breeders attempt to achieve."

When the woman is done speaking, the lecture hall is silent. The pro-evolutionists have nothing to cheer for, and the Academy students do not wish to appear like obnoxious guests, so they also remain quiet.

After a short pause, Heather walks stiffly to the microphone on stage-right and announces to the audience, "Well, on that note, we'll take an intermission break. We'll commence with the second half of the debate in fifteen minutes."

Some students rise from their seats to stretch. Others leave the room to go outside for some fresh air. The members of the micro-cohort, along with many of their Academy peers, climb the stairs up to the exit and gather in a small lounge fifty feet from the lecture hall.

As they stand around drinking from water bottles and cans of juice they purchased from the lounge vending machines, Rachel announces, "Drew is on his way over. He had a lab this afternoon but left early to come here. He says he has something to tell me."

"Wow, that doesn't sound good," Armando says. "Unless he misses you so much that he's coming to say he can't live without you for another minute."

Before anyone can respond to another Armando jest, an unprecedented event occurs, rarer than a blue moon or a February with twenty-nine days.

"Shut up!" a raised voice exclaims. "Just shut up, Armando! You make everything into a joke even when it could be serious. I'm so done with your ill-timed sarcastic humor!"

The Screaming Eagles think they recognize the voice but assume they must be mistaken. It is not until they turn and look at the speaker that the owner of the voice is confirmed as Stewart. His face, which is so incapable of expressions of emotion, is as flat as ever. The bespectacled man's eyes, however, are twin erupting volcanos.

Less than four months ago, Stewart's words would have been highly inflammatory, the proverbial fuel on the fire. But Armando is not the same man he was before winter break. Ever since the trip to LA to encounter his brother's killer, he has been noticeably different. He still has the ready sense of humor, but he no longer is quick to be critical of those he perceives as weak or explosive toward those who touch his pockets of shame.

Jack is the only one who fully knows what happened in LA, namely, that Armando finally forgave himself for his long-standing self-hatred at being the cowardly brother who abandoned Raul in that bloody alley in Valencia. Since he has now forgiven himself and Sniper and surrendered his anger to God, there is now very little negative emotion left for those he perceives as weak or cowardly.

The ex-gang member considers Stewart with a level gaze as he fingers the teardrop of death beneath his eye. No one says anything. Jack, who feels most prepared to interject a comment, purposely holds back. He senses that the two young men need to resolve this moment between themselves. He does not miss the flash of anger in his roommate's eyes.

Finally, Armando takes a deep breath and lets it out slowly. "Okay," he says in a matter-of-fact voice, "it's good to know how you feel, ese. I'll try to be more careful with my humor in the future. It's an old coping skill I learned as a boy and still fall into easily, often without premeditation."

There is another moment of silence before Armando adds, "I'm impressed, Stewart. I feel like I know you a lot better now than I did a minute ago. Life's about being known and loved, right?"

Stewart does not reply. His eyes are still smoldering. Rachel touches his arm and begins to speak when a large man approaches the group of Academy students and taps her on the shoulder. Rachel turns around, and her face immediately brightens when she sees Drew. Her smile fades quickly, however, when she observes the anguish etched in shadowed lines across his face.

"What is it, Drew?" Jack inquires even before Rachel can speak.

"Sorry to bother you guys," the imposing man says breathlessly. "It's— it's my father. He had a heart attack this morning, and I'm going to fly home to see him. He's in the ICU and not doing very well. He's been intubated, my mom says. She's really broken up. I just wanted to come by and ask you guys for prayer before I leave."

"Oh, Drew," Rachel says, "I'm so sorry to hear about your dad." Armando glances sidelong at Stewart, hesitates, and then says, "It's okay, Rachel. It's okay to hug him. It looks like he could use one."

Rachel's cheeks flood with color, but she does not hesitate. She steps toward the big man and hugs him gently. Drew is quick to wrap her in his arms. "Just like the bridge in Mystic," he says quietly into her ear, his voice faltering ever so slightly.

"Let's all gather around and pray for Drew," Jack suggests.

Soon the university student who met Jesus not long before Christmas is surrounded by six members of his new family. They lay comforting hands on the young believer. Several other Academy students who overheard the conversation join the impromptu prayer group as well. Soon thirteen and then twenty and finally thirty-three people are gathered around the young man. They pray for his father's health, his mother's anxiety, and for Drew to have strength to be present for both of his parents during this crisis. University students walking through the lounge stare at the unusual gathering and wonder what is going on.

When the prayers are over and the group breaks up, Rachel wipes tears from her face and looks up at Drew. "I'd like to come with you," she announces, "if I can get a ticket, that is. I'd need to go back to the dorm and pack, but I can do that in ten minutes. What do you think?"

Drew smiles warmly at the woman who has rapidly become his best friend and says, "I'd like that. Just be aware that the flight leaves at six, and it's already two-thirty."

"That'll work," the woman with the shoulder-length brunette hair replies. "The Academy is on the way to the airport, so we can swing by my dorm and grab my stuff."

"Great," Drew remarks with as much enthusiasm as he can muster under the circumstances. "My friend, Sam, will drive us. I'll book a ticket for you online while we're on our way."

Aly and Emily give Rachel a hug and wish her a safe trip to New York. Aly tells her friend that she will keep praying for Drew and his family. Emily smiles but says nothing. She looks like she is a thousand miles away. Jack observes her and randomly wonders if she is thinking about her own father. What Jack knows for sure is that he has been thinking about his father ever since Drew informed them that his dad was in the hospital.

A few minutes later, the micro-cohort is back in the lecture hall, minus one member. Even before they are in their seats, the debate begins again. Heather is reading a question texted to the four participants from a listener in the audience. The question addresses whether the fossil record is an asset or a liability to the evolutionary position, whether Darwinian evolution or Neo-Darwinism.

Dr. Aspen Woods tackles the question first. She explains that there is an extensive array of fossil findings that support natural selection. She discusses at length a handful of famous examples, including the Tiktaalik of Nunavut, the Archaeopteryx, and the Pakicetus. She finishes by stating that while the fossil record may be somewhat imperfect when it comes to the presence of transitional forms between species, it is still "good enough." Also, if a person studies the evidence from the past 540 million years, the fossil record demonstrates consistently good support for Darwin's theory.

Dr. Greenlay is already on his feet, pacing back and forth on the platform, when Dr. Woods' words are still echoing in the lecture hall. Both Drs. Woods and Hawkstern appear irritated. Aspen repeatedly glances at Heather as if demanding that she do something to rein in the man's obnoxious antics. Heather does not appear to notice.

"Whoever asked the fossil evidence question is very wise indeed," the portly man announces as he raises his right hand and points with his index finger toward the gold-tiled ceiling. "It may be the most critical question of the evening."

As the professor continues to pace, his mouth forms the round shape that always reminds Jack of a fish. *Evidence that Dr. Greenlay evolved from both fish and penguins,* he facetiously thinks to himself with a smile. A few seconds later, the anticipated torrent of words bursts from the man's mouth.

"The fossil record is critical to Darwin's theory," the professor announces as he struts across the stage, now looking more like the rooster that often appears in the aquarium classroom. "Evolution theorizes that natural selection over time coupled with small mutations leads not just to adaptations within a species but ultimately to macroevolution where one species eventually, by blind chance, evolves into another species. Accordingly, one would expect to find many transitional fossils, otherwise known as intermediate links, that exhibit the progression from one species to the next. Even Darwin himself initially claimed that the number of intermediate links must be truly enormous.

"However, over time, Darwin himself discovered to his chagrin that these links were not present in every geological formation or stratum."

The short man pauses and turns to look at the audience. His glasses have slid halfway down his nose.

"Some of your parents have drawers full of clothes back home that prove you didn't just leap from being an infant to an adult," he says. "You had six-month-old clothes, twelve-month, two-year-old, five-year-old, seven-year-old, and so on and so on. So, if your dear parents have evidence that you evolved from a baby into an adult, why doesn't geology have evidence in its drawers that clearly points to this slow mutation process?"

Dr. Greenlay takes three steps closer to the audience. He gets so close to the edge of the platform that his wife, Nancy, rises to her feet, and several students in the audience gasp. The professor, true to form, is so engrossed in his topic that he is only marginally aware of his surroundings.

Looking down at the students seated five feet below the platform, he asks, "Do you want to hear what Darwin himself said about the fossil record in his book, *The Origin of the Species?* On page 292, he writes, 'Geology assuredly does not reveal any such finely graduated organic chain; and this, perhaps, is the most obvious and gravest objection which can be urged against my theory.'"

Oblivious as ever, when he is engrossed in thinking and speaking, Dr. Greenlay takes one more step toward the audience.

Now he is mere inches from stepping into thin air. The students seated just below the platform raise their hands as if readying themselves to catch the man should he fall.

This time Nancy Greenlay stands up and yells with urgency, "Alan, you're too close to the edge!"

Without turning his head, the professor takes one step backward. Nancy sits down, and her husband launches into his next comment.

"Naturally, Darwin attempted to save his fragile theory from extinction—please forgive the pun. He argued that the fossil record was currently imperfect but would one day be more complete as additional fossils were discovered. Today, however, one hundred fifty years after Darwin, only a small fraction of fossils has been found that qualify as intermediate links."

The professor pauses to wipe his forehead with a handkerchief and then adds, "Paleontologists must finally admit that the fossil record supporting evolution is spotty at best and atrocious at worst. As much as dedicated evolutionists would like to object to this truth or continue to trot out questionable transitional fossils, the geological evidence disproves Darwin's theory far more than it affirms it."

"All the honest paleontologists I know, which admittedly aren't many—I don't mean that there aren't many honest paleontologists, just that I don't know many paleontologists—admit that saltation is a grave issue for Darwin's theory of gradual change occurring over millions of years."

At this point, a voice in the lecture hall yells out, "What the heck is saltation?"

"Saltation?" the portly professor repeats as he cups his hand behind his ear and takes two steps toward the voice. Then he is gone. Overboard.

Several spectators in the lecture hall scream. One of them is Nancy Greenlay. Dr. Woods gasps and rises to her feet. Dr. Hawkstern rushes over to the edge of the platform as fast as his gigantic frame allows and peers down into the audience. Heather's hand is over her mouth, and her eyes are large with surprise. Everyone in the hall is on their feet, craning their necks to learn the fate of the fallen man.

Before long, loud laughter breaks out in the room at the spectacle of the professor being crowd-surfed over to the aisle. Jack imagines that the Academy professor, who is being transported belly-up with his limbs splayed, looks like a small pig on the giant platter of the audience.

It takes several minutes for order to be restored. In the end, Dr. Greenlay returns to the platform, appearing none the worse for his mishap except that his clothes are disheveled, and his hair now looks like a wild brown mop on his head. He walks within four feet of the platform's edge and looks down at the people in the first several rows.

"Thanks for saving me from serious injury," he says, pressing his palms together and bowing his head to the audience. "I'm reminded of the time in third grade when I fell out of the attic window in my parents' three-story house and rolled off the roof. On that occasion, my fall was broken by a plum tree. I survived with only a few bruises and fifty-seven puncture holes in my body from the thorns. I was sore for a month. Since that inauspicious day, my older brother has called me 'plum crazy' Al."

Some spectators in the lecture hall groan and shake their heads. Several laugh.

A few stare blankly at the man, clueless to the meaning of "plum-crazy."

Jack also shakes his head and thinks, *I don't know how he does it, but he always seems to win over a crowd. He should have been a stand-up comedian or a clown in the circus.*

"Okay," the professor says as he presses the lips of his small mouth together and wrinkles his forehead. "Where were we? Ah, yes, saltation. Saltation is the word used to describe the fossil record 'jumping' from one species to the next without intermediates." The indomitable professor begins strutting across the stage again with his finger pointed in the air.

"As I was mentioning before 'the Fall,'" the professor says with a smile and twinkling eyes, "honest paleontologists now acknowledge that these jumps are not just a reflection of an incomplete fossil record. They now admit that they represent explosions of different species as opposed to the gradual evolution of living organisms. The most renowned of these explosions occurred during the Cambrian Period, when many major organisms appeared for the first time simultaneously. During this period, the organisms appeared suddenly—in geological terms—and were fully formed. To this day, we have not discovered intermediate links for these organisms."

The professor stops pacing and walks toward the front of the platform. Once again, the diminutive man is careful to stop well back from the edge as he says, "One thing you need to know is that dedicated Darwinian evolutionists are never deterred by negative evidence or a lack of evidence. Predictably, the lack of transitional fossils simply led these philosophers—I hesitate to call them scientists because true scientists honestly follow where the evidence leads—simply led them to create the inane phenomenon of Punctuated Equilibrium to explain these jumps.

"This fabricated construct says that after a stable period covering millions of years, a species may undergo a rapid burst of change that leads to the development of a new species with little to no fossil evidence. Why does this rapid burst occur? Nobody knows. It's just another example of the creative intellectual gymnastics Darwinians will resort to if the facts do not support their theory.

"If evolution encounters a legitimate challenge, its proponents just add further confusing complexity to the theory that props it up for a few more years as they await a better naturalistic explanation to come along. They know that if Darwinism becomes extinct, there's only one other 'theory' available to explain the existence of the universe, namely, miraculous creation by an intelligent designer otherwise known as God. No wonder they feel compelled to revive the corpse of Darwinism time and time again."

The debate continues for another thirty minutes even though the climax of the event clearly occurred when the professor took his nose-dive into the audience. Everything after that moment feels anticlimactic. Nonetheless, the crowd in the lecture hall seems at least moderately interested in the arguments between the four participants.

The final topic addressed is the advent of microbiology, a new science that was born after the successive appearance of the microscope, the electron microscope, and X-ray crystallography. These developments were followed by the significant discovery in the 1950s that the protein myoglobin was much more complex than first thought.

Dr. Hawkstern presents what he appears to believe is airtight evidence of evolution on a molecular level when he discusses the mutation of viruses to evade the human immune system. Nancy Greenlay counters with the argument that the viruses altering to avoid eradication is an example of *adaptation* within organisms and does nothing to prove the existence of macroevolutionary changes that produce new species.

Nancy expands further. She argues that in the nineteenth century,

Darwin knew nothing of what was in the "black box" of the cell. Lacking the technology to peer into the cell, Darwin and his early disciples proposed that cells were merely lumps of material that easily evolved via the evolutionary process of natural selection with mutations over time.

However, once microbiology was born in the middle of the twentieth century, the black box was finally opened for close examination, and the astounding complexity of the human cell was observed for the first time. Quite surprisingly, it was discovered that molecular machines guided every cellular process with such complexity and advanced calibration that a blind, accidental evolutionary process could not have developed such intelligent designs.

Nancy alludes to the amazing complexity of the eye, the 'miracle' of flight, the blood clotting process, the immune system, and even the chemical protective system of the Bombardier beetle as examples of "irreducibly complex" systems composed of several interacting parts that could only have formed all at once, not one by one through blind chance. There are only two ways these complex systems could have come into existence, she asserts: either by winning the lottery, i.e., having all proteins appear at once against all odds, or by intelligent design.

"And so, I conclude," Nancy says, "where my husband began this debate. I appeal to the principle of Occam's razor, which states that when seeking an explanation, the simplest of two competing theories is to be preferred. In this case, it is clear that the creative intelligence of God is a far simpler, logical, and obvious explanation for the existence of the universe than is blind, unguided naturalistic evolution where everything comes into being by sheer accident."

The woman, who is about three inches taller than her husband and appears much more athletic, adds, "Believing that naturalistic evolution is responsible for the existence of the universe is similar to believing that a tornado careening chaotically and destructively through a junkyard is capable of leaving in its wake a fully operational Boeing 777 passenger aircraft replete with functioning Rolls Royce engines, crew members, pilots, and passengers."

Nancy pauses and smiles at her audience. "To be completely honest, I agree with the author who said that he doesn't have enough faith to be an atheist. For me, God is the clear choice for the existence of reality, and all that composes it. I propose that it takes less faith to believe in a God-created universe than one that came about by sheer accident."

When Nancy Greenlay retreats to her chair, Heather walks up to the podium and announces, "Both tables are now asked to close the debate by summarizing their position in one sentence here at the main microphone. Then we'll take a vote from the members of the audience to see who won the debate."

Dr. Woods presses her lips together and nods toward the man sitting next to her without looking at him. Apparently, she has not yet forgiven her co-debater for his gaffe regarding artificial selection. With a grunt, the mammoth Dr. Hawkstern rises from the table and lumbers to the microphone.

The polar bear dressed in human clothes clears his throat, and the sound vibrates through the lecture hall like a dozen bowling balls rumbling over bolts on a metal floor. He fixes his gaze on the back of the large hall and is silent for a long time. His billowy eyebrows twitch as he runs his mammoth hand down the dirty avalanche of his beard that covers his barrel chest.

Finally, he states, "Contrary to what our adversaries have argued this afternoon, fully naturalistic evolution is the simpler explanation. It is supported by observable evidence that explains the existence of the universe with the welcome bonus of removing from the equation of life a meddling

God whose only purpose is to accuse us of being guilty of sin and declare us worthy of hell."

The titan stands at the podium for a long time after his closing statement soaking in the loud applause. He gazes over the heads of the audience and majestically nods his lion-sized head with its generous white mane.

"You may be seated, Dr. Hawkstern," Heather is finally compelled to say. Then she invites the "anti-evolutionary" team representative to approach the microphone and deliver their final statement.

Nancy turns to the man sitting next to her with his tousled hair and disheveled clothes and says, "Take us home, Alan. Just stay on the platform this time," she says sternly. Her mike is still on, so everyone in the audience hears the warning she utters to her husband.

There is a smattering of laughter as Dr. Greenlay walks around the table and approaches the podium. When he reaches the microphone, applause begins to ripple across the lecture hall like the sound of a gently flowing stream and slowly builds to the more robust noise of a whitewater river. The few scattered derisive comments are mostly muffled by the clapping.

"When Nancy and I were at home this morning preparing for this debate," the smaller man begins, "she told me not to be too witty or too academic or too charming but to just be myself." A few people catch the self-deprecating humor and laugh.

When the large hall falls silent, Dr. Greenlay slowly scans the sea of faces before him. It appears that he is attempting to make eye contact with everyone in the audience.

After a lengthy silence, he says in a voice that breaks with emotion, "My closing statement to you precious men and women is that if I agree to the purely naturalistic evolutionary process proposed by Woods and Hawkstern, then I must view you as accidents, as animals no better than pigs and hyenas—as walking dust. I simply cannot do that with a clear conscience when I know that every single one of you has been designed and created by a loving God before time began *who knows you all by name!* He also has a wonderful plan for your lives if you but turn to him in repentance and believe in his son, Jesus."

The short, portly man pulls a handkerchief from his pocket and wipes away tears, and then blows his nose. He turns to go back to his chair next to his wife but abruptly pivots back toward the audience and mumbles into the microphone, "I love you, people. I love every single one of you."

On that note, the semi-annual debate concludes. For some reason, the moderator, Heather, does not call for a vote to determine the winner. Instead, she summarily dismisses everyone and hurriedly retreats from the microphone, and exits the stage.

As the members of the audience rise from their seats and file toward the door, Armando remarks, surprisingly without humor, "Small man, huge heart. I respect him as the wise father I never had."

CHAPTER 16

CLYDE AND DONNIE

Clyde Kildaire and Donnie Caruso, cousins in blood and crime, rendezvous with the DaFoe brothers in a parking lot behind a deserted warehouse not far from the gloomy bar where they met last time. The asphalt beneath their feet is cracked like a mirror punched by the fist of an angry giant. Radiating lines run in every direction around them. Evening is stalking the world, and the long shadows cast by adjacent buildings fall over the men like harbingers of death as they stand in the space between the gray Silverado pickup and the late-model burgundy sedan at least partially hand-made in Germany.

Half-Dome Clyde, diminutive Donnie, no-neck Aamon, and dead-eyes Daemon all believe that soon they will be wealthy by using the very men they are staring at.

"We want 24/7 surveillance from here on out," Daemon announces to the two hired thugs. "We've applied pressure to this Jack character very recently and expect him to make a move soon. We suspect he'll lead us to the 'Ladies' any day now, so don't let him out of your sight. Especially keep a close watch on them around that school. Savvy?" The man's tone is condescending and harsh.

Clyde has served enough time in the big house and has otherwise lived around unsavory characters on the outside to know what kind of men the two brothers are. They are not simply selfish and greedy men. They are evil.

271

They would just as soon kill him and Donnie as they would swat a fly or step on a beetle. He would never admit it to his cousin, but he fears the brothers as much as he despises them. He might not be the smartest ex-con on the block, but he has street smarts, as they say, and plenty of them, accrued the hard way—through the school of hard knocks.

Clyde spits on the fractured pavement and nods his head. "We'll be on that dude like white on a picket fence," he says, uttering one of his famous or—as his cousin would say—infamous 'Clydeisms.' "If we have to, we'll follow him until the pigs fly home," he adds.

Out of the corner of his eye, Clyde notices his cousin roll his eyes at him for the tenth time in the last five minutes. The big man jerks his head threateningly toward his cousin and curses him with a glare from the Kildaire "evil eye."

"We're serious about this Jack Sutherington," Damon states coldly. "We don't want you fools bumbling this operation for us. There's a lot riding on this." For us.

Clyde bites his lip until his cheek twitches. "I got the message the first time, loud and clear," he says, barely keeping a straight face.

"Okay, then," Damon growls. "Keep us posted, day or night. You've got the number to my burner phone. Call as soon as you know anything. It just better be soon. The big guy is getting really impatient with you buffoons."

"Ten-four," is all that Clyde says. Apparently satisfied, the two men—the bulldog and the alligator-man—jump and slither, respectively, into the luxury automobile and drive away.

Clyde watches the retreating car and curses loudly. "It never makes no sense in my brain how men like that deserve anythin' good in this world. It ain't fair. They deserve to be locked up for the rest of their lives along with the rest of the lyin' thieves in the world."

Somehow it is lost on Clyde that, by his own definition, he also should be transported to prison in the back of a police squad at that very moment.

"I don't trust those two apes," Donnie says as he wipes his mouth with the back of his hairy hand.

Clyde's upper lip curls into a sneer, and he replies, "Neither do I, cuz. I don't trust neither of them any further than they can throw me."

Donnie turns away and feigns a cough. He knows that his big cousin is at the end of his patience with the eye-rolling, and so he hides it masterfully.

As they climb into the gray truck that Clyde affectionately calls the "Hillbilly Hooch," the large man with crooked teeth and stringy hair fires up the truck, and they motor out of the parking lot.

As they cruise over the dusky streets, Clyde glances at Donnie and says, "Those two men are executioners. They're fixin' to kill us, cuz. When they're done usin' us, they're gonna rub us out and bury our bodies in the woods as sure as the pope is Lutheran."

Donnie looks at Clyde with bloodshot eyes and three days of stubble on his face. As he pictures a cathedral in his mind, he says, "So what are we supposed to do? Get out when the gettin's good, or wait around and take our chances?"

"Did you hear the bigger guy slip up tonight?" Clyde inquires of his cousin. "What're ya talkin' about?" Donnie asks.

"He said somethin' about findin' the 'ladies,' and I don't think he's talkin' about a visit to the cathouse," Clyde remarks.

"Maybe it's a code word for somethin'," Donnie comments, looking at his cousin's face that is alternately bathed with illumination and then covered in shadows as they roll under the streetlights.

"Yeah, a darn-tootin' code word for money," Clyde says, elongating the last word as he nods his big head.

"So, we're not gettin' out, then," Donnie says to his cousin.

"Not when we're this close," the big man says, glancing at his cousin as he rubs his crooked nose. "We could go a whole lifetime and not have another chance like this one come along. We hafta take the risk. If we find the treasure, we'll be on easy avenue for life."

Donnie turns and looks out the window into the night. It's "easy street," he murmurs at the window without making a sound.

"We just need to plan how we're goin' to watch that Jack clown," Clyde says.

Eventually, Donnie turns away from the window and stares at his cousin out of the corner of his eyes. The big man has that telltale look on his face that says he is counting money—and lots of it. His large eyes bulge from their sockets, and his massive tongue slides back and forth over his sizeable lips.

Donnie shakes his head almost imperceptibly and thinks, *How in the world did I end up with a cousin like Clyde?* Donnie is not angry; merely philosophical. *It's weird what life can bring your way. I wonder if I'll be happy at the end of it all.* Then he's done with his philosophizing because his mind never goes any deeper than that.

Out of nowhere, Clyde announces, "My dang moral hurts." One of his long, stained fingers is groping around in his mouth.

"That's because you never go to the dentist," Donnie comments as the knobby tread of the off-road tires growl over the darkening road. "I'll bet it's been a month of Sundays since you went last time."

"Not true!" Clyde snaps at his cousin. "I went just last...last...Lemme think. Oh yeah, I went when I was in the joint the last time."

274

"That was four years ago," Donnie says, shaking his head. "Four years ago, Clyde! In four more years, all your teeth are goin' to have to be yanked out of your skull, and you'll be wearin' dime store teeth like your granny did."

"Will not!" Clyde disagrees. There is a short silence before he adds, "Well, if you're right, which I highly doubt since you're never right, then at least I won't have to brush 'em anymore."

"You don't brush them the way it is, Clydesdale!" Donnie exclaims. "It's no wonder they're as yellow as a canary sittin' on a banana."

Clyde mumbles something under his breath, and his cousin knows he is angry and searching his mind for the most derogatory comeback he can imagine.

Finally, his bulky cousin turns and snarls, "Don't go off complainin', Donnie! Life's easy for you! You only gotta put up with me. Now, me—I gotta put up with you every cotton-plantin'...every nose-pickin'...every dang second of my life!"

Donnie's face contorts, and he quickly turns to look out the window of the truck, but this time he cannot help himself. He breaks out into raucous laughter and cries, "Seriously, cuz? 'Nose-pickin'? Who raised you, anyway? A pack of wild boars?"

A split second later, a large hand flies across the cab of the truck and smacks him hard in the face.

"Hey!" Donnie exclaims angrily as he glares at his cousin. "What was that for? I was just jokin'!"

"There's jokin', and there's disrespectin'," Clyde insists as he navigates the truck onto the interstate. "Your words are disrespectin'. I don't take none too kindly to disrespect. Sometimes you just get too big for your bridges,

Donnie, and I got to put you back in your place."

Donnie is so angry that he uncharacteristically misses his cousin's verbal blunder. Fuming, he folds his arms tightly across his chest and stares out the window.

Under his breath, he mumbles, "I sure don't know what the good Lord was thinkin' when He made you, my cousin. I would've been better off hangin' with that pack of boars that raised you—rabid ones at that."

CHAPTER 17

———

A FATHER'S LEGACY IN PAINT

———

Drew and Rachel run down the hallway and into the intensive care unit at the hospital in Schenectady, New York. The clock on the wall behind the counter reads 4:13 in the morning, three numbers that will remain etched in Drew's memory for decades to come. Breathlessly, he asks the charge nurse for directions to his father's room. Before the harried woman can answer, Suzie Johnson drifts up to him like a specter.

The son takes one look at his mother's granite face, and his eyes grow large. "No," he says in a pleading voice as he shakes his head. "No, Mom. No! He can't be gone. I didn't get to say goodbye."

Suzie sighs and closes her eyes. She presses the palms of both hands against her forehead. The woman looks dazed, lost in a fog of exhaustion.

"He passed an hour ago," the new widow mumbles. "I didn't want to tell you until you got here."

Drew sighs and stares at the clock on the wall. "Where is he?" he asks without even looking at his mother.

Suzie nods her head toward the hallway on their right. "Down there. Room 2017. No, 2011. I don't remember. On the right, about six doors down."

Drew turns to go but then throws his hands into the air and says aloud, "What're you doing, Drew? Think, man, think."

The big young man wheels around and takes his much smaller mother into his arms and holds her close to himself. Neither Mother nor son utter a word. They have had no practice for such a moment as this—death or hugging—and are at a total loss for words.

When Drew finally releases his mother, he says, "Mom, this is Rachel, the woman I've talked to you about. Rachel, this is my mother, Suzie Johnson."

Rachel tentatively extends a hand to the dazed woman and says, "I'm so sorry for your loss. This must all be so surreal for you."

Suzie eyes the young woman stonily and says, "I've been better." She does not take Rachel's hand.

Drew leads his mother over to the small lounge area adjacent to the desk and tells her to sit down on a gray couch decorated with seagulls in flight. Then he flags down a nursing assistant and asks him if he could bring his mother a cup of coffee. He tells his mother that he will be back soon.

Rachel volunteers to stay with Suzie, but Drew gently takes her arm in his large hand and steers her down the hallway. As they walk forward under the glaring fluorescents, Drew says quietly, "Mom isn't much for giving or receiving comfort. Besides, I need you with me."

They arrive at room 2013, and Drew hesitates. The placard fixed next to the door reads, "Don Johnson."

"I can't believe my father is in there, and he's not breathing," the hulking man says quietly. He looks Rachel in the eye and adds, "This day came way too soon. You never had a chance to meet him." His square face is pale and expressionless.

Rachel takes the large hand of the grieving son in hers and prays, "Jesus, be with Drew as he walks into this room. Give him your strength at this terrible time. If he can receive it, remind him that you are the resurrection and the life. You are the only one who gives us comfort when death, the great interrupter, darkens our path. Yes, comfort Drew, Father. Death is so wrong, and you are so good."

Drew nods his head. He takes a deep breath and lets it out slowly. Then he walks into the single occupancy room with Rachel's hand still in his.

A curtain prevents them from seeing anything when they first enter. Then they move past the thin partition that flimsily separates them from death and see Don Johnson lying still on the hospital bed. A sheet covers his body up to his neck. He looks peaceful, as if in a deep sleep. No tubes or IVs snake toward his body. His face is pasty, almost colorless. His mouth is open, and his eyes are closed.

Drew stands at the foot of the bed and forces himself to look at the body that is or was his father. He watches his chest for a long time. "This is the first time I've ever seen him not breathing," Drew comments. The words are not for Rachel, and she knows it. She remains silent and squeezes the large hand that engulfs hers.

Eventually, the young man coughs softly. Out of the corner of her eye, Rachel sees tears rolling down Drew's broad cheeks.

After a long time, Drew reluctantly releases Rachel's hand. He takes another deep breath and then walks around to the side of the bed so that he is standing directly over his father's unmoving body. He reaches down and touches the hand that has painted dozens of nature scenes and thrown hundreds of objects on the potter's wheel, and pruned thousands of plants. He stifles a sob when he realizes that he cannot remember the last time the hand touched him with affection.

Drew's shoulders shake, and he covers his eyes with one of his hands. "Why—" he begins to speak but cannot go on. Eventually, he recovers enough to begin again. "Why do I feel like I'm looking at a stranger?" he asks in a tight voice that is half an octave higher than his normal deep voice. "I've known Rachel for only three months, and I already know her ten times better than I ever knew you. A hundred times better. I even know a God I cannot see far better than you. Why is that?"

The next words catch in his throat, and he pauses. A minute later, he asks in a trembling voice, "Why didn't you ever let me in, Father? I ate breakfast and supper with you for twenty years, and yet I can't remember a time when you looked across the table and smiled at me as if you liked me or at least really saw me. Wasn't I good enough for you...or was it that you didn't know how to love?"

Rachel is weeping openly now, and the room is blurry through her tears. She slides over next to Drew and puts her arm around his waist. "I'm here," she says in a voice husky with emotion. Then she adds, "I see you, Drew. I see you."

The big man puts his arm around Rachel's shoulders and then glances at her as if to say, "I see you, too." Then he turns back to the reclining body in front of him, and his mind races with so many thoughts. He thinks that his father will never walk again on this planet or open his mouth to take a bite of a hamburger or smell the lilacs in the springtime or behold the rising sun or hear the buzzing of the bees around their hives behind the greenhouse or shave or scratch an itch on his cheek or brush his teeth or—

Drew shakes his head and groans softly. "Well, Father—" He stops abruptly, and there is a short silence. Then he exclaims bitterly, "Who am I kidding? It doesn't even feel natural to call you Father. You're a stranger to me—a distant acquaintance at best. You never were a Father to me."

Drew sighs again and snorts loudly. "Well, Don," he begins again, "it's too late for you and me now." He pauses and then says, "It's totally unnatural that I'm even talking to you this way. How sad that the most intimate words I've ever spoken to you come after you're dead."

The young man swallows hard and clears his throat. Then he says, "If there's one thing I swear—and Rachel Biandi is here as my witness—it's that I'm going to learn something from you, even if it's after you're dead. I'm going to learn from you what not to do. I'm going to do just the opposite of what you did or didn't do with your family so that my wife and kids know that I see them and love them. I'm not going to spend hours and hours in the greenhouse or garage or shed or even on the golf course at the expense of my family. Life's too short to never get close to people, Don. Life's way too short."

Torn between anger and grief, Drew reaches down and gently runs his fingers through his father's thinning hair over and over. Then he touches the colorless cheeks with the back of his hand.

Eventually, he pulls Rachel close and says, "Jesus, I put my father into your hands. He's all yours now. Please give me the power to fulfill the vow I just made. I need you to make me the best father and husband that a man can be. I want my children to know beyond any doubt that I love them and that they can approach me anywhere, anytime."

Drew touches his father's hand one last time. Then he bends over and hugs the body gently, and rests his cheek on the cool forehead. "Goodbye," he says. "It sucks that you had to leave just when I was beginning to love you instead of hate you."

The big man straightens up and turns to Rachel. He smiles down at the woman with the attractive face with its field of freckles. "Let's go, babe," he says warmly. Rachel smiles back at him and takes his hand again. Hot tears roll down her cheeks and neck, this time not out of grief.

Rachel will always remember that the first time a man spoke a term of endearment to her was in a hospital room in Schenectady, New York—in the presence of a dead man, no less.

The next morning, Rachel wakes up in Drew's room outside of Lake Luzerne and not far from the Hudson River. Drew is not with her. He is sleeping in the small room above his mother's veterinary clinic. Rachel reads her devotions and talks with God, primarily about how to shore up Drew's young faith during such a difficult time. Then she showers, gets dressed, and walks out into the kitchen.

Drew and his mother are nowhere to be seen. Rachel peers out the latticed window at the hodge-podge of buildings a hundred feet from the old farmhouse. She sees the greenhouse Drew has spoken of in the past and decides to see if he is there. She grabs her light winter jacket and heads out the back door, crunching her way over the thin layer of old snow that covers the ground.

"I'm sorry I didn't get back to see him before he died," Drew remarks to his mother as he approaches her.

Suzie Johnson is pruning plants in the greenhouse as if today is like any other day. She is wearing a small gardening hat, gloves, and denim coveralls. Her graying hair, unbrushed, flows down to the middle of her back. Granny glasses perch on her small nose. She does not immediately reply to her son but continues to busy herself with her climbing cucumber plants.

Drew allows a short silence and then inquires, "Did you hear me, Mom?"

Suzie does not look at her son as she replies coolly, "I have ears."

There is another silence before Drew asks, "Where did he have the heart attack?"

"Right where you're standing," the rigid woman says without hesitation.

Drew closes his eyes momentarily and sighs. Then he rubs a hand over his unshaven chin and says softly, "I wish I'd been here."

Suzie finally turns away from her pruning and looks at her son. "Why?" she asks impatiently. "You wouldn't have been any help."

"It must have been awful for you," the large young man comments.

Suzie turns back to her work and mumbles just loud enough for Drew to hear, "Wouldn't have happened in the first place if you hadn't created all the extra stress."

"What did you say?" Drew asks, tilting his head. "What extra stress?"

"You know," his mother says as she lifts her chin to look more closely at the plant she is pruning.

"No, Mom," he says, "I don't know."

This time Suzie sets down her pruning shears and turns to level her gaze on her son. "Are you telling me you didn't see how worried your father was after you got religion?"

"No," Drew responds, pulling back and crinkling his forehead. "He never said a word to me about it one way or the other. I know he probably wasn't pleased, but he never complained to me. Did he say something to you?"

"You know your father was never a man for many words," his mother replies, looking farm-like in her blue-denim bib overalls and straw hat but sounding business-like in her tone. "So, no, he didn't say much to me about it, but I could tell he was deeply disturbed by it all."

Drew inhales deeply. Then he puffs out his cheeks and blows out the air from his lungs. "Are you saying what I think you're saying, mom? Are you blaming his heart attack on my belief in Jesus?"

"I'm not blaming," Suzie retorts, her eyes briefly flitting across his face. "I'm just telling you what your irrational belief did to your father."

"You're not just suggesting a positive correlation here, but claiming causation," Drew says. "You're saying that my new faith *caused* his death."

The fifty-year-old woman looks at her son with gray, stony eyes that are similar in color to her long hair and says slowly, "Okay, now that you've spoken it, I agree. I honestly believe that your stubborn belief in Jesus caused your father's death."

Drew shakes his head and says, "I don't think this is about him; it's about you, mother. *You're* the one who's deeply disturbed and thinks I'm hard-headed about it all."

Suzie nods her head and admits, "I do think you were selfish to cling to your belief in some mythical deity when your father and I raised you to see the world rationally. All you could think about was yourself and what you wanted. You didn't give one thought to us."

"Selfish?" Drew repeats incredulously, his voice rising. "Ever since I gave my heart to Jesus, I've been nothing but kind to you, guys," he insists. "Hands down, you've gotten the best version of Drew you've ever had over the last three months. I went out of my way to help you two over winter break, and since I went back to the university, I've checked on you guys every few days."

His mother offers no reply, so Drew keeps talking. "Even for you,

Mom," he says with restraint, "this is a low blow—blaming me for his death. Maybe you need to look in the mirror. Maybe you're the selfish one who wants everyone to see the world the way you do, and if they don't, you guilt them to death."

"Eye for an eye, is that how it's going to be?" his mother snaps.

Drew looks up at the glass ceiling of the greenhouse and groans. "Sorry, mom," he says. "That's not the way I want to talk to you."

He pauses and then looks back down at his slender mother, who stands half a foot shorter than him. He registers how fragile the woman looks. Has she always appeared so wispy?

"What I do want to ask you, though, is why you're so opposed to my faith in Jesus. I still don't get why you're so antagonistic about it. I know you're holding on to anger toward your father, but it almost feels like there's more to it than that. Could it be that your default position is defiance against God?"

The woman stares at her brazen son. The two gray pools that are her eyes freeze over even as she looks at her challenger.

"I'm an intelligent woman who has no time for crutches," she snaps. "My beliefs have nothing to do with defiance. How can I defy something that doesn't even exist?"

"I'm just saying that you exhibit a lot of emotion whenever the subject of Jesus comes up," Drew observes. "It's almost like you're angry with him about something."

"You're not even in the right time zone," the woman says, sidestepping her son's comment. "I get angry whenever anybody tells me that I need to depend on somebody outside myself. I don't need anyone's help. My life is going just fine without Jesus."

"Really, Mom? Life is going just fine?"

Suzie begins to reply but then stops. Her face softens ever so slightly as she admits, "I misspoke. No, life is not just fine right now. But I can manage things. I'm going to be okay."

Drew gazes at his mother and studies her wan face with its high cheekbones and pointed chin. Neither one of them speaks for a long time. Finally, the son inquires gently of his mother, "Did you need—my father? Did you ever let yourself depend on him?"

Suzie lifts her chin and stares down her nose at Drew. She clears her throat and says, "Your father and I are—" The woman pauses and swallows hard. "I am, and he was—we both were very independent people," she says. "We didn't need much from each other. We got by just fine."

Drew shakes his head at the words, *We got by just fine,* but he doesn't allow himself to roll his eyes. Instead, he touches the sleeve of his mother's shirt and says, "That's exactly why I can't stop believing in Jesus, Mom—because I don't want to live the rest of my life just getting by. I want more. I want love and joy and hope and a river of excitement that runs through the middle of my life every day. I want to depend on Him and need others not as crutches but as people I love and want to be with.

"I tried living life at a distance and settling for fleeting pleasures like—" He pauses and looks closely at his mother because he knows his words will strike very close to home for her. "Like alcohol and drugs," he says, completing his thought. "But that didn't work for me. Something was off. A relationship with the God who created me is what I was missing."

Drew looks into his mother's eyes and sees a flash of emotion. She clenches her jaw, and her hand grabs the worktable next to her as if to steady herself.

"Are you okay, Mom?" Drew asks as he grasps her arm firmly.

Suzie takes a deep breath and lifts her chin once again. "I'm fine," she says unconvincingly. "I'm just fine."

Just then, the door of the greenhouse squeaks. Drew turns, expecting to see his father. When his eyes fall on Rachel, he remembers that his father will never enter the greenhouse again.

The young woman with the bobbed brunette hair hesitates just inside the solar-heated structure and looks questioningly at Drew and his mother. He nods at her that it is safe to approach.

As Rachel walks among the plants toward the mother and son, Suzie sees her opportunity to escape. She dismisses herself with a parting glance at her son and turns to leave. She does not look at Rachel as she breezes past her.

"Is your mom okay?" Rachel inquires, walking up to Drew. "I mean, I know she's not okay at a time like this. It's just that she looked kind of... angry."

"She thinks she's fine," the tall and broad-shouldered young man replies, his eyes watching the retreating figure of his mother, "but she's not. How do you tell someone who thinks she's fine that deep down inside, she's sad and lonely and scared and hopeless? How do you convince her that she's anything but fine?"

Rachel looks up at Drew but says nothing. Her eyes are wide with compassion, and her lips are compressed with concern.

When the door of the greenhouse closes behind Suzie Johnson, Drew looks down at Rachel and says abruptly, "Come with me." His voice sounds strangely expectant. He grabs Rachel's hand and leads her in the same direction his mother had just departed. "I've got something to show you, I think; something that might be amazing."

Rachel opens her mouth to inquire what he means, but Drew looks at her with a smile and says, "I couldn't show my mother, but I can't wait to show you. And no, I haven't seen it yet, so I'm not totally sure what it is, but it sounds—hopeful."

Even more confused than before, Rachel is tempted to speak again. Instead, she mirrors Drew's smile and says, "Whatever it is, it better not be far away because I'm going to explode with curiosity any second now."

Drew laughs, and again, Rachel is confused by the young man's positive mood after what she discerns was a difficult encounter with his mother.

The new believer in Jesus leads her out of the greenhouse and through an adjacent door that takes them into another room that is smaller and much colder. Rachel is amazed at what she sees. The room is an art studio filled with pottery pieces, paintings, charcoal sketches, and a handful of sculptures.

"Who's the artist?" Rachel asks, wide-eyed. "Some of these nature scenes are really impressive!" she says as she slowly scans the room.

"Everything in this studio comes from the creative hand of Don Johnson," Drew remarks, his deep voice unusually tight.

"Your dad!" Rachel exclaims, turning to look at Drew. "I had no idea he was an artist. I pictured him as a crotchety man who lived a very narrow, black-and-white life. This artwork totally blows away my impression of your dad!"

As Drew walks slowly around the room, he observes wistfully, "Yeah, this room was his sanctuary. He retreated here whenever he wasn't preoccupied with the greenhouse or his other odd jobs. This studio is the only place where my father expressed himself. I believe that his deeply hidden true self could only emerge in a place that was safe and isolated."

"Did you ever hang out with him in here?" Rachel asks.

"Not often," Drew admits as he zips up his winter vest. "Even inside this studio, he was in his own little world. Sometimes I wandered in here to see what he was doing, but he never said much to me. It seemed like wherever my father was, he was inaccessible to other humans."

"That's really sad," Rachel comments as she touches Drew's arm. Drew looks around the room a while longer, his face flushed with grief.

Then, remembering why they came into the studio in the first place, he says, "I almost forgot. I'm not here to grieve. I'm here to look for something."

"Look for something," Rachel repeats.

"Yes," he says. "I haven't had a chance to tell you, but I got a phone call this morning from a man I've never met. In fact, I never knew he existed."

"Okay," Rachel says, elongating the word. "Who was he, and what did he say?"

"You're not going to believe this, Rach," Drew says, his face shifting from grief to excitement. "He was the pastor of a church in Lake Luzerne, and he was calling to say that he had been meeting with my father every week since January."

"What? Seriously?" Rachel asks, tilting her head to the right as is her custom when she asks a question.

"I know, right?" Drew replies.

"Why?"

"His name is Pastor Zhou," Drew says, "and he was calling to tell me that—" He abruptly stops talking and looks at the woman next to him with a blank face.

"Stop it Drew!" Rachel immediately demands with feigned sternness. "I know what you're doing. Don't you dare!"

"You want me to stop talking?" Drew asks.

Rachel punches the man's muscular arm and displays the radiant smile Drew was hoping to see, the one that makes him feel like the sun is rising and will never set.

"You know what I mean," she says. "Stop holding out on me, big guy. Tell me now, or else."

Drew cannot wait any longer to speak, even if he wanted to keep Rachel in suspense a while longer. He replies, "Pastor Zhou told me three things, basically. First, he told me that my father had called to set up an appointment with him when I returned to school after winter break. Can you imagine *that*? My father called a pastor!"

"Second," Drew says in a louder voice before Rachel can respond, "the pastor said that my father was very curious about my new faith; so curious, in fact, that he began meeting with Pastor Zhou weekly to ask questions about Jesus and the Bible. Can you believe *that*?

"And finally, at their last meeting, my father offhandedly informed the pastor that he wasn't feeling well. The pastor encouraged him to see a doctor right away. My dad agreed that he would. As he was leaving the church office that day, my father told the pastor that if anything ever happened to him, he should contact me and tell me that he left something for me in the studio.

"So, that's why we're here, Rach," Drew announces, "to find what my father left for me. The last thing I remember him giving me was a pair of Yaktrax for Christmas when I was twelve, so this is kind of a big deal."

Rachel stares at Drew while she absorbs his weighty revelation. When it all sinks in, her eyes immediately begin to scan the room. "What do you think he left you?" she asks.

"Your guess is as good as mine," the son of Don Johnson says. "My only thought is that if he left it in the studio, it might be some sort of artwork he created. Maybe."

Rachel nods her head, and her reddish hair sways back and forth like rich velvet. "Do you mind if I help you look?" she inquires, still looking around the studio. "I like to find things."

"Not at all," the big man says. "In fact, it might be better if you looked for it.

I'm feeling kind of uneasy about it. On the one hand, I'm pumped. On the other hand, I'm afraid I'm expecting something he could never deliver."

Rachel's eyes find Drew's face, and she studies it. "Okay," she says, knitting her eyebrows and pursing her lips. "I can do that."

Rachel begins to make her way around the studio. She looks at dozens of paintings on easels, drawings pinned to the walls, ceramic mugs, and decanters sitting adjacent to the kiln in the back of the room. She examines small sculptures of animals and birds resting on the floor. She inspects the countertops that are cluttered with photographs of lakes and streams and golden aspens set against purple mountains with snow-covered peaks. Her search is careful and exhaustive.

As Rachel conducts her search, Drew informs her that she will find no sign of humanity in any of his father's artistic expressions. Don Johnson was all about landscapes, still life, wildlife—not human life. To her surprise, she soon discovers that Drew is correct.

Rachel is ready to tell Drew that she cannot find anything his father might have left him—at least nothing that is clearly labeled for him—when she spots the three legs of a lonely easel tucked in the far corner of the studio. A white sheet covers a large rectangular object resting on it. Rachel carefully weaves her way among the scattered items on the floor until she reaches the easel.

Rachel stands in front of the shrouded object for a long time. She takes a deep breath and closes her eyes. Finally, she whispers, "Please, Jesus, may there be something here for Drew that will mean something to his grieving heart. I pray that his father left a message or some personal legacy that Drew can hold onto forever."

Rachel turns and looks at Drew, who is standing across the room like a little boy with wide eyes. He licks his lips slowly, then nods his head.

Rachel carefully lifts aside the sheet and lets it float to the floor. Even before it alights on the oak floor of the studio, Rachel's eyes grow wide, and she covers her mouth with her hand.

Seconds later, she says with reverence in her voice, "Drew."

"What is it, Rachel?" he inquires. He cannot see what Rachel is looking at since her body and several other easels stand between him and the revealed object in the corner of the studio.

"You have to see this," she says without moving her riveted eyes from the object that has mesmerized her.

Drew navigates the cluttered studio over to where Rachel is standing. He purposefully does not look at the easel. He stops behind the woman who helped bring him to faith and rests his huge hands on her shoulders. Then he looks down at the object that has so captured her attention.

It is a painting. It is large. Drew knows the size: 48" wide by 36" tall. It is absolutely unlike anything he has ever seen his father paint. Three magnificent white stallions jump off the canvas toward him. Their eyes are large and ablaze with passion, and their long manes wildly blow in the stiff wind. As he stares at them, he imagines their noble heads tossing and hears their nostrils snorting and their feet stomping impatiently on the lush grass of the expansive meadow.

But there is something even more breathtaking than the stallions.

Sitting bareback on the majestic steeds are three men dressed for battle. Yes, humans. Amazingly, Don Johnson has permitted people to make an appearance in his painting! All three men have a bow hung over one shoulder, a quiver of arrows over the other, and a forbidding, sheathed sword hanging from their waists. Like the manes of their intrepid war horses, their hair flows freely in the wind. Their eyes, wild with adventure, are lifted toward the distant horizon where an unseen battle is raging. Their faces are fixed in the resolute expression that princes and warriors wear when they have abandoned themselves to the mission of a lifetime—come life or death.

Drew examines the faces of the men more closely. His jaw drops. The bearded man in the middle, who sits gloriously on the largest of the three stallions, has a crown of gold on his head and is dressed in a white garment. On the robe is written the words, "King of kings and Lord of lords." His eyes burn like fire. His left hand is resting on the shoulder of the man next to him as if he is his best friend. His right hand grips the shoulder of the larger but younger man on his other flank as if he will never let him go.

Of course, Drew knows who the riders are. The painting is not of three princes among men—only two of them are mere mortals. The rider in the middle is no human prince. He is *the* King, *the* Immortal and Eternal One. He is the God-man who created the two men on either side of Him. He is the General of all generals leading his armies into the battle of battles: not against flesh and blood but against the spiritual powers of darkness whose wicked leader is ravenous for the destruction of God's image in every man and woman.

The man on Jesus' left is Drew's father, although his face is much younger and infused with a passion Drew never witnessed when the man was alive. Drew is the large man on the right of the eternal General with burning eyes.

The painting is not complete. It will never be finished. The mountains rising in the background are only partially formed, and the fiery horizon toward which the three men are about to ride is awaiting final touches. Drew will own it until the day he dies and then passes it on to his children and his children's children.

There is no personal note addressed to Drew from his father. No letter or card—only the title of the painting: *Riding in Revelation with our Lord of Lords*. But it is enough for Drew.

The only child of Don Johnson, who climbed atop his stallion less than four months earlier, smiles through tears as his eyes linger on one word.

Our.

The large prince standing behind Rachel nods his head and simply says, "Thanks for letting me know, Dad."

Drew pauses and takes a deep breath. Something crashes through his body that transcends anything he has ever felt before a hundred times over. It is not a fleeting counterfeit rush. Finally, what he feels is real—a great joy that takes up residence in his heart as if it is going to stay for a while, maybe even forever.

The rejoicing man looks up at the low ceiling of the studio and utters another word of gratitude to a different father, "Above all, I praise you, my awesome heavenly Father, for bringing salvation to this house.

"To both a son and his dad."

CHAPTER 18

THE ODD COUPLE

David Abramovich, Mossad agent from Israel, flies into the MCI airport in mid-March. His arrival has been anticipated for a week now by the Screaming Eagles, several Academy professors, and two special guests. Due to commitments at the Silver Bay Lodge, classes and other academic activities, Jack and Aly are the sole representatives who travel to the airport to retrieve the foreign visitor.

As they pull over to the curb in the baggage claim area, Jack glances at the young Saudi-Thai woman and detects a glow on her face that appears a bit more pronounced than usual.

"You like him, don't you," Jack comments matter-of-factly.

Without turning to look at Jack, Aly nods her head slowly and replies, "I can't help but think it's because of the nightmare at the King David."

The young woman shivers and closes her eyes. Then she says, "I've heard that experiencing an event above and beyond normal human experience bonds hearts together in a way that nothing else can. So, I don't know if I like him, or love him, or if I've simply attached to him as a co-survivor of a shared tragedy."

"I can't imagine what it was like for you guys over there," Jack says. "I mean, I've been to Israel for a few weeks with a church group and heard a bomb go off a mile away, but I've never experienced an attack where someone actually died, and I was badly injured. I'm so sorry you had to go through that, Aly. At times like that, trusting God can be challenging."

Aly turns her heart-shaped face to Jack and looks at him with her large brown eyes. "If Jesus can deliver me and my brother from Islam and from our own dark hearts, I can and will trust Him with anything," she says resolutely. "My life is now His, and He can do with it as He pleases. I'm convinced that whatever He gives me will be for the best, whether it be pain or pleasure, sadness or joy. I'm fully surrendered to Him."

Jack nods his head and replies, "I've witnessed that trust in you since the day I met you, Aly. Passion for Jesus burns hot inside of you. I'm convinced that God will do and already has done great things through your life. You'll lead many out of the Darkness and into the Light."

Aly turns and looks toward the glass doors leading into the baggage area. "None of us at the Academy is common, Jack," she reflects. "We're here because Jesus has called us to special service for Him. I wish every believer were more uncommon; I wish they all would see the world through Jesus' eyes instead of seeing Jesus through the eyes of the world."

"Amen to that," Jack replies as he leans forward and joins Aly in looking toward the terminal doors. "As our culture here in America continues to decline, it'll take an uncommon believer to communicate God's love as well as His truth. Those who don't stand on the solid rock of God's Word will either fall away from faith or they'll live disillusioned by the lack of His presence."

Aly shakes her head, and her black hair slides back and forth on her shoulders. "Sometimes I do not understand," she comments. "How can believers who know they're going to die in fifty or sixty years invest so much in this world when they'll soon be with Jesus in heaven for a million years...a billion years...forever? Why are they so in love with the things of this world that will be gone in the blink of an eye?"

"I think it all comes down to our affections," Jack says. "If our affections are for the things of this world, we'll love the world more. If our affections are for Jesus, we'll love Jesus more."

Aly laughs softly and replies, "Sounds circular, Jack."

"I think it is," he says, tapping his fingers on the steering wheel. "If we love anything, it'll capture our attention and occupy more of our time. I don't care what it is. I've been around guys who focus massive attention on sports, fantasy leagues, pornography, or getting a good job and making lots of money. What they love demands their time and becomes increasingly important to them until other things take a backseat or totally suffer—even their relationship with Jesus.

"Shoot, I know a few thirty-year-old guys still living in their parents' basements who go to work and then come home and play video games for the next five to eight hours. Even worse, they might watch some other dude online as he plays video games. Lots of young women are complaining about the thin crop of respectable men out there because so many boys have never grown up."

Jack pauses and then adds, "Are any of those things I mentioned wrong in and of themselves? In one sense, no—except for pornography. But I don't want men to get off the hook that easily. Any of the activities I mentioned are dead wrong if they distract them from loving God and others above everything else. They're living wasted lives."

Jack watches an airport security officer walking down the sidewalk and says, "I can't throw stones at these men because I'm not perfect, either. But that doesn't mean we can't challenge each other to be soldiers for Jesus instead of civilians, to be lighthouses in this world instead of pen flashlights."

Aly turns to Jack and smiles. "I can see you're uncommon, too."

"I hope so," Jack says. "The problem is that nonbelievers don't necessarily like uncommon Christians. Maybe they feel judged by the children of the light or maybe they simply feel ashamed next to the light because they're walking in darkness. Just as misery loves company, so sinning people prefer fellow sinners but not the believers who make them look bad. That was true of me before I believed in Jesus. I thought all Christians were holier than thou. But now that I'm a believer, I don't want to dim my light for Jesus so others will feel comfortable. They need to see the light so they know there's another option in this world."

Jack pauses and stares through the windshield at the cars queued up in front of them. "I certainly don't want to communicate condemnation to those who don't know Jesus," he says. "I would never want that to be my agenda. However, if sharing the love of God makes others feel bad because they become aware that they're falling short of God's glory, I'm not going to stop. None of us turns to Jesus until we're made conscious of our sin and realize that we need someone to save us from it."

Aly nods her head at Jack as she looks back toward the terminal building. A second later, she announces, "He's here!"

The young Saudi-Thai woman immediately climbs out of the Jeep and begins waving in her petite feminine manner—her arm does not move, only her hand as if it is a fast-swinging pendulum on a metronome. Jack smiles at his classmate's excitement as he gets out of the vehicle.

When Jack steps up onto the sidewalk, Aly is already embracing a man who looks to be about half a foot taller than her. They hug for a long time. Jack stands next to the curb and looks away from the reunited couple. He focuses his attention on the crowd of people who are spilling out of the glass doors with rolling suitcases, bulging backpacks, golf clubs, and even a bicycle or two.

These people are all going places, Jack reflects to himself. Most of them seem to be in such a hurry. But do they know why they're here on the planet in the first place or where they're going besides geographical locations? How tragic that this fleeting world so easily distracts us from the eternal things.

Jack shakes his head and asks, *Am I being weird, Jesus? Is it bad for my attention to be so focused on you that I don't feel at home in this world?*

Someone is standing in front of him. Jack's eyes turn several inches and focus on the figure of a man. His olive-skinned face has a congenial look to it and his eyes radiate the joy that exists only in those inhabited by the living Spirit of God. His wavy black hair seems to speak of freedom and life. In an instant, Jack knows that he likes this man. He understands why Aly is drawn to him.

"David Abramovich," the man announces in a thick accent as he extends his hand. His voice is as friendly as his face.

Jack grabs the man's hand and shakes it vigorously. He does not want to communicate dominance but does wish to thank the courageous man for his part in saving his friend, Aly, and her brother.

"It's good to finally meet you, brother," Jack says with a broad smile. "I hear you and I are members of the same family."

David chuckles and says, "You've heard correctly. We both bow the knee to Jesus of Nazareth. That's in Israel, you know," he adds as the joy in his eyes now mingles with mirth. "Nazareth, that is."

Jack nods his head and glances at Aly. Tears are flowing down her cheeks. In that moment, he experiences a powerful confidence that she and David will be more than friends.

Jack opens the gate of the Jeep and throws David's luggage in the back. Several minutes later, they are on the interstate heading back to the Academy.

"I forgot to ask Aly if you've been to America before," Jack says without taking his eyes off the road.

"Once, many years ago," the man replies from the backseat. "My family came to visit some of my mother's relatives."

They make small talk most of the way back to the Academy until Jack finally broaches the topic that brings the man from Israel to Missouri.

"Aly told us that your father may have a lead on the suspect behind the bombing in Jerusalem," he says.

David nods his head. In the rearview mirror, Jack observes a man whose face looks young but whose eyes appear more mature, as if they have been transplanted from an older man's body.

"The reason I'm here, of course, is that Aly informed me you may have met the man responsible for the King David attack," the Mossad agent replies.

"I don't know for certain," Jack says to the mirror as he glances back at the Israeli. "However, he did make some unmistakable reference to his power extending all the way to the city of my messiah."

"Those were his words?" David inquires as he leans toward the front seat.

"To the best of my memory," Jack replies as his forehead wrinkles in concentration. "He certainly had a powerful presence, the kind of man who's afraid of no one. He struck me as what a dictator would be like if I were ever unfortunate enough to meet one."

David nods his head, then asks, "Did he seem capable of murder? I know you can't get into the man's head and know his thoughts after one encounter. I'm just asking what you intuited after being around him."

Jack does not hesitate before he replies, "Without a doubt. He is a man capable of killing others and not thinking twice about it." He pauses and then adds, "This may sound a bit extreme, but he felt like the personification of evil. I don't think the Devil's presence would feel much darker."

The Mossad agent nods his head and glances at Aly. "I hope he's the one. It would give me deep satisfaction to apprehend the man who killed Daniel."

Jack nods his head but says nothing. His passenger's face betrays that he has gone to some distant place in his mind, and Jack does not wish to interrupt the journey.

When they arrive at the Academy, Jack pulls the Jeep into the parking lot and unloads the luggage. Then he and Aly lead David through the porticoed front entrance of the citadel and up four flights of stairs to a room that Jack has only seen once before during a tour of the school.

Dr. Windsor calls it the War room. It is reserved for Academy board meetings and for school emergencies that require serious deliberation. Jack has been told that few students even know of its existence. Today, Jack and Aly, and David enter the room that is roughly twenty-feet wide by forty-feet long with a cathedral ceiling two stories high and a striated gray-marble floor. Ensconced in the walls are alcoves occupied by crosses and figurines and other biblical symbols fashioned from stone.

As Jack scans the room, he sees the sword of faith, the helmet of salvation, the breastplate of righteousness, and the shield of faith. But the objects around the room do not hold Jack's attention for long. It is the people in the room that his eyes gravitate to.

Sitting around the conference table that runs half the length of the room are thirteen people who have been waiting for the three new arrivals. Jack recognizes most of them. His eyes travel quickly over the faces of the other four mini-cohort members and professors McNeely, Fagani,

Livingstone aka Embee, Greenlay, Windsor, and the prophetess, Miriam. Nancy Greenlay is also at the table along with Sonny Livingstone. One other man is sitting at the far end of the oak table, someone Jack does not recognize. Before he can inquire about the man's presence, he hears David exclaim from behind him, "Chaplain? Chaplain Bloomstrom?"

A middle-aged man at the far end of the table dressed in military fatigues rises quickly and strides over to the young Israeli. The two men embrace and hold each other for a long time, slapping each other on the back.

"David Abramovich!" the man announces as they finally separate. "How long has it been? Fifteen years? Twenty? Young David is not so young anymore. You've become a man. No doubt your father is very proud of you."

The man pauses, and his face darkens. "I'm so sorry to hear about Daniel," he says, shaking his head. "What a loss for you. What a loss for the world. He was such a special young man."

David nods his head but does not speak. Jack can only imagine that the reunion with the chaplain Aly had told him about is emotionally powerful for the Mossad agent. After all, here is the man who introduced David, Daniel, and Kameel to Jesus when they were young boys back in Sharm el Sheikh.

Chaplain Joshua Bloomstrom slaps David on the shoulder and says, "We'll catch up later." Then he walks back to his chair.

Before he sits down, he looks at David, Aly, and Jack and says, "If any of you are wondering why I'm here, I was invited by Dr. Windsor. We have a mutual friend in the 82nd Airborne Division. The professor thought that my military experience as a ranger and with troops in the Middle East might be helpful as the Academy assesses the level of threat to the members of the school."

The three new arrivals nod their heads.

While David is introduced to everyone seated around the table, Jack marvels at the quickly organized response to the person of Draegan DaFoe. It sobers him to see that one evil personality is taken so seriously. He feels comforted by the presence of Dr. Windsor, of course, but also by the presence of David Abramovich and Chaplain Bloomstrom.

He is aware that everyone in the room is present because of his great-great grandfather's sin and his relationship with Philip DaFoe. He senses a growing conviction that he must step up and do his part in this developing situation.

Aly's conversation with David Abramovich ten days earlier was the initial catalyst for this meeting. During that phone call, she informed the Mossad agent of Jack and Emily's encounter with the eccentric man who obliquely alluded to being involved in the attack in Jerusalem.

After her conversation with the Israeli agent, Aly relayed to Jack—with David's permission—what Colonel Moshe Abramovich discovered during his interrogation with the fourth assailant. Jack and Aly then met with their four fellow students along with Drs. Livingstone, Windsor, and McNeely to discuss their plan of action. At that meeting in the "Moses Room," it was decided that a larger assembly was necessary to respond proactively and professionally to the person of Draegan DaFoe.

Emily's testimony regarding the threatening demeanor of the corpulent man was the tipping point that motivated Dr. Windsor's strong response to Philip's great, great grandson.

Today's meeting in the War room has been convened to address a handful of issues not the least of which are the possible connection between Draegan DaFoe and the man who attacked Jack on the university campus before Christmas, as well as the motivation behind Draegan's encounter with Jack. The wisdom of contacting law enforcement is also discussed at length since Draegan is the police commissioner.

An analysis of the attack at the King David consumes an hour. Most of the time is spent listening to David Abramovich and the evidence his father asked him to share with involved parties at the Academy. Chaplain Bloomstrom especially is mystified about what unusual motive would have prompted someone in America to carry out an attack on Israeli soil. Another topic that is bandied about briefly is the possible exhumation of Agatha Sutherington.

After four hours of discussion, disagreement, accord, and the formulation of an action plan, Dr. Windsor looks up over his reading glasses from his comprehensive notes and says, "Okay, people, I'm going to summarize our conversations here tonight."

After adjusting his glasses, he says, "First of all, we decided that there's a ninety-five percent probability that Draegan DaFoe is the mastermind behind the attack at the King David hotel. Secondly, the motivation for the aforementioned attack is not at all clear to us. At this juncture, our far-ranging, imaginative brainstorming has left us with what amounts to educated guesses at best and pure speculation at worst.

"One possibility we generated was that the attack was a strong-arm tactic to intimidate Jack into revealing the whereabouts of Philip's body," the professor summarizes. "But why cross the globe to create such intimidation when he could simply plant a bomb in Jack's vehicle or kidnap one of his friends here in America?

"A second possibility is that Mr. DaFoe has some vendetta against Ms. Ahmed and her brother. However, Aly attests that she has never met the man before and knows of no connection between Draegan and anyone in her family. She and her brother, Moussa, spoke earlier today, and he knows of no history with DaFoe, either.

A third possibility is that the big man hates both Christians and Jews, and the attack at the King David provided a unique opportunity for him to inflict damage on both religious groups—two birds with one stone."

Dr. Windsor presses his fingertips together and then comments, "None of these options concerning the motivation for the attack seem particularly compelling. We can only hope that as we move forward, the truth will emerge."

The retired colonel looks down at his notes and says, "Beyond the overwhelming certainty of Draegan DaFoe's involvement in the King David attack and the total uncertainty of his motivation for such an attack, the next conviction we arrived at is that the man who attacked Jack last December is most likely connected to Draegan. We have no hard evidence to substantiate this belief, but we're convinced that the timing of the assault by the 'cemetery man' and Draegan's appearance are not coincidental. They occurred too close together to be unrelated.

"The 'cemetery man' demanded the journal of Jacob Sutherington while Draegan demanded to know the location of the body of his great-great-grandfather. What we have here are two different objectives with the strong possibility of them being related.

"We concluded that the 'cemetery man' was hired by DaFoe to track down the journal because he believes it contains more than clues about the silver dollars. He appears to believe that the journal will help him locate the body of his great-great-grandfather Philip and a treasure that is buried with him. This treasure must be substantial since Draegan is willing to sacrifice the coins for it."

Dr. Windsor pauses to rub his eyes under his glasses with his long fingers.

Then he further summarizes, "Next, we decided that Draegan DaFoe has a substantial support system capable of international impact as witnessed by the operation in Israel that involved the hiring of overseas mercenaries. His position as police commissioner could conceivably grant him access to impressive financial support from the dark underbelly of society as well as from ostensibly reputable citizens."

The retired colonel pauses to emphasize his point before he states gravely, "We can only begin to imagine who is in his camp." The war professor scans the faces of the people gathered around the table, his face stern and his eyes hard.

"Mr. Fagani suggested that the rumors swirling around our city for the last century about the existence of a coven of Satan worshippers could suggest that Draegan is involved in such a covert organization," the retired paratrooper says. "If that's true, he probably has extensive underground support that I dread to even think about. It certainly would explain why he hates Jews and Christians."

The professor slides his notes aside and folds his hands. Then he looks over his glasses again and says, "We decided not to involve law enforcement at this time since there currently is no clear evidence for criminal activity by DaFoe here in America. In addition, we're not certain who we can trust in the police force.

"We also reached the unanimous decision to give Jack and the other Screaming Eagles the green light to dig up the grave of his great-great-great grandmother as part of a larger plan to apprehend the cemetery man. We're not going to sit around on our helpless hands and wait for Draegan DaFoe and his henchmen to dictate future events. We're going to take the battle to him by enticing one of his thugs into a carefully laid trap."

Dr. Windsor takes off his glasses and lays them on the table. Then he rubs his eyes for the tenth time and says, "That's everything."

"I still don't like it that we're unable to include the local police," Lieutenant Colonel Joshua Bloomstrom says. "That's like going into a major firefight without the support of artillery and air support."

"Do you think I like it?" Dr. Windsor replies a bit too harshly. "I always hated it when the order came down to go into battle without adequate resources. This situation feels very similar. I'm never comfortable being placed in a position where I can't protect my people the way I'd like. As it is, we've already lost one of our own," he says, glancing at the Mossad agent.

David smiles sadly at the reference to Daniel. "Three, actually," the Mossad agent corrects. "Four, if we include the bellhop."

"Four," Dr. Windsor affirms with a nod of his head.

There is a long silence in the room. Finally, Sonny Livingstone speaks up in his quiet manner that nonetheless commands the attention of everyone in the War Room. "Only one thing left to do before we call it a night," he says.

Dr. Windsor nods his head and says, "Okay, people, let's set this trap. But—" he begins and then falls silent. "But let's not be motivated by a spirit of revenge. I feel that dark spirit yanking on a chain in my heart as much as the rest of you. We need to pursue justice in the name of Him who loves everyone and who wants to set everything right."

He pauses and then turns to the lieutenant colonel and inquires, "Chaplain, will you ask God to infuse our planning and strategizing with His wisdom?"

"I was afraid you'd never ask," the man in fatigues comments with a smile. "Let's pray, gentlemen."

Sonny removes his tired red farm machinery hat and smiles.

When the trap for the cemetery man is in place, and the lengthy war council finally ends, no one is in a hurry to leave. David moves to the chair next to Chaplain Bloomstrom and engages in a face-to-face conversation for the first time in two decades. No one is in a hurry to leave. Armando, Rachel, Emily, Aly, and Stewart sit around the long oak table interacting with the professors and their spouses; Jack leans back in his chair and takes it all in. He contemplates the impressive war room with its towering ceiling and the accouterments of faith that line its walls. He imagines angels and demons lined up in battle formation around the room, uttering curses and hateful accusations or words of encouragement and power.

Suddenly, the heavy feeling that has crushed his chest so many times in the past descends on him yet again. Jack abruptly sits up in his chair as the darkness attempts to penetrate the protective wall around his mind. *Jesus* is all he can cry out in his oppressed mind.

Almost immediately, Jack hears words of comfort with the ears of his heart. They are words from Joshua 1: "Have I not commanded you? Be strong and courageous. Do not be frightened, and do not be dismayed, for the LORD your God is with you wherever you go."

For a fleeting moment, Jack is transported to a different time and place. He is sitting around the fire with Sniper and Armando in Valinda. The heavily tattooed gang leader is jumping around like a crazy man. Something brilliant radiates from his face as if a star is buried beneath his skin. Angela Rose is crying, and Carmelita is singing and dancing around the fire. Jack looks at Armando, and both men shake their heads and look up to the heavens. Jesus feels so close to Jesus that he laughs for joy.

Jack returns to the war room. He feels the familiar power surging through him that he felt back in the gang leader's backyard. But it is not the power that captures his attention. Rather, it is the presence. He senses the person of the living God inside of him, a friend who is closer than a brother.

Thanks for hearing my cry, Jesus, he says in his head. *Thanks for promising that you'll never leave me.*

He laughs again, this time apparently more loudly than he realized.

Everyone sitting around the table in the war room stops talking and looks at him. Somehow, they all discern that Jack is in the presence of their God and King.

They all smile and laugh with him.

Aly and David walk out on the dock that leads to the submerged aquarium classroom. The sun had set hours ago, and darkness now blankets the campus and the adjacent lake.

When they arrive at the end of the dock, the young woman from Thailand says, "This is the place. This is where the prophetess Miriam spoke to me about going to Jerusalem with Mahmoud—Moussa. Then back there," she says, pointing toward the shore, "is where she stopped and yelled at me not to rush away from King David."

David shakes his head as he gazes down the long dock toward the dark outline of the shore. "May Yeshua our Messiah be praised!" he exclaims. "He is the God of angel armies who goes before us in every battle."

Aly sits down on the bench at the end of the dock, and David joins her. They gaze across the midnight waters that are frosted with moonlight filtered through clouds. The moment feels holy and powerful. Aly shivers from the cold and from the presence of God.

After a long silence, the Mossad agent says to the quiet waters of the lake, "He saved our lives through you and Miriam that night at the King David."

He pauses, then turns to look at Aly and observes, "Do you realize that neither one of us would be sitting here at this precise moment if you hadn't been sitting on this very same bench five months ago and been obedient to the message you received from Miriam?"

"We serve a mighty God," Aly replies with a smile and a pleasant sigh as she smooths out the folds of her skirt.

David nods his head and turns his attention back to the silver water. After another long silence, the young man remarks casually as he continues to look out over the lake, "For some reason, sitting here reminds me of the night we dined on the garden terrace behind the King David. Do you remember that night, Aly?"

Aly wants to say, *I've only thought about that night every day for the last three months.* Out loud, she replies, "Yes, that was a special night. How were we to know that it would be followed by such unexpected tragedy."

Once again, David nods his head as he stares out on the lake and listens to the gentle lapping of the water against the dock. "I also remember the night up on the roof of Mahmoud Dajani's store in the Old City," he says.

Aly laughs and says, "I'll never forget sitting around those old kerosene heaters after walking through the streets of the city dressed up like Arabs going to the marketplace. I felt like a spy that night."

David smiles and says offhandedly, "You looked beautiful with that *kaffiyeh* on your head."

Aly feels herself blush. She laughs nervously and replies, "Really? Honestly, I felt like I had my hijab on that night, something that was supposed to hide my beauty from men instead of revealing it."

"Do you miss anything about being a Muslim?" the young man asks Aly abruptly as he turns to look at her.

Aly stares up into the dark heavens and sees several persistent stars peeking through the clouds. "I haven't missed Islam except maybe for the familiar and safe hedge I felt around me when I was immersed in it. Of course, I now realize that the hedge was a prison that hemmed me in and prevented me from escaping."

Aly folds her arms across her thin sweater and shivers again. David sees it and covers her shoulders and back with his jacket lying beside him on the bench.

"Thanks," she says as she glances into eyes that shimmer with moonlight.

"What a beautiful night," the young man remarks as he looks across the lake at the lights of the Silver Bay Lodge in the distance.

Aly nods her head in agreement and then inquires, "How is your father?"

David clasps his hands behind his head and leans back on the bench. "My dad is...my dad. Stubborn, strong, extremely independent, born in Israel and destined to guard his country like a bulldog until the day he dies."

Aly looks down at her hands and says, "He was so faithful about visiting me in the hospital." She hesitates and then adds, "He felt like a father to me."

David nods his head and remarks, "Yes, Moishe Abramovich has a softer side, but men never see it. Not even his son. That side of him is reserved for the women in his life. I can still remember him dancing with my mother in the kitchen on many nights. He actually had a smile on his face back

311

then," David says wistfully.

Aly turns to look at the young man and asks, "What happened to your mother? I mean, how did she die, if you don't mind me asking. I've never heard you talk about her."

David sighs and turns his face away from Aly. "She died of a broken heart," he answers as if announcing it to the lake.

"A broken heart? What happened?" Aly inquires gently as she leans toward David.

"She never recovered...after my sister died," the young man says softly.

Aly gasps and places a hand over her mouth. "What? You had a sister! You never mentioned her before."

"The colonel and I never talk about her," David replies without emotion. "Between us, it is like she never existed."

"What... what happened?"

David rubs his face with both hands, and Aly is reminded of the very same response she saw from his father in the hospital room in Jerusalem.

"She was only seventeen," David reminisces thoughtfully, "and the joy of my father's heart." He shakes his head and then sits up rigidly on the bench. "One night, she was driving home from a friend's house. Somehow, she got turned around and ended up driving into a part of the city known to be unsafe."

David rubs his face again. This time he leaves one hand over his nose and mouth. Eventually, he mumbles through his hand, "When they found her the next morning, the police discovered that someone had thrown a large rock through the windshield. They found it in the backseat. Apparently, it knocked her unconscious, or at least stunned her. Her car collided with a concrete barrier.

"They said she was traveling at least eighty miles an hour when she hit the wall, so they surmised she must have inadvertently stepped on the accelerator. She died instantly. She never knew what happened."

Aly slides close to the young man who grew up on the opposite end of the religious world as her. She rests her right hand on David's shoulder as the two lovers of Jesus sit quietly under the silvery canopy of the night.

Minutes pass before the young man speaks again. "I was thirteen at the time," he says with a sigh. "We had just moved to Jerusalem from the Sinai six months earlier. Life was good. I loved the big city. I mean, I know Jerusalem isn't even a million people, but to me, it felt huge at the time after being in small cities for most of my life."

He pauses and then says, "Being the protector that he is, whether it be for his country or his family, my father never forgave himself for my sister's death. He obsessively second-guessed himself for letting her go out alone with the car since she hardly knew the city. Dad was so careful with her that he rarely let her drive alone—especially in the dark.

"Of course, when my mother died eighteen months later from a broken heart, he found a way to blame himself for her death as well."

"How awful," Aly says, shaking her head. "Your poor father. And how terrible for you to lose the two women in your life in less than two years. I can't imagine what that was like for you."

The survivors of the King David Hotel attack sit quietly and listen to the water whispering against the shore. Besides the rhythmic, mesmerizing sound of the lake, the night is quiet. The few crickets that have ventured out on this early spring night are far away and cannot be heard on the dock.

"What was her name?" Aly inquires as she looks at the man sitting, unmoving, next to her. "Your sister's name, I mean, although I don't think I know your mother's name either."

"Esther," David answers quietly. "A queen among lesser women."

"You must have admired her," Aly observes as a large cloud entirely obscures the moon and the night around them becomes darker.

David laughs softly and nods his head. "She was an amazing sister. Compassionate, beautiful, strong, brave and—"

Aly waits for a few moments before she prompts the young man. "And?"

"And she was the only person in our family who believed in Jesus at the time," David says as he runs a hand through his wavy hair. "I've always comforted myself by believing that God chose to bring her home because she was the only one in the Abramovich family who was ready to die."

The young man chuckles softly and remarks, "One of the reasons I finally surrendered to Jesus was because I thought it was a way to be closer to Esther."

"Did your mother also believe?" Aly asks.

David looks down at his feet. He shakes his head and says, "Not that I ever knew. She was too angry at her version of God. She couldn't forgive Him for taking away her beloved daughter. I told her that the way she would be guaranteed of seeing Esther again was to believe in Jesus. So maybe she did, as she was dying."

The Mossad agent hesitates and then says, "She died of a malignant tumor in her heart—and probably from the side-effects of chemotherapy."

Aly gazes at the man next to her, who is probably five years older than her. "That explains a lot," she comments, "I mean about your father and his attitude toward Jesus."

David nods his head. Aly can barely make out the young man's face because thicker clouds roll over the already obscured orb above them.

"The problem with suffering and death is that they'll either make you a believer or an atheist," he states flatly. "It's the great divide. I suppose a few people might settle into the middle ground where they view God as a version of themselves—good and loving but powerless against the evil in this world. But most of us will settle into one of the extremes: faith or unbelief.

Aly turns and pulls her legs up beneath her on the bench so she can see the young man better in the darkness. "What about you?" she inquires quietly as she pulls David's jacket more tightly around petite body. "The death of your sister and then your mother—and now Daniel—how are you doing with losing so many people you love?"

David turns and looks at Aly. "The Israeli in me says that it is what it is," he answers. "I've spent my whole life in a country that never feels safe. At any time, we can be attacked from the north or the east or occasionally the south and even from the ocean on the west. And then there's the threat of internal terrorist attack.

"One way to deal with the ever-present specter of death is to hold life loosely. Never love anyone too much. Leave the house in the morning, knowing you might not come home that night."

"Did not loving anyone too much help you when you lost your mother and sister?" Aly asks.

David laughs without mirth and says, "It's one thing to be a philosopher in the classroom but another thing altogether to live out your worldview in the trenches of everyday life. So, no, I wasn't able to detach emotionally from my loved ones. When my sister died, I was overwhelmed with grief and anger. When my mother died, I wanted to die, too. But by then, I was a young believer in Yeshua. His love comforted me during months of depression and even thoughts of suicide. Daniel helped, too, of course. He was a brother who never left my side."

David looks down at the dock and massages his neck. "As a Christian, I know that Daniel and Esther are safely home, so I don't grieve as those who have no hope. I worry more about my mother, of course, but I'm at peace even with her because I know that my God in heaven is the only perfect judge in the universe. His justice is always fair, always unbiased. Besides, I'm hoping that my mother had a good conversation with Jesus after she slipped into a coma."

David pauses and then adds, "My only regret about losing Esther and Daniel is that I didn't get to say goodbye to either of them. They left this world far too abruptly."

Aly glances at David just as the full moon appears from behind the blankets of clouds like a lightbulb. The young man's face glows in its illumination. Aly clears her throat and then announces, "I have something to tell you about Daniel that might help."

She goes on to recount the dream she had during the flight from Rome to Atlanta. She tells David that in the dream, she was back at the garden terrace restaurant behind the King David hotel. She mentions the four shekels, the appearance of Jesus, and Daniel's comment about Christians never having to say goodbye, just "see you later."

David turns toward Aly, clearly interested in the dream. The face that has been, at best, impassive that evening, finally appears more alive.

The Mossad agent is thanking her for sharing the uplifting dream when Aly gasps abruptly.

"What is it?" David asks, alarmed. Automatically, he scans the immediate environment with eyes that are fully alert, searching for a potential threat to their safety.

"I just remembered something," the Thai-Saudi woman with the fine-featured heart-face announces. Her eyes are large with surprise, and her voice is filled with excitement.

"What?" David inquires.

"A young woman!" Aly exclaims. "She was in my dream, at the King David hotel, on the terrace. She was standing behind Jesus when he came to tell Daniel it was time to come home."

David tilts his head to one side, mildly curious. "Is there anything else you remember about her?" he asks.

Aly pauses and grabs the hand of the young man sitting next to her. "I wonder—" She hesitates and shakes her head. "I wonder if it could have been your sister."

David's face communicates skepticism, but his eyes reflect mild interest as he leans toward the dreamer beside him on the bench. "What did she look like?" he inquires as his eyes narrow.

"Well," Aly says and hesitates. "I wasn't exactly focusing on her. She was the lowest person on the totem pole, as they say here in America. My eyes were on Jesus and Daniel."

"Of course," David remarks. "Do you remember anything about her?" he asks with growing urgency in his voice.

"She had long black hair," Aly recalls, "and her face was glowing as she looked at Daniel. It was like she knew him from somewhere."

"Okay," David says with some impatience. "Anything else?"

Aly closes her eyes and attempts to recreate the scene at the garden terrace on a cool night, very much like the one she is presently sharing with David on the dock.

Then, she remembers.

"It seemed kind of strange at the time," she begins slowly as she opens her eyes and looks out on the molten silver waves.

"What seemed strange?" David asks. "What was it?"

"It was a tattoo. It looked like a dove," she says thoughtfully, narrowing her eyes as she turns to look into David's eyes. "It was a strange color for a dove—red with a yellow border around it like it was glowing with light. It was on her neck, on the right side, the side closest to where Jesus was standing."

Even before she is done speaking the last word, the Mossad agent, with the young face and the old eyes, leaps to his feet and begins jumping up and down like a seven-year-old boy whose parents have just told him he does not have to attend school for a year. His hands are raised above his head, and he is shouting, "Thank you, Jesus! Thank you! Thank you for this amazing gift!"

The young man stops jumping long enough to grab Aly's hand. He pulls her up off the bench and begins dancing with her on the dock under the soft light of the moon that is smiling down on the world. Aly cannot help but picture Moshe Abramovich dancing in the kitchen with his wife back in Jerusalem. Aly still does not know her name.

As they continue the animated dance on the dock that resembles a hybrid version of the hora, David exclaims breathlessly, "You saw Esther! In your dream, you saw my sister! She got that tattoo only weeks after we moved to Jerusalem! She told me that the dove was the Holy Spirit, and the red color was the blood of Jesus, and the yellow border around it represented the Father's glory. That was Esther!"

After what seems like a long time to Aly, the dock dance finally slows from the exhausting tempo of the hora to a slow waltz. The young Mossad agent has fallen silent, and he is crying.

Aly knows because she feels David's warm tears mingling with her own on her cheek that is cool from the night air.

CHAPTER 19

―――

THE STRIKER AND THE OUTSIDE MIDFIELDER

―――――――――――――――――――――――――――――――

Nancy did not grow up as a girly-girl. As a middle-aged woman, she is adventurous, highly energetic, an ardent camper and spelunker, confident, and in another lifetime was a starting outside midfielder for a professional women's football team. All these characteristics about the wife of Dr. Greenlay appeal to Emily, especially her football experience since Emily herself has played soccer since she was four.

The forty-seven-year-old woman is 5'8"——three inches taller than her husband—and has a shorter bob haircut with highlights in her chestnut brown hair. Her eyes radiate intelligence, her body is strong, and she is afraid of no one, as she demonstrated at the debate a few days earlier.

She and Emily are taking a break on a small bleacher beside a soccer practice field. The pitch is not chalked except for the goal lines and the penalty areas. However, there are two serviceable goals with nets—necessary equipment for a productive practice unless shooting is not on the day's schedule.

When Emily contacted Nancy at Embee's recommendation, the older woman suggested meeting on the pitch since she knew through her husband that Emily had played soccer in college. Nancy mentioned to the Academy student that if she shakes some of the rust off, she is welcome to join a women's team she coaches in the city. League play begins in a few weeks.

Nancy runs through some drills with Emily. The last one before their water break involves coach Nancy striking a ball toward the corner flag with pace—they enlisted a gym bag to serve as a flag. Emily's job is to chase down the ball, do a Cruyff turn, and then center the ball toward the net, first from the left corner and then from the right. Emily is exhilarated by being out on the pitch, and Nancy is genuinely impressed with the young woman's "touch" on the ball. She is a natural athlete.

"So, why now?" the coach asks the player as they relax on the metal bleachers. "Why did you seek me out now? Embee told me she gave you my number six weeks ago."

Emily shrugs and says, "Probably the debate. When I saw how you handled Dr. Hawkstern, I knew you were someone I could respect."

Nancy Greenlay's face breaks out into a broad smile, and she laughs. "Ah, yes, the night Alan took the dive off the platform. He's the epitome of the absent-minded professor at times—especially when he's talking!"

There is a pause in the conversation, and Nancy demonstrates two aspects of her character: she does not tolerate extended silence well, and she asks pointed questions instead of wasting time on "fluff," as she calls it. So it is that when the pause in the conversation between the two women endures for a little too long, the outside midfielder asks, "So, what's on your mind?"

Emily looks across the pitch and replies, "Embee thought I should speak with you."

"About what?"

"She didn't tell you?" Emily stammers.

"No, she didn't," Nancy replies. "She values confidentiality."

"Okay," Emily says, looking at Nancy. "I—"

"But I can imagine what it might be about," the coach says without hesitation.

"How would you—" Emily begins.

"Is it about sexual identity?" Nancy asks matter-of-factly, as if she were asking Emily what she had for breakfast that morning.

Emily pauses and looks over the woman's shoulder. "Maybe," she replies.

"You're not the first young woman Embee has sent my way," Nancy informs her listener with a smile. "I'm considered the resident expert at the Academy on gay, lesbian, and transgender issues. I identified as a lesbian myself for fifteen years."

Emily pauses to digest Nancy's admission and then says, "I had no idea," with more surprise than she had hoped to express.

Nancy nods her head and takes a swallow from her water bottle. "I don't look it now, but back in the day, I sported the classic butch appearance. I still have the tattoo of a bulldog bitch on my right rib cage."

Nancy pauses briefly and then says, "The short version of my story is that growing up, I didn't experience any of the classic sexual abuse that often accompanies lesbianism. However, when I later looked back on my childhood, I realized that my mother was merged with me emotionally— she was way too close to me. She was extremely dependent on me, and I felt like it was my job to take care of her. I saw her as weak and grew up trying not to be her. To be honest, I hated her neediness and had no respect for her. Hate is not too strong a word for what I felt.

"Whenever I could get away from my mother," Nancy continues, "I would escape to the garage and watch my father restore the latest automobile in his endless parade of classic cars. What he did out in that garage was much more exciting than the boring domestic things my mother did in the house. Unlike my overwhelmed mother, my dad took the time to show me how to do things like weld a joint or throw a football or rebuild the engine of a '55 Chevy wagon."

Nancy laughs and says, "If I had the interest, I could probably rebuild an engine today. Of course, I'd have to rent a hydraulic hoist," the woman comments with a wry smile.

"My father welcomed me into his world," the woman says as she holds Emily's eyes with her steady gaze. "But therein lay the problem. I had to enter his world. He didn't pursue me into mine. Neither of my parents knew me emotionally—partly because they didn't know how to do intimacy and partly because I had detached from my mother. I wouldn't have let her know me even if she had tried. She never tried, so it was a moot point."

Nancy steps on a nearby soccer ball and rolls it back and forth under her shoe as she says, "There were other contributing factors that greased the track for me to identify as a lesbian later on. First, I experienced gender nonconformity beginning early. I was a tomboy. I preferred hanging out with my older brother and his friends more than any of the prissy girls.

"When I became a teenager, I felt more and more on the outside of the adolescent female world. I was still figuring out how to have one close female friend—just one, mind you. I didn't wear makeup like the rest of the girls, nor did I care to. Remember, my mother—and therefore, all women, in my mind—were weak and undesirable, and so I didn't want to embrace femininity as it was portrayed to me.

"Another complicating factor was that my father was prone to anger," Nancy explains, "especially toward inanimate objects like the tools in the garage but also toward my older brother. No, my brother wasn't an inanimate object," she says with a laugh, "but he had a way of getting under my father's skin.

322

"When I saw my father direct his explosive anger toward my brother, I made a vow to myself that I would never do anything to trigger that anger toward me. So, I became a good girl, a nice girl."

Nancy pauses to drink from her water bottle again and then says, "So, if it doesn't sound too confusing, I believe that I divorced myself from myself—twice. I didn't want to be my weak, dependent mother, so I divorced myself from my needs—primarily the emotional ones—because they reminded me too much of my mother.

"And like I said, I never wanted my father to be angry with me, so I divorced myself from me a second time. I abandoned behaviors and opinions that might trigger my father's unpredictable rage. Certainly, I never talked back to him. I was my father's favorite child because he never had to feel guilty about being enraged around me since I did everything I could to never make him angry. I always left him with positive associations of me and also of himself for not losing it."

Emily adjusts her omnipresent white headband and asks, "Was there anything you could positively do to please your father, or were you just trying to avoid his negative reactions?"

"Good question," Nancy replies. "It was very clear to me from a young age that my dad was marginally pleased when I excelled in academics. However, sports was king for him. He coached me in football for many years and vicariously lived through my achievements on the pitch. Over time, the athletic and academic Nancy became the self I showed to the world since the one parent I respected valued me for my performance in those two areas.

"An added bonus was that *I* was pleased with me because the smart and athletic Nancy was strong and respectable, unlike the weak woman who birthed me."

The older woman waves her hand to fend off a bee and says, "My father never knew my heart, of course, but he liked what I did on the outside. No one knew me on the inside. I was so alone, but I tried to convince myself that everything was fine."

Emily nods her head and says in a vulnerable moment, "Hiding your real self is lonely."

Nancy nods her head in agreement, then continues her brief autobiography.

"Somehow, I made it through high school even though I never felt like I had an identity. Other girls seemed so sure of themselves, even around boys, but I didn't even know who I was. I had one dating experience with a guy I had always idealized from afar, but he turned out to be a creep. He just wanted sex. I ended up feeling used, something I felt with my father, too. He didn't use me sexually, but I often felt like he used my achievements to reassure himself he wasn't a total failure as a father.

"When I finished secondary school, I began abusing alcohol," Nancy admits. "Way too many times, I put myself in vulnerable situations where guys used me. After several years of that, I finally got to the point where I was totally done with men. They didn't care to know me or love me. They just wanted my body. Bluntly said, I came to hate the male sexual organ."

Emily nods her head in agreement with Nancy's assessment of men.

The older woman shifts the ball from her right foot to her left and says, "About that same time, my mother fell ill and died within six weeks. My father coped with his grief by retreating to the garage every free moment he had. He didn't want me around anymore—or maybe I didn't want to be around him. Probably both. Maybe I reminded him of my mother.

"Shortly after that, I began attending university not far from home. It was there that I met an upperclassman on the football team who took me under her wing. She was one of the team captains. She had lost her own mother when she was eleven years old. Understandably, she was very sympathetic to my loss."

Emily's eyes are fixed on Nancy even as she attempts to appear disinterested in the woman's story.

"One night, while we were hanging out in her dorm room," Nancy says, "the team captain held me. She stroked my hair and held my hand. It felt so incredibly good—almost electric—to be touched by a woman who was so much stronger than my weak, dependent mother that I leaned into the experience, you might say. I felt like female touch is what I had been missing all along. In some ways, it was.

"My teammate and I cuddled many times in the weeks that followed," Nancy admits. "Then, one night, it turned sexual. I was initially shocked and felt immense shame, but it felt so good that I didn't resist. Certainly, I enjoyed the physical touch, but more importantly than that, I loved being with this woman who I admired. I felt taken care of, desired, and known.

"In the following days, she introduced me to other women on campus who were lesbians, and I soon became part of their community. For the first time, I felt like I finally belonged somewhere. That was huge for me—belonging. Not long after that, I began to think of myself as a lesbian. I was groomed by several of the upperclassmen who were already lesbian identified."

Emily nods her head as she chews on a fingernail.

"At the end of the academic year, my queer partner graduated from university and left for grad school—without me. I was devastated, but what could I do? She was ready to move on. Just like when my mother died, I was abandoned by a woman.

"That fall, I hooked up with another woman on the soccer team who identified as a lesbian. We ended up in a committed relationship that lasted twelve years."

"So, what happened?" Emily inquires with narrowed eyes.

"I'm convinced I would've remained in that relationship for life if my partner hadn't cheated on me," Nancy replies. "She didn't cheat on me with who you'd normally think of—another woman or maybe even a man. Oh, no. She cheated on me with Jesus."

Emily stares at the woman with short brown hair but says nothing. Nancy keeps sharing her story.

"My partner, Kate, had grown up in a religious home and occasionally felt guilt about being in a relationship with another woman, but it never seemed to impact her too much. But then, one night, she came home and told me she had been experiencing major dissonance for a while. That was her exact word—"dissonance."

"Several weeks earlier, she had been invited by a co-worker to hear a speaker at a local church, a woman who had met Jesus and subsequently left her gay identity behind. Ever since that night when she heard the woman's testimony, Kate had begun to experience the nagging dissonance.

"This same woman was scheduled to speak at another church across town," Nancy continues. "Kate said that both of us should go this time. I agreed to attend but only because I secretly planned to undermine everything this woman said to help Kate put this meddlesome dissonance behind her forever. I hoped to extinguish the small spark of doubt before it grew into something dangerous."

Nancy shakes her head and laughs softly. "God is such a strategist," she comments. "He had a trap set for me when I thought I had a trap set for Him. That night as this ex-lesbian spoke and read scripture, the emptiness of my heart was exposed. I left the church aware that something was missing in my life. Kate sensed the same emptiness. I did nothing about it. However, Kate gave her heart to Jesus, claiming she had been missing Him for years."

Emily stares at the older woman with her intense green eyes. A dissonance begins to stir within her heart as well—an old, familiar one.

"When we got home that night, we sat and talked until the sun came up. We also cried our eyes out. Kate felt this strong conviction that we should break up. She claimed that she now knew beyond any doubt that our relationship was not what God wanted for us. Our emotional bond was so strong, however, that we stayed together for several more months. Our sexual relationship ended immediately, however, because of Kate's new faith. To be honest, the sex wasn't a huge loss for me because it had never been as important to me as being close to her and feeling her non-erotic touch.

"I didn't see it until later," Nancy confesses, "but Kate and I were two half people looking for someone to complete us. When we became lovers, our two halves made a whole. We were emotionally one person—merged in an unhealthy union that felt amazingly good. Honestly, it felt addicting to me. I couldn't imagine being without her. She filled me up. When Kate met Jesus, I began to experience this terrifying fear of being empty and alone forever. I had several severe panic attacks."

"So, what happened next?" Emily asks, pulling her knees up to her chest as if building a wall against an answer she does not want to hear.

Nancy lifts the soccer ball into the air on her instep and catches it in her right hand. Then she replies, "Kate spent the next few months talking about moving out, but every time she did, I would do something to manipulate her into staying. I even threatened that I would kill myself if she left."

Nancy sighs and says, "One night, I laid awake and thought about who

I had become. Sometime in the middle of the night, I had this epiphany that I had become my mother. I was shocked and so ashamed. I hated myself. I realized I had become the dependent and manipulative woman I had despised for so many years.

"A week later," Nancy says with a sigh, "Kate and I mutually agreed to separate. I was devastated and scared. Initially, we decided to remain friends, but we soon discovered that a clean break was needed because of our emotional oneness. Kate moved across town, and I moved back home with my father. I felt totally empty like I'd been ripped in half. I contemplated suicide for months. I believed my life was over. All I could think of was Kate.

"Eventually, I realized how obsessed I was with even the thought of her. Later, I would admit that she had become my idol, my god. There was no way there was room for Jesus in my heart as long as Kate was the goddess of my life."

Emily looks out across the soccer field and mumbles, "How could someone who loves you hurt you so badly?"

Nancy does not seem to hear the younger woman. "I knew Kate was already in therapy with a woman of faith," she says. "I decided to follow in her footsteps and began meeting with a counselor at the same clinic. She listened well. I opened like a bud exposed to sunlight. The first five sessions, I don't think I let her say more than ten words. The two things I liked about her were that she didn't judge me, and she genuinely seemed to care about me. I could tell she cared by the look on her face and by her amazing patience with me. She didn't try to change me. She was simply *with* me."

Emily looks at Nancy but says nothing.

"She didn't pressure me about anything," the woman says. "I was the one who eventually asked her about God. She answered my questions honestly. She didn't try to convince me to embrace my same-sex attraction like some therapists would do. Neither did she push me toward God."

Nancy smiles, and two wrinkle lines appear around both sides of her mouth. "Six months after I began therapy, I gave my life to Jesus. I still can't believe it! I realized that Jesus was the person I had been missing all along. For so long, I had tried to fill the emptiness inside of me with something else that felt so good in the moment but left me aching for something more.

"I attended a group for women who were moving away from their same-sex attraction because they loved Jesus more. This group was helpful, but I had to be careful, so I wouldn't become unhealthily attached to any of the group members or let them attach to me. In the end, it was my attachment to Jesus that empowered me to detach from Kate—even in the world of my imagination."

"How did you meet Dr. Greenlay?" Emily inquires. She wants to move the conversation to safer ground.

Nancy laughs and replies, "Believe it or not—you probably will believe it—we met while traveling with a group that was exploring famous caves in Europe. We specifically met in a huge limestone ice cave in Austria known as Eisriesenwelt. I was attracted to Alan's infectiously joyful spirit, and he was attracted to what he called my 'indomitable will.' He called me 'the unsinkable Nancy Brown.' Brown was my maiden name."

Nancy laughs and says, "Neither of us experienced love at first sight. I was not sexually attracted to men, and Alan wasn't exactly Don Juan. Alan was Alan and seemed more interested in God and the Bible and caves. We 'dated,' if you could call it that, for six years. Together, we traveled to caves all over the world.

"Then one day, he—how do I say it—it dawned on him that we should be married. It wasn't exactly high romance. We were married six weeks later, in the Cathedral."

"Oh," Emily replies, "because you're Catholic?"

"No," Nancy says with a laugh. "Our wedding took place at Cathedral Caverns in Alabama! Believe it or not"—Emily is beginning to notice that the phrase is a favorite of Nancy's—"ninety guests joined us in the largest room of the cave for our wedding. Alan thought it appropriate to be married in a cave since we both loved spelunking. Milner McNeely performed the ceremony. Milner, Alan, and Harley Hawkstern were buddies back in college days."

Before Emily can comment on her surprise about the friendship of the three professors, Nancy asks the young woman, "So, what's your story? Where are you in your journey with SSA?"

Emily takes a deep breath and looks down at the ground beneath the aluminum bleacher. "A very different place than you," she says.

Nancy gets right to the point. "Have you decided that lesbianism is your identity, or are you seeking restoration?"

"You make it sound like SSA is something I'm choosing," Emily remarks coolly as she abruptly gets up and jumps down from the bleacher. "Well, I didn't choose it. I was born this way."

"Hmm," the spelunker says as she tilts her head down and eyes Emily from the tops of her eyes. "The way I see it today, being queer is the practice of same-sex behaviors, not an identity you were born with. I certainly don't believe I was born gay. Many of my lesbian friends don't believe that either. But neither did I wake up one morning and tell myself that I was going to be attracted to women. In other words, while I believe the strong pull toward women is usually not intentionally chosen, I do think a woman has a choice to practice that attraction or not."

Emily pulls a soccer ball out of the bag in front of the bleachers and rolls it under her foot, just like the coach had done earlier. Looking down at the ball, she comments, "There's a lot of women out there who would disagree with you. Like, totally."

"I'm aware of that," the coach says. "There was a time in my journey when I believed with all my heart that I was born gay and had no choice but to be a lesbian. That's what coming out was all about for me—admitting who I was to myself and the world.

"Is it possible that some people are born with an inherent inclination to be attracted to the opposite sex? Maybe, although there is no research at the current time to suggest that. Yes, there have been several studies that claim evidence of biological cause—everything from studies focusing on twins, amygdalae, and prenatal hormone exposure. But if you examine these studies closely without bias, the research is clearly flawed, and the findings are unsupported."

Nancy looks at the young woman beside her, who is still gazing down at the ball under her foot. "My belief is that everyone in this fallen world is born with inclinations to certain temptations," she says. "For one person, it might be alcohol; for another, a food addiction; for yet another, strong sexual desire for the opposite sex or for same-sex relationships; and for someone else, maybe it's the temptation to gamble or play video games day and night."

"So, you don't believe that queer people are born gay," Emily states as she glances up at Nancy with a passionless face but with eyes that are throwing off sparks.

"As I just said, they might be born with an attraction to the same sex, but that does not equal an identity," Nancy replies. "God didn't create lesbians any more than He created alcoholics. We all have temptations to sin embedded in us as a result of the Fall, but we have the choice to practice that sin or fight against it. Me saying I was born gay and that's who I am is like a person addicted to meth saying she was born that way, so she must identify as a meth user and continue to embrace that identity for the rest of her life."

Emily's eyes blaze as she retorts, "You're equating an addiction to meth with lesbianism? I resent that. Loving someone is not the same as an addiction to meth." She pauses and then says icily, "And by the way, right now, you're sounding a lot like my judgmental father."

"You're right, Emily," the other woman says, nodding her head, "they're not the same thing. I'm just saying that both of them are temptations to practice something God didn't intend for us. Both are potential idols that take the place of our affection for Jesus."

Nancy pauses and then inquires directly, "Do you believe you're honoring God with your lesbianism?"

"Like I tried to say earlier," Emily snaps, "I believe that being gay is who I am, that God made me this way. So, yeah, I'm honoring Him by practicing same-sex attraction."

"What do you do with the passages in the Bible that say that homosexuality is the practice of exchanging God for an idol?" Nancy asks. "And what about the ones that clearly point out that it's a sin against God?"

"I guess I interpret them differently than you," Emily says, bristling. "I don't think God would condemn someone for being gay if that's the way he made them. I think those passages in the Bible were only meant for the culture back then, or they're referring to gay prostitution."

The older woman says, "Some theologians, both gay and straight, have tried to explain these passages differently than the church has for the last two thousand years, but unbiased scholars who read the text in the original languages agree that these references are clearly referring to the practice of homosexuality."

Nancy pauses and then says, "There's one thing you need to know, Emily. Yes, homosexual sin is about sexual behaviors with a person of the same sex. But even more than that, homosexual sin goes beyond external behaviors to internal choices and attitudes. At its core, it has to do with worshiping a person above God or choosing her over obedience to God. In that sense, it's idolatry."

"I'm not making her an idol," Emily says, shaking her head. "I'm simply loving someone and choosing to be with her."

"But that's what idolatry is," Nancy says. "Idolatry is loving something or someone more than God to the point that we're willing to disobey God to hold onto that desired idol. At that point, there's no way we'll let God tell us our affections are misplaced. All that matters is what we want. God must defer to us, or we'll cut Him out of our lives—or we'll fashion God into a deity made in our image who loves us but makes no demands on us."

"I still don't understand why you think being a lesbian is so bad," Emily says edgily. "After all, it feels better than anything I've ever done, and besides, it's all about loving someone."

"I believe some gay individuals are attracted to the same sex because they've divorced from something inside themselves, and so they must find that missing piece in another person of the same gender," Nancy replies. "I don't know what your story is, Emily, but I detached from my femininity when I was very young because I despised my mother, who represented the feminine to me. Then, when I was old enough to make my own choices, I went out and found that divorced part of me in another, stronger woman who I could admire."

Nancy drops the ball that had been resting in her hand and begins juggling it from foot to foot and then to her knee and her chest and her head. She smiles as she concentrates on the ball and says, "Do you remember from the debate how Alan and I made the point that Darwinian evolution is an interesting theory but has very little evidence to support it beyond examples that are actually about adaptation or microevolution within species?

"I'm not sure how convincingly I made the point, but I believe that many people will defend evolution to the death. They create amazingly non-scientific arguments such as Punctuated Equilibrium to prop up a wobbling theory on the verge of collapse. Why? Because it's not about science at that point. It's all about creating an explanation for the universe that excludes the Creator. For many reasons, some people don't want a God to be behind it all. They want to be free from accountability to sovereign authority."

Emily, out of some compulsive habit, is counting the number of juggling touches the coach has accrued. So far, she's at thirty-three.

"The point I'm trying to make, Emily, is that I think there's a parallel between people's belief in naturalistic evolution and their support of gay and lesbian identity," Nancy says. "Both beliefs represent people defending a position that often dismisses accountability to divine authority because they insist God doesn't exist or He agrees with their version of reality.

"We kill God off, or we write the playwright out of the play, or we subjugate his authority to ours, or we say that His commands don't really mean what they appear to say, or we make His words say what we want them to say," Nancy says, beginning to breathe a bit harder. "In short, we make ourselves god. We become the authority in the universe. We call the red light green, and the green light red. We ignore the objective color and call it the color we want it to be. We take the black and white unhealthiness of SSA and depict it as a beautiful rainbow. That's called relativism. Absolute truth dies on the altar of our demand to choose what we want since we are now the new sheriff in town."

Emily is still counting. Sixty-one touches. She tries to keep counting as she says, "You believe what you want to believe about lesbianism, and I'll believe what I want to believe. Just don't force your belief on me."

"What you just said is an example of relativism," Nancy observes. "Everybody does what's right in their own eyes. Do you know what will happen if we continue to live by relativism?"

"What?" Emily replies sharply as she counts in her head, seventy-seven.

"If this trend continues," Nancy says, continuing to keep her eyes on the ball, "soon child pornography will be permissible, as well as adults engaging in sex with consenting minors. There will be no moral code left since it has all been rewritten by people who don't want any rules interfering with what they desire. And that's saying it mildly. What I should say is that the moral code will be toppled to the ground like the statue of a hated dictator."

When Emily does not reply but simply tracks the ball as Nancy juggles it from foot to chest, to thigh, to foot, the older woman concludes breathlessly, "If absolute truth is shooed away like a pesky fly, there will be no more guardrails to warn people from doing anything they want to do at any time even if it literally kills them—or someone else."

The young woman's eyes flash, and she says, "I'm not opposed to morality or truth. I'm just angry that you think you can tell me who I can love and who I can't love. That's not your right. I get to decide who I want to love. I'm not telling you that you can't love Dr. Greenlay."

Nancy traps the ball on the instep of her right foot and balances it there after the one-hundredth juggle.

Then she looks at Emily and explains, "I'm not saying that your partner isn't your best friend, or that you're not genuinely liked and known by her, or even that you're not growing in this relationship. And I'm not saying that your self-esteem hasn't developed at all or that you haven't found a community of friends, maybe for the first time in your life. I'm not denying any of that. After all, I experienced all those things."

Nancy transfers the ball to the instep of her left foot and balances it there. She says, "I'm not here to tell you to stop sinning or to immediately leave your partner. Not at all. I'm here to invite you to trust Jesus and surrender to Him and allow His love to transform your heart. Only then would I ask you to listen to what He has to say about your affections and your behaviors.

"Even God doesn't call on you to give up your idolatry first and then come to Him. He says, *First, come to me, and I will become the One you worship. Only then will I teach you the truths to obey that will give you the greatest joy and help you become the Emily I created you to be from the beginning.*

"He doesn't want you to settle for being an old rusty Chevette when He created you to be a Corvette."

Nancy passes the ball from the instep of her foot up toward Emily's knee.

The younger woman traps the ball on her thigh and then begins to juggle it just as the coach had done. Eventually, she kicks the ball over her shoulder high into the air. Then she wheels around and tracks the ball as it falls toward the ground. At the last second, she kicks it with violence. The ball travels thirty yards into the top right corner of the goal.

"Thanks for running me through drills," Emily says flatly with her back to the older woman. "I'm done here. I've got to get back to campus and get ready for work."

As she strides toward the parking lot, she retorts over her shoulder, "By the way, you'll have to find another striker for your team. I refuse to play for haters."

As Nancy watches Emily walk away, she sighs deeply and thinks to herself, *I blew it, didn't I, Jesus? I came down too hard on her. I went for the jugular when I should've just loved on her. Me and my big mouth. When will I ever learn to let you be God and not think that I must win every battle in my own strength?*

Nancy walks over to the net and retrieves the ball Emily kicked. "Nicely done, young lady," she says aloud. "Nicely done."

As she gathers the other soccer balls and places them into the bag, Nancy continues to pray.

I would feel hopeless about that young woman if I didn't remember my own rebellion against you. When I was her age, my ears didn't want to hear anything you had to say to me, and my eyes certainly didn't want to see what your plans were for my life. I wanted to do my own thing. "Don't fence me in with any rules" was my mantra! No way was I going to give up the one thing that made me feel loved and gave me a sense of belonging.

But then...you showed up so inconveniently in my life. Nancy chuckles and shakes her head. *And I've loved every minute since then. I certainly haven't liked how difficult life has been at times, but I've loved every minute I've had with you.*

Oh, Jesus, please speak to Emily's heart like you spoke to mine. Capture her attention, Holy Spirit. Whatever it takes. I personally know that a devastating hurricane is what it can take to blow a woman into that safe harbor where she discovers the most amazing treasure in the universe—you. Only then will she stop clutching the idols in her heart and open her fingers to release them. She'll never regret the decision to trust you. For you are the great lover of her soul who gave your life for hers so she might live forever.

A rare tear escapes Nancy's eye and rolls down her cheek as she cinches up the ball bag and then looks up into the sky. "Jesus," she says aloud, "Emily is right about one thing—it's all about love. Show me how to love this young woman the way you loved me."

CHAPTER 20

JULIANNA AND MISS MARPLE MEET AGAIN

"I agree with Mahatma Gandhi when he said something like, 'I like Christ, but I don't like His followers.' I've always experienced Christians as condemning—even hateful. I despise it when they talk about the love of God and then tell other people they're sinners. Who are they to judge someone else? Didn't Jesus himself say not to judge others but to accept all people?"

Julianna, the daughter of Harley Hawkstern, is speaking. She and Rachel are sitting on the patio outside the cafeteria at the university. This is now the second time they are sharing a meal together, counting the initial "serendipitous" meeting at the fast-food restaurant a month ago.

Rachel had met Drew earlier that morning on campus and was on her way to the parking lot when she ran into Julianna in the student commons building. The English professor insisted that Rachel join her for lunch. She appeared pleased to see "Miss Marple" again.

Of course, appearances can be deceiving.

Once again, Rachel does not agree with everything the daughter of Dr. Hawkstern is saying, but she decides that it is best to choose her battles carefully—to be quick to listen but slow to argue. Like the last time they met, the professor needs someone to listen to her talk. And talk. And talk. So it is that Rachel nods her head, listens, and waits. She does not have to wait long.

"That's why I was attracted to Buddhism," the university professor says, continuing her monologue. "There was no judgment. There was no impossible standard I had to live up to like there was with Christianity."

The professor pauses as she takes a bite of her salad.

"But then I studied karma more," she explains. "As I dug deeper, I discovered that there wasn't such a thing as good karma in pure Buddhism, only bad. I became particularly disillusioned when some of Buddha's disciples asked him what rules they needed to follow to escape their sins. Buddha told them to throw an ox's yoke into the river and let it float downstream for three years. Then when the three years were over, he told them to release a blind turtle into the river to search for the yoke. When the turtle finds the yoke, he instructed, that is when your sins will be forgiven."

Julianna takes a sip from her water bottle and says, "Isn't that crazy?"

"Buddha is basically saying that none of us can escape our sins by trying to be good or by following the rules. Getting rid of bad karma is impossible," the professor states, looking directly into Rachel's eyes instead of at her forehead.

"But what felt like strike three to me was when I discovered that Buddha—his name was Siddhartha Guatama, if you didn't know—actually abandoned his young wife and newborn child," Julianna says with no attempt to hide the disgust in her voice. "When he was twenty-nine years old, Buddha decided that the way to enlightenment was to become a monk. So, he left his wife and child and began the journey of escaping the cycle of suffering."

Julianna pops a cherry tomato into her mouth and chews it with great energy. "I simply can't respect a man who turns his back on his family. Family abandonment is too reminiscent of my father's actions."

340

As Rachel listens to the loquacious professor, she examines Julianna's face. The woman has clearly gained weight. Her cheek bones do not protrude as sharply as they did a month ago, and the concave space below them is not as pronounced. In addition, the appendages attached to her shoulders now look less like oversized golf clubs and more like arms. All in all, she does not appear to be an ambulatory skeleton anymore. She looks much more alive to Rachel.

"I flirted with Hinduism, but I wasn't highly enamored of a religion that has over thirty million gods," the tall woman remarks as she takes another bite of her Cobb salad. "I had already dismissed Islam due to its blatant anti-feminism. And atheism, as you know, was not on the table for me because of my father. So, what was left? New Age spirituality was the next viable option, at least in my mind.

"I pursued it for a while, but it didn't deliver; it never gave me the power to live life with purpose and vigor. So, at the end of my New Age quest, I found myself empty—a battery without a charge."

Rachel sips her iced tea and looks at the woman sitting across from her beneath the blue and red umbrella that hovers over them like a parachute for two. She is thinking that the professor's eyes connect with hers much more frequently than during their first encounter when they preferred to drill holes in her forehead.

After fifteen more minutes of meandering through the labyrinth of her religious quest, Julianna pauses and shifts gears. She glances into Rachel's eyes and comments, "I reread *The Mirror Crack'd from Side to Side* last weekend for like the seventh time. Have you ever read that Christie novel?"

Rachel chews her lower lip and stares up at the multi-colored parachute. "I think so," she replies tentatively. "Was that the mystery about the movie star who poisoned someone?"

"Yes, that's correct," Julianna confirms with a smile, obviously pleased that her Academy acquaintance is familiar with the book. "World famous movie star Marina Gregg and her husband move to St. Mary Mead where Marina encounters an avid fan who had visited her years earlier." The professor chews on another tomato and then says, "This time through the book, I saw something I never noticed in earlier readings: I am Marina Gregg."

"How so?" Rachel inquires as a gentle breeze teases her reddish hair and fills her nose with the heavy fragrance of gardenias.

The daughter of Harley Hawkstern dumps four packets of sweetener into her black coffee and inquires, "Do you remember the motive for the murder in that story?"

"Not clearly," Rachel says. "I do remember that Marina poisons someone—maybe the fan you mentioned earlier."

Julianna nods her head. "During a garden party at her new house in St. Mary Mead, Marina encounters an old fan, Heather Badcock. During their conversation, Heather divulges that she was ill when she came to visit the pregnant Marina years earlier. Marina puts two plus two together and realizes that it must have been Heather who infected her with the German measles during her earlier visit, which ultimately led to mental defects in her newborn son.

"Marina is immediately possessed by a spirit of revenge toward the culprit responsible for damaging her son. At the garden party, she poisons her own drink and then gives it to Heather, who later dies."

"Yeah, I do remember the plot now," Rachel says, nodding her head. "She poisoned her own drink to make it look like someone was trying to kill her." Rachel pauses and then says, "But I don't get it. How are you like Marina Gregg?"

Julianna pushes her coffee cup aside and massages her long neck. She stares out across the green lawn of the campus and sighs. "Just as Marina blamed Heather for the birth defects of her son and killed her for it," she says, "so, I've blamed my husband again and again for the general malaise in my life. My bitterness has become a dangerous poison that is killing my marriage—and my heart."

The daughter of Harley Hawkstern sighs again and confesses, "I've taught myself to despise him. Is it any wonder that he stays at work as late as he can, and when he does come home, he ignores me and devotes all his time and energy to our kids? Heck, he treats the server at the restaurant better than me and speaks more compassionately to the telemarketer who's selling time-shares in Siberia.

"I've become an anchor around his neck. If I hold my own feet to the fire, I hate to admit it, but I've become the critical mother he grew up with, and he's become the father I hated so much."

Julianna turns to look at Rachel and says, "Last night, he told me he was meeting with a divorce lawyer today. He wants us to be done." The woman who was so cold the first time she sat at a table with Rachel removes the napkin from her lap and dabs at her eyes.

"I don't know what to do," she confesses. "I don't think that even wise old Miss Marple can help with this murder mystery. She can't solve the imminent death of my marriage."

Rachel reaches across the table and pats the distraught woman on the arm. "I'm so sorry," she says softly.

"What am I going to do?" Julianna inquires as more tears begin to flow. "What will happen to the kids? I swore I would never allow them to suffer the same fate I did as a girl. I hate that the very thing I wanted so desperately to avoid is going to be repeated in another generation on my watch. I'm both grieved and enraged that the legacy rolls on."

Rachel clears her throat and looks at the professor with eyes as clear as the sky after rain. "Do you mind if I share one thing with you?"

The grieving woman stops dabbing her eyes and stares at Rachel. "What now? Are you going to tell me that Jesus will deliver me from anorexia nervosa and then save me and my marriage?" she asks, her mouth suddenly petulant.

"I was going to share with you something my mentor at the Academy told me," Rachel says. "It's about marriage."

"Oh," Julianna says, the sarcasm draining from her face.

"Her name is Dr. M. B. Livingstone, but we call her Embee after the initials of her first and middle names."

Julianna nods her head but says nothing. Her wide eyes appear expectant as opposed to defensive.

Maybe this woman is really looking for something to save her marriage, Rachel thinks to herself. *Jesus, may this be that dark hour just before the dawn when Julianna opens her bitter heart to truth.*

"Embee was telling us in her love class—" Rachel pauses and then explains, "Dr. Livingstone teaches a class in our program on love, both God's love and our love for each other." She smiles nervously, fearing a negative response from Julianna about such an intangible topic as love, but the professor says nothing.

"Anyway," Rachel continues, "one day in class, Embee told us that early in her marriage, she saw herself becoming increasingly negative toward her husband. At first, she didn't understand why. She did have an awareness that after growing up with unpredictable parents who always overstimulated her with their intense arguments, she had married Sunny because he was much quieter and laid-back.

"At first, things were fine, but after a while, she began to dislike the very thing that had attracted her to her husband. He was passive and didn't seem to be that interested in her. He rarely pursued her. Over the years, she became more critical of him until her negative thoughts, like growing weeds, strangled her love for Sunny."

Rachel notices that Dr. Hawkstern's daughter does not have a look of disgust on her face, so she keeps talking.

"Embee told us that those weeds in a marriage begin as small frustrations but then slowly grow into anger. After anger, bitterness comes, and then resentment, followed by hatred, and finally, contempt. Embee told us that over time, a woman who doesn't feel loved by her husband will eventually despise the man she used to gaze at with stars in her eyes.

"The day will come when this contempt leaks out during every interaction she has with her husband. At this point, there's no way her husband is going to approach her. He will pull away from his wife and escape to work, sports, pornography, and maybe even an affair."

Julianna nods her head. "Sounds like my marriage," she says scornfully. "Before Ryan gets seven words out, I've fired a thousand back at him, all of them hateful. But I resent it if you're suggesting that he's the innocent husband and I'm the bad wife. I've felt from the beginning that he doesn't love well."

"You're right, Julianna," Rachel affirms. "He needs to own his part. Embee would say that he must move toward you with love instead of moving away from you with detachment. She would also say that you need to respect him instead of eroding his confidence with your contempt."

"Well, love and respect certainly aren't the hallmarks of our marriage," Julianna announces. "Quite the opposite. He pulls away because of my disrespect, and I get angry. Then my anger leads him to pull even farther away.

At that point, I communicate more anger and disrespect, and he pulls away so far I can't even see him anymore.

"What a pathetic cycle," she snaps. "I end up feeling utterly unloved, and he feels totally disrespected. Neither of us get what we want, so why even try, especially when we don't even like each other anymore? I hate the whole mess and just might welcome a divorce."

Rachel says a quick prayer asking God for wisdom and then says, "I think you and your husband need a love beyond your own limited human affection that will transcend your contempt and his withdrawal. That kind of love only comes from Jesus. He gives you the ability to love your husband with a divine love."

"Sounds like more of that same magic we talked about last time we met," Julianna comments sarcastically.

Rachel perceives that the woman's heart is not fully invested in her criticism. She does not appear to be nearly as dedicated to her dismissal of God as she was during their earlier encounter at the fast-food chicken restaurant.

Before Rachel can reply, Julianna sets her fork on the table and stares at her salad. Her face is expressionless.

"I'm getting very tired, Rachel," she confesses. "I'm tired of being my mother's ally against my father. I'm tired of hating my husband. I'm tired of structuring my life around food. I'm weary of exercising excessively and abusing laxatives, ipecac, and diuretics every day. I'm sick and tired of competing with the beauty of far younger students on campus. I'm convinced that my body is too large, I struggle with osteoporosis and dental disease, and I live in constant dread of gaining weight.

"Yes, the treatment program is helping," Julianna says, picking up her fork and stabbing at a cherry tomato. "I'm restricting calories less—that terrifies me, as you must know from your own experience. I'm not avoiding certain foods as much as I used to, and I haven't been in the ER in the last five weeks. Some of my eating behaviors are obviously getting better. But I still hate my life."

The daughter of Dr. Hawkstern clenches her teeth and stabs at the elusive tomato for the tenth time. Two of the tines on the plastic fork break, and Julianna curses loudly. She tosses the plastic utensil onto the concrete patio, and her shoulders slump.

Rachel eyes the woman across from her with compassion, unsure of what to say next. She rests her folded hands on the napkin in her lap and clears her throat. "Do you know what I finally figured out five years ago that totally changed my depression?"

"As a matter of fact, I do," Julianna snaps, exasperated. "I already know that the answer to all of your questions, rhetorical or not, is Jesus." She pronounces the name with derision.

Rachel feels anger rise in her throat, and she knows her face is two shades redder than five seconds ago. Swallowing her anger, she says, "I discovered that at the end of everything, the only important thing in life is relationships. I realized that even my eating disorder symptoms were about difficulties in my relationships with others, with God, and even with myself. I was too close to some people, too distant from others, hated some people, and feared others. I disliked myself and wished I were someone else.

"Above all, my anger and shame cut me off from God. How could I love a God who kept wounding me with rejection and abandonment? And how could I approach him when I was so shameful and unlovable? For years, I had no interest in approaching God, people, and even my own worthless self."

"That's when you finally decided to get religion," Julianna comments. She elongates the word *finally* and raises her voice an octave when she pronounces it.

Rachel shakes her head. "I didn't want religion," she says. "No, it was then that God reached out to me. A girl in my Health class that I met after school invited me to a Bible study. I was so alone and depressed that I didn't even have the self-respect and assertiveness to say no. So, I went. A month later, I asked Jesus into my heart with the help of my English teacher, believe it or not."

Rachel smiles to herself when she realizes that she is using one of Julianna's favorite phrases.

Julianna actually smiles. "Nothing like an English teacher to bring love and adventure into your life," she comments.

"I can't disagree," Rachel says with a laugh. Then she goes on to say, "My ED behaviors didn't disappear overnight, that's for sure. To this day, I still struggle at times when my deepest wounds get touched.

"But far more important than my occasional regression back to old eating behaviors are the new things that are going on in my heart. Increasingly, joy lives in my heart, and I'm learning to love not only other people and God but also my own self. Amazingly, my anxiety and depression are slowly becoming distant memories. The Holy Spirit living inside me speaks poems of peace that wash away the songs of sorrow."

Before Rachel can speak her next thought, Julianna leans back in her chair and looks down her long, thin nose at the young woman across from her. She says, "Nice reference to poems. I know what you're trying to do—you're trying to butter up an English prof." She pauses and then adds, "I also know what you're going to say next." The hostility in her voice has downgraded from a two-edged sword to a paring knife.

"What's that?" Rachel inquires, bracing herself for the cutting comment that is sure to follow.

"You're going to ask me if I'm ready to believe in Jesus," she says with a mirthless chuckle. "Instead of the English professor praying with the student to believe in Jesus, you want to be the student who prays with the English professor to believe in Jesus. How cute would that be," Julianna says with a smirk.

"I will have you know that I have no desire to engage in any such religious hocus pocus at this juncture in my journey. I have more thinking and calculating to do. Finance isn't the only arena where you add things up to see if you can afford to do something or if you're making a smart investment."

The daughter of Dr. Hawkstern looks at the steady parade of students making their way over the university sidewalks and says, "I do have one question for you, Miss Marple."

Rachel leans forward on her plastic patio chair and gives the professor her full attention.

"I need to know if loving Jesus is practical," she comments. "I need to know not only if believing in him is doable but if it would give me a better life. I'm too much of a pragmatist and maybe even a mercenary to believe in something unless it's going to get me something. In other words, I don't want to do something because I *should* but because it will be a wise choice for me."

"Well," Rachel replies as she closes her eyes and attempts to think of a good response, "would it help if I told you that believing in Jesus is not about obeying a bunch of stifling rules but about entering into a personal relationship that makes all of your other relationships not only better but restores them to what they were meant to be all along?"

Rachel pauses, and her mind gropes for a fitting metaphor. In the end, she digs deep into her musical background to come up with something marginally credible. "Believing in Jesus is like writing a four-part symphony about love and not settling to have it played by a single sousaphone in a basement closet but having it performed by a ten-thousand-piece orchestra in a massive concert hall directed by the most accomplished conductor in the universe."

Julianna shakes her head with its spiky hair and picks up the recalcitrant tomato with her fingers. "Wow," she says as she inserts the small fruit into her mouth, "now that's an interesting word picture. I love word pictures. I would obviously vote for the ten-thousand-piece orchestra."

"Another way to say it is that asking Jesus into your heart is like not just viewing distant stars through a telescope but holding them in your hands," Rachel says.

"Or, lastly," she adds, "believing in Jesus is like being loved by a king who died rescuing you from certain death. Then, rising from the grave, He loves you perfectly and never forgets you for even a second. On top of all that, He escorts you to his mansion to be presented before His whole kingdom as his bride who will rule with Him forever and ever."

"Is that even true?" Julianna asks, her eyebrows twisted by doubt.

"It's in the Bible," Rachel answers. "You can read it for yourself."

"Okay, you've given me a lot to think about," the angular woman says as she dabs at her lips with her napkin and then pushes away from the table. "The image I can't get out of my mind is the sousaphone 'oompahing' in my basement closet. Obviously, I don't want to settle for that. Anybody who knows me knows that I love to hear the classics played by a philharmonic orchestra."

Julianna and Rachel rise from their chairs and push them back under the small table.

"Just so you know," Rachel says, her eyes squinting against the bright sunlight as she looks up into the face of the taller woman, "if you'd ever want to do it, I'd love to have you over to the Academy some time, so I can play your favorite classical piece on the organ in the sanctuary. The sound that reverberates in that cavernous room is enough to drive the music into every fiber of your being." A tingle runs up her spine just thinking about it.

"I might take you up on that someday," Julianna comments, "but first things first. I need to resolve this whole Jesus mystery before I make any other significant decisions. Besides, as you should know, Miss Marple, I'm still adamantly opposed to going anywhere where I might encounter Harley Hawkstern."

"I understand," Rachel replies. "Just remember as you think through the whole Jesus decision that He specializes in raising things back to life—even dead marriages. After all, he referred to himself as 'the resurrection and the life.'"

Julianna tilts her head at Rachel's words and comments, "A bold claim for someone living in a human body." Then she tilts her head and nods a goodbye to her lunch partner.

As the tall woman turns to walk away, a gust of wind blows through her sawtooth hair, and the individual spikes bend like javelins lowered for battle.

Speaking of battles, over the next few weeks, there will be a fight for Julianna Hawkstern's soul. The kingdom of darkness salivates to bring the dead woman to hell, the place of terrible separation from her loving Creator.

The King has other plans.

CHAPTER 21

GRAVE ROBBERS

The Screaming Eagles have been waiting a long time to dig up Agatha Sutherington's grave. They are not seeking primarily to exhume a body or to remove any contents but to discover if there is more than one body in the grave.

Mr. Fagani has assembled a genealogy supported by a detailed paper trail to show that Jack is Agatha's legal descendent on the off chance that the exhumation would be discovered and questioned. Everyone involved wants to avoid being accused of grave robbery, an activity that is considered a felony in certain states if any items removed are valued above a certain dollar amount.

Dr. Windsor researched the legal ramifications of the exhumation of a gravesite and discovered that while it is customary to petition for the dis-interring of a body, there most likely will be no untoward consequences for the action if conducted without such permission. Petitions are almost always granted if there is a valid reason for the exhumation. If worst comes to worst and the exhumation comes under public scrutiny, Jack and his friends will offer the defense that they are seeking to solve a century-old murder mystery—sketchy but legitimate.

The reason the Screaming Eagles will not be applying for an exhuma-tion petition is that they do not want the police commissioner to be aware of their plans. Draegan DaFoe has proven himself to be untrustworthy at minimum and a murderous criminal at worst.

Mr. Fagani and several other professors from the Academy, as well as David Abramovich and Joshua Bloomstrom, have met with the students a handful of times over the past ten days to plan the details of the excavation.

Fagani, the nonagenarian cemetery professor, possesses a wealth of information related to exhumations—more than anyone needs to know. He informs Jack and his mini-cohort members in his plodding, halting manner that there are certain variables to consider when considering the decomposition stage of a buried body.

Many factors indicate that the exhumation party will not be dealing with a messy decomp, the professor states with confidence. Even though a thorough search of records left by a meticulous cemetery director named Elijah Skaggs reveals that Agatha Sutherington was buried in a high-quality oak-wood casket, the passing of one-hundred-twenty-years guarantees a fully decomposed body.

In addition to the factor of time, Mr. Fagani feels the need to speak at length about other variables that point to a complete decomp: the soil conditions in the immediate area, which contain little clay, the higher humidity and temperature levels in the region, the higher moisture levels (the elderly professor states that moisture is kryptonite to a buried body), the lack of embalming at the time of Agatha's burial, and the additional note from Elijah's records that indicates a shallower burial depth than is customary due to rocky conditions. All these factors predict that the body—or *bodies*—will be reduced to dry skeletons or possibly even mere bone fragments.

Mr. Fagani informs the students that because of the natural chemical processes set in motion after death by the bacteria within the body as well as the presence of other flesh-eating organisms in the soil around the coffin, the body—or bodies—undoubtedly experienced significant decomp during just the first twelve months after death.

"Just imagine what another one-hundred-nineteen years have done to whatever is down there in the ground," he says.

Mr. Fagani's belief is that when the Screaming Eagles dig up the gravesite, they will not find the coffin or its cover but only the iron handles and screws along with bone fragments. They may also find a few clothing fragments accompanied by any jewelry the body or bodies were wearing at the time of internment. The professor advises them to be prepared even for hydroxyapatite, the condition that occurs when the bones have turned fully to dust.

Mr. Fagani pauses—for a long time—to take a bite of his daily snack of choice: a chocolate-frosted peanut donut washed down with black coffee. Then he waxes on about the stages of decomposition after death and the impact of embalming on the rate of decomp. He even wanders far off the path and discusses the topic of body farms.

Additionally, he describes what happens to a body when it is buried in a wooden coffin as opposed to being placed in a sealed casket and then interred in a concrete vault with a plastic liner. Lastly, he explains the phenomenon of exploding caskets, otherwise known as burping.

During the burping and exploding part of the cemetery professor's presentation, Rachel makes a face at Aly and whispers, "TMI."

The Saudi-Thai woman nods her head and wrinkles her small nose.

Mr. Fagani ends his monologue by stating that it does not bother him to talk about decaying bodies even though he knows his wife's body is in an advanced state of decomp by now and that his own body will soon be undergoing decomposition.

The elderly professor explains that he has always viewed his body metaphorically. "I see the human body," he says, "as either the vehicle...our spirits drive around in until God gives us new models...in heaven that will never die or rust, or as...a cocoon that the caterpillar inhabits until it dies and...later emerges as a beautiful butterfly."

At their last staging meeting just two days ago, the students and professors involved in the excavation—whom Armando has aggregately named the Grave Reapers—met and reviewed the steps of exhumation. It was decided that the digging should commence at 6 p.m. on the evening of April 4th, when traffic at the cemetery should be minimal and, weather-permitting, there will be two hours of daylight before any artificial lighting will be required.

At the end of the meeting, Dr. Windsor points out that the location of the cemetery will minimize detection: it is situated in a depression on the hillside and largely hidden by the massive structure of the citadel as well as the stone wall that encircles it. Sunny then interjects that a green tarp erected around the gravesite will further protect the grave diggers from detection. Yes, the tarp may draw some attention, but it will blend in well with the grass of the cemetery lawn and help contain any artificial light that may be required. Besides, anyone who sees the tarp will likely assume it has been erected for an imminent burial. No one will suspect a disinterment.

Thursday, April 4th, finally arrives to the excitement of the students who have been waiting months to dig up Agatha Sutherington's grave. This specific day was selected because the extended forecast called for dry conditions and favorable temperatures.

As often happens with meteorological predictions, however, unexpected weather patterns develop. Clouds move into the area late in the afternoon, and a steady mist falls from the sky, as pesky and unwelcome as mice in a cheese factory.

Possibly even worse than the moisture, the temperature drops to fifty-five degrees, and a cool breeze begins to blow. Fortunately, the dormitory building serves as a welcome windbreak between the students and the lake. Also, since the cemetery has the added protection of the stone wall around most of its perimeter, it is largely unaffected by the wind.

Component B of *Operation Grave Robbers* conducted by the *Grave Reapers* is set in motion at precisely 5:50 p.m. Rachel and Emily walk into the cemetery sharing an umbrella. The mist is not miserable, just obnoxious. Anyone who sees the two women would assume that they are relatives visiting the grave of a deceased family member.

As they enter the arched rod-iron gateway, Rachel glances over at her classmate. The woman who normally loves mysteries and solving them is subdued. Her face is as overcast as the pewter skies above them.

"I thought this day would never come," Rachel offers to her fellow grave digger.

Emily glances at her fellow student and nods her head. She says nothing. The saga of the mysterious Emily continues.

A few minutes later, Aly and Armando, who look like they could be husband and wife, enter the cemetery as well.

At 5:55 p.m, Jack and Stewart drive up the gravel trail from the citadel toward the cemetery. They are riding in a 4x4 UTV with a trailer in tow. The trailer is loaded with tarps, tall posts, shovels, a stepstool, and miscellaneous other items such as water bottles and snacks.

As they approach the gate, Jack spots a man and a woman walking down the hillside toward the cemetery from their left. Jack groans and twists the throttle on the UTV, hoping to avoid a rendezvous with the untimely visitors.

Jack thinks his strategy is going to be successful until the woman suddenly begins running toward the UTV and waving her hands as if she is flagging down a fire truck to report a fire. Jack cannot hear what the approaching woman is saying over the grumble of the engine, but he can see her mouth moving. He has no choice but to stop and speak to her.

Jack twists back on the throttle and brakes slowly. The engine falls to a soft idle.

"Just what we needed," he mutters to his roommate.

"Yoo-hoo!" the woman cries, still running toward them. She is older than Jack first thought, maybe sixty years old. "Yoo-hoo!" she cries again, even when Jack and Stewart have already come to a stop and are staring at her.

When she approaches the UTV, the woman stops running and bends over. She places her hands on her knees, attempting to catch her breath, apparently after an unusual level of exertion for her. Eventually, she looks up and asks breathlessly, "Where is Russell Bertrand's grave?"

Jack glances at Stewart for help, but his cemetery assistant simply turns and looks in the other direction. Finding his friend to be no help whatsoever, Jack turns back to the breathless woman who now has been joined by a man even older than herself. They look like siblings, Jack decides.

"Russell Bertrand?" Jack says, rubbing his chin and pushing his baseball cap back on his head. "Russell Bertrand."

"Yes," the woman says. "He was buried here about four weeks ago. Isn't that correct, Ed?" she asks, turning to her male counterpart. Ed begins to answer, "Yes, Margaret—" but the woman is already speaking to Jack again. "Certainly, you must know where our older brother is."

Jack looks away from the woman and begins to cough, the only stalling technique he can think of in the moment. Out of the corner of his eye, he sees Stewart speaking into his phone. *Thanks a lot, buddy,* he thinks to himself. *Who could you be talking to at a time like this when I need your help?*

Jack turns back to the woman who is already talking at him again and engages her in conversation. After finding out how long they are going to be in town and the specifics about how Russell Bertrand died, he asks, "By the way, where are you folks from?" he inquires.

"We're not from these parts," she says, her voice now growing impatient, "so we've never been to this cemetery before. We need your help. Where is our beloved brother buried, young man? If you work here, you must know."

Jack is thinking in his head that Bertrand must not be that beloved to the two siblings if they missed his funeral when he hears Stewart interject, "Welcome to Sunrise Cemetery, Margaret and Ed. Mr. Russell Bertrand is at rest in the northwest sector of the cemetery. After entering the gate, take your first left and walk down twelve rows. Then turn right and walk six plots in. As you know, it's a fresh gravesite with no monument erected yet. You can't miss it."

Jack stares at the Intellect, who somehow knows the answer yet again. Ed and Margaret turn and walk away without even a word of gratitude to Stewart. When they are out of earshot, Jack asks his friend, "How in the world?"

Stewart's owl eyes peer at Jack from behind his large black glasses. "I called Mr. Fagani," he explains. "He knew exactly where Mr. Bertrand was interred. It just took him a while to get the words out."

Jack stares at his assistant a while longer and then begins to laugh. "Stewart, man, you're absolutely amazing," he says. As he continues to gaze at his friend with admiration, he thinks he sees a rare twinkle in the young man's eyes. The Intellect's face, however, remains stoic, as impenetrable as ever.

Jack throttles up the UTV, and they motor forward through the gate and over a six-foot wide asphalt path that leads to the far side of the cemetery, toward Violet Windsor's grave. The fine mist continues to fall. The low-hanging, leaden ceiling of clouds makes it feel like it's 8:00 p.m. instead of 6:00 p.m.

Soon, another wrench is unexpectedly thrown into their well-laid plans. As Jack and Stewart are cruising over the asphalt, the UTV abruptly dies, and they coast to a stop. Jack attempts to start the vehicle repeatedly, but the engine refuses to turn over. He checks the fuel level and the spark plug wires and then tries to start the 4x4 again to no avail.

Shaking his head, Jack turns to Stewart and says, "I suppose you can't call someone on that phone of yours and ask for roadside assistance." He looks at his friend for several seconds with no expression on his face. Then he breaks into a smile and winks at Stewart.

The Intellect stares back at him and says nothing.

Once again, Stew, you're sadly out of touch with the world of relationships, Jack thinks to himself.

But then, a moment later, Jack hears a voice next to him say, "I guess we can't be too surprised that our UTV died in a cemetery."

Jack turns and stares at his friend in astonishment. "Stew," he says, "that's the best humor I've ever heard from you! Nicely done! Especially when you had that *grave* look on your face."

Stewart does not appear to register Jack's attempt at humor. *I guess one for two isn't too bad,* Jack thinks as he chuckles at his own pun.

Momentarily ignoring the pressure to figure out an immediate solution, Jack places his hands on the steering wheel in front of him and confides, "You know, Stew, I remember very few things my dad told me when I was young. One thing I do remember him saying was something like, 'Plan on life being difficult. Plan on things going wrong and breaking down. Then you won't waste your time bellyaching about life being hard. Instead, you'll spend your energy focusing on solutions.'"

Stewart adjusts his glasses by pinching the right bow and responds, "Your dad sounds like a wise man."

Jack looks up at the asphalt path and nods his head. "I think you're right, Stew," he comments wistfully. "He really was."

A second later, urgency grabs Jack's attention, and he slides out of the UTV. "Looks like we're going to have to pack-mule it to the gravesite. Can you call the others to help?"

Three minutes later, all six members of the micro-cohort are hauling the contents of the trailer up the slightly ascending path toward the Sutherington monument. After fifty yards, they turn left and trudge past Violet Windsor's grave that now has a small monument and flowers. Jack begins to empathize with the breathless Margaret who they met earlier. He adjusts the heavy green tarp on his shoulder and keeps trudging forward.

Eventually, they arrive at their destination—thirteen minutes behind schedule. Rachel and Aly look exhausted. Emily is unreadable. Despite some lost time, everything seems to be going according to plan.

"Oh yeah, somethin's developin' down there all right, like film in a camera," the big man says.

He adjusts his binoculars and then comments, "I guess those two suits were right, for a change. They put some pressure on good ol' Jack, and Jack is deliverin' for us. The only problem is those five other people with Jack. But we'll figure somethin' out, right Donnie? Clyde the Glide always has a plan up his shirt. The possibility of a little lateral damage never stopped us before."

"Let me look," Donnie insists, reaching for the binoculars.

"Wait your turn," his cousin growls as he continues to look through the binoculars.

"When is my turn goin' to come?" the smaller man asks. "You've hogged the binoculars since we got here."

"So?" Clyde retorts. "Is there some law sayin' when I should give 'em to you?"

Donnie lets out an exasperated sigh and tries to see what is going on in the cemetery without the aid of the binoculars. He can see six people moving down the path, but he cannot make out what they are carrying. The cousins' vantage point on top of the hill above the dormitory is not ideal, but it is the only place they can observe what is happening in the cemetery short of entering the huge church building and watching from one of the upper story windows. Unfortunately, several trees prevent an unobstructed view of the gravesite.

"They're gonna do it!" Clyde exclaims. "They're gonna do what I thought."

"What's that?" Donnie asks.

"They're gonna dig up the Sutherington grave!"

"You never said they were goin' to do that," Donnie protests. "You told me they were goin' to search for the hidden grave of that DaFoe fellow."

"Funny how every great mind always has its nay-slayer," Clyde mumbles as he continues to observe the six students. "You're my nay-slayer!"

Donnie is completely fed up with his selfish, blowhard cousin. "If you had such a great mind," he snaps, "then you'd know its 'nay-sayer,' not 'nay-slayer.'"

"That's what I said," Clyde says matter-of-factly.

Donnie shakes his head and spits in disgust. "Has anybody ever told you that you're the most impossible person in the universe?"

"Nope," Clyde responds as he continues to observe through the binoculars what is unfolding in the cemetery. "You're the one and only. More evidence that you're my nay-slayer."

Donnie curses under his breath and shakes his head again. Then he looks up into the branches above him and then down at the ground beneath him. "I gotta take a whiz, cuz," he says.

"Go ahead," the big man with the Half-Dome head replies. "I ain't gonna look."

"There's no way I'm taking a whiz up here," Donnie objects.

"Have it your way," Clyde says as he continues to stare through the binoculars.

———

David Abramovich, dressed in a cobalt blue suit, is looking out the window of the greenhouse classroom on the fourth floor of the edifice building. Chaplain Joshua Bloomstrom of the 82nd Airborne is standing next to him in army fatigues. Unlike Clyde and Donnie, they each have their own pair of binoculars.

As David scans the campus grounds, his binoculars stop their slow scan of the forest above the dormitory. Suddenly, he laughs loudly. "What is that?" he asks. "Are you seeing what I'm seeing?"

"Where?" Joshua asks as he briefly disengages from his binoculars to look at David.

"Nine o'clock, up on the hill behind the dormitory," the Mossad agent replies.

Joshua lifts his digital camo binoculars to his eyes and focuses on the area indicated by David. A few seconds later, he exclaims, "Are you kidding me! There are two goons up in those trees!"

"That's what I'm seeing," David replies. "I'm glad you see them too, or I'd think I'm hallucinating."

"What are those turkeys doing up there?" Joshua asks his binoculars. "Oh, I get it," he mumbles a second later. "The bigger guy has field glasses and is surveilling the students in the cemetery."

"If I had a rifle, I could shoot them out of that tree without a scope," David remarks, laughing.

"Yeah, they're not exactly conducting secret surveillance," the lieutenant colonel quips.

"What do you recommend?" David asks.

"I was just going to ask you that," Joshua says.

"You outrank me," the Mossad agent replies. "Besides, this is your country, not mine. I'm here for recon only. Unless, of course, the monster shows himself, and I have no choice but to apprehend him, dead or alive."

"Well, then," Joshua says, as he slaps his spiritual son on the shoulder, "as a chaplain, I recommend we pray for God's wisdom. Then, as a military officer, I'd say we need to radio our findings to the others and prepare to spring the trap. We just need to confirm there aren't any other unfriendlies lurking around. I'm not convinced those two tree-huggers are the only spooks around tonight. So, keep your eyes open."

"Yes, sir!" David replies with a broad smile as he salutes the man who planted the seed of Jesus' love in his heart when he was just a boy back in Sharm el Sheikh. He lifts his binoculars to his eyes once again to observe the two men who are about twenty feet up in the trees.

Suddenly, he laughs and asks incredulously, "Is the smaller guy doing what I think he's doing?"

———

Jack issues instructions, and soon the eight poles designed to support the tarp are spaced around the disfigured gray-granite Sutherington monument and the six sunken gravestones. The sharpened ends of the poles are insert-ed into the ground, and then Stewart, who has proven to be the strongest of them all, climbs up on the stepladder and pounds them into the ground with a short-handled sledgehammer.

Stewart informs his peers that he acquired his impressive strength from splitting wood when he was a boy.

When the poles are secured in the ground, the six students staple tarps to the poles. Soon, the 20x20 site is encircled by a green, plastic wall that is almost as opaque as a rock. It will serve its purpose well. In only fifteen minutes, the area has been properly prepared for the exhumation of great-great-great grandmother Agatha Sutherington's grave.

The Academy students gather inside the area encased by the green wall around them and the gray ceiling above them. They stare down at the six markers that have been all but swallowed by the ground. The barely visible graves are spaced about four feet apart.

"Before we dig," Jack says, "keep in mind that the JLS journal might be a hoax and that the only thing we'll find in this grave will be what's left of Agatha. Madeline DaFoe may not be buried here. Maybe she had to escape her husband's abuse and ran off to New York City."

Jack pauses and adjusts his hoodie to keep the mist off his face. "On the other hand, Jacob Lane Sutherington's journal seems legitimate so far. In addition, the newspaper articles from the late 1800s do report that my great-great grandfather's wife and children were killed execution-style by someone who appears to have been seeking revenge against Jacob. Who had a motive for such vile acts except for Philip DaFoe, a man exacting revenge against the killer of his wife?"

"Madeline DaFoe is buried beneath our feet," Armando announces with conviction. "I feel it in my bones."

Three of the other Grave Reapers groan and then laugh. Emily remains disengaged, strangely unexcited by one of her favorite activities—sleuthing. Stewart nods his head—once.

"Okay, then," Jack says. "Let's pray before we dig. Jesus, what we're doing now may or may not have any eternal significance. I sure don't know. My prayer, however, is that what we're about to do here will somehow bring glory to your name. If nothing else, may our digging here in this place that honors the dead remind us of the brevity of life so that we might be reminded to live every moment with eternity in view."

He pauses and then adds, "Help us not to store up treasures on this earth where moths consume, and rust destroys, and thieves break in and steal. Help us instead to store up treasures in heaven where moths and rust and thieves do not even exist. For where our treasures are...there our hearts will be as well. Amen."

Jack checks his phone. The digital display announces 6:31 p.m. They are now sixteen minutes behind their target time. Motivated to hurry, Jack says, "Stew and Manny, let's pull the sod aside. Be careful not to rip it too much; we need to roll it back afterwards and make this site look undisturbed."

The three men pull out long, stiff knives and carefully cut an outline in the grass that is six feet wide and ten feet long. They practiced the technique in Dr. Windsor's backyard just yesterday, so they are adept at the task. Then they rip up the edge of the sod all along the ten-foot length.

Next, all six students get down on their knees and, by a process of ripping and rolling, remove the grass carpet from the grave. When they are done, they have a large roll of sod that looks like a big pipe.

When the heavy sod has been moved out of the way, the three young men grab spades and begin digging into the soil that has not been disturbed in over a century. Recent rains have softened the ground, and any frost that may have been in the topsoil has long since melted, so the digging is not difficult beyond the sheer effort of removing it. The clay in the soil is minimal, so their spades slice easily into the black earth and remove sizeable chunks with each bite.

"Can you imagine Jacob digging this grave up by himself?" Emily comments to her fellow grave diggers. She is transferring excavated soil onto a tarp lying next to the grave.

"And in the middle of the night," Rachel adds.

"And after he had killed a woman," Aly says. "I think this necropolis would be even more terrifying when you are burying someone you just killed."

The radio attached to Jack's belt squawks. He detaches it from his belt and thumbs the PTT button on the side of the walkie-talkie. "Jack, here. Go again."

"We have eyes on two intruders coming your way," he hears Joshua warn. "I advise sending someone out to ward them off."

Jack looks around at the other Grave Reapers, who are eyeing him with concern. "Copy and 10-4. We'll take care of it. Over and out."

Jack smiles as he reattaches the radio to his belt. "I've always wanted to say '10-4' and 'over and out,'" he says with a laugh. Turning serious, he asks, "Do I have any volunteers to check out the intruders coming our way? It's probably Ed and Margaret."

"I'll go," Rachel says, raising her hand."

Armando laughs and says, "Rachel, this isn't third grade. You don't have to raise your hand here in cemetery class. Just say, 'I'll go.'"

The man known as Syko Loco in another lifetime—before he was born to new life—glances at The Intellect and adds, "No disrespect intended, Stewart." He sounds genuinely apologetic.

Stewart looks at him but says nothing. No erupting volcanos burn in his eyes tonight.

"I'll go with Rachel," Emily says without raising her hand.

"Okay," Jack replies with a smile, "go ward off those intruders. If one of them happens to look like the cemetery man I described to you this morning, get back here right away."

"On it," Rachel says with a smirk.

Jack shakes his head and smiles. "Get moving, private," he orders in an exaggerated commanding voice.

After the two women have left, Armando, Stewart, and Jack continue to dig while Aly sifts through the soil, searching for artifacts. The three men are now up to their knees in the grave.

"Is it weird knowing you're digging up your great-great-great grandmother?" Armando asks as he throws a shovelful of dirt on one of the tarps beside the grave.

Jack wipes sweat from his forehead with the arm of his hoodie. "Haven't thought about it much, to be honest," he responds.

"I dug up several graves back in the day," Armando confesses.

"Why?" Aly asks, wrinkling her nose.

"Looking for pieces," he says. "Guns. Rumor had it that a rival gang had buried them with one of their homies and planned to come back and dig them up after the heat cooled off a bit. Thought we'd beat them to it."

"It is hot out in Los Angeles," Aly agrees with a nod of her head. "I do remember a lot of hot days when I lived out there as a young child."

Armando breaks out in loud laughter. Jack chuckles and shakes his head. Stewart's eyes notably glimmer in the misty evening air.

"What's so funny?" the small Saudi-Thai woman asks as she looks up from her sifting. "I made another language mistake, didn't I."

"Armando, it's your story," Jack comments. "Tell Aly what's so funny."

The believer in Christ, who has the images of Raul, Miguel, and Jesus tattooed on his body, smiles at the wide-eyed woman who is kneeling on the ground beside the three diggers. "My dear Aliyah," he says, "whenever a gangbanger mentions the 'heat,' he's never referring to the air temperature. He's always talking about members of law enforcement, i.e., the police."

"Oh," Aly says as she attempts to wipe dirt off her nose with the back of her hand, only to inadvertently rub dirt on her forehead. "Thanks for explaining it to me," she says with rare sarcasm. "Next time you guys make a mistake, I'll laugh at you, too. That includes you, Stewart Olson," she says with a smile.

Jack notices that Aly seems extra perky. Then he remembers that David Abramovich is in town, and he smiles to himself.

By now, the rectangular hole has been dug to a depth of three feet. Only

Jack and Stewart remain in the grave. Armando happily exited the hole a few minutes earlier when Jack asked him to get out and begin carving away dirt from the sides of the grave. Aly continues to rake through the extracted soil with a small garden tool.

"We're back," Rachel's voice announces as she and Emily walk back into the small enclosure.

"It was Margaret and Ed," Emily informs the others, "the couple that spoke with Jack and Stewart earlier. They don't seem to be the type of people who would be Draegan's spies."

"But, wow, that Margaret is one curious woman," Rachel says, slowly running her fingers through her misted auburn hair. "And sharp. She actually asked us if a body was being exhumed over here!"

"Seriously?" Armando asks as he gets up off his knees. "What did you tell her?"

Rachel looks over at her sidekick and says, "Emily proved to be even smarter than Margaret," she reports with a laugh. "She told the curious woman that a grave was being excavated to look for the presence of a flesh-eating bacteria."

Stewart, who has been unusually quiet, interjects, "Every grave has flesh-eating bacteria, at least the more recent burials."

Emily nods her head and replies, "Yes, Mr. Fagani told us yesterday that during the initial stage of decay, the cells in the bodies of the deceased begin to self-digest, and bacteria increases. We'll check for the presence of bacteria in Agatha's grave, but it should be long gone by now."

"Looks like you guys are making good progress," Rachel says as she walks up to the deepening hole. "Any signs of the casket yet?"

"Nope," Jack replies as he pulls up the sleeves of his hoodie and begins to dig again. "But we're deep enough now that we're being more careful how hard we drive the spades into the dirt. As Fagani told us, Elijah Skaggs' records show that this grave wasn't as deep as many others due to a shelf of rock that runs beneath this part of the cemetery."

It is now 8:00 p.m. The sun had set fifteen minutes ago behind the hill above the dormitory, and twilight is creeping through the place of the dead. The cemetery feels eerie with the persistent mist, the settling darkness, and the vault of low-hanging clouds above them.

"We're going to need the lights," Aly says. "I can't see much of anything in this dirt anymore."

"Soil," Armando says.

Aly stares at Armando and says, "What?"

"It's soil, not dirt," the man from LA responds. "Dirt is what you sweep up in your garage. Soil is what you plant things in. This is soil, mi amiga, not dirt. Those words come directly from Mr. Fagani," he says with a laugh.

Emily and Rachel each grab a battery-operated work light from the pile of work gear and walk over to the hole that is looking more and more like a grave. They switch on the lights, and the whole enclosure comes alive with illumination. When the lights have been optimally situated, the two women begin assisting Aly to comb through the dirt that is being removed from the grave.

Fifteen minutes go by, and the night changes from dusk to darkness. The mist turns into a persistent drizzle, and before long, everything is soaking wet. Armando stops digging and directs Emily and Rachel to help him hold a tarp over the grave. Jack and Stewart keep digging carefully. Now they are over four feet down.

Jack opens his mouth to wonder aloud if they have been hornswoggled by Jacob, but just then, his fellow grave digger announces, "I may have found something. Shine one of those light over here."

Emily releases her corner of the tarp and adjusts the angle of the work light that sits on the ground beside the grave. "What is it, Stewart?" she inquires as she looks down at the Intellect, who now is on his knees in the rectangular shaft.

Stewart busies himself with something at the bottom of the hole, then stands up and holds out his hand. "We're definitely standing on top of somebody's decayed body," he says.

Emily shines the work light on Stewart's hand. The bright light exposes several slivers of dark wood and what appears to be tiny fragments of much lighter wood.

"Them thar is bones," Armando says, peeking beneath the tarp he is holding. "Bone shards," to be exact. "And I'm glad you're touching them and not me."

"We're in," Jack states as he looks at his fellow Grave Reapers with solemn eyes. "We're in the casket now. These bone fragments are either from my great-great-great grandmother or Madeline or both." He looks at Stewart and adds, "We need to be extra careful now. And maybe we should put the latex gloves on."

The bespectacled man standing in the grave beside Jack nods his head and gazes at him with the owl eyes. Then he extracts the gloves from his pocket and pulls them on. Soon, he bends down and begins digging again but now with a smaller spade equipped with a much shorter handle. Jack pulls on his latex gloves as well. As he does so, he does not notice that he accidentally turns down the volume on the walkie-talkie. Armando drops a medium-sized plastic bin into the grave to collect any remains or artifacts the two diggers might encounter.

A few minutes later, Jack looks up into Emily's face. She is miles away, emotionally detached, looking disinterested. He looks from Emily over to the Intellect, who is digging beside him. Then he asks Stewart if Emily could spell him for a while, hoping that she might engage a bit more. The man from Minnesota hesitates but then nods his head and defers to Emily. He climbs out of the deepening grave, and Emily slides down next to Jack.

For the next fifteen minutes, the students work together, digging and sifting. More bone shards are discovered, along with larger splinters of wood. Several displaced teeth are unearthed, and later, they discover a skull with a few molars still attached to the jaws. Emily and Jack eye each other solemnly and set the skull aside carefully in one corner of the grave since they have no plans to remove it from the burial site.

Shortly after the skull is found, Emily unearths a necklace of dirt-en-crusted gems, which she places in the plastic bin. Then she finds small piec-es of cloth that mostly disintegrate in her hands.

As Jack continues to dig carefully in the artificially illuminated grave, his mind keeps returning to thoughts of death. Against his will, he remem-bers the day of his father's funeral.

He felt so lost that day, so scared—like a rudderless ship tossed about by Himalayan- sized waves. He had no idea who he was, and there was no one around to lead him forward into his unknown future.

It was hot and windy the day his father went into the ground. Seven-year-old Jack was the last one at the gravesite following the brief service. He sat on his knees on one of the white wooden folding chairs under the funeral tent that flapped violently in the stiff breeze like it was in the throes of death.

As everyone turned their backs on his father and trudged back to their cars with heavy feet and even heavier hearts, Jack watched them. Weirdly, their legs and arms appeared to swing in slow motion as they walked through the shimmering heat. His eyes especially followed his mother and three younger sisters as they retreated farther and farther away among the tombstones until he could no longer see them.

He never told anyone what he felt inside that day, how he wanted everyone he loved to leave him at the cemetery and never come back. He was feeling the throat-strangling, heart-crushing presence of grief and wanted everyone to go away now so he would not have to feel their loss in the future. He wanted to get all the pain and sadness over with on the same miserable day. He could not imagine how he would ever survive if he had to go through death again. He struggled to breathe, and he could not swallow.

His eyes blurred with tears as he slid off the disgusting white chair that lied about the beauty of things and stumbled over to the coffin that rested on green straps stretched across the terrifying hole. In the distance, he saw the graveyard man lurking next to a tree, smoking. Jack knew the man was going to crank his father's body down into the ground as soon as he left, and he would never see him again. Jack was not going to let that happen. So, he lingered next to the coffin, protecting it. Protecting his father.

He knew his mother would not come for him. As always, she was overwhelmed and unavailable. Besides, his sisters needed her. They were like three piglets he had seen at the state fair sucking everything out of the recumbent sow who had such meager supplies, to begin with, that she could not even remain standing on her four feet.

And he remembered what his father had told him with his final words: *Take care of your mother, Jack.*

Jack rested his cheek against the hot steel skin of the sunbaked casket and wept. He hugged it as if it were his father's chest. And he thought. He thought the thoughts of a seven-year-old boy ...

He thought about the last time he had seen his father—normal, that is. They had thrown the football in the backyard, and his dad had tackled him again and again. He always wondered how such a big man could tackle him without ever hurting him. And then he and his dad went to get ice cream sundaes. How he loved eating ice cream with his dad. It hurt his chest remembering that day.

He thought his dad was invincible...

Alone at the gravesite, hugging the terrible steel maggot that had swallowed his dad's body, he decided two things in his young mind. No, they were bigger and more binding than decisions: they were life-long vows that carried the same gravity as when he swore to be blood brothers with Steve Goodspeed, the boy who lived across the street from his house. To make the promise real, the two boys had cut their fingers in the treehouse with a small pocketknife and rubbed them together, mingling their blood.

The first blood vow he made at the coffin was that he was going to get crazy good at football. His father would be so proud of him when he made it to the pros. Every time he ran out on the field, his dad would think of him, and he would think of his dad. Every time. They would remain connected forever through football.

And then there was the second blood vow: He would never love anyone again—not even Goldie, his golden retriever. He would like Goldie, but he would not love her.

No, he must never let anyone get close to his heart. He could not risk the terrible pain of loss, so he could not allow what came before the loss: love. And he would certainly never permit himself to need anyone. How awful it felt to depend on someone and then have him go away, never to come back again. It made his chest throb, and his throat burn like lava was gurgling up from his stomach. He could not get enough air in his lungs, and the blasted tears prevented him from seeing the world clearly.

And then there was the ache he felt in his whole body. It seemed related to but somehow separate from the physical pain in his chest. It was unbearable. He was afraid it would never go away. If it never did, he was not sure what he was going to do. But if it did go away, he could not allow it to return. The simple solution was to never love anything again.

Jack swallows hard as he carefully removes a thin layer of soil from Agatha's grave. He sighs as the drizzle drips off the edge of his hood and onto his hand, creating clean rivulets on the dirty latex gloves. He remembers from the journal readings how terribly Jacob missed his wife and children when they were buried beneath the ground, and he wonders if his great-great-grandfather ever made a vow not to love again ...

One day, years after his father's funeral, something unexpectedly scaled the walls of Jack's impregnable fortress. He was not planning on it. He was not looking for it. It was not like it came out of nowhere. The siege ramp that finally rose to the top of his fortress wall had been under construction for years at the direction of a God who specialized in wise and timely campaigns waged against the most guarded hearts.

He was seventeen years old and began the day like any other Friday in autumn—looking forward to the football game that night as a brief reprieve from the heaviness that resided in his chest. Many years ago, it had been the ache.

Over time, it had become heaviness. He could never escape it. Like his grandmother used to tell him before she would read him a Bible story, "In life, it's always something, Jacky. It's always something."

She had left him, too, dying only a year after her son. But her leaving did not hurt Jack nearly as much as his father's departure. By then, his heart was already partially protected by the wall that was under construction.

After the football game that Friday night, he was invited to a party at a different house than the usual ones. Several of his teammates discouraged him from going to that house, but he decided to go anyway. He always left the other party houses buzzed but still feeling empty and lonely anyway, so why not try something new?

There was no alcohol at this new house, and therefore none of the familiar drinking games and flirtatious girls with their hungry eyes and macho males flaunting their antics designed to impress the flirtatious girls. The parents were even home at this new house, hanging out with the kids! How strange was that.

At this version of a "party," Jack encountered three guys from school that he considered acquaintances at best. They played basketball for the team that finished runner-up in the state tournament the previous winter. (Jack never wanted to play basketball simply because it was not football, the sport that connected him and his dad.) The three ballers seemed genuine. They were not intimidated by the quarterback who had already broken school records for touchdowns—both passing and rushing—and total yards thrown. No, they treated him like just a regular guy.

The four of them talked for hours—about life. Then, unexpectedly, the topic shifted to Jesus. Jack's father had talked to him several times about Jesus, and his mother had always been what some referred to as a nominal believer, but Jack himself had walked away from religion not long after completing confirmation class in the ninth grade. He got nothing out of going to church except some vanilla sermons about loving the world and being a good person, and becoming a responsible steward of mother earth.

Church never solved the heaviness inside of him; if anything, it contributed to it by stirring up the emptiness inside him but never filling it. Whenever he talked with the pastor at the church, he was reminded of his mother. After an encounter with her, he usually felt disappointed. He was hoping for a steak dinner but walked away with a cold hot dog on a day-old bun.

The three guys at the party were not empty or disappointing. They spoke a language he had never heard before. They told him that he must never settle for knowing about God but to know him personally, like a friend. The phrase that riveted Jack's attention was when one of the guys, Gene, told him that being a Christian was not about practicing a religion or going to church but about knowing God like a son knows his dad.

Those words were a hook for Jack. He did not know it at the time, but after hearing what Gene said, something entered his mind that he would never forget or successfully resist.

After he left the party that night, he went home and prayed in the darkness of his lonely bedroom in the basement. No, he did not *pray*. As Dave, one of the guys at the party, told him to do, he simply *talked* to Jesus.

Communicating with Jesus as he would with a friend seemed strange and awkward at the time. Nonetheless, Jack told Jesus that he was not even sure He existed but that his life was not going very well, and he needed all the help he could get. He said something about being sorry for the things he had done wrong against God and other people and expressed a desire to be a better person.

"Please, come into my heart," were his final words before he climbed into bed that early morning and went to sleep.

When he woke up the next morning, discouragingly, nothing felt different. Over the next several weeks, he repeated his prayer over and over, but he still felt the same. Then one day, when he was sitting at his desk in one of his classes, he randomly looked out the window and into the cloudless October sky.

At that precise and unexpected moment, he sensed that Jesus was living inside of him instead of far off in the distant heavens. It was on that day that his heart began its long journey back from the isolated place where his childhood vow had exiled him. The ultimate Grave Robber had saved him from the place of the dead.

Jack realizes that he has stopped digging. He refocuses on the trowel in his

hand and begins to scrape away the dirt again and transport it to the five-gallon bucket sitting next to him. As he works, he talks to his best friend in his mind. He thanks Jesus for pursuing him seven years ago, leaving the ninety-nine other sheep to come after him, the one lost sheep.

He also thanks his Deliverer, even as he unearths more bone slivers, that death is not the end. When his heart stops beating, his lungs stop filling with air, and his brain experiences one last burst of activity before shutting down and beginning to decay, he now knows he is not at the end of it all but at the beginning.

The words, "I am the resurrection and the life," flow through Jack's mind like the rushing stream in Colorado near the camp where he had worked for years. In that moment, it is not lost on him that while he is physically in the bowels of a grave filled with all the evidence of death, he is spiritually in the presence of his loving Father in heaven, who has promised him that he will live forever. Yes, knowing Jesus is reward enough for Jack. But the added benefit that death no longer scares him is also amazing! Especially after little Jack's earlier experiences.

Then comes the moment the Screaming Eagles have been anticipating, even though by highly disciplined intention, none of them has spoken of it during the exhumation. Jack pushes aside a thin layer of dirt and finds himself staring into the eye socket of a second skull.

CHAPTER 22

THE DISCOVERY OF THE CENTURY

Hey, guys," he says far too calmly to the other Grave Reapers. Stewart has already seen Jack's discovery because he has been adjusting the small work light that illuminates the grave. Rare for the Intellect, his eyes are large with excitement.

Emily twists around on her knees, and the other three students peer over the edge of the grave.

"Ay, *caramba*!" Armando cries.

"A second skull!" Rachel exclaims. "Jacob's journal is legit! It must be Agatha since it's located over a foot beneath the other skull."

Aly is already on her knees next to the hole. When she sees the skull, she allows her body to sag down on her elbows as she releases a long sigh. "Finally," she says, her voice flooded with relief, "after waiting and imagining it for so many weeks, we now see it with our eyes. This is amazing! Thank you, Lord!"

Emily looks at Jack and comments with more energy than she has shown all day, "We have Agatha and Madeline. Let's find the other ladies."

Jack looks up at the four heads hanging over the edge of the grave. Eerily, in the weak light, they look like they are floating in the air, disconnected from their bodies. For a moment, he remembers his nightmare with the crooked-nosed, stringy-haired cemetery man, and he feels a wave of panic crest in his chest. He feels a sudden urge to climb out of the grave. Instead, he closes his eyes and takes a deep breath.

"Are you okay, Jack?" Emily asks, leaning closer to him.

Jack nods his head unconvincingly and says, "Just...a bad memory," he says. "I'll be okay." He takes a deep breath and glances up at Armando. "Manny, take a look outside the enclosure to see if the coast is clear. I don't want to be surprised by anyone, even Margaret and Ed."

"10-4, Juan," his roommate says with a wink and a smile.

Jack and Emily return to excavating the grave as the drizzle continues and the cold night air seeks out the lowest pockets in the greasy burial cavity. As they carefully remove the soil with small trowels, they unearth several metal buttons, an iron handle undoubtedly belonging to the disintegrated casket, two rings, another necklace, several screws, and a hinge.

Jack swivels around on his knees and begins scraping away dirt about three feet from where he had found the skull. A minute later, his efforts are rewarded as his trowel strikes something firm. A rock? No, it sounds metallic.

He lays aside his tool and begins digging with his fingers. Armando, who has just returned from his reconnaissance, asks, "What is it, Juan?"

He continues to dig as he replies, "I thought I was looking for a leather purse or something like that—not that it would still be intact, of course. But I've found something hard instead. I think it's a box."

Jack pries a tin container from the fingers of the earth that have clutched it for over a century. It is half the size of an old cigar box, approximately 4" wide by 5" long and less than 3" deep. It looks ancient. It is heavy. Directly beneath it, he spots the corner of another box peeking out of the dirt. He digs it up as well. It, too, is heavy. Jack's heart begins to beat faster. Five sets of curious eyes follow his gloved hands as he places both boxes into the plastic bin.

Jack and Emily dig around the grave to a depth of four or five more inches but find nothing except for more slivers of wood and bone. "It looks like we're done here," Jack announces as he surveys the floor of the grave around him. He leaves the second skull in situ.

He takes one last look into the eyeless orbits of his great-great-great grandmother, Agatha Sutherington, and says, "I hope to see you in heaven, Agatha. We'll have a lot to talk about." Then he gets to his feet.

When he is fully erect, his chest is level with the lip of the grave. He notices that the world around the gravesite has become extremely dark compared to the illuminated grave he has been working in. Not even the light of the moon or the stars temper the darkness obscured as they are by the invisible clouds.

"I have to believe we found everything we were after," he says to his fellow exhumers.

"Just make sure you're absolutely certain you're done," Stewart advises. "We're going to backfill the grave immediately after you and Emily climb out of there."

Jack looks down into the grave as he ponders Stewart's wise advice. Just then, a shadow rushes across his line of vision, and he pictures the two women lying in the single casket, Madeline on top and Agatha beneath. Out of nowhere, he hears a mantra chanted in his head. *Two for one. Two in one. Two-one.*

Jack immediately thrusts himself up and out of the grave as if it had suddenly been overrun by scorpions.

"We're done," he announces without hesitation.

"Take a few pictures, Jack," Rachel suggests, "of the skulls and the inside of the grave."

"I've taken lots already," Emily comments flatly. "I think we're good."

"Well, okay then," Rachel replies, rubbing her hands together. "I, for one, am ready to get out of this place. It's beginning to feel a bit creepy out here. All those middle school cemetery stories have been flooding my mind for the last hour.

"I can't seem to get rid of the one where the teenager is locked in a mausoleum overnight by his amazing friends—not. When they return to let him out in the morning, he doesn't say a word but only stares around with vacant eyes like a zombie. He can't even blink anymore. One version of the story says his hair had turned as white as snow. He never speaks again, and he lives out the rest of his days in an insane asylum."

Armando's eyes grow large. "Yeah, let's pack it up," he says with too much enthusiasm.

Emily lifts the blue plastic bin up to Jack, and he sets it beside the open grave. He is reaching down to help his archaeological assistant out of the hole when a voice from his not-so-distant past growls, "I'll take that, Jack."

Jack wheels around and sees a large figure standing at the entrance of the enclosure. He cannot see the man's facial features because the work lights are shining in his eyes, but he knows who it is. In a déjà vu moment right out of his nightmare, the big bear-man is back—the same one who attacked him on the university campus. He is wearing the same trench coat he had on the last time Jack was unfortunate enough to encounter him.

"Give it to me!" the man growls.

Jack glances around at his fellow Grave Reapers. Their faces are all frozen with fear—except for Stewart, of course, whose countenance is also frozen but with the usual impassivity. Emily is still standing in the grave. Jack imagines six more bodies buried on top of Agatha and Madeline.

The whole scene strikes Jack as surreal. He has a fleeting picture of where he would be right now if God had not called him to the Academy, namely, working at the familiar camp nestled among beautiful mountains with the whitewater stream rushing over the rocks behind the chapel. But here he is instead, standing in a cemetery with five people he had never even met seven months ago, exhuming two bodies under the cover of night. What a difference one decision can make ...

Jack looks down at Emily, who is still in the grave, and at his four other friends, who are standing around in the steady drizzle. They are all here out of allegiance to him and in obedience to God. They are true friends—sisters and brothers he would die for in a heartbeat. Yes, he realizes in that moment that he would die for any one of them.

He turns his attention back to the hulking figure who is blocking the entrance—and the exit—to the enclosure. For some reason, most likely because the Grave Reapers' team has decided that the police commissioner is the boss of this man standing in front of him, he thinks of Draegan DaFoe and how he had looked at Emily. He remembers his arrogant voice and the small eyes that shifted from bemused to flat to violent in a moment's time. He recalls how the man cruelly maligned his father. He will not forget his bloody attack in Jerusalem and his threats promising future violence if Jack refuses his demands.

He also wonders where the rest of the team is. They should have intervened by now ...

"Do you still want the journal?" Jack asks as a stalling technique.

"You know what I want," the man says as he steps into the small enclosure. It is only then that Jack sees the smaller man behind him.

385

Jack is now able to see the big man's features more clearly. His head is impressively large. The front half is bald, while the sides and back are plastered with long stringy hair that falls past his shoulders. A straggly beard mingles with his hair in an unholy union. His nose is bent to the right, and his teeth are in significant disarray in his mouth. For some reason, the partly yellowed and blackened teeth remind Jack of the monuments in this older part of the cemetery that lean cockeyed in every which direction.

The man standing before him in the long trench coat is unquestionably the same one who attacked him at the university and who appeared in Violet's dreams. More relevant to Jack in the moment, he is the "cemetery man" Jack saw in his nightmare that took place here in this very cemetery; the nightmare where the big man stabbed him and shoved him into an empty grave—maybe the one where Emily is standing at this moment. Maybe his dream was prophetic...

"No, I don't know what you want," Jack replies.

"I want what's in there," he demands, pointing a large dirty finger at the blue plastic bin.

"It's not yours," Jack parries.

"Maybe it is, and maybe it isn't," the big man says, his voice beginning to rise with anger. Jack recognizes the harsh tone from the university and feels adrenaline begin to course through his body.

Out of the corner of his eye, Jack sees Emily slide the bin back into the grave. He smiles at her courage.

"It doesn't belong to you," Jack persists.

"Neither does this knife I stole from the man I shanked in the alley last night," he lies, patting a hunting knife hidden beneath his long coat.

Clyde has never stabbed a man—except, ironically, the time he attacked

Jack on that night back in December when the big man was under the influence of meth. Never has he killed anyone. Those who are closest to him know that he is like one of those dogs with a vicious bark that rarely, if ever, bites. Of course, he does look and sound threatening, and he will use his bare hands to remove anyone who gets in his way, especially if they are smaller than him.

"Move out of the way!" the man barks.

Jack glances down at Emily. Her eyes are fixed on the intruder. They appear young. They are filled with fear. An anger rises inside of Jack as he realizes that he is weary of Emily being threatened by men. Inspired by a passionate desire to protect her, he turns back to confront the big man more forcefully this time.

The large fist strikes him hard on the chin. Jack stumbles backward and, like a strange fulfillment of his nightmare, falls into the grave, somehow missing Emily, and lands squarely on his back. Emily screams as Jack gasps for air. She bends over him, looking panicked. Jack knows the wind has only been knocked out of him, but Emily must think he has been stabbed.

Jack does not see what happens next as he lies on the bottom of the grave, grasping for air. Armando later gives him a blow-by-blow account.

When the trench coat man strikes Jack, Stewart shouts, "No!" which in and of itself is a rare display of emotion for the Intellect only matched by his anger toward Armando at the university debate. (Stewart himself will admit later that the large man reminded him of a bully he knew back in high school named Billy Reisch.) But what Stewart does next is even more amazingly unusual for him—and very unintellectual.

Stewart leaps toward the big man "with the agility of a mountain lion," as Armando describes it to Jack later.

Surprised, the intruder swings impulsively at his unexpected attacker.

Stewart ducks under the man's undisciplined strike and launches his body and right fist at the attacker's lower chest. The combination of the big man's body following his punch coupled with Stewart's fist flying at the man's chest is the perfect storm for a violent collision.

When the Intellect's blow strikes the man's solar plexus, he literally crumples to the ground. Armando will swear after the incident that he has never seen a punch to the chest knock a man out, but that is exactly what Stewart's strike accomplishes. The man is not only down, but he is out.

Nobody moves. Everyone is in shock. Seconds pass.

Eventually, the wide-eyed smaller man who had been standing behind the larger man starts backing up slowly with his hands held out in front of him. He mumbles something to Stewart about not hurting him, then abruptly turns and disappears into the darkness of the night. He is not gone long.

A moment later, David Abramovich and Joshua Bloomstrom appear at the entrance to the enclosure with the smaller man between them. The Mossad agent and the army chaplain both have a firm grip on one of the man's arms.

They shove him toward his fallen crony and then follow him into the enclosure. Directly on their heels are Dr. Windsor and Sunny Livingstone, who is wearing his red baseball hat with the initials IH sewn in black letters. The retired colonel and the owner of Lighthouse Farm rush into the small compound as breathlessly as if they had just run the hundred-yard dash.

"Sorry we're late," Dr. Windsor says apologetically. "We were checking out a suspicious SUV in the parking lot, and you were not responding to our calls on the walkie-talkie."

Jack staggers to his feet in the grave and stands up next to Emily. Sunny jumps three steps backwards. "What in the world!" he exclaims.

"Just me, guys," Jack says, still trying to recover his breath. "What happened?"

Armando smiles, and his white teeth glow in the gloomy conditions. "Chuck Norris showed up and took down the bad guy with one blow," he exclaims. "It was Stewart," he goes on to add. "I'm serious," he says, his face looking very convincing.

"What are you doing in there, Jack?" Joshua inquires. "While the rest of us are risking our lives, you're taking a dirt nap?"

"Lol," is all Jack can think to say in the moment with notable lackluster. His face still feels like he got hit by a truck. *At least I didn't get knocked out this time,* he thinks to himself. He stares at the fallen man, who is now groaning, and then at Stewart and shakes his head. "Who would've guessed," he says aloud.

Armando pulls Jack and Emily out of the grave, and they join the rest of the Grave Reapers in Grand Central Station. The small enclosure is filled with bodies, all alive except for the two in the exhumed grave.

Ever the soldier, Dr. Windsor, looks at Jack with his colonel's eyes and announces, "Alan Greenlay and his brother-in-law are still maintaining the perimeter. It's time for us to fall back to the war room."

Jack nods his head and pulls his soaked hood off his head. He runs his fingers through his medium-length damp hair and looks around at the scene that will be etched in his memory forever. Randomly, he counts the people in the small compound, including the cemetery man and his sidekick. Twelve altogether. Twelve disciples? No, two of them are not the master's men. But then, even Jesus' band of twelve disciples had one seriously bad apple. In this gathering, there just happens to be two.

"Give us fifteen minutes, Colonel," Jack says, even though he knows that Dr. Windsor does not prefer to be addressed any longer by his military rank. In the moment, however, it feels entirely appropriate to be more formal.

While the large heap on the ground moans and then finally rolls over on his back, Jack and his five peers begin shoveling the piles of dirt that had been heaped up on tarp back into the grave.

The backfilling proceeds quickly. They make sure to pack the soil down as they go. At the end, they lift the tarps and shake the remaining dirt on top of the grave. Once the excavated grave is refilled, they pack it down some more. Then they roll the displaced sod back over the barren rectangular spot and step it down with their feet.

After they dismantle the green wall and pull the poles out of the ground, they pack up the lights and miscellaneous tools employed in the disinterment mission. By this time, the large intruder is sitting up and staring at Stewart. There is a distinct expression on the large man's face. It is not anger. It looks more like wary respect.

"Where's the UTV?" Dr. Windsor inquires, glancing around the dark cemetery.

Jack glances at Stewart in the waning illumination of the battery-powered work lights and says, "We had to abandon it, sir. It broke down two hundred feet from here."

Before Jack or Dr. Windsor can say anything else, Stewart announces gravely, "It was a God thing. He wanted Jack to remember something his father told him when he was a boy."

The professor with the square shoulders and ramrod back looks from Stewart to Jack with his austere eyes and nods his head. He decides that this is not the time for more interrogatories.

As they leave the gravesite, Jack looks back over his shoulder one last time.

In the darkness, the ground in front of the large, fractured monument looks mostly undisturbed. The mist-turned-to-drizzle-turned-to-sprinkles did wet the dirt, which then stuck to the bottom of their shoes which ended up on the grass around the gravesite. Hopefully, by morning, the dirt will be washed away. Certainly, no one would ever guess that an exhumation had taken place at the gravesite the previous evening.

Little does Jack know that over a century earlier, his great-great-grandfather had the same exact thought in the same exact spot.

Instead of returning to the war room, the members of the Grave Reapers and their two detainees congregate in the Agatha room on the main floor of the edifice. There are no elevators in the massive four-story building except for one old service elevator that has been temporarily out of service for fifteen years. Since Mr. Fagani is well past using the stairs, they decide to meet in the huge cafeteria with the cupola floating above their heads like a giant, deployed parachute.

Dr. Greenlay and his wife Nancy join the twelve disciples, as do Embee, Dr. McNeely, and his wife, Sandy. Miriam is not in attendance. Although she famously stays up into the wee morning hours, she has no time for such meetings. She is at her home five blocks from campus, undoubtedly kneeling beside her bed. She has other battles to fight—in prayer.

A debriefing is held around three round tables that have been pushed together. On the middle table rests the blue plastic bin, mute but prominent. Everyone who has been in the cemetery is wet or at least still damp from the unexpected moisture of the evening. Coffee and hot tea are prepared by Dr. Windsor and the Livingstones to warm the chilled bodies.

Mr. Fagani's favorite food has been secured from an all-night bakery and is served along with the hot beverages.

Alan Greenlay's brother-in-law has been tasked with watching the apprehended unfriendlies in an adjacent room. It has been decided that the two men do not need to hear the details of the debriefing.

One by one, the three teams share their observations. Dr. Windsor and Sunny had been in a surveillance position located in Sunny's pickup truck up by the main parking lot. They had seen no activity from their position. David and Joshua, of course, amidst smiles and laughter, share about their "recon"—the lieutenant colonel's word—and their discovery of the two intruders in the tree.

"At first, I thought they were black bears," David reports with a laugh that elicits a big smile from Aly. "Then I noticed they were wearing clothes. At that point, I knew I was looking at humans, not bears."

The Mossad agent pauses and shakes his head. "I still don't know how the big guy climbed that tree wearing cowboy boots and that long, heavy trench coat," he says with another laugh.

Mr. Fagani clutches the lapels of his own ever-present trench coat and rasps with a twinkle in his faded eyes, "At least you didn't think it was me."

Everyone around the three tables laughs. Then Joshua responds, "When I saw him, I knew it wasn't you, Mr. Fagani. The bear wasn't wearing a fedora."

Everyone laughs again, hard and long. Mr. Fagani pulls a handkerchief out of his pocket and dabs at his eyes.

A minute later, the students are taking turns sharing details about the exhumation. As they talk, their listeners nod their heads, shake their heads, gasp here and there—especially Embee—and utter words like "amazing" and "thank God" and "nicely done" and "mission accomplished."

Armando concludes their portion of the debriefing with the account of Stewart taking down the big man with a single blow. When David mentions that it must have been a calculated blow to the solar plexus delivered with tremendous force, Stewart nods his head. He informs his listeners that he learned how to administer the punch at a small dojo in Duluth in anticipation of a showdown with Billy Reisch.

Everyone is impressed by Stewart's courage. Armando, who had a front-row seat to the whole encounter, is especially excited about his classmate's feat. He says, "Never in all my life have I seen a man strike as quickly or as hard as Stewart did. He was muy magnifica! Just as Goliath was felled by one of David's small stones, the cemetery man was felled with one blow from Stewart!"

The Intellect is not accustomed to public acclaim. His cheeks turn a bright red, but his face remains impassive. He clearly does not know what to do with the generous affirmation. He looks down at his hands and says nothing. Rachel pats him on the back and says, "Way to go, Stewart. You saved the day."

When the debriefing is finally complete, and the clock on the stone wall tells them that midnight is only a few minutes away, Dr. Windsor looks over at Jack and the other Screaming Eagles and says, "We're going to interrogate the two bad guys now. Why don't you go examine what you found during the exhumation? I'll call you when we're finished so we can fill you in on anything you should know. I'm not at all pleased with the big man who has found it necessary to attack you twice now."

Jack and Armando each grab a handle of the blue bin and walk toward the exit. As the six students are leaving the room, the two apprehended men are brought in. The larger man is still wearing his brown trench coat while the smaller man is dressed in army fatigues with a matching baseball cap that he wears backward on his head. They are seated at the tables in front of Dr. Windsor, David Abramovich, Joshua Bloomstrom, Mr. Fagani, Sunny and Embee Livingstone, Milner McNeely and his wife, Sandy, Alan and Nancy Greenlay, and Alan's brother-in-law, the state patrol officer. Jack glances at the big man in the trench coat. He notices that the unkempt man is eyeing Stewart closely.

A short time later, the six students convene their own debriefing up in the familiar fireside room, otherwise known as Hawkstern's Aerie or the Moses room. The blue bin is sitting on the floor next to the large square coffee table in the lounge area. Rachel spreads out paper towels on the table that she grabbed from the woman's restroom down the hall. Jack and Armando sit on the couch while the other four Grave Reapers find comfortable perches in the overstuffed chairs.

Jack begins the meeting simply by praying, "Be glorified in our midst and be honored in our discoveries, Jesus." Then he begins removing the items from the bin and sets them on the paper towels. When he is done, the tabletop exhibit includes two necklaces, a bracelet, one broach, four rings, the two tin boxes, and a single small skeleton key. All the items are covered with dirt and corrosion. Some of them have been partially washed by last night's rain. Everyone is leaning over the table to get a closer look at the objects recovered from the grave cohabited by Agatha Sutherington and Madeleine DaFoe.

"Well," Rachel says, her eyes bright with excitement, "are you going to open the boxes today or tomorrow?"

Jack glances over at the young woman with the burning curiosity and says with a smile, "Which one do you think I should open first?"

Rachel hesitates a moment and then points to the box on the right.

"That one," she says with resolve.

Jack reaches over and picks up the box, and sets it in front of him. He stares at it for a while and then comments without looking up, "If this box contains the Lady Libertys, they're not going to be nice and shiny, are they, Stew?"

The Intellect replies, "I did some research in preparation for the exhumation. I discovered that silver is a moderately reactive metal. If buried underground for more than a century, it will corrode. Both chlorine and sulfur eat silver, leaving a deposit that will change the appearance of the coin often to a black color.

"Depending on the soil conditions, the coins will most likely range from slightly black to very black. The bad news is that when you clean them chemically, they might end up pitted due to corrosion or appear blotchy with gray spots. The good news is that sometimes, with professional cleaning, they can be restored to their original pristine appearance."

"Okay, then," Jack says, "let's have a look inside and see if these are the Lady Libertys Jacob mentioned and, if so, what condition they're in."

While Jack attempts to open the lid on the first box, an audience of five watches with great anticipation. They know that a rare treasure might be sitting on the table in front of them.

The tin container is highly corroded, so the lid proves impossible to remove with hands alone. Armando gives Jack a large pliers he had borrowed from Zeke at the Silver Lake Lodge hotel several days earlier for this exact eventuality. With assistance from Stewart, he forces all four sides open one by one. Fortunately, there are no hinges on the box.

When the lid is loose, Jack lifts it off the small box. Then, one by one, he removes coins that are in various states of corrosion. Before long, twenty-six coins are resting on the table. Jack picks one up and attempts to rub it so he can read the inscription better.

"Be careful not to scratch it," Stewart comments. "Hairlines reduce the value."

Jack rubs the coin softly with a paper towel and then bends over to examine it more closely. "Well, the one side certainly looks like a seated Lady Liberty," he observes. "The other side—" he pauses as he turns the coin over carefully— "has an eagle facing toward my left."

"Can you see a mint mark?" Stewart inquires as his hand creeps toward the coin.

Jack rubs the coin ever so gently and then squints at it under the light of his phone. "Yes, I see a mint mark." He lifts the coin up close to his right eye and then says, "It appears to be an 'S.'"

Aly smiles at Emily, and Rachel squeals in excitement. Armando announces, "Eureka! We have found them! The 1870 S Seated Lady Liberty Silver Dollars!"

Aly's face glows as she remarks, "Just think, up until now, it was believed that there were only what—twelve of them in existence? These coins more than triple that number."

"The good news is that these are the coins we hoped to recover," Jack comments. "The bad news is that with twenty-six more of them in existence, maybe their value will lessen."

"What are they worth, Stewart?" Armando asks as he slaps the man on the back playfully. "Just a good ballpark estimate."

Stewart looks sidelong at his classmate and adjusts his glasses. After a short pause, he says, "In mint condition, well over a million dollars apiece. Maybe closer to two million. But the condition of these coins is anything but mint, at least in their current state. They need to be professionally cleaned, and then their value can be accurately determined. It's likely the value of each coin will vary widely depending on their final condition."

"Open the other box," Rachel says with a feisty grin.

Jack shakes his head at his classmate with the bobbed brunette hair and smiles. He picks up the other box and sets it in front of him on the table. "This one's heavy, too," he announces. He repeats the process with the pliers, loosening the four corners of the corroded box. Then, he removes the lid and stares inside.

"What is it, Jack?" Rachel inquires. "Are there more coins?"

Jack nods his head. "They look older than the other ones. Medieval or Roman, perhaps. Yes, definitely more ancient."

Slowly, he removes the coins from their tin coffin and sets them next to the Lady Libertys. Fifteen coins this time. On the bottom of the box, he sees something that looks like a liner, and he removes it as well. It is stained with corrosion from the coins as well as the tin box.

"Almost looks like papyrus," Stewart comments as he leans in and looks at what appears to be a flat piece of leather.

"Pirate who?" Armando asks facetiously.

Stewart's eyes rivet on the group's humorist. Not unusual lately, when Armando is the trigger, they betray disgust. "Papyrus," he repeats slowly. "It's a type of writing material made from plant stalks common in Egypt. Thousands of years ago, the earliest paper was made by pounding these stalks together."

"It's very blotchy," Aly observes with her large almond eyes. "Is there anything on it?"

"Yes," Jack affirms as he carefully unfolds the papyrus. "It almost looks like a rudimentary map, but I can't be sure due to the stains. "Hold on, guys," he adds as he continues to examine the small papyrus fragment.

"There's initials in the right bottom corner—PWD."

"Philip DaFoe," Emily volunteers in a subdued voice, "along with the initial of his middle name, whatever that is."

"Maybe it's a map to the hidden DaFoe treasure trove," Rachel interjects.

"Possibly," Jack mumbles as he studies the map even more closely. "It does look like there's a trail here that turns right at the fifth or sixth arm of a path and then crosses a double line, whatever that means."

"Railroad tracks," Emily initially volunteers. "No," she corrects herself, "a river. The river that Jacob mentioned in his final communication. Do you remember what he said about the 'river room'?"

"It must be a map to the cave room where Jacob met Philip!" Aly asserts. "That means there's an underground river, just as Jacob mentioned."

"It's so badly stained that it's difficult to tell how many passages are forking off from the main road," Jack says.

"Don't you mean the main tunnel?" Armando says.

"We can't assume it's a tunnel," Jack replies. "Maybe it's a map of aboveground roads."

"Possibly," Stewart interjects with hesitation. "However, after Jacob's final 'missive' we read, I'd have to agree with Emily and Armando that it points to the cave system."

"Jacob and Philip might have had their final encounter in the cave system beneath this citadel," Aly persists. "It's possible that sitting six stories beneath us is both the tomb and treasure trove of the man who murdered your great-great grandfather's family."

Jack sits back on the couch and contemplates the fair-complexioned face of the Thai woman. Then he replies, "Draegan DaFoe does seem to think I know where the body of his great-great-grandfather is, so I suppose it's fair to assume that he thinks the body is somewhere near the Academy and that the treasure is nearby."

Rachel leans over the table to get a closer look at all the coins. She carefully picks up one of the Lady Libertys and says, "It's heavy." Then she sets it back down. As she continues to examine the coins, she says so quietly that only Emily hears her, "I think we need to clear the cave-in caused by Jacob's second stick of dynamite."

Jack interlaces his fingers behind his neck and scans the faces of his fellow Grave Reapers. "Before we deal with these coins," Jack says, looking up at the ornate ceiling of the Hawkstern Aerie, "we need to figure out a schedule for the next six weeks. The spring semester will end by the middle of May. What do we need to get done before the academic year ends?"

"Like Rachel said, the tunnel needs to be excavated," Emily comments with conviction but little enthusiasm. Jack remains puzzled by the young woman's uncharacteristic lack of excitement regarding the resolution of the Sutherington mystery.

"After what Jazz told us about her great-grandmother, I think we also need to explore the woods behind Philip DaFoe's house," Armando suggests.

"First, of course, we need to determine the location of Philip's house," Stewart interjects, "to see if the house and the woods still exist today."

"We should have the coins professionally restored so their worth can be accurately appraised," Aly offers.

"After excavating the tunnel," Rachel says, "we need to locate the river room."

"And after you locate the river room," Emily adds, "you'll have to remove the blockage from the entrance to the cave room where Jacob and Philip had their duel."

Jack stares at the woman with the wide headband that hides her beautiful golden hair. He wonders if he is the only one who picked up on the pronoun Emily used. *You. Why didn't she say 'we?'* Jack asks himself. *And why am I always so attuned to what she says or doesn't say?*

"Let's also remember to pray," Armando says. "For sure, we need to pray for our safety. With that Draegan guy around—and who knows how many friends he has—we could be in great danger. We probably *are* in great danger even as we sit here."

Aly comments softly but with resolve, "And we need to be praying for David as he investigates Draegan DaFoe. If he's behind the King David bombing, he's responsible for the death of four people, including David's best friend, Daniel." The young woman's voice is calm, but it has a slight edge to it.

"Can we also remember to pray for Julianna, the daughter of Dr. Hawkstern?" Rachel says. "She's so sad and angry. She needs the love of Jesus."

"And we can't forget to pray for Drew's ongoing growth in his new faith and his relationship with his mother—especially after his father's recent death," Jack interjects.

Rachel smiles approvingly at Jack when she hears his concern for their mutual friend.

"Also, remember my brother, Moussa, as he grows deeper in his relationship with Jesus," Aly comments.

"Since we're praying for half the known world," Armando says, "pray also for Sniper-become-Miguel. He needs all the wisdom he can get to do the right thing out there in Valinda."

There is a pause. Everybody in the small circle is nodding their heads and uttering words of agreement.

Eventually, Stewart clears his throat and looks at Jack. He says, "Pray for Dr. Windsor, who is still grieving his wife, Violet. And—" the man from Minnesota stops abruptly and looks down at the coffee table. "And... and pray that the Holy Spirit will keep opening the door of my heart to trust God and other people."

The Intellect's five listeners glance around at each other with raised eyebrows and understated smiles, but no one remarks about Stewart's comment because they do not wish to embarrass their typically turtled friend who is showing increasing signs of coming out into the world.

Jack thinks to himself, *Another Stewart-sighting. Something is clearly going on with the Intellect.*

There is a long silence before Jack says, "Well, okay then, let's talk to our Father right now. We've got a lot to figure out in the next six weeks, and we need God's perfect wisdom to guide us along the way. Oh, one last thing," he adds with a grimace, "please pray for my splitting headache."

A moment later, Armando begins the prayer time by thanking Jesus for his protection in the cemetery and for wisdom to know how to proceed in the days ahead. Everyone has their eyes closed as they listen to Armando's prayer.

So it is that no one notices Emily rise from her chair and quickly exit the room.

The two apprehended men are questioned by the son of the master interrogator, Moshe Abramovich. As amiable and compassionate as the Mossad agent can be around Aly and the other Academy students, David is a

Doberman around the two men. His ears are pricked up, listening closely to every spoken word as well as every unspoken word, and his eyes scrutinize every facial expression and movement of their bodies. He is so much like his father, just not quite as intimidating. But then, nobody is as intimidating as the colonel.

The trench coat man and his crony are not forthcoming. They have no idea who David Abramovich is, but they must discern that their interrogator, with his thick accent, has little authority in America, so they reveal nothing to the Mossad agent. Neither of the men's names would have been known except that the smaller man, when addressing his partner in villainy, speaks his name as nonchalantly as if they were at a Sunday afternoon picnic.

When the smaller man—who appears very nervous—utters the name, Clyde, the larger man is highly displeased. He attempts to slap him with the back of his hand but pulls up suddenly and grabs his chest where Stewart had punched him earlier.

Limited to words as a medium for castigation, the big man scolds "Donnie Caruso" severely, calling him several choice names. He also assassinates several aspects of his character. Along the way, he butchers several idioms and uses the wrong word at least three times. He concludes by exclaiming, "Just shut up and let the head poncho do the talking around here!"

The smaller man takes exception to the harsh words. Instead of heeding the threats of his partner, he turns to the larger man and says, "No, you shut up, Clyde! I'm tired of your Half-Dome insults! You're nothin' but a tick on a warthog to the whole Kildaire family. And for your information, grandma Hazel didn't say, 'You don't have the sense you were baptized with'. She said, 'You don't have the sense you were *born* with.'"

The big man, who everybody in the room now knows is Clyde Kildaire, thanks to the big mouth of Donnie Caruso, throws his huge head back in his chair and says, "Stupid, stupid, stupid!" He pauses and then adds another idiom that he slaughters, "'Stupid is as stupid was.'"

By this time, everyone in the Agatha room is smiling and attempting to suppress laughter. The bantering between the two men is worth the price of admission.

Clyde turns to look at Donnie and barks, "Are you goin' to give them my social security number and home address, too? You might as well; you've already let the pig out of the bag!"

Now, most of the people in the room are laughing openly at the three stooges minus one. Even Dr. Windsor's normally severe face is wearing a smile. Only Mr. Fagani is not sharing in the humor of the moment. He has extracted a thick folder from his small briefcase and is slowly thumbing through the pages. His glasses are propped on the end of his long nose with the ladybug growths, and his head is tilted upward so he can read his notes through the bottoms of his bifocal lenses.

As he reads, he occasionally licks his thumb with his tongue so he can achieve better traction on the uncooperative sheets of paper. Eventually, he stops on a page midway through the thick stack and examines it closely. As he scrutinizes his notes, he mutters to himself. Everyone in the room has fallen silent by now. They know that their resident historian is onto something like a bloodhound on an hour-old scent trail.

After several minutes, the Academy "cemetery man" sets aside the papers that are covered with copious scribbling and looks across the table. He points the long bony index finger of his right hand at the man with the half-bald head and announces, "You are Clyde Kildaire, son of the late William Kildaire."

Everyone in the room looks at the man in the trench coat.

Clyde folds his arms across his chest and stares straight ahead. Then he retorts, "I'm admittin' to nothin'. It's for you to know and me to find out." The smaller man sitting next to him snorts in disbelief and disgust.

Mr. Fagani massages the top of his cane that stands next to him on its tripod base and says, "Sadly, you don't even know your mother's name."

Clyde abruptly turns to look at the elderly man but says nothing. His silence—which is a rare phenomenon for the large man—only serves to confirm the accuracy of Mr. Fagani's observation.

"When your cousin, Donnie, mentioned your name, I instantly knew that it sounded familiar," the cemetery professor explains.

The church historian runs shaking fingers over the rim of the chocolate-brown fedora lying on the table in front of him. Both his gaze and his long index finger then shift their focus from Clyde to the more diminutive Donnie. The eyes of everyone in the room follow the elderly man's finger and look at Donnie.

"You," he says, speaking quietly and without accusation, "you are the son of Rachel Kildaire, the sister of the previously mentioned Bill Kildaire. That makes you and Clyde cousins, as you already revealed. Your father's name is Doug Caruso."

Donnie stares at the historian, who stares back at him unwaveringly. Finally, the smaller of the two cemetery intruders nods his head slightly. "I know, I know," he says with a sigh and a shrug of his shoulders. "You're wonderin' how someone like me could be related to someone like Clyde. Believe me, I've been askin' myself that for thirty years now."

Clyde's eyes burn holes through his cousin's skull.

Everybody in the large unconventional cafeteria turns their eyes on Mr. Fagani. They all sense that he is not done. He is building up to something.

They are not disappointed.

The cemetery professor looks from Clyde to Donnie and then back at Clyde again. Then he looks over to where Jack had been sitting a few minutes ago.

Everybody in the room follows the elderly man's eyes from Clyde to Donnie to Clyde and then to the empty chair.

"You mentioned that you and your cousin share a grandmother named Hazel, is that correct?" the historian inquires of Donnie.

Apparently feeling left out, Clyde answers for his cousin. In his inimitable manner, he retorts, "Maybe, maybe not."

Donnie nods his head and says to one-up his cousin, "Yep, Grandma Hazel is on my mom's side."

The cemetery professor nods his head slowly. He nods for a long time.

Everyone in the room waits for the pronouncement that is certain to come. They wait for a long time. All eyes are on the elderly man.

Finally, their patience is rewarded. Mr. Fagani looks at Clyde and then at Donnie. He clears his throat loudly and asks, "Do either of you have any idea what your grandmother's maiden name was?"

The two cousins share a rare moment free of antagonistic sentiments. They glance at each other and shake their heads.

Mr. Fagani falls silent and, to the great chagrin of everyone in the Agatha room, pauses to lift his coffee cup to his mouth with a hand that shakes like glassware during a major earthquake. After several eternal swallows followed by the perfunctory dabbing at his thin, pasty lips with his napkin, he lifts his watering eyes and addresses the two cousins along with everyone else in the room.

"Ladies and gentlemen," the cemetery professor announces with as much volume as his lungs can muster, which is not much, "the maiden name of Hazel, the grandmother who Clyde and Donnie share, was...none other than *Sutherington*. Her only sibling was her older brother, Joseph, who is...the deceased grandfather of—"

Here the elderly man pauses and attempts to clear an impressive collection of phlegm from his throat. After a full minute, he is finally successful. Collecting himself, Mr. Fagani takes a deep breath and finishes his earlier thought.

"Joseph is the grandfather of...of our beloved Jack Sutherington," he declares. "By blood, Jack is, therefore, a second cousin of...Clyde Kildaire and Donnie Caruso."

"What!" Isaiah Windsor exclaims with a combination of shock and disgust in his stern voice. Many other reactions fill the Agatha room as the people around the tables digest the news that seems too incredible to believe.

"Are you certain, Louis?" Embee asks the nonagenarian as she fingers the cross dangling from her neck. "Absolutely certain?"

"My research is as right as rain," the old church historian replies. Donnie and Clyde stare at each other, then shrug their shoulders.

The retired colonel recovers from his initial shock and turns to look at Jack's newly identified cousins. "Well," he says, still sounding a bit disgusted, "this casts a new light on this whole matter. Potentially. You two hirelings can continue to remain loyal to whoever is paying you or—or you can switch your allegiances and come alongside your cousin Jack to help him. We can find a way to protect you in exchange for any information that might lead to the arrest of Draegan DaFoe."

"Who's Draegan DaFoe?" Donnie asks.

"We believe he's the man who hired you," lieutenant major Joshua Bloomstrom replies. "He's been implicated in an act of international terrorism that resulted in the murder of four men. If you have any connection to him, you could be headed to Israel for trial."

"We don't know any Draegan DaFoe!" Donnie exclaims. He looks over at his cousin and says, "Do we, Clyde."

"Shut up, Donnie," the big man says threateningly.

Donnie ignores his cousin and says, "We've been meeting with two suits who referred to each other as Daemon and...and Aaron, maybe. We don't know anyone named Draegan," Donnie insists.

"I said, shut up!" Clyde yells as anger floods his eyes and twists his mouth.

"I don't know about you, cuz," Donnie announces, leaning forward in his chair and slapping the table, "but I'm surely not goin' to get sent over to Israel for murders I had nothin' to do with."

Half Dome licks his lips and glances around the room. He rubs his chest again and then scratches his crooked nose.

"Okay, this is the deal," he finally says. "My cousin and I walk outta here tonight. You give us twenty-four hours to decide what we're gonna do. Make it eighteen. We'll get back to you tomorrow night by 6:00 and let you know our final decision. If you keep us here, we give you nothin'. Zilch. Zero. Nostradamus."

"Nada," Donnie says with a pained expression on his face. "It's nada, not Nostradamus."

"Shut up!" Clyde snaps. Then he looks back at the council of ten and asks, "Do we have a deal?"

Isaiah Windsor glances at Joshua and David. Then his eyes travel over the faces of the Greenlays, the Livingstones, the McNeelys, and Alan Greenlay's brother-in-law, Bill. Of all the faces, David's is the most hesitant. When Milner McNeely nods his head at Isaiah, the warfare professor turns back to the two detained men and says, "Okay, we have a deal. You can leave tonight. We'll plan to hear from you by supper time tomorrow."

Clyde smiles, and his teeth that are checkered with varying shades of yellow and black are on full display for all to see. "Dandy," he says as he gets to his feet.

"Just know one thing," David says gravely in his accented voice. "Even if you don't know it, you might be connected to Draegan DaFoe through those two contacts you mentioned. And if that's true, you're dealing with an assassin who kills whomever he pleases."

Donnie, clearly hesitant, glances up at his cousin and opens his mouth to speak.

"Shut up!" the big man says as he buttons up the trench coat that permeates the room with a sweaty, musty odor. "We need time to think on this. Let's get outta here, Donnie!"

Clyde's cousin gets up reluctantly and rotates his hat so that the bill extends over his forehead instead of the back of his neck. He nods at Chaplain Bloomstrom, who is dressed in military fatigues like himself, and then turns to follow his cousin. A lamb summoned to slaughter would look less dour than Donnie's face.

Dr. Windsor holds up his hand and says, "Hold on one more minute. I don't think you're taking the threat of Draegan DaFoe seriously. Let me tell you what your cousin, Jack, said about this man."

The German luxury car is still lurking in the parking lot thirty feet behind Sunny's truck. The two brothers have seen most of what transpired that evening in the cemetery except for what went down behind the 'green screen' as Aamon called it, cursing at the tarp that was erected around the gravesite.

Now the two DaFoes are impatiently waiting to see what the personnel at the Academy are going to do with their goons—men, who, in a matter of a few hours, have gone from assets to major liabilities.

There are three options, the way the brothers see it. It really is not complicated. If the two cousins are handed over to the local police, Draegan will find a way to get them released immediately. If the two goons are cut loose tonight, Aamon and Daemon will pick them up. If they remain in the custody of those inside the castle—well, that is the only way the bumbling cousins will live to see another day. Even then, their lives are over. It is only a matter of time.

Of course, the brothers report everything they saw that evening to a disgruntled Draegan, their cousin who is the offspring of their mother's brother and the mastermind behind all their missions.

After speaking with his two cousins, Draegan sits back in the leather desk chair in his home library. He analyzes the oral reports from Aamon and Daemon concerning the activities in the cemetery that evening. He must make no mistakes at this stage in the unfolding of events.

After much thought and half a cigar, Draegan decides that all the hullaballoo at the gravesite was limited to the discovery of Philip's measly coins. Nothing bigger. Philip's treasure trove is still in play. He believes it will only be a matter of time until the elusive journal leads him to the ultimate object of his quest.

The man adjusts his massive body in the chair that groans under his weight. He stares out the window into the heavy darkness. Abruptly, he slams his massive fist on the desk and curses loudly. He still must find a way to make Jack Sutherington squeal. Squeal like a pig skewered with a hot poker. But how?

He ponders the topic while he finishes his cigar. When he finally thrusts the head of the spent cigar into the large ashtray and crushes it violently against the glass, his brilliant mind captures an idea that had proved elusive until that moment.

"Of course!" he exclaims loudly. *Now, why didn't I think of that before*, he wonders to himself as he leans back in his chair and smiles at the darkness.

———

After the Academy students have finished praying, Jack is the first to notice the absence of their sixth colleague. "Where's Emily?" he inquires as his eyes scan the room. The only eyes that meet his are the burning eyes of Moses that stare at him from the far side of the fireside room.

No one knows what happened to Emily. No one saw her leave. It is like she was whisked away in a flaming chariot like Elijah.

Just when Jack decides to get up and go look for Emily, he hears Rachel's voice asking, "What are you going to do with the coins?"

Jack's attention returns to the group gathered around the coffee table, and he shakes his head. "I don't know, Rach," he replies, looking into the brown eyes set in a field of cinnamon freckles. "Technically, they don't belong to me. They belong to Philip and Madeline DaFoe."

"But those people are long gone, Juan," Armando comments. "Just tonight," he says with a smile, "we found clear evidence that Madeline is dead, and I think it's safe to assume that her husband has been reduced to dust as well. So, am I wrong when I say that it's finders-keepers at this point?

Besides, they were found in your great-great-great-grandmother's grave. I hope I got enough 'greats' in there."

"I'm not entirely sure how all that works," Jack says, rubbing his eyes. "Draegan DaFoe could certainly argue that they belong to him since he claims to be the offspring of Philip."

"What if you find out that you can keep them?" Aly inquires. "If the coins can be restored to mint condition, you will be a millionaire many times over."

Stewart nods his head and rubs his aquiline nose. "She's right, Jack," he says. "You would have a tidy sum that could range from twenty to thirty million dollars or more."

Armando's eyes grow large, and he whistles softly. "From a nobody to a prince overnight," he announces.

"Thanks, I think," Jack says, shaking his head.

"And we don't even know the value of the other coins," Rachel comments.

"Plus, we may have in our possession a map that might lead us to Philip's bigger treasure," Stewart says.

"Your great-great-grandfather could turn out to be really great," Armando says with a laugh.

There is a short silence, and then Aly asks, "What's wrong, Jack?"

Jack runs both of his hands through his damp, flaxen hair. "I'm not going to lie to you," he sighs, "the sound of all that money feels—exhilarating. I feel like I just won the lottery. I can have everything I've ever wanted and more. What's not exciting about that? Isn't that the American dream—to have it all?"

Jack grows quiet, and his troubled blue eyes scan the faces of his friends.

"But I'm conflicted. I hate it that money makes me feel that excited. I just spent two hours digging up bone fragments from a grave where two women were buried, one old and one young. What good did money do for either of them—in the end? Not a red cent of good. It didn't give them ultimate happiness or protect them from death. So, I refuse to be seduced by the lure of wealth. I reject it. I want to fix my affections on what will last forever, beyond the grave."

Aly is the first to respond. She nods her head and says, "My father slaved day and night at the factory in Yala and became a wealthy man, but at what cost? He doesn't know his children, and he doesn't even know how to love his wife. Besides, all those material things never gave him joy. He is not a happy man. I believe that his wealth, instead of being a good thing, distracted him from the most important things in life."

Armando chimes in with the comment, "Okay, I agree. But let's face it, money is a temptation. It can buy you things that are very appealing to the senses, like Lamborghinis and boats and houses and nasty threads and fine wines and status and popularity and pleasures from A to Z. Did I mention Lamborghinis? If I had all that money, I could travel to a different exotic location every week. I could be in Sydney tomorrow, Bali next week, and Abu Dhabi the week after."

Jack nods his head. "True, Manny, money can be very appealing. In and of itself, it is not bad. Even God's Word doesn't say that money is bad. It just warns about the love of money."

He pauses and then says, "But do you know what I think? I'm almost certain that if everyone believed in Jesus and lived to obey him, I don't think there would be any poverty in the world because everyone would share their resources as He commanded us to do. And when you know this world is not your home, that you're just passing through, money is not that important. It's a lot easier to share your wealth with others when you know you won't be taking it with you anyway."

"So, you might give away all thirty million dollars? You wouldn't buy even one thing for yourself?" Armando inquires.

Jack hesitates and glances over at the Hawkstern-sized fireplace. He smiles sheepishly and replies, "Maybe I'd pay off my outstanding college loans and buy a new Wrangler."

Everybody laughs, and then Stewart comments, "What about us? Wouldn't you do the same for us?"

Jack smiles broadly at his friend, who continues to emerge from his hiding place, and says, "Sure, Stew. I'd pay off your college loans, too."

"What about the Jeep?" Armando asks.

More laughter ensues. Jack tries to fully enter into the levity of the moment, but Emily is on his mind.

A few minutes later, the Screaming Eagles, aka Grave Reapers, post-exhumation debriefing comes to an end, but only after they all decide to meet again tomorrow in the old greenhouse classroom to plan their next steps. Jack immediately dismisses himself and goes off to find Emily to ask her why she left so abruptly.

It is not long before he discovers the answer to his question. As he walks through the door from the umbilical cord hallway and into the dormitory, he encounters Naomi, a student who lives in the room next to Emily's. When Jack asks her if she has seen Emily, Naomi replies, "Didn't she tell you? She's leaving the Academy."

"Leaving the Academy," Jack repeats. "Where's she going?'

"She's leaving for good," Naomi says with a shake of her head. "She's going back to Florida. She shipped off most of her stuff yesterday and took the rest with her tonight."

"She's already gone?" Jack asks incredulously.

"Five minutes ago," the upperclassman replies. "An Uber is taking her to the airport."

Jack turns while Naomi is still speaking and sprints back through the door into the umbilical cord. As he runs, he thinks he hears the woman say behind him, "She doesn't belong here anyway."

———

At 1:03 a.m., Emily wheels her two suitcases to the edge of the road that runs in front of the imposing castle and looks for her ride. Three old streetlights provide minimal illumination to the dark campus driveway.

At 1:04 a.m., a nondescript black SUV occupied by two large men rolls up beside the vehicle belonging to the DaFoe brothers.

At 1:05:00 a.m., Clyde and Donnie emerge from the double doors beneath the portico and amble into the dark night. Clyde's grey truck is parked a block away from campus.

At 1:05:10 a.m., Jack bursts around the side of the Citadel nearest the lake and sprints toward the road in pursuit of Emily.

The first thing Jack sees as he approaches the campus drive that runs between the Citadel and the parking lot are two familiar figures. One is short, and one is tall. The taller figure is wearing a trench coat and walks in an awkward manner that looks more like he is stomping. Even from forty feet away, he hears the bigger man say, "Shut up, Donnie!"

Jack is beginning to slow down as he scans the dark driveway for some sign of Emily. As he looks up and down the road, he hears tires squeal loudly and a powerful engine accelerate. A block away, a dark vehicle begins speeding toward Donnie and Clyde. Somehow, the two men do not hear it or see it.

Discerning the evil intent of the charging SUV that is briefly illuminated by a distant streetlight, Jack immediately breaks into a dead run and begins screaming at the two men, "Look out!" He is within twenty feet of the cousins when glaring headlights—like the eyes of an angry demon—pierce the darkness and blind the two men.

Jack knows the oncoming vehicle is not going to stop. Its intent is to run down the two men. Jack does not hesitate.

He races toward the speeding vehicle and the men who literally look like the figurative deer in the headlights. At the last second, he hurtles his body toward the nearest man. He hits him hard, just like he would tackle a linebacker returning an intercepted pass Jack had thrown behind his receiver. He hears an ugly thud and feels something unyielding strike his leg. Then he is in the air, spinning through the darkness.

Emily stares out the backseat window of the car into the bleakness of the night. She has made it clear to the driver that she is not in any mood to talk. As she watches the intermittent waterfalls of light pour down from the streetlights and pool on the road, she tries not to think because there is no safe place to go in her brain.

Her eyes refocus, and she sees a dreary image of herself reflected in the window. She recognizes the face but does not know who it is. The light in the young woman's eyes has gone out.

Who am I? she screams in her head.

Her anger, like a terminal cancer, has continued to grow inside of her in recent days, corrupting her heart. She is angry at Nancy Greenlay. She is angry at Embee. She is angry at men as a corporate entity.

More importantly, her anger reached a crucial tipping point when she was hanging out with some young women after church the previous Sunday. One of them was watching a video on her phone and made some off-hand-ed comments about gay people. She said that God hated them and would surely send them to hell along with everyone in Sodom and Gomorrah.

Emily did not say a word in remonstrance, but her heart burned, and something snapped inside her. She was so tired of feeling judged by people. Only hours later, she made up her mind to leave the Academy for good—or for bad.

Emily closes her eyes and shuts out the night.

She cannot stay out of her brain completely. She shakes her head as if to clear it of cobwebs.

This version of me doesn't work, she thinks bitterly. *I tried, and I can't be this Emily. I can't be the good Christian girl. I feel so different from everyone around me. I don't fit in at the Academy or in my family. I'm different than all of them. I'm queer. I have to be who I was born to be. I have to go where I belong, where I'm welcomed with open arms, where I fit.*

Emily opens her eyes again and stares out at the desolate world. She thinks she should be crying at this moment, but there are no tears. She feels nothing.

"Goodbye, Jack," she mumbles. "Goodbye, Mom and Dad. Goodbye, Rachel and Aly." She has a vague awareness that she must see these people who love her as bad in order to justify her surrender to the new Emily, but the awareness is quickly whisked from her brain.

As the car hurtles through the darkness, she adds, "Farewell, Jesus. I'm going to miss you."

The only divorce she fails to acknowledge is the one that has been transacted within her own heart. She has detached from the Emily she has been since birth. No surgical amputation has ever been more severing.

In that moment of farewells, the dissonance that has dogged Emily for so long finally melts away, and she feels free for the first time in years. Since she has now exiled "good girl" Emily with all her pain and bad memories and pathetic weakness to a dungeon so deep inside herself that she is virtually inaccessible, the longstanding tension of being a house divided against herself resolves. There is no more shame. No need to repent of her sin. She is only the one Emily now that her true self has been sentenced to annihilation.

The cost of Emily's false peace is high. Freedom has been purchased at a terrible price, at the greatest price: Divorce from God, others, and her own heart. The unholy trifecta has been realized.

Like a tarry sludge, a tangible darkness fills the car Emily is riding in. It drives out all the remaining light. The young woman is unaware of it because she is no longer aware of spiritual presences.

The same profound darkness descends over the Academy as well. It floats down soundlessly, like a massive shroud falling from the sky. No, it is not a bright sheet radiating hope and purity. It is as black as the cave where Philip DaFoe's body lies entombed. Its name is rebellion and death.

Thirteen students comfortably asleep in their dorm rooms experience nightmares during the night. On the drive home from the meeting of the Grave Reapers, Nancy Greenlay asks Allen to pull over to the side of the road because she is suddenly overcome by a wave of nausea. Dr. Embee Livingstone is rushed to the hospital at 4:30 a.m. by her husband, Sunny, for what turns out to be a ruptured appendix.

The sound of rumbling voices begins to echo through the night outside the world of physical hearing. It is a victory chant. The unearthly chorus is beyond eerie. It is terrifying.

The prophetess, Miriam, is kneeling on the living room floor in her small house only blocks away from the Academy. She is alone—physically, that is. The room is dark except for three candles burning unwaveringly on the coffee table.

Something disturbs the prayers of the elderly woman, and her eyes fly open. She hears the voices. A shiver rolls through her body. She knows why they are chanting.

Minutes pass. The flames of two of the candles bend oddly. Then they die. The woman finally speaks.

"Yes, Lord," she says quietly, "I hear your voice above all the others. The great battle for your precious one has intensified. And yes, I will pray for the daughter whom you love so deeply—the one living in great darkness, the one guarded by a legion of dark warriors."

The prophetess closes her eyes again and prays, "Jesus, open her ears to hear your voice so that she might turn back to you and know your love. Arouse her to come to her senses so she might escape the snare of the devil, the dark, defiant one who has taken her prisoner to do his will. But give her endurance because deliverance will not come immediately."

The woman who is old and weak in body but young and strong in spirit pauses and groans softly. Then she nods her sagacious head with its silver crown and says, "Yes, you have plans for your lost daughter that not even she knows of yet. Send forth your mighty messengers to ensure the fulfillment of these plans, for the enemy is strong, and she is so weak."

Miriam raises her eyes to the ceiling and smiles. "What is impossible for a child of the flesh is possible for you, Lord. Nothing is too hard for you, my dear Jesus.

"Nothing."

Hell flinches at the prayer of the prophetess, and the prince of darkness raises a defiant fist toward heaven.

"Watch and see," the creature of sin and death growls. "This time, I am a step ahead of you, oh, mighty ruler," the voice utters, dripping with hate. "Like a furious lion, I will scatter and devour the pathetic sheep you appear to love so deeply—so inexplicably."

"How sad," the voice from the darkness mocks. "How very, very sad. Their rejoicing will be turned to mourning, and their day will become as the night."

The flame of the last candle is extinguished, and the room is swallowed by darkness.